Sean Stamos:
Blue Purge Revelation

An Epic Espionage Thriller Series

Acknowledgment

I am blessed to have had many thoughtful and dedicated teachers in my life. To those who have nurtured the creativity and love for science and truth that I possess today, I thank you. A small-town Iowa boy doesn't just become an accomplished physician, entrepreneur, author, and world traveler on his own without the inspiration of great teachers.

I did not get here alone.

SEAN STAMOS:
BLUE PURGE REVELATION

by

Brent W. Laartz, MD

CARIBE ID
PUBLISHING
FLORIDA • NEW YORK
®

Publisher: CARIBE ID, LLC

ISBN-13: 978-0-9982054-7-2
Publisher: Caribe ID Publishing, LLC

For information on distribution, translations, or bulk sales, please contact Caribe ID Publishing, LLC directly:

Caribe ID Publishing, LLC
P.O. Box 75304
Tampa, FL 33675

Library of Congress Cataloging
Laartz, Brent W
Sean Stamos: Blue Purge Revelation
ISBN 978-0-9982054-6-5 (hardback), 978-0-9982054-7-2 (paperback), 978-0-9982054-8-9 (epub), 978-0-9982054-9-6 (audiobook)

www.drlaartz.com

https://www.linkedin.com/in/brent-w-laartz-md/

Ig: @brentwlaartzmd

Contents

I dedicate this figment of my imagination to my lovely children, who inspire me through their energy and passion. When I see them embarking on so many thrilling adventures, I am vain to think that I played a part in instilling that roaming spirit within them. Keep it up, my loves.

CHAPTER 1: NATALIA THE MENTOR

Natalia Volkov knew herself well enough to appreciate she could not and would not sit idle for long. It had barely been two years since she, her old confidante Chip Merlin, and the rest of the Merlin Commerce team had saved the free world from a Russian catastrophe. To cap things off, the pair prevailed as the home team yacht for the America's Cup on the Solent near the Isle of Wight in England. After several months of secret hearings in the House Intelligence Committee, Natalia now found herself facing an existential crisis. Her revolutionary artificial intelligence stock market trading program had taken on a life of its own, with the Journal hiring several computer scientists to utilize its predictive algorithms for the public good.

The project that consumed an uncountable number of years of her life was now out of her hands and she felt a soothing yet exhausted relief that was akin to a divorce from a lover turned psychopath. She knew this breakup was for the good of her sanity, though for the time being, it left a gaping hole in her heart. That void paled in comparison to the anguish she experienced as a castoff from her family, which had little care for her life, having tried to end it here in her adopted home of New York City. As with any void, you could bet your retirement fund the hole would not stay empty for long. For the first time in her life, she felt a lack of direction, aimlessly performing financial research for those friends who were nice enough to hand her some menial tasks.

Recently, however, she and Chip had found the release they so desperately needed. And it was none too soon for Chip, for he had experienced the same disenchantment with the world order and the injustices of modern society. Indeed, while they had vanquished the adversaries of free humanity, many of the perpetrators and beneficiaries of this global transgression would go unpunished, free to commit further misdeeds in the future. One only had to look at Natalia's family as a shining example.

Her family's shipping and logistics company had suddenly become the subject of scrutiny from around the world, with mounting pressure from its customers to break ties with it and its mother Russia. Her father was able to sell off pieces of the company and her uncle was in exile, or perhaps a worse fate that often befell those who failed the President of Russia. Her brothers, who had distanced themselves from the affair, continued to wield some power in Russia as oligarchs. They were repaid in kind for their unending loyalty to the motherland, no matter the circumstances. While at times she was heartbroken that she had not spoken to her father since before those fateful events, she was more than comfortable severing the umbilical cord and the suffocating hold that he and the rest of her family had on her for years. It was just another wound to heal for the strong-willed, tall brunette former Olympian sailor from St. Petersburg.

Elections had come and gone in the year since the scandals had rocked those who would sell their freedom to the most unscrupulous country on Earth. Those who continued to stoke fear in the populace and promote draconian punishments for the less powerful in society had not lost much power in the U.S. In fact, they had gained a substantial element of popularity in many circles, with vocal calls for prosecuting and persecuting those "woke" individuals increasing in volume in social media.

For the last year, she and Chip had received invitations from all over the world to skipper and co-skipper various challenging boats for world-class sailing regattas. Owners of super yacht racing sailboats were more than willing to give up the helm of their boats to these newly anointed superstars of the racing scene. Flattering as it was to be invited and then win, it was not accolades these two were after. Yet, with their innate skill and choice selection of invitations from the swiftest of yachts, that was exactly what came pouring in.

With the welcome respite from responsibility, they jumped at the chance to compete once again against the pre-eminent sailing community. Simultaneously, the erstwhile off-and-on romance between these two blossomed into a genuine partnership of a sailing power couple. Their true love was whirling around on the fair winds of success, enveloping them in a euphoria that helped mend their souls from those bottomless wounds recently inflicted.

To say sailing was the ultimate release from all that encumbered her spirit was the understatement of the century. For all the glory, here they were, their faces suntanned, with saltwater spray dripping off their wet, bright-red sailing gear and their hair flowing in the brisk breeze, on a Maxi 72 in Newport, Rhode Island for Race Week. For the week-long series of races, they took turns as skipper and tactician/navigator on this extremely fast and nimble yacht, as they proved their fortitude against the challenging rough weather conditions of this open water regatta.

"I can't believe we have never raced here!" exclaimed Natalia as she called out the next tack. "Tacking in 3... 2... 1... Helm's over!" Her long brunette locks were tied in a ponytail through the back of her navy-blue Merlin Commerce ballcap. Her hands and forearms were sinewy steel clamps on the gigantic wheel of this 72-foot yacht. Though it was not as fast as the AC75 that they had just won the America's Cup with, it was incredibly sensitive to the touch, and she felt as much at ease and in control of this long slender sloop as she had the tiny 470 sailboat with which she had won the Olympics less than twenty years ago.

There was a flurry of the crew called grinders rotating the gargantuan winches and those crew who were not manning those machines ambled across the hatches to the port side of the sleek yacht. As was characteristic of a Chip Merlin and Natalia Volkov helmed boat, there was not a lot of yelling. The crew had only raced together for five days, but it seemed to all spectators they had been crew mates for years. The fluid motions of 14 sailors acting as one instantly flung the sail from the port to the starboard side, filling it instantaneously with the wind and launching the boat toward the final mark.

"Well-oiled machine this crew is!" Chip shouted as he also called a few coordinates for Natalia as she skippered this final race of the week. "Everyone, keep the sail tight. Don't let it pinch on this last leg! You guys are awesome!"

As they rounded the final mark, the magnificent black Kevlar sails were trimmed tight, and Natalia felt the refreshing bite of the Northeast breeze as over her shoulder she could now visualize the many boat lengths that they held over the IRC 72, their closest competition, a similar-sized 70-plus foot sailing yacht. The crew of 14 young sailors was beaming with one giant smile as most were straddling the upper rail, with feet dangling an adrenaline-provoking 15 feet above the cobalt blue sea. For many, this was their first flirtation with championship yachting, and for all the crew, it certainly would not be their last. Once you were bitten by the maritime bug, coming down with regatta fever on such awe-inspiring yachts, you could not help becoming hooked for life.

Among this crew were two familiar faces from the Oxford women's sailing team and potential Olympic champions if they lived up to their potential. Natalia had invited them for this short break from their training at Oxford's Farmoor Reservoir, as she knew that sometimes small boat competitors needed to experience the feel of a yacht to bring some perspective to their seamanship training. Kate and Celine were the favorites to win the Olympics next year in the 49er class of sailing due to their strength and sailing knowledge. Both had demonstrated their sailing mettle in the small boat classes but had not yet experienced these larger boats. The pair, soaked to the core in sweat and sea spray, were having the time of their lives.

Each time the foaming waves jettisoned off the bow of the boat, the crew on the rail howled as though they had never sailed before, laughing as they stared out at the ocean blue. Natalia and Chip soaked all of this in as they crossed the finish line for the victory in both the final race and the entire series. In dominating fashion, the sleek yacht and crew had won all eight races of the week, and there wasn't even one close finish.

Natalia rounded the long, slender sloop down off the wind, brought it down off the plane, then slowed it considerably so she could steer the yacht straight into the wind to begin to douse the sails. With the sleek, black sails dropping to the deck in the background, Chip embraced Natalia with a heartfelt side hug since she still required room to steer the sailboat to the dock. Normally, on their own boats, she and Chip would ask one of the younger crew if they wanted to captain the boat to shore, but this was not their boat to risk. Once back at the docks, the celebration began in earnest, and she turned to the crew with a champagne glass high in the air. "Flawless, gentlemen and women. Flawless. Thanks for showing us an exciting challenge on this side of the Atlantic!"

After the deck was tidied up, Natalia and Chip strolled arm-in-arm up the dock to the famous New York Yacht Club in Newport Harbor. As the champion of the week, they earned a reserved slip on the small dock and all other sailboats scattered to their respective marinas throughout Newport Harbor. It was a short walk to the lawn of the opulent mansion that had been repurposed into the clubhouse for the New York Yacht Club. In an hour, this would be the location where the awards ceremony would take place for the Cup. Geographically out of place in this Rhode Island harbor, the NYYC and Newport Harbor were the epicenter of sailing in the United States, and the whole sailing world was watching. The grueling week of seamanship was livestreamed worldwide with drones flying overhead and their cameras zoomed in on the boats to catch the action.

Natalia pointed upward, "Look at the drones! You're on TV!"

The two stopped as if to pose, but were really just fascinated by the drone technology being deployed by the streaming company. "It's amazing those drones are so stable in the gusts of the Atlantic! You know Sam is utilizing these sophisticated drones more and more for our security!" Chip exclaimed.

"Well, this is the life! I could get used to doing this full-time. Where next? After D.C., that is." Natalia was still in dream mode. She would have to snap out of it for this next trip back to D.C. Their last trips to the capital city were under some stress with days of intense hearings, but the enticing event invitation Natalia received could not be declined. The hidden, tertiary purpose of their return stateside was a less formal yet exciting appointment with an old friend. Since the pair planned to accept the invite to this get-together in Washington, naturally they arranged a detour after the end of the races to see Sean Stamos, now the darling of the clandestine world.

"Hmmmm, first the America's Cup, now we just won the Rolex? We would have to win some TransAtlantic or Trans-Pacific races to top this." Chip thought the idea insane, but a race across an entire ocean might just be the escape from civilization they needed. "Maybe we could enter one of my J boats in Trans Pac. We could get the RYS members to crew. Or better yet, we solicit an invitation to skipper someone else's boat again. Maybe this one! She would make a fine winner in Waikiki!"

"How about Capri? The Mediterranean sounds lovely. We could stop in Cannes. But first, before we get too far ahead of ourselves, do you want to head to D.C. tonight or hang out with the crew for the evening?" Natalia queried.

"Let's wake up early tomorrow. We deserve some celebration for once. Georgetown will still be there tomorrow." Chip was not sure what they were getting themselves into at Georgetown but an old journalism mentor from the Oxford years had offered an open invitation for this week. He understood the undertones that the exploratory meeting had in their business journalism world. Yet wisely he thought it best to leave that discussion with Natalia for later.

The festivities would fly by as quickly as the races that evening. As they joined the crew on stage at the awards ceremony, there were cheers and an occasional chant of "USA", for the billionaire yacht owner was mentioned as a potential sponsor for the next America's Cup challenger. There were champagne toasts all around as Natalia and Chip were arm-in-arm once again, enveloped in the spirit of the moment. The American owner of the Maxi 72 beamed proudly beside the beaming British and Russian skippers and the bubbly was exploding and pouring all over everyone. Naturally, some of the younger crew became a little over-exuberant with their shouting and dancing on the stage.

The accolades were numerous and seemed to last forever, and as they descended the stairs off the stage, the familiar and trusted faces of their security detail were waiting at stage right. The ex-Army Ranger Torey Severin, who was the director of security for North America, had now become Natalia's go-to for security detail leader. Their trusted confidante and Chief of Operations for Merlin Commerce, Sam Steed should have been there by now, thought Natalia, as her eyes searched the nearby crowd.

"Is Sam here yet?" Natalia, nearly out of breath from the excitement, looked up at Torey as she struggled to gain her footing, still swaying from being tossed in the waves all day long.

"Not yet, we are expecting him any minute," Torey mentioned, eyes scanning the crowd. Chip's right hand, Sam was once again attending to some side business. With the stability of the world still in the balance, business was booming for the security division of Merlin Commerce. As with any business, they could always use more action to flow their way, but part of that boom resulted from the insecurity of nervous Russian oligarchs. For the time being and for obvious reasons, Russia would remain off limits, however. Sam and

Torey, out of business and personal necessity, had recently developed technology to listen and tune in for any and all security threats around the world for their clients, based in part on some of Natalia's artificial intelligence programs. Always testing the limits of technology in its application to their shipping and logistics company, Sam would continue to be occupied all day today testing its capabilities.

As the celebration continued into the evening, Chip and Natalia couldn't have felt closer to the happiness they had always yearned for. Maybe they should have been racing yachts worldwide all these years instead of the insane concentration on their careers, Natalia thought for a fleeting moment.

Sam would not make a presence that evening, and the word finally came that he would meet them on the plane tomorrow. During their many excursions, Sam had a habit of sleeping on their opulent corporate jet, which served as his command center when he accompanied Chip and Natalia.

After a long list of hugs and goodbyes, in what seemed like just minutes they were whisked away to their hotel with their security detail in tow, and, only a few hours later, with little sleep, escaped the tiny, romantic island under cover of darkness to the awaiting plane at Providence International Airport. Natalia and Chip hoped they would be able to catch another hour of sleep on the short flight to Reagan National Airport in the aptly named Merlin Guinevere, the oversized ACJ380 that was the flagship of the security operations team of Merlin Commerce. As they greeted Sam and Torey at the bottom of the stairs, Natalia felt safe in the familiar confines of this colossal airplane that only a year earlier was the headquarters of their save-the-world from financial ruin campaign.

As they alighted the flight stairs, Natalia looked down at Chip in the quiet darkness and took in the peaceful early morning sounds of this small, seemingly dormant northeastern airport. She put her arms tightly around his neck as they finally consummated the full embrace that she desperately craved all night. Chip reciprocated with even more emotion as the love he had wanted was finally his. All these years of friendship and occasional romance had proved very frustrating as neither could convince the other to settle down. But maybe. Just maybe, now was the time.

When they finally made their way into the spacious cabin, Sam was already seated in the reclining chair facing the door and Torey was standing next to the cockpit door. Sam suddenly donned a serious look on his face. He looked over, first at Chip and then at Natalia, whose smiles were also replaced by a stern appearance. The tailing security personnel ushered them into the cabin and out of the open doorway.

"So, are you going to tell me what this excursion to Georgetown is all about?" Sam queried. After all, the Chief Operating Officer and Director of Security of Merlin Commerce felt like he needed to know these things. Planning the jet-setting couple's security always proved complicated and their safety could depend on it. He had only cursorily been informed and with business on his mind distracting him, he had not fully comprehended why they were heading back to the city of politics and division.

"There are two items on our agenda. First, visiting our old mentor from Oxford, Dean Smythe, and then we are going to pay a visit to Sean Stamos." Just saying his name brought a smile to her face as Natalia explained in more detail the purpose of the trip.

"Okay, so Torey do you have the logistics lined up I am assuming? I haven't been around much lately but I think I have all of the loose ends of Merlin Security and Investigations tied up. It seems the billionaires and sheiks of the world are getting more nervous, not less after the syndicate was destroyed." He caught himself for a moment. "Nay, destroyed is too strong of a term. Let's call it injured. Maybe not even truly injured. Maybe just a minor case of injured pride."

Natalia demurred. "I'm not really sure what the purpose of the invitation from Dean Smythe is. She billed it as a meet and greet with the faculty of the school of business there. I have a feeling it is something more and could be the new beginning that we've been looking for. And as for Stamos, I think he just misses us. I wonder if he would ever join the security division. Chip, what do you think?"

"I think he would be bored working for us. We would probably be dragging him around to stuffy regattas from one ocean to another. I, for one, hope our life will remain as boring as it is from now on." Chip was hopeful but not optimistic about that statement.

Sam's ears perked up, sensitive to the sarcasm, "Stamos might like some of our new technological developments in the security division. You're right, though. He might be bored with you guys sailing all around the world. But then again, we do need to get you guys back to some semblance of work. Perchance he could help with that?" That brought a smirky grin to his face, and then he added, "D.C, huh? Well, here's to new opportunities!"

A few short hours later, there Natalia was, already bouncing back with another adventure. Sitting in the office of the Dean of the School of Business at Georgetown University, with several faculty in attendance, the discussion was lively but meandering from politics, then business, then developing countries, and finally to journalism. The corner office was of considerable size and the chairs Victorian and as uncomfortable as the small talk that delayed the Dean's inevitable endgame. The afternoon sunlight shone at an angle through all windows in hazy beams that suggested a divine aura to the room at this venerable Jesuit university. The stuffy faculty resembled amorphous seraphim figures in the shadows, but the tone of their questions and conversation was cordial enough.

"So where will your stratospheric trajectory take you from here, and can we persuade you to bring your expertise in business and business journalism to Georgetown?" With that pointed question, the Dean willfully steered the conversation from a vague exchange to a decidedly direct intonation.

"Why, I haven't given it much thought, except I appreciate the first prerequisite for any opportunity would be the leeway to travel for research. The offer is intriguing, as I have recently enjoyed mentoring a few brilliant interns at the New York Journal, and I would love to expand on that experience by advising and shaping young journalists and business majors." Natalia's immediate thought echoed in her head that her editor at the Journal, who had provided her immense latitude with her present nautical sabbatical, would not share in her excitement about this fresh academic direction in her career.

"The faculty here have been following your career for some time now, and I have been given a wide indulgence to ascertain what would bring you to Georgetown. We have also been granted some discretion from the Washington Chronicle for an endowed faculty position which would also give you some financial backing from their end."

This was positively a dramatic turn of events. The Washington Chronicle was known for literary freedom for its journalists and while it would be a lateral shift, she thought it would be nice to escape the stifling confines of New York City. At Georgetown, journalism was not offered as a major, but the business college and international relations program were second to none, which could confer a boost to her research on developing economies. The weakness of the journalism program notwithstanding, some of the brightest business journalists in the country had hatched their careers from this venerable, grey limestone building in the New North section of campus.

The Dean's office of the School of Business overlooked some of the wide sidewalks and thick greenery of campus. Natalia stood up and walked through the hazy rays of sunlight to the towering windows to gaze down below at the lush landscape. The sight of the undergraduates lying about the vast lawn brought back memories of her times at Oxford. The collegiate atmosphere of Georgetown and the substantial political clout wielded in D.C. by the Chronicle would certainly be a welcome change from New York and its anonymous living.

Auspiciously, the invitation to this meeting was proffered under the guise of wanting to get to know a colleague while she was in DC, but Natalia had a premonition that there was more to it than just dialogue. The thought crossed her mind that she should have researched her demands more thoroughly. It was never a wise business decision to walk into a negotiation without previously scrutinizing the positions and exigencies of the opposing side. Nevertheless, evidently she held the high ground in this transaction, so she hastily pondered her primary demands before accepting the offer. Interrupting those thoughts was the desire to work with this former mentor, who had risen through the ranks of business journalism like a rocket, seemingly blazing a trail for Natalia. That path stood before her now and was hers for the taking.

"Technology. Technology and business journalism and business analytics. I know you have a data science program. Can we dovetail something with the computer science department?" Natalia knew this demand would probably end up rehashing her research at the Journal, so she was hesitant to make this a steadfast requirement.

It so happened, present in the corner of the room, was a professor of data science and artificial intelligence, who concurred regarding some form of collaboration between the two departments. That was almost too easy, thought Natalia as she spied some undergraduates walking on the quadrangle below, who could easily have been her twenty years ago on the Oxford campus.

It seemed like just yesterday during a fateful trip to visit her family in England, when she and Chip were reminiscing in the sacred halls of Balliol College on the Oxford campus, observing and remarking on many of their old classmates' pictures in the vestibule. At that moment she had decided to reconnect with some of her former mentors and mentees. Those Oxford Blue men and women displayed on those walls had already in their short careers made some real differences in a world that, at times, appeared to be spiraling out of control with nationalist and isolationist agendas. The resulting cruel and heartless wars had created refugee crises across the globe in recent years. Hence, the real heroes on those walls were those who were the champions of the downtrodden of the world.

Probably most prominent among the international business majors that had their pictures hung in the foyer of Balliol Hall was sitting before Natalia, a continuously rising star of journalism and business. The Dean had now reached the pinnacle here at Georgetown. Her area of specialty was in developing economies and just like Natalia, her achievements in predicting investment success had brought her worldwide notoriety. The paths of the Dean and Natalia could not have been a more parallel road to becoming accomplished journalists.   Her name was Erin Smythe, and she was Chip's classmate and another mentor to Natalia when she was an underclassman at Balliol College. She had taught Natalia to believe in herself even during the grueling first year at Oxford. Natalia had followed in her footsteps to the Journal, believing that, like her mentor, she could make a difference.

Between the two of them, they dramatically changed the way countries in the developing world were seen by the institutional investor. Prior to a decade or two before, there was only a fringe investor who was interested in putting their money into what was perceived at the time to be too high a risk. What Dean Smythe and subsequently Natalia changed was the quantification of that risk and advising those countries how to minimize that risk to enable greater investment in their future by outside forces - forces that improved the economic situation in those regions for the most part, with some notable exceptions. Those exceptions were becoming more frequent in the past few years with some large institutional and whole governmental investments taking over the economies of some small African countries to their detriment overall.

Natalia turned from the window with what she knew would be a slam dunk request from her mentor. "What I really want to do is precipitate some real change in Africa and Asia to realize some of our objectives with non-aligned, non-BRICS by the end of the decade. Thus far I see some failures in our estimates of where they should be by now." Natalia was going for the jugular. "Can we add some institutional investment research into preventing the takeovers by the opportunistic carnivore investors out there?"

Dean Smythe was indeed impressed with the demand. "I think we can achieve this on a small scale. As you know, Georgetown has some benefactors that share some of these goals. And the Chronicle I know has some interest in these areas." The Dean paused for a second, "And I can tell that there is something else on your mind?"

"Why yes, there is. During the past year, I have also become interested in our own underdeveloped economy of the rural and urban areas. In some ways, the economy of these areas is worse off than some underdeveloped countries and could destabilize the macro economy of our country. The educational systems in these areas have less investment and there are forces at work that undermine any real efforts to improve this. I would also like to undertake some research into methods to reform investment decisions in the American rural sector."

While rural America as an underdeveloped economy was not a novel concept as a whole, the poverty of middle America and the South, as well as urban centers was increasing. Methods to mitigate this poverty were not being considered outside of infrastructure investment. It seemed the only educational investments being accomplished involved deconstructing the public school systems and replacing them with religious or for-profit private schools.

The Dean agreed with her, "There must be some answers that institutional investment can ascertain regarding different investment vehicles. Charter schools seemed to be the answer in the early 2000s. I wonder where this will take us."

Natalia took a drink from the bottled water she held in her hand and continued, "The inequities of the working poor in the United States have been a travesty. They're the backbone and the engine of the American economy. They are the small businesses of America, the farmers, plumbers, electricians, gun shops, shoe stores, small newspapers, et

14

cetera. They employ an astronomical number of Americans and they are under siege from every direction. Increased taxes, insurance costs, labor costs, education costs, etc. Increased investment in this section of America at this moment in time is equivalent to investing in the small businesses in underdeveloped countries."

The Dean was impressed, "Well, that is certainly a passionate opinion. I gather you are correct that, in some ways, rural America is doing worse than some underdeveloped countries."

Natalia felt she had to restate her opinion more succinctly, "The problems of the rural poor and rural small businesses can be summed up in their difficulty competing against global conglomerate companies that employ economies of scale, monopolistic practices, and just plain criminal activity to tip the scales in their favor."

"Yes, if we can work as a team for these two goals, I don't see how we could fail. Do we have a deal?" The Dean wasn't going to take no for an answer.

"I don't think I have ever been more flattered and flabbergasted at the enormity of this opportunity. And I have had many extremely generous offers from the private sector over the years. However, I have one more request. I understand the Georgetown sailing team only has one head coach for men's and women's sailing. I would like to avail my services to Georgetown in that regard." If this request was granted, Natalia would have everything she ever wanted. Over the past several months, she had won the America's Cup for Great Britain, had flown around the globe for regattas as far away as Australia, and had reveled in molding young sailors to conquer the winds and the oceans. Sailing was her zen.

"You have a deal; I will discuss it with the athletic director today. You are the embodiment of Georgetown's vigor and achievement and we would love to have you aboard." With that statement, the Dean finished with some collegial talk about their old stomping grounds south of London in the venerable halls of Balliol College at Oxford and the idealism of their youth.

As all in attendance stood to leave, one of the younger female faculty members stopped her at the doorway, "You know there is an old-time schooner regatta on the Chesapeake Bay this weekend if you are still in town. You should see if you can get on a boat. It's the most magnificent sight to see the wooden masted boats of yesteryear out there on the Chesapeake."

"Wow, that sounds delightful. We were just on the Chesapeake yesterday! Let me check with Chip, who is my first mate and captain, all in one. I am sure he would enjoy that. Do you have a boat in mind that needs some crew?" The only thing Natalia knew was that their plans were open for the next week, but had no idea if that could change, as it often did on a dime.

"I do," her new-found sailing friend said, offering to connect her with a boat captain.

Natalia couldn't help daydreaming for a second or two about her future life here in the capital where she and Chip could finally settle down a little while still being able to enjoy sailing in the most idyllic setting. Well, she thought, she had better consult her partner, who had already agreed to a relocation stateside. Excited for a cool change, she set out on her path to destiny.

—•❯❯ ❮❮•—

CHAPTER 2: HATCHING THE PLAN

—•❯❯ ❮❮•—

Tucked in the southern end of the Blue Ridge Mountains of Northern Georgia, numerous log cabins dotted the landscape at the base of the Appalachian Trail, each tucked neatly into the tall green pines, with easy access to streams, ponds, and reservoirs. Historically, Southerners from Georgia, Alabama, and South Carolina flocked to these areas due to the universal attraction of peaceful relaxation and the lure of the great outdoors. Hunting and fishing had been abundant and there were large plantations for hunting wild boar and deer. At least that was the way it used to be when life was good in these parts. Now there were throngs of Northerners who were hiking and bicycling the trails, camping, glamping, and bringing along with them marijuana, drugs, and their crazy Northern belief systems.

According to some people in the South, this was an unfathomable sin against God and their forefathers. How could these people not like to hunt or fish? Why would they smoke marijuana and not cigarettes, tobacco being a life-sustaining staple in these parts after all? There was a growing resentment among Southerners in Georgia and South Carolina for these types who were invading their land and ways of life. They had already taken over the coastland but now were trying to take over the Appalachian and Smoky Mountains. What was worse, some of them didn't leave each fall and were taking up permanent residence, building bigger log cabins on acreages that would break up the wide-open hunting lands. That meant life in these areas would change forever from the way things had always been. Plantations were disappearing and along with them went the hunting and fishing opportunities locals had counted on for generations. It was not just that, centuries of history and the Southern way of life were disappearing.

Moreover, with permanent residence came voting and with that, loss of control over that Southern way of life. Waging the war over power at the ballot box had become an arduous task for those remaining in authority in these lands, but that was an art best left to the back rooms and the alleyways. It was not a pretty sight, and the unwritten code of the established networks of the old guard was not to talk about opposition suppression publicly. Code words of integrity of the vote and ballot security were paramount. However, the established Southern order also knew that these techniques would not prevail forever, as the flourishing minority population in these parts would eventually become a majority. Namely, they couldn't gerrymander their way to hegemony eternally.

It was the heart of summer, and the heat could be stifling in the lower lands of Georgia, but here in the mountains at its border with South Carolina, the elevated heights brought a little cooler weather to those who took respite among these majestic views. The modern world was hours away in Atlanta, and to those who frequented these areas, couldn't be farther away. Most cabins had sparse comforts of modern society, no telephone, no cell coverage, and no satellite TV. This was what the modern adventure traveler yearned for - to get away for a few days. A few of these escapes had no running water or electricity, bringing a whole new meaning to leaving civilization behind. The distance from the modern, progressive civilization was also what every Southerner appreciated about these lands.

The sheer number of trails that emanated from here and wound hundreds of miles north into South Carolina and North Carolina was so extensive that every year dozens of hikers became lost and a few died of heat exhaustion or hypothermia depending on the season. You could hike for an hour and not see a single other person, even if you were close to a road. Nearby Amicalola Falls or Tallulah Falls were considered by many to be the beginning of the Appalachian Trail and the number of tourists in the area was on the increase.

On this particularly humid, sunny summer afternoon, three bearded men, each with a sun-soaked, leathery face, sat with somber faces around the dining room table of one of these sparse cabins. Each was, in his own right, but more so in his own mind, a brave leader for the freedom of men. Each had garnered the following of thousands of Americans through social media. They had spent the morning lamenting the growth of Yankee beliefs in each of their homelands.

This was Virgil Burns' backyard of sorts. He lived only a few hours from here at the end of a gravel road on forty wooded acres that had been in his family's hands since before the Civil War. His parents were able to eke out a small living by farming twenty of those acres for tobacco, but his father had to work two jobs in town to make ends meet for the kids and grandkids. Virgil was an electrician and turned to hunting for entertainment. His father was active in local politics and was well-connected in these parts. If it wasn't for his father and the family's historical ties to local organizations, with only forty acres, the family would have been destitute.

But Virgil, through his father, managed to build a network of like-minded individuals who were sick and tired of the whining modern American. With local groups who no longer wished to quietly participate in politics, there was an upwelling of those willing to take matters into their own hands. They policed their own neighborhoods to protect themselves from the crime emanating from the cities, which they believed was becoming all too common. Growing out of that concept of vigilante justice, throughout the South, the network was becoming better organized. They no longer liked to be called militias which were considered too offensive to the average Joe. They preferred to be called protectors of the realm.

Without much sense of history, though, Virgil's groups were organized almost identically to the old confederations of the 19th and 20th centuries, such as the Ku Klux Klan. While there were some of the older members, like Virgil's father, who had participated in the KKK and wished it would rise again, most members, like Virgil, knew they couldn't go by that name. And those who were lucky to be around during the bygone era when that old infamous collective was active perhaps subconsciously guided the structure of these protector groups into familiar sects that were called realms. The term realm conjured up a king ruling over an area he owned. The younger members like Virgil didn't make any connection to the past because they didn't even bother to learn the history they were defending. For Virgil, it was just about fighting against change that was coming from cities like Atlanta and others farther north.

Virgil was in the middle of extolling the achievements of his organizations in the South during the last elections. While in some areas the forces of the liberal elites in the cities had won, in the rural areas of Georgia and South Carolina, the protectors had beat back the tide and still held majorities in the state houses and governorships. Virgil put his fingers in his side belt loops and puffed out his barrel chest as he bragged about some of the misdeeds he had done to accomplish just that.

"But these investigations have taken a toll on my organization," interjected one of the men, Rodney Baylor, the leader of the American Action Men, probably the largest white nationalist outfit in the country. They were based in the wild lands of Idaho and had subsisted without the federal government for almost two centuries. And they could not stand the elites in the cities of the East Coast telling them what to do with their lands. Rodney himself only owned a few acres of land and was not rich by any means, but he represented a group that had the backing of the larger landowners and political leaders of Idaho, Utah, and Montana. "The Feds have gone too far and we need to have control over our domains. You guys here and those in Arizona, Nevada, Michigan, and Pennsylvania had better whoop some ass and bring everyone else in line or this country will be overrun by this nonsense."

The man from Idaho stroked his wiry graying beard in thought for a few seconds, and then continued, "And if you don't do it, the Action Men will do it for you!" He stroked his beard some more, revealing one of many tattoos barely visible on his neck behind his beard, the Don't Tread on Me snake with its tongue extending under his ear toward the back. In so doing, he flexed his aging bicep and awkwardly admired the multitude of fading tattoos there. "Brother, this confederate flag shows our solidarity with you southern folk!"

The room was quiet for almost a whole minute, but the third man broke the silence, "Yeah, it's taken a toll on us too. And these Feds aren't even legally authorized by the Constitution to bring these investigations. They won't be able to trace the money to us anyway. Our investments in President Zorin's movement were hidden by crypto. The best thing ever invented. Even with the loss of our investment. It will only be temporary. I've heard that the movement is already reorganizing with funding from our czarist friends. The new plan will bring victory to the movement." A real-life backwoods survivor, Woody Nelson had turned his following into an investment vehicle, aided by advertisements on social media and his purchases of cryptocurrency.

For a short time, he and his movement, the Silver Eagle Militia, were flush with cash, and Woody was fast becoming a celebrity in Central Michigan. He had social media followers across the world and in his mind's eye was completely invincible, even with the temporary failure of the movement's fundraising mechanism. Several years ago, upon hearing the movement's plan to finance their activities with astronomical returns of 200% and 400%, Woody jumped on board the moving train without hesitation. For four years, that gravy train was coming home with a skyrocketing balance in his accounts at the hedge fund in Detroit that held their so-called money. After the debacles of the last few years, the election losses in Michigan, and the loss of all of their capital, a regrouping was required. While he was ultimately disappointed, the defeat made him more determined to conquer the urban blight. And in the depths of his mind, Woody believed it would strengthen the movement, not weaken it as the world believed.

"What's this so-called plan and how are we going to bring about the victory you speak of? We already have control in our areas using our own means. We just need to double our efforts," Virgil Burns interrupted Woody's daydreaming with a reality check.

"The thing is, the czarists and the movement are still our friends, and they want to help us with our goal of keeping America white and Christian," Woody began. He stuttered for a few seconds, "If, if it wasn't for the meddling media elites, the market meltdown would have never occurred for our funds. You see, the Russians had the right idea in controlling the markets for our purposes. That door is closed. Now we just need to take matters into our own hands. What we need is to take this plan out to the streets and implement it without anyone finding out, and victory will be ours in the next election. But we need to strengthen and reorganize our groups with grassroots control of the plan. The movement has acquired information that will defeat the enemies of history."

"It's going to be difficult as hell to reorganize when many of our members are serving time, on probation, or probably under surveillance but I see your point. We can't give up now. Our republic is counting on it." Virgil gave a wry smile as he stood up, then ambled over with a noticeable limp to the refrigerator, the wood-planked floor creaking with each step as he did so. He pulled out a beer from a lone twelve-pack situated between three small brown boxes and slammed the door. He cracked it open with a splash, and sat back down at the table, letting out a groan as he grimaced from the pain.

These were hard times for the movement, and the three graying leaders were getting older not younger. The saving grace of their leadership was the young blood that they were recruiting every day in Michigan, Pennsylvania, the entire South, and the Western highlands. Their message was being received loud and clear with a purpose in the youth that was less educated with fewer opportunities in the modern economy.

At the same time, the movement taught them to nimbly harness technology for their clandestine purposes. They were already communicating in encrypted methods that were more difficult to trace or document for proof of any activities. This they learned from their friends in the movement, but the real game changer would be staying off the grid entirely with satellite infrastructure to hide their communication and movements.

Woody continued, "Each of us represents a large swath of America and we need to execute this plan to take back America for the Heartland. Virgil, you are going to be in charge of the movement in the South. Georgia and South Carolina and a few other areas will be yours to stop the evil from gaining any foothold in the South. Rodney, you are going to contain the corruption and pestilence in your realms, especially Arizona and Nevada. We can't have anyone there trying to steal the next election the way they have the last few times. I will organize Wisconsin, Michigan, Ohio, and Pennsylvania. If we can block the spread of their lies in these states, then victory will be ours."

"Understood," Rodney, who was normally a man of few words in person, stood up, looked out the window, and turned back toward the table, all the while continuing to run his fingers through his wiry beard. As an online persona, he could command an audience but he was not comfortable speaking in public. He managed to form his thoughts and frustrations about the previous debacle into words finally. "But once we set the plan in motion, each of our realms will be self-governing then, right? And each of us needs to fund these splinter groups to make this operation work. It needs to be top-down and no-holds-barred with total autonomy. None of this 'Wait for orders' bullshit. And no communication once we leave here unless it's on the apps you say they've created on these tablets. Communication from the movement will also come from the apps or is it directly on the tablets? I am sure more information will follow but this is my demand. Full autonomy. Especially with the Final Play."

That was a lot of words for the Idaho outlaw, who could command a barfight and was a formidable man at several inches over six feet, but normally could not speak a full sentence without either forgetting the point or stuttering. He was not a man of education, but a man of the ropes and reigns. And now he was commanding a group online the size of a Fortune 500 company. But you didn't need to be a great orator online as his average communication on those apps was only ten words long.

As Virgil looked across the room at the rustic decor of the cabin and the wild boar head that was mounted above the fireplace, he knew the plan was necessary to save the once great nation they grew up with and loved. For they would be seen as patriots in the end, saving the heritage of their ancestors and returning the glory to those who had built this land. He had stayed in this cabin once before on a hunting trip and had used other cabins in Northern Georgia as staging for the Georgia Militia activities. This bold mission was going to require a new set of rules and regs. Virgil loved rules and regs, for his organization needed to have a backbone of discipline to succeed.

His gaze came back to the thirty modest, unmarked brown boxes that lay neatly stacked on the coffee table across the room. This was the new technology that would resurrect the movement. And this was the reason for the whole new operating protocols.

Rodney also stood up, walked across the room, then turned back toward the group, bringing one hand up to his chin and the other held up in the air with one finger pointing to the ceiling as if he was talking to himself. "Each of us will have ten leaders loyal to the movement." He stuttered for a second, "I... I... I know my ten already."

"Agreed," Woody began, "and all ten will need to submit to monitoring by the movement. No more trusting that they will do the right thing. No more moles. If they were loyal to the last movement then they will be loyal now. There can be no infiltration at this level. Each of those ten will organize in their areas for fundraising and operations. Again, each of those ten must be fully autonomous. We will communicate only on the app."

Bristling at the interruptions, Rodney began to become irritated and raised his voice, "Well, what about... " he said but sat back down when he sensed Woody's anger boiling over.

"Would you listen to me?" Woody continued, "All names and birthdates will be entered into the database for our allies to run background checks. Bank account usernames and passwords will be required information. Social media usernames and passwords. All family members' names and addresses. They aren't messing around this time. And no local leaders, the movement wants this to be grassroots."

Both Virgil and Rodney raised their eyebrows simultaneously, nodding their heads in agreement.

Virgil then piped up, raising his voice even further, and stood up again for dramatics, "Where this republic will be and where each of us will be in ten years depends on this mission. We start with a few test cases in each of these thirty realms, then bring about a steady grinding war using the information that each of us will be given by the allies in the movement."

The use of the word "realm" was absolutely lost on the men in this room. None of them had any cognizance of the historical meaning, but the word sounded cool and commanding. The movement in the South was organized into these realms for a reason. Keeping the organization local allowed local leaders to control the movement. But the movement now sought to distance itself from the normal local leadership which was political in nature. These realms would be separate.

The old realms were built around old customs, old nationalist groups, and the 20th-century verbiage of their ancestors before them who once wore robes to disguise themselves. The new realms were about to change leadership without the leadership knowing. They could not know because they were political leaders subject to control by outside sources, the media, and their own financial aspirations. Going forward they would disguise themselves in these realms using technology and utilize better communication to recruit the future of their race.

Heritage was of the utmost importance not only to these three but to the entire movement. Their allies had the history of the czars on their side, and each of their realms had the legacies of their own local birth rights to look to for inspiration. Their ancestors and their descendants were all counting on this mission to succeed.

"Just one more thing before we go." Woody hesitated. "We have one more tactic that only a select few will be privy to. This will ensure the blame is properly laid."

Over the next few hours, as the sun set over the beautiful Georgia mountains, these three would cement the plan and the participants who would carry it out. Now all they needed was direction from their allies. They would not need to wait long, for most of the instructions were already compartmentalized into these different realms from the movement. The timing would be controlled by the movement. But the lively, pointed discussion left the trio eager for the fight to come.

Final instructions were provided to return to their respective realms to begin the recruitment process for the ultimate plan to take back their country.

The three men departed unceremoniously that night never to see each other again.

—•≫ ≪•—

CHAPTER 3:
OPERATION TITAN REALM

—•≫ ≪•—

These two salty veterans had been down this rebuilding road many times before and it was never easy to move on to the next case or mission. Neither Sean Stamos nor Steven Point could rest on their laurels after their financial transaction tracking program, Artificial Reconnaissance of Transactions Intelligence, or ARTI had used artificial intelligence to track patterns of stock selling to unearth a conspiracy of epic proportions.

What culminated in two years of congressional and International Criminal Court proceedings was now winding down, and Stamos was wondering if he could just have one day of rest. True to the form of his life, in the early morning of another sweltering summer day at the beginning of his only vacation in two years, the FBI was a flurry of activity around his old offices. He and Point had just been notified of an urgent planning meeting in the director's office. Stamos received the confusing message while he was sitting at his favorite coffee shop in Quantico, The Q Café, reminiscing the old days with his mentor, Bret Chelsvig, who was now retired and contemplating a move to some remote island.

Sitting beneath a trellis of fragrant jasmine on the shady patio, Stamos lightened the conversation, "Well, I may be fast behind you. I really need this vacation. I've been spending too much time in front of grandstanding congressmen and prosecutors. I just need to take a little time to relax and visit an old friend."

Chelsvig, never one to mince words, retorted, "There seems to be no ending to the stupidity of D.C. I can't believe there are congressmen backing these Russians and saying that it was a good thing for them to prop up our economy. I'm just glad to be getting out while the getting is good."

As the text message came in, Stamos let out a guttural sound that caught Chelsvig's attention. "That doesn't sound too good. What is it?"

"The Director wants a meeting. Today. That could be either good or bad, and neither of those is really good. I changed my mind. Probably only a choice between bad or worse."

"Well, looks like your vacation decision is made for you. I'll see you before I head south in a few months." Chelsvig stood up and set his empty coffee on the table.

Short goodbyes were common between these two old friends. This time, the parting hug lasted decidedly a few seconds longer than usual. Stamos could sense reluctance on the part of his old mentor regarding his decision to retire. Certainly, the last few missions were too close for comfort and had taken a drastic toll on his body and his mind. To tell the truth, the friendly fire and double-crossing agents had the same retirement-contemplating effect on Stamos. He just thought Chelsvig had a few more good years to contribute, and who knows how many he himself had in him.

"Are you sure about this retirement thing?" Stamos asked with a grin, to which Chelsvig could only smile and shake his head.

Stamos wasn't really dressed for a meeting with the Director, wearing jeans and a dark blue T-shirt, the stereotypical classic bomber jacket, and riding cowboy boots. At least he had a light blue button-down shirt and tie in his office in D.C. It would go with the blue T-shirt, he thought. He picked up his helmet and brown leather jacket off the table and walked outside. His favorite highway driving machine was parked in the shade of a tree right outside the front door. Thank goodness for that. Albeit short, the ride to D.C. was sure to be a burning furnace. At least he had the meandering back roads to soothe his mind to keep from thinking about the meeting.

Effortlessly, he tilted the red Ducati Superleggera upright and placed his helmet over his head. With a short growl of the ignition, he was off into the heat of the day. The faster the superbike went, the cooler it would be, so he was sure this would be a quick drive. He was not wrong about the curves keeping his mind occupied as the rocket hugged the lines of the road. The hour-long drive seemed like only twenty minutes as he zoned out to classic Jackson Browne in his headset.

The heavy bike jumped barely an inch when he hit the speed bump at the gate for the garage as security waved him through on sight. It didn't take long to turn the bike down the half level to the motorcycle parking area. When he arrived at his office, he didn't realize he had slightly wadded his shirt up on the chair, so he had to brush the wrinkles off with his hands when he put it on. It'll do, he thought as he headed up the elevator to the Director's office. His old buddy Steven Point was waiting, leaning heavily on the door in the hallway with his classic black suit and black tie.

The Director, who was famous for the dramatic, was sitting on the corner of his desk facing away from the door, staring down Pennsylvania Avenue. He had barely even said, "Come In," when Stamos and Point were announced by his secretary. The secretary sat them in the soft leather chairs across from his desk. It seemed like more than a few minutes ticked by and the two were reduced to looking at each other in silence, as the Director did not turn his head one inch. The two were reduced to guessing silently as to what the Director's gaze was concentrating on, if anything.

"Men!" the director startled them with a scowl, "I don't

have to tell you again what I think of the future of your signals intelligence gathering machine. I came up the ranks without these fancy computers you have nowadays. But I'll tell you what, I think I have the perfect use for it. The Attorney General has it stuck in his head that there are a thousand threats to our nation that may or may not be there. The threats he thinks he sees come from within, our very own people, for God's sake. The media is calling it domestic terrorism. What a dumb name that is! Hell, I think each one of these isolated episodes is totally unrelated to the others. But, my hands are tied by what he has ordered. Gentlemen, by the orders on my desk, I have named you co-directors of the new Office of Domestic Counterintelligence, which will seek to detect and counteract domestic terrorism threats."

As both looked on with jaw-dropped, incredulous looks on their faces, Stamos made the first attempt to utter a word. Neither of them had expected to be anywhere close to division director status any time soon. "Well, sir, that is an incredible honor and could be one of the most significant changes of direction for the bureau." He knew the FBI director was a stodgy curmudgeon who was more of a political appointee than anything, even though he was a former agent. But that was a lifetime ago, which was why he said the words "fancy computers" like they were brand new. The real leadership of the bureau was vested in the division directors anyway.

"Don't go teary-eyed on me. This is going to be the shortest-lived division in the bureau. I don't think you'll find much. As a matter of fact, I will make sure to keep your office here fully furnished for your return."

Point cleared his throat to speak but was interrupted by the director. "That's not to say you won't find a few rednecks somewhere out there plotting to put pipe bombs in mailboxes and such."

"Well, sir, then why put the world's finest artificial intelligence algorithm on this, if you don't think we are going to find anything?" Point, previously a polite, mild-mannered

SEC agent, was definitely developing the sardonic wit required of an FBI agent. Stamos mused to himself that Point would do just fine in the transition.

The Director did not seem to be listening. He was still staring out the window from the corner of his desk. He hadn't even glanced in the direction of his new division chiefs. He looked down at his desk, picked up a candy from the candy bowl, and popped one in his mouth. With a mouth half full of candy, he muttered loudly, "I've already taken the liberty of assembling a staff of good agents for you. As a matter of fact, they should be in your office now. We will develop the field agents assigned to your team next week. Are you both on board?" It seemed to both Point and Stamos that the decision was already made for them.

Stamos felt he needed to negotiate some autonomy for this mission. He could sense the director was not on board with this new division under his command. A mission without support from above would be destined to fail. "Sir, I would need full autonomy. And I would need carte blanche on the need for agents, budgeting, and equipment. We will need a full travel setup. If I call and need something, I need to know you have my back. I am not going to go on a shopping spree and I won't come to you unless I feel it is necessary. Based on our recent mission and the Russians' cultivation of assets here in the United States, the threats inside this country are a real possibility. What we won't know until we dig deep will be how organized they are and whether they are stupid enough to get caught again."

"Stamos, I know you are a straight shooter. I give you my word. You guys will have my complete support." The Director still had not looked their way.

"How can we pass up the opportunity?" Stamos asked. He was ready for this change after the damage his body had been through during the past few missions. He pledged to himself at that moment that he would delegate to others so he wouldn't be ambushed or shot at this time.

Stamos stood up and walked over to the window behind Point and to his right, he could see the Washington Monument stretching majestically toward the blue sky over the nation's capital.   He then looked back over at Point and from the look on his face, Stamos knew his answer too.

"Let's get this operation on the road," Point blurted out, while rising to his feet, buttoning his black suit jacket.

Well, there it was, Stamos reflected as he continued to stare out at the skyline of the District of Columbia and its historic monuments. His official retirement from field espionage missions. And none too soon, he figured. No more near-death experiences at the hands of foreign agents. His body could not take any more abuse, just like his old friend, Chelsvig

Regardless, his storied deep-cover career was involuntarily, completely caput. With his new-found worldwide notoriety from the congressional hearings, gone were the days of investigations in disguise in faraway lands. Alas, there were newbie Quantico and Langley graduates who, with their youth and vigor, would fulfill that role in the future. While he surely would miss the excitement of field work, perhaps his resignation to desk work and delegation would be a good decision. He and Point were now tasked with leading a team to uncover the next threats to the stability of the United States of America.

As Point and Stamos slowly exited the director's office, the director gave a cursory, "Good luck, men," and they were on their way to Stamos' office to determine what ragtag group of agents the Director had assigned to their team.

Their old offices were stately but sparsely decorated and as Stamos walked through the door, he could see they now had several attorneys and investigators in their 6th-floor wing of the Hoover FBI Headquarters. These investigators all crammed into the small office and while it was a little crowded, this was just a welcome meeting consisting of their newest staff. Stamos walked over to the window and looked down on Pennsylvania Avenue for a second time. This time he watched silently as a small group of protesters with Second Amendment signs gathered across the street. This was no ordinary time in the history of the United States, as the sentiment of the masses could be described as restless to put it lightly. Extremists from both the left and the right were destabilizing the security of the United States and caught in the middle were law-abiding citizens trying to build upon the successes of this great nation. The Director couldn't have judged the importance of this new division more wrongly.

One of the agents, a slightly heavy-set middle-aged man, was sitting at Stamos' desk. He jumped to his feet and walked toward Stamos. "Hello, my name is Bill Hanson. I will be your assistant. We've all been talking about the meaning behind our assignment. I have been canvassing the group, finding out their strengths and level of experience. They are not all newbies. I think this team is well suited to this mission."

Stamos had overlooked that one hard fact. He, as a division director now, would require an assistant, that would also essentially be his shadow, a bodyguard of sorts. Hanson looked the part, perhaps a little older, slightly larger build, maybe would look more at home in Secret Service garb, Stamos mused. He wondered which of these other blokes would be Point's bodyguard.

Steven Point, who had lingered outside for a minute, now entered quickly and stood in the only empty corner of the room, while the junior investigators sat in chairs they had brought in from the other offices. He was still dressed in his characteristic black suit, thin black tie, and white pressed shirt, with short blonde hair spiked with hair gel that made it look like he was an actor playing the part.

Stamos cleared his throat with a short cough. "Thanks. Alright Steven, looks like it's you and me now, with this crew. This is going to be the biggest shift in our careers. We can't use some of the surveillance tactics we used in the past but where we lack in field stakeouts we can make up with some artificial intelligence tools. Do you think we can retool ARTI to accomplish this?"

Point couldn't wait to retool ARTI for this mission. He was more than ready to prove this would be a new challenge he could meet head-on. "First, we need to determine where these threats are emanating from. The way I see it, there are threats from both sides of the spectrum so it will be difficult to pin down the exact phenotype of the person or persons or groups that will turn out to be the real threats."

Steven Point's analytical mind was eerily similar to his own, Stamos thought, but they were also as different as night and day. Steven had advanced through the financial world of analytics and enforcement of securities law and Stamos had moved up through the ranks of spies with a legal twist. On the last mission, and now moving into the future, their different mindsets would complement each other nicely with Point's utilization of computerized analysis of possible perpetrators tied into Stamos' in-the-field investigation experience. They both had perceived that the movement that they had taken down last year was still alive and well, yet hidden from immediate view.

Point continued, strolling across the room in front of Stamos' substantial solid oak desk, then stopped and turned around, looking pointedly at each investigator, "We need to compile some dossiers on both groups and individuals, monitor their interactions among each other and see what ARTI can gather from all of the legally available information we have. And given the threats and the severity of those threats, we can skirt the legal avenues that we have at our disposal. If we need to we should deploy drone surveillance teams as these guys like to meet in very rural places to avoid detection. It will be difficult to get approval for that, I know."

Stamos countered, "I don't want to be sitting in front of a committee asking why we are spying on our own people, but we have certain people for which we will have probable cause for warrants. Let's bring into the fold of groups some of the foreign actors that we know want to promote division. To that end, we can see if there are any interactions among them also. Remember the cross-chatter we encountered during our last mission between the "movement" in Russia and some of these stateside groups."

"You know, there is no reason we can't use some field surveillance on the foreign actors that could ensnare these groups. We still have the location and IP addresses of the movement and all of their US-based servers. They still have not taken down these assets." Point was really good at sensing where Stamos' investigative mind was headed.

"Do they really not know they were compromised?" Stamos asked incredulously.

"I don't think so. When we were closing down the operation, Sebastian installed some malware on their servers as we thought they were monitoring our incursions into their servers anyway. Turns out they were not as protective of their own security as we thought."

"Do you think he could pass the security clearances that he would need to become part of our team?" Stamos knew that Sebastian was a hacker and lived with his parents, not to mention a recent college graduate, so he was not sure if he would pass the financial and background checks that were needed for top-secret clearance.

"I already took the liberty of setting that up because I was hoping to steal him for myself if I moved back to the SEC. He passed with flying colors, straight as an arrow! He jumped at the chance to join us at the SEC, I don't see why he wouldn't do the same here. I think he would enjoy the thrill of the chase that exists on this side of the government world."

Again, Point was three steps ahead. Stamos turned around shaking his head. "Well, let's start assembling a team around us three and these fine recruits once we have the new iteration of ARTI up and running. While we are doing that, let's assemble the first round of probables. Feed them and our known "movement" actors into the system first. Their communications may expose them before we even get started."

Steven Point needed to clarify something, as he did not want to be based here at the Hoover Building in downtown D.C. "Let's base our systems down at Quantico. All of you investigators will be commuting between field offices and Quantico. I kind of like being away from the city for this operation. Our operators are sure to be located in the sticks and we need to be closer to them." Steven was starting to sound more like an FBI agent than an SEC computer analyst.

Quantico was becoming the epicenter of counterintelligence training and signal intelligence because its rural location allowed the FBI to evade detection by foreign agents. Stamos thought it was a great idea, and approved the move, conditional upon finding a location. "We need a secure location for ARTI, though."

"Most definitely," Point replied curtly.

Stamos now finally turned away from the window and addressed the agents before him. "Well then, gentlemen and women, it's official now. This is going to be our first mission. I am going to call it Operation Titan Realm. I've named it after some of the verbiage and organization of the extremist groups that go way back to the 1920s. We will need to watch our backs as these groups are becoming more and more offensive in their tactics. They will know we are watching them and they will be looking for us. And they are armed."

There was a lot of nodding and affirmative banter around the room as there were a lot of opinions as to the locations and targets of the first surveillance. These were junior agents, some of whom were getting their first assignments after making top-secret clearance and Stamos mused to himself that he rather fancied their overenthusiasm and the team could use it to their advantage.

Point's mind was already racing a quarter mile down the runway after the green light was given. "We will have a lot of prep work, first and foremost moving ARTI down to Quantico. This will be no small feat. I think we can accomplish the dismantling, moving, and re-installation in about a week. I will arrange for the secure compartmentalized location."

Hanson interjected, "With my last division we had space in Quantico. I know there is room in the Fiber Building, which has an encrypted trunk internet connection to the outside world. It also is essentially a SCIF building in itself. But I will arrange a modular SCIF conference room in case we have visitors. And we need to start getting set up with regional office space. What do you think about Atlanta, Phoenix, and Detroit for starters?"

"I like that. Let's get the information on the footprint of this location in Quantico," said Point.

Stamos expected this transition to take weeks, but within minutes the mission was off the starting block and in a full sprint. "Great, it's settled. You and Sebastian can arrange the logistics of bringing ARTI to Quantico. And let's get all of these regional offices set up in the next few days. Since my vacation was just canceled, I want to travel to Atlanta as soon as I can to get the lay of the land, so to speak. I was hoping to go there anyway to see an old friend I haven't seen in a while."

As Point turned to leave, he looked back at Stamos, and said, "This could get messy, but I think there is a lot more that we will discover than the Director thinks. Let's get this up and running as soon as possible. You know what they say about the oxymoron of a political hack getting involved in intelligence. The word about the mission tends to get out and we don't want to wait until that happens."

"Right. First, I need to stay in the city to see Natalia and Chip. Then I will meet all of you down at Quantico tomorrow. I arranged the rendezvous somewhere quiet. Do you want to go? She says she has some news for me, and I wanted to tie up some loose ends with the last operation. Sort of an informal debriefing."

Point had not seen them since one of the early hearings. "Sure. I wonder what new adventure she will be cooking up."

"That's a good question. I heard they have been capitalizing on their sailing fame." Stamos rose to leave. "Alright let's go. If we don't leave soon, we'll be late."

A voice from the corner gave a subtle, yet loud, "Ahem." Then a pause, "How would you like to be, um, accompanied?"

Stamos had already forgotten about his newly acquired assistant who he now realized would accompany him even on this unofficial business. If it slowed him down the tiniest bit, this was going to get old really fast. There was not much privacy for those who had attained the title of division director.

These agents even accompanied single directors on dates and attended family functions for those who were married. Along the same vein, he supposed from now on there would be a car or two posted outside of his home.

"Hanson, what kind of car do you drive? Is it fast?"

"I have a decent car, an Audi A6. I try to avoid government-issued cars just like you. James here is also going to join us."

"Perfect, a crowd. You're Point's assistant?" He pointed to James, a slightly younger, athletic African-American man who looked more like an Olympic wrestler than an FBI agent. "Okay, keep up with me, we aren't going far, a little blues club in an alley near Georgetown. First, I have to change."

A few minutes later, they were off, and as Stamos engaged the clutch and shifted gears, once again the bike seemed to lift his soul to a higher level. He took a few slow deep breaths and contemplated the events of today. Akin to meditation that he had practiced a few times before, the bike made him feel at one with the earth and sky at the same time, thus clearing any unnecessary thoughts.

His thoughts rose to a higher level than those on the city streets around him and began to flash back to people who had helped him attain his dream of fighting for righteousness. He took the long route along the scenic tree-lined streets along the Potomac River to breathe in the spirit of the historic waterway. Old stone bridges crossed it with the respect it deserved. Some of those who had guided him along his journey were no longer with him in the physical world, but he still felt their hands guiding him. People like his first CIA paramilitary commander in Pakistan, through whom he had learned how to survive when there was no possibility of surviving.

Ostensibly, most would think this assignment would be a step down from international espionage and intrigue, but to Stamos, this was a logical extension of the last several years of work. There had been warnings flashed in his travels through the clandestine world that the same forces that were at play in

Russia from his past two missions could bubble up through the underbelly of middle America in a far more dangerous way. Who better to investigate than those who had foiled the most sinister plot to destroy first America's democracy and then America's financial infrastructure?

If there was one thing he believed in, it was the opportunities that America and other free countries offered to everyone, no matter their background. Equality was the backbone of a free market system since it gave everyone the same chance to succeed and therefore to pass that torch of the American dream on to their children.

There would be equal opportunities for danger on this mission, he thought. He glanced to the side at his mirror, and there was the A6 not more than twenty yards back. "Not bad," he thought as he looked forward, and with a slight twist of his right hand, it was more like a hundred yards.

—◆}} {{◆—

CHAPTER 4: CLOSURE

—◆}} {{◆—

A hefty dose of adrenaline flowed steadily through Natalia's veins as she confidently skipped down the worn marble steps of Georgetown's business college building. She fully recognized her decades of hard work and persistence, yet she sometimes felt she must have crazy luck to win the opportunities that always seemed to fall before her feet. Each rung on the ladder she had attained continued to pay off in dividends that led to ever more extraordinary experiences and exceptional people. Materialistic success mattered so little, even to this daughter of a Russian oligarch. What truly defined her life were the friends who were now family to her. Despite the excitement that she felt regarding this newest big break, she promised herself at this moment to appreciate them more. She held a rich belief that these investments had already made her life rich beyond belief

She emerged from this deep thought just in time to behold her favorite co-pilot along this enchanted journey, who was waiting in suspense at the curb with arms raised and stretched out to the sky. The sight of the genuinely loving smile on Chip's face brought her heart rate down from the stratosphere to a more manageable level. Dressed in dark blue jeans and a blue patterned dress shirt, accentuated by aviator sunglasses, he epitomized business casual style and easily could have been mistaken for one of the business professors that she had just left behind.   Simultaneously, the pair appeared to leap slightly into each other's arms as they embraced on the promenade at the base of the steps.

Chip inquired about the results of the meeting, exclaiming, "From the color on your cheeks and the sparkle in your eyes, I'd say that went quite well!"

"Oh my God, it went so well! Better than we could have ever expected. As we thought, they extended a generous proposition to come here to Georgetown, which would involve the Chronicle too. I think it may be something we can't refuse."

"Wow, that's great! Congratulations! It couldn't have happened to a more deserving person! They are capturing the brightest star in business journalism. We should celebrate!"

"Yes, you are right! We can celebrate when we meet with Stamos! Look at that! We're almost late! This meeting took longer than I thought. It seemed like the entire faculty of Georgetown was in attendance."

Her new opportunity added to her desperate need for the closure this informal debriefing with Stamos would bring to her. But in actuality, it was Stamos who asked for the meeting, so maybe it was he who needed the closure. Or perhaps the daring attorney-turned-spy had some other news or information for them. Chip was now standing with his hand propped atop the thick, open door of the black, armored Suburban, motioning for her to climb in. Under his arm, she spied Sam, busy on his phone in the front seat. While the three of them had participated in dozens of interviews at FBI headquarters, they had not had a chance to decompress and debrief in private with Sean Stamos, their old friend. And, frankly, they had become more than just casual friends in those few days of battle against global tyranny. This informal exchange was long overdue.

"Well, hello, Sam!" Natalia greeted her second favorite

Brit.

"Cheerio, my sweet sister!" came the response from the front, with fingers still typing. It took a few more seconds of contorting his face in a way that showed serious twisting of the written word to say, "Okay, I'm done. How was it?" He let out a deep breath of relief from whatever stress previously occupied him.

"Very successful! We may need a real estate agent here in D.C.!" Natalia nervously revealed.

"That was quick! Congratulations! I am sure you will bring your real-world practicality to all of these bright students," Sam pointed to a group of what seemed like children to him strolling down the sidewalk.

"I love the atmosphere here! Almost seems like old times in Oxford, don't you think?" she asked.

"It does have an old-world appeal to it." Sam then commanded and motioned to the driver to make some time.

In a matter of minutes, the world-famous trio would finally get the chance to reconnect with Sean Stamos. The setting was quite unconventional, a little blues club tucked way back in an alley just a block off the ritzy M Street corridor of Georgetown. As they passed the ancient dark red brick three and four-story buildings, they were instantly transported more than two hundred years to the beginnings of these neighborhoods after the Revolutionary War. It didn't take much of an imagination to envision John Adams or Thomas Jefferson trotting down the cobblestone streets to the Potomac. Natalia and Chip pointed out the historic markers on each side and the old church, wishing they could join a historical tour of the locale.

To tell the truth, though, at the culmination of this long day of storytelling, Natalia really just needed to relax and was looking forward to sitting back and listening to some good, old blues or jazz. Her mind conjured up a jazzy saxophone number just then to settle her mood with a cupful of meditation to balance the adrenaline. Rarely did she drink, but her taste buds were joyfully anticipating a cool sparkling wine as the perfect ending to close out this chapter of her life.

For a few seconds, she sank down in her seat, with her eyes closed, clearing her mind. There were two techniques she had always leaned on to promote a higher plane of existence. The first involved visualization of her state of mind if it were to exist with only positive inputs and no negatives. To accomplish the positive meant the negative needed to be exhaled into the ether that surrounded her, exiting to who knows where. She desired this meeting to be the positive closure she longed for from her former life. Though she had said her own personal, inner goodbyes to her family long ago, this was a professional closure. She followed this with the second method of elevation, affirmations of self-determination, which was accomplished easily with today's events.

Ignoring all caution regarding hasty decisions, Natalia's mind was prematurely embarking on her exciting next phase of life, mentoring young journalists and business majors who were ready to make their mark in this world. In a way, this offer made the transition away from New York and the hectic city life easy for her. She loved Georgetown. It felt like her old home at Oxford with the architecture of the campus and the small-town charm of the tree-lined neighborhoods. And she couldn't wait to sail single-handed boats on the Potomac and the Chesapeake, teaching the lost art of the wind to these undergraduates.

She opened her affirmative mind to the world, followed soon thereafter by her green, radiant eyes. As the frontmost of the two armored Suburbans slowly turned down the side street in front of them, their coach dutifully followed. This was the minimal security package when she traveled nowadays. Even the smallest errands took on complex logistics, but she barely noticed the inconvenience, since, from early childhood, she had always been accompanied by security, and her detail was treated like an extended family. The alleyway was in view now, and they slowed to a stop on the street to await the decoy assessing the situation as it crept down the narrow alleyway. There was barely room for the SUVs to pass through. Not ideal, but Sam motioned to proceed.

Their chariots for the evening came to a stop in the alleyway, letting their passengers duck into the small vine-framed doorway with playbills posted on the nearby wall. As they paused at the entryway, Natalia, arm in arm with Chip, let out a laugh that was a smidgen more than a giggle and tossed her hair back as she gazed into Chip's eyes just long enough to see through to his heart.

"This is SO romantic!" she exclaimed, as her curls glistened in the setting sun.

Chip had always known these deep green eyes were his future, with the warm, inviting embrace bringing him closer to happiness than he had ever been in his life. Those eyes were the love he had wished for his whole adult life. The exuberance that was flashing in her eyes was a joyous sight, given the torture she had endured these past few years at the hands of her family.

As they entered the club down several tiled steps and through another doorway, they were suddenly, uncomfortably blind in the darkness that was the Georgetown Blues Club. Comfortingly, Natalia and Chip could feel the shoulders of their preceding security detail with their outstretched hands. As they squinted their eyes for a few seconds, suddenly they could make out shapes and then those shapes came into better focus. It seemed there was not a single light on in the place at first. There were only a few patrons savoring the music this early in the evening, and at the back of the club, on stage, their ears could detect a crooning saxophonist gently serenading them.

There he sat, quiet, unassuming, and underdressed, with his black MK V-neck shirt and dark blue jeans, with black cowboy boots neatly accessorizing the look, nestled into a deep red velvet seat in the shadowy corner. The large booth was walled off from the rest of the room, almost a separate room in and of itself. The saxophone and haziness certainly added to the mystery of the night, as Natalia imagined they were meeting a clandestine spy here for information exchange. She was sure he had to have security or a junior agent who was in charge of his security. As she glanced around the room, sure enough, there were two younger men in suits across the room with club sodas, conspicuously out of place.

She was not expecting to see the blonde gentleman next to him, wearing a black suit with a thin black tie like he was a 1960s FBI agent. In Natalia's vivid imagination, Steven Point had a way of dressing his part as if he were the star of a classic avant-garde detective thriller. The only thing missing was the dark sunglasses that would have completed the ensemble. Natalia felt relieved that it was more than just Stamos they were meeting. She had an uncomfortable attraction to him, that she could feel was mutual but unmentionable between them. She knew she was in love with Chip and there existed more than enough attraction there but that didn't mean she was dead. This guy was everyone's dream. She privately wondered why he was still single.

Stamos and Point shot out of the booth simultaneously, as Natalia, Chip, and Sam neared the table. Sam motioned to the table with the two junior agents and their security detail took the hint, departing in search of matching club sodas. Sam then rejoined the group and there was an awkward silence as they started to fill in the seats of the booth.

Natalia and Stamos were the last to sit, and, as they exchanged the customary European distant cheek kisses, the mood lightened and the months of absence melted into oblivion.

"You two are sights for sore eyes, you know that?" Natalia blurted out nervously. "We never brought closure to our adventures last year. First off, how are you?"

Greetings were exchanged around the table as though they had just seen each other last week, but the time and distance were soon readily apparent as a stiff silence ensued. Apart from the salutations, no one knew what to say, which could have deteriorated the situation. Stamos stared across the room at their assistants, uncomfortable in their hard chairs near the bar. Without moving his eyes, he canvassed the room's attendance and eyed the stairs with a black iron railing and dark red walls leading to the second floor at the back of the room. That would be his escape if needed and he already had a few routes he had rehearsed for years gone by. His eyes darted back to his guests as he felt the painful silence. Then, uncontrollably, Natalia's heart-on-her-sleeve mentality lightened the situation.

Tears glistened in everyone's eyes but they flowed forth from Natalia's eyes as the floodgate let loose and they poured down her reddened cheeks like two rivers of emotion. She paused for a few seconds to catch her breath. With her sleeve, she wiped the tears, and with a soft laugh, continued, "I don't think I have truly cried since, you know, the events. I know we have to be professional and can't talk about anything, but I feel like there is some connection that we need to maintain for all of our professional lives. There is unfinished business in the world. I don't think we have defeated the Hydra just yet. People like my uncle don't just fade into the black and disappear. They will be back, and sooner than you think."

Stamos could feel some excess dampness in his eyes, and, with his mind and the tips of his fingers, willfully forced the tears back in. "Yes, unfortunately, we didn't completely wipe out their wealth. But Point here and I are embarking on a different but similar path with ARTI as the backbone. I am sure we will tell you soon enough. I too want to make sure we don't lose this connection. And we are going to have a connection through Sebastian, who is joining us at the bureau."

"No, are you serious? That is amazing. He will be a perfect fit with you two. Though he can be a bit corny with his barely pubescent humor. I have to warn you about that. I am not sure he has had a real girlfriend yet."

Point chimed in his two cents on the subject, "Oh, we already have some hearty experience with his wit on the airplane in Teterboro." He was right about that. Probably one of the more memorable moments apart from the RPGs being fired at them by the Secret Service, was Sebastian's witty exchange.

"Well, you have your hands full. Chip and I have some news for you, too. We may be moving to Georgetown if all of the cards fall right. They've offered me a position in the school of business and the sailing team as a coach. All with a research program sponsor."

"Well, you will now be right down the road, though I have a feeling we will be traveling a lot for this upcoming mission." Stamos would turn out to have quite a premonition on that point. At least for the time being they would almost be neighbors in the capital at the top of the Potomac River. "I live near Quantico, Virginia which is the training base for the FBI and a U.S. Marine Base about an hour away, and we are moving some of our offices there."

Natalia reciprocated, "Well hopefully we can catch up periodically, that is, when you are in between world-saving missions. Chip and I plan on continuing our peaceful life here for a while."

Stamos blushed a little, "Well if you are going to set up a domicile here in Georgetown you will have to spend some time here in this little club. They have the best jazz and blues singers from all over. I have spent many a Friday night here, relaxing and getting my mind off the outside world. A friend and I used to perform here every once in a while. You guys should meet her, she holds the rhythm of soul in her heart."

"Oh, really? I was wondering who had your heart?" Natalia was more than curious now. That was the answer to the question she had on her mind for months. Where did his heart lie?

"She's a best friend from home. Fiery, sexy, but nomadic. Rolling stone. Just like me. We are perfect, but not so perfect for each other. Just friends." he said, lying through his teeth.

"Do you have any musical talents?" Natalia asked.

"I can play the sax and the harmonica. She and I used to play in some small bands back home or just impromptu drum circles. Her music was better suited for the drum circles. But I kept up with all of them pretty well." Stamos stared at the brick wall behind Natalia, reminiscing about the old days. The black iron bars on the windows close to the black painted tin ceiling added to the ancient mystery of the club, which in a former lifetime was a horse stable. Black lights on the walls illuminated posters from a bygone era of jazz and big band stars who had once graced these halls with their sinewy tunes. A lone oxidized saxophone hung between the two windows and Stamos could feel the urge to remove it to start playing if only his love was here to sing along.

Chip could sense the longing and interrupted his train of thought, "We would have never known. Somewhere under the stoic James Bond type, is a creative artist, just waiting to shatter and break through the tough outer shell? I take it this is blues you play, too?"

"Yes, both blues and jazz. Normally I just play in the privacy of my home. I'm not much of an entertainer, more of an introverted artist. She is the extrovert. She brings me out of my comfort zone creatively."

Natalia was fascinated, but changed the subject, "Let's get back to business. Anything you need from us regarding my family and maintaining surveillance on them, just let me know. I may not be able to travel back to Russia anymore but I have some old classmates who are part of the resistance."

Stamos bit on the morsel offered, "We can always use connections if they are vetted right. I will let you know. Let's plan to meet again at our new offices in a few weeks once we find out what we are dealing with in this new mission. We can bring you in as consultants. We will have to background check and clear the vetting from the outside vendors. This time it will have to be run through the proper channels. I am sure your family may present some problems for your security checks, but we will just have to compartmentalize any secret information."

"Yes, my family always presents some kind of problem. Don't they?"

"I have to travel to Atlanta soon but we will circle back to this when I return." Stamos was already giving away mission information with this statement and he stopped for a few seconds to think about what more to say about that. "What I can say is we have some new investigations starting up."

There was an awkward silence that was broken when the

singer's voice and the saxophonist became louder and more upbeat and a guitarist joined in with an old B.B. King song, Rock Me Baby. The deep, guttural female voice presented an impeccable feminine version of the iconic blues singer. The four of them turned and just sat there quietly for several minutes and took in the next few songs without a word spoken. A few of the early patrons began to dance in front of the band and all four were tempted but thought better of it, especially this early in the evening.

As the tempo and volume decreased once again, the opportunity to talk returned. Always forward, and a bundle of curiosity, Natalia looked over at Point. He was even more unemotional than Stamos. There was something more casual about him today, though, despite his dress code. He appeared to be getting into the music, tapping his fingers on the table, sometimes even rocking his shoulders back and forth.

"Steven, what about you? What is your passion?" The question half-startled Point, as he previously maintained a policy not to engage in much personal talk. Natalia could sense the discomfort and rephrased the question. "What kind of music do you like?"

Point felt a little more comfortable, "This is great music. I have dabbled in electronic music in the past. It's like programming a computer. There's a logic to it."

"Aha, that's interesting. There's a whole scene in New York for EDM. DJ Point could be a good moniker."

He just smiled and a hint of laughter escaped his lips. "Hmmm, that would be interesting. It's all about the data. The beat is just a bunch of ones and zeros of programming really when you think about it logically."

The five of them had quite a chuckle at Point's expense. Even Sam and Chip laughed out loud at the thought. The image of the black suit, thin tie, and black hat could be quite a persona in the clubs of Manhattan.

As it turned out, the evening would be quite enjoyable for all, and as the party wound down, Natalia felt as though she had accomplished what she set out to do. They were able to meet these two in an informal situation and maintain their connection. And most importantly, she felt relaxed and rejuvenated by the decisions she would soon have to make. She realized that she had forgotten to tell Sam and Chip about the offer of sailing on the Chesapeake and plans were made to delay their departure for New York.

As Stamos left, he gave a hearty embrace to the whole crowd and mounted his Ducati with a final goodbye of the evening reserved for his junior agent, with some special instructions on their route home through the countryside. He informed Hanson that he would take it easy on him before revving the throaty V4 engine. Hanson quickly ran for his vehicle, knowing he would never keep up, but at least he could try with the V6 German engineering.

That scene of scrambling assistants was quite comical to the three visitors as they climbed into the heavy awaiting Suburbans. Stamos allowed maybe thirty seconds for Hanson to get to the car, and seeing the headlights turn on, the superbike shot down the alleyway and onto the side street. Chip, Natalia, and their gang of security waited for the Audi to depart in front of them and followed them out of the downtown neighborhood.

Chip looked over at Natalia, "You are looking more relaxed than I have seen you in a long while. Are you sure you want to interrupt your sabbatical?"

Natalia replied confidently, "Yes, I think it is time. And this opportunity affords me everything I need, including you. Teaching young journalists is going to be so fulfilling and relaxing for a change and will give us a chance to build a life out of the limelight and away from my family. But first, let's sail the Chesapeake this weekend."

—⸱⸱⸱—

CHAPTER 5: CLAIRE

—⸱⸱⸱—

After a beautiful pink sunset, dusk had descended on an antiquated, red brick industrial building in midtown Atlanta that had been converted into a dozen lofts with an open elevator. Claire Taub, with her fiery auburn dreads in tow, paused for a few minutes to watch the sunset from her parked car, taking stock of the day's accomplishments. Now, she hastily ascended the antique freight elevator from the parking lot below. Her hands were overflowing with that day's sushi leftovers, her handbag, and a stainless steel water bottle, as she was fumbling to extract her keys from the oversized hobo handbag. As she placed her keys on the hook next to her notebooks, she let out a sigh as she noticed some boxes that her two blue-point Siamese cats had been in the process of destroying. She pulled her incomplete dreads back in a ponytail of sorts, put her sushi dinner in the refrigerator, and set about cleaning up the mess. Her feline children, Sammy and Gio, were trying their best to interrupt the process to show their appreciation for the return of their owner. Their olfactory senses kicked into overdrive detecting the raw fish that had just been put away as they expressed their desire to be fed with persistent vocal begging.

As she extracted the natural pet food from the refrigerator and began to spoon it into two hand-made pottery dishes, she scolded her children, "Boys, you know that sushi is too spicy for you. This is better for you, full of vitamins so you grow big and strong!"

Apparently, that would suffice for the two felines, as they appeared to fight over which bowl was whose, each inspecting the other's bowl to be sure they were not missing out on any of the fish they could still clearly smell.

If she was going to get in a quick four-mile sprint through Piedmont Park, she would need to hurry. Her diminutive size belied her quickness, as she was actually quite a swift runner. Tonight, her goal was to carry a six-minute pace through the park, which for her was quite slow, but with her relatively new, momentous position at Worldwide News Network, she found it difficult to find time for exercise. She always found time for two things, running and her love for performance arts and music of the deep, expressive genres. If she could find a drum circle, no matter where or what time, she was always down for it.

Growing up in Belfast, Maine, she always found herself in the mountains or down by the shore, with a myriad of friends, creating bohemian, free-thinking music that reverberated through her soul. Her specialty was rhythm as she had taught herself how to play various drums in her childhood. She didn't like band in high school, as the rhythms the band teacher taught at the small school she attended did not speak to her. She preferred blues, island music, and reggae to the stodgy old standards that her parents wanted her to play. It wasn't until college that she was able to take some lessons from a reggae master drummer. In her small town, there just wasn't the opportunity, though the rhythms just naturally came to her. No, flowed from inside her.

During her formative years at Bowdoin College, she studied art and music and dabbled in writing poetry and short stories, as well as reporting on local music and art events for the school's paper. It wasn't until her senior year that she decided to switch to a journalism major, as it suddenly became her dream to travel the world, reporting on music and art scenes of different cultures. She had already traveled extensively for a year abroad, splitting time between Colombia, Trinidad, and Jamaica. After graduation, she made the move to D.C. for a short stint of a few years at an international online news outlet, before she finally attained her dream job at WNN. She had been making waves as a newbie journalist in Atlanta for only four months, but she truly believed she was building inroads into a permanent position in the culture section.

As she gathered her running clothes and sat down at the chair in her living room that overlooked the midtown area with large, almost floor-to-ceiling windows, she thought to herself that the year was already so full of sunshine for her spirit. She had met so many positive people at WNN, so many like-minded individuals who cared deeply about the human race. There was no doubt in her mind, this was where she was meant to be. Traveling around the country (and hopefully the world soon enough) reporting on the creative energy of the best of our society was the miso soup for her soul.

She hurriedly changed into her running shoes and shorts, and her favorite Bowdoin dry-fit tank. With her headphones in place and a smooth reggae beat, she was almost primed for her nightly outing. But first, she had to return a text to an old friend. It looked like he was going to be in Atlanta sometime soon. She sighed and gazed out at the Atlanta skyline beginning to light up. Claire was not the attached type, but if there was one person she could see herself with long-term, this was the one. They had grown up together along the shores of Maine and were often running partners in D.C., but now they were separated by long distances for the past few months. Neither of them had time for a relationship, and that suited Claire just fine, for she knew if her destiny was to travel the world, there would be no chance to be attached, let alone married and raise a family.

She took a few minutes to get the text right. She offered an invitation to get together upon arrival. They had continued to stay in touch by text, but with their busy travel schedules, there was scarcely time for even a short Hi, opting instead for pics and emojis. She added that she was going to be traveling this week and to be sure to confirm the dates when they were known.

With the text sent, she briefly glanced in the round mirror in the hallway to affirm her goal for this evening's run and gave the green eyes that stared back at her a brief affirmation. She closed them, inhaled a deep breath, and concentrated on the physiology of the muscles in her legs, priming them. She opened them again to see the same sparkling orbs, this time with a fiery determined look. She bent down to pay sequential attention to each of her offspring, who were agitated at the lack of affection from this one. "Okay, I'll be back in a few minutes. Here's some vittles for you," she said as she cracked open an envelope of delectable treats.

With that, she descended the creaky elevator, and with a short stretch on the sidewalk below, she was off like a shot. Her dreads were bouncing lightly in the air as she strode through the park effortlessly. The paths in the park were well-lighted and were considered very safe for women joggers, and there was a lot of activity on the soccer fields and volleyball courts in the twilight. Her halfway point at two miles and the highlight of her run through the park was climbing the stairs at the fountain on the far north side of the park. Her watch was telling her the pace was just a little bit off her goal, so she decided to kick it in gear a little on the way home.

This week, she knew she had to keep to her running schedule, as she was due to fly to Red Rocks, Colorado to report on a festival there this weekend. The altitude there, with its lower oxygen levels, would challenge her pace. She had only stayed in Denver once, but she loved the trails along the creek near her hotel and was looking forward to a few days of the extra elevation.

As she returned to her rustic brick domicile, she noticed one of her neighbors, Mía, was also just getting home. They had just met a few weeks ago but immediately struck up a friendship due to their many shared interests. It seemed to

Claire that they were sisters from different mothers. Mía had just landed an internship for the year at the prestigious Atlanta Sentinel and had just moved from D.C. as well, and they both enjoyed writing poetry and listening to music.

"Hi, Mía, how was work today?" Claire's shoulders were glistening with only a minimal sweat even though it was quite warm out this evening.

"Amazing! I have just been offered a new assignment over the past week that could be a byline. That would be my second by-line in two weeks. I need to get some more research done on it right away." Mía could not contain her excitement, and her face beamed with pride at her accomplishment.

"Already? Congratulations! You'll have to tell me about it! I was going to invite you out with the crew tonight. Sounds like you're going to be busy. How about sushi tomorrow before I leave for Denver?"

"That sounds great! I'll text you. Have a great night!"

Claire had a lot to accomplish in performing background research and contacting band management tomorrow before she left, so she may have overscheduled herself once again. Innately likable and inquisitive, Claire had always been a social butterfly and could fit in with any crowd. This evening's plans were not going to wait. She needed to hurry to fit them all in. She managed a hasty shower, threw on a beautiful red dress and her only pair of Jimmy Choos to attend a birthday dinner for a colleague at a swank Italian restaurant. She was liked by so many because of her genuine, fun-loving attitude, and she equally loved their company. She glanced down at her watch as she fussed over the little make-up that she knew she didn't want or need. Well, everyone knew she would be running late anyway, as usual.

Tonight would be no different as she sat down at the already-full table at her reserved spot, right next to the blissfully happy birthday girl. Claire was the life of the party, animatedly telling stories of Colombian Andean music festivals she had attended in her years abroad. Her only glass of chianti sat almost untouched in front of her. She was not a drinker as the most she would ever drink was a half glass of whatever it was she chose on any given night. She went through phases, at times choosing tequila and other times vodka, but never beer. It was cheese wheel pasta all around as the celebration continued. The waiters were sweating as they rolled bowl after bowl of pasta through the enormous cheese wheel, soaking up cheese into the noodles by the pound as they did. At the end of the feast, the gifts were delivered around the table to the jubilant recipient of honor.

Despite being able to accommodate any attire, Claire did not feel as comfortable in the red satin dress, as she did in a Jamaican red, yellow, and green Madras dress. Planning ahead, she had brought along her favorite dress as well as some flats to change into prior to the next venue, which would be less formal. The Madras dress was the perfect expression of her personality as it included the colors of green for eternal hope and connection to the earth, gold for stolen wealth and rebellion against those oppressors, and red for the needless bloodshed around the world. If there was a religion she felt closest to, it would definitely be Rasta, while Buddhism was a close second.

Since it was Wednesday, as was traditional, or as traditional as four months in this new home could be, the party shifted to their friend Kat's place where it was open mic poetry night. Claire often found herself here on Wednesdays for hours, practicing some of her college beat and zen poetry, as she could get some great feedback from the crowd. She wished she could bring her Congas tonight, but they were reserved for times when she had more preparation. She nourished her soul off the creativeness of others here as well.

Claire had an innate skill of expressing her profound passion through her art, and tonight she brought the rapture of the spoken word. And though you could feel the affliction in her voice, she always managed to bring out the positive aspects of emotion like empathy, sympathy, and the fate of one's destiny. Now at the microphone, without any cheat sheet, head down, eyes closed tightly, arms folded across her chest, she held her own shoulders in a tight embrace. Eyes

still closed, she opened her arms wide and began slowly, methodically, rhythmically.

"I learned.
I grew.
Lost it all again in you.
I sought you.
Thought I found you.
Through you.
Letting you in.
Giving in to you, strong you.
So hard to find.
Running away.
Lost me."

A short pause. She opened her eyes, closed her arms
tightly across her chest, embracing her shoulders with her
hands, and started again, even slower this time.

"Learned more.
Grew more.
Lost in me.
I sought me.
Thought I found me.
Through me.
Letting me in,
Giving in to me, strong me.
So hard to find.
Running to me.
To me.
Found it all again,
In me."

What came next was the usual response to her intense
introspection. There was a long pause when she finished,
as some were not sure if she was finished. As the crowd
processed her emotion and passion that was common to the
human spirit, especially of womanhood, you could hear a

few of those in attendance choke up, a few ahs, and then the applause would begin slowly, then loudly. Claire, eyes welling up with tears, fought them back, closed her eyes while opening her arms widely again, and stepped back from the microphone.

She stepped forward again, the decrescendo of adoration faded, and silence enveloped the venue. Her dress flowed behind her as she moved from side to side, humming melodically. She looked down, eyes closed still.

"Overcome by positive
Thought it was love
Embraced now close to live
As though 'twas from above

With all my heart
Raised up from the fall
Ne'er be apart
Ne'er ere heard such love call

Would I believe a one
Love me with tender touch
Help me become my one?
Raised me up so much

Healed each other new
Stoked love with fire
Partners in life true
How much desire?

A few slights of hand
Love would not abate
Blind to the remand
Remember the date

Blue crash little lie
Sell me talents abound
Promises to try

Little truth be found

One innocent mistake
Find knowledge of not
Second, address to take
Lust for another begot

Belief yields disbelief
Denial offered time to bide
Face of said facts relief
Holds fast to the side

Surface sounds so glib
Not rip us apart the roil
Dishonesty. Yet 'twas the fib
Not getting caught was the goal

Digital slight of hand
Learned was master of all
Apps to obscure the rand
How can I cope the fall

Example to bring
To stand now being tall
Sovereign to my being
Promise to never enthrall

Lone me calls out
Wish I wouldn't stand
Small steps be about
From underfoot I can

Learned from me
Underfoot tears burst
Now me again to be
Live with me only first"

Again the applause, slowly at first as before, as most only

followed bits and parts, but the gist was there, of heartache and pain. Of lies and deceit. Heartache and recovery. They got it. She could tell.

As she exited the stage, she immediately transformed, from her artistic mask to her public persona. First a smile, her green eyes beaming in absolute positivity, then laughter when the birthday girl erupted from the table, tearfully rushing toward her, and opening up in a genuine embrace at the foot of the stage.

As the evening came to a close, she knew she needed to get home so that she could finish those calls tomorrow before embarking on her assignment. She was not going to the office in the morning for she knew the perfect place, this quiet coffee shop with multiple private workspaces that was her go-to for those busy days.

Arriving home late at night was always worrisome, even in the nice neighborhood in which Claire lived. She made it a habit to drive through the parking lot once with her brights on, then returned to her assigned parking spot. There was that same unusual, black car parked at the end of the parking lot in the visitors' space, and she thought she saw some movement inside the darkened windows. She had seen that car every night for the past week, and it looked even more suspicious tonight. It was extra humid tonight so she could see some condensation on the windows. She noted the make and model, a small Toyota, and decided to carefully monitor the situation. She had her keys out and ready before she exited the car. The night was unusually silent as she ascended the few steps and entered the well-lit but ancient elevator.

She noticed that her neighbor's lights were still on. Probably still working on her assignment. She could tell Mía was a bright kid, a hard worker, the kind you would want on your investigative team. What new assignment was she so excited about? She couldn't wait to hear about it tomorrow evening.

The next morning commenced with an early launch out the door just before sunrise. She took notice of the surrounding area before reaching her car. Again the air was very humid, and only a few crickets could be heard in the neigh-
62

borhood. Thankfully, the suspicious car was gone so she let her guard down the slightest bit. The coffee shop was starting to spring to life at first light this morning with students and business people alike collecting their pick-me-up for the day ahead. She took her place in the corner room that luckily was not occupied as yet.

From her chair on the opposite side of the room, she garnered a view through the glass window of a large screen television that was silent but had closed captions on. This small distraction allowed her to occasionally check out the headlines for the day. As she opened her laptop, she could see some of the headlines that were concentrating on the up-coming elections still months away. There was more and more at stake in every election, but the election seasons were becoming longer and longer. "Too Much, Too Soon!" she thought. She organized the day's phone calls and researched her questions. She knew she would not be able to call any of her contacts until at least 11 a.m. since the vast majority were located either in California or Colorado.

Four mocha grandes and fourteen telephone calls later, Claire was judging by the increasing afternoon crowd, that it was near quitting time for the rest of the world. She only had a few more calls to make. She decided to text her neighbor that it would be about 7:00 before she would be done and to query whether that would be too late.

Mía answered quickly, "Np, can we meet there? Running late too."

Claire responded with a simple, "Ok."

It seemed like only a few minutes later and it was already 6:30. The calls went well. Laptop closed. The satisfaction of a full day's work and a successful beginning brought her positive energy for her short journey home. All was good in the world. These artists knew the game. They all sounded genuine. Tomorrow was going to be the start of something wonderful, new music, new environment. To minimize logistics, they would be traveling as a crew of only two. The cameraman acted as producer and the pair would both be in charge of editing.

Despite the heavy Atlanta traffic, she managed to make it to the sushi restaurant near her condo before 7. She entered the small, white brick building on the corner bordering her neighborhood barely on time. As she sat down in the small booth near the window, she ordered some miso soup to start. As she looked down at her watch, it had just struck 7 even. She decided to text Mía, just to make sure she was on her way. She gazed out the vine-covered window at the passersby who were scurrying off to unknown destinations, staring down at the gray sidewalk. Their facial expressions seemed to be wrapped up in their troubles and not focusing on the present, their peace. She doubted any of them were at peace with themselves.

By the time her soup arrived, it was only five minutes later, and Mía came bouncing through the front door. "Sorry, I'm late!"

"No problem. How is your research going? You said it was an interesting story?"

"Oh my god, yes! It is regarding some election irregularities from last year. I'm really just getting started on the background. Some of these rural Georgia areas are really backward. Living in the past kind of thing. Creepy stuff."

"You're right. You know you need to be careful. These backward areas have skeletons, and their past and present are not pretty."

"I know, right? I spent the past few days in a library and at the city hall in a small town just north of here. This county north of here has more black people than white, but yet somehow they elect the same good ole boys every election."

As they ordered their spicy tuna rolls, eel rolls, and sashimi, Mía explained that it had always been her dream to become a journalist and help fight the good fight for those who could not fight for themselves. "You know you work your way up the ladder, in school for what seems like forever, learning, but always feeling like you are being held back. Then you finally get your chance, step up to the plate, and I feel like I am finally getting to do what I always wanted to do. There's no holding me back, no stopping the train. I am part of a movement. I feel it. There are millions of women just like me, fighting for our rights and there are millions of café-colored people doing the same."

"That's inspirational! I think the Sentinel is the perfect place for you. They have a lot of support. Let me introduce you to some people at WNN. They can support you also. They have the full power of a juggernaut global media company, one thousand times the support of the Sentinel. You can collaborate."

Mía was staring out the window at the fading daylight and the few people walking by the street-side window. "That would be awesome. You are right. Sometimes I feel like the Sentinel is too small to take on the big fight."

"When I get back from Colorado next week, let's get together with my editor, to see who we need to get you hooked up with at WNN. We do a lot of combination pieces with the Sentinel I think."

At that point, Mía was still lost in thought but grasped the points Claire had laid down before her that she realized required an answer. She turned from the window, noticing the sushi roll that she thought was in the grips of her chopstick had fallen on the table beside her plate. "Oops! That would be perfect! I will text you then. I don't mean to be a party pooper, but I need to get home early for bed. I have some more research to do tonight and tomorrow."

"Yes, and I have an early flight. I'll get the tab, I have an expense account. Since you may be working with us on collaborative pieces, I think that more than qualifies."

Claire stayed behind to finish her sushi and paid the bill. As she waited, she watched as Mía walked by with her face looking up, searching for stars, then disappeared around the corner, out of sight. She again watched as a few distracted people passed by and speculated that, as opposed to these individuals, Mía was probably in a beneficial state of mindfulness. She was sure she would enjoy working with her in the future.

As she exited the restaurant, she paused to breathe in the fresh air with all of the scents of the restaurant and the jasmine vines covering the white brick pungent in her nostrils and held it in. She could feel the energy of renewal as the next few days would bring a positive change in her world. However, she also had to consciously fight back the negative auras of the human spirits around her, breathing them out. Move forward, upward she commanded her mind. Exhale all the negative.

She moved on, not noticing or even feeling the sidewalk beneath her feet, walking on air, purposefully only conscious of the regenerative greens and blues surrounding her. Upward.

—•❯❯ ❮❮•—

Chapter 6:
Natalia And Chip
Sail The Chesapeake

—•❯❯ ❮❮•—

The sailing on the Chesapeake Bay this time of year was hit or miss, but luckily a steady blow was forecast for this weekend. The short drive to Baltimore was a great chance for Chip, Sam, and Natalia to catch up and strategize the impact of moving both of their operations to the capital city in the next few weeks. Both Natalia and Chip were ready, Sam not so much, but he could make it work. He lived, breathed, and worked by video conference anyway. If Chip was forced to choose one area of the United States to live, it would have been the Chesapeake Bay area, and soon the trio would forge a homestead within an hour-long sail to the open bay. This was as close to home as there was stateside.

Chip mused, "There went our sailing career! We had better live it up this weekend on the boat, soak in the salty sprays. I will ship at least one of the J boats across the pond and let's see what happens, sailing-wise. Can you believe you will soon be back to your old single-handing days?"

Sam took a more serious tack and interrupted the question, "I have begun looking into the yacht clubs and marinas along the Potomac. It appears that a lot of them are full, with waiting lists, but I have inquired about the strictness of the rules. And I will begin shipping the J-45. And what about the Wizard II? We haven't spent much time on her since she was christened." The 110-meter triple-masted schooner was launched by her makers barely a month ago with much fanfare and sailed across the channel to England on her maiden voyage. The only schooner longer than the Wizard II was Ben Longley's yacht, owned by the world's richest man.

"Yes, let's bring her over. I love the tranquility and beauty of those tall sails," Natalia looked at Chip for confirmation. "She would probably have to dock in deeper waters. Norfolk?"

"She will be put to best use here anyway. Norfolk is a great possibility, but a good distance from D.C. She cannot dock here in D.C., for she won't fit under any bridges. I've already found two potential tall-ship docking locations there in Norfolk. The closest possibility is Annapolis, where she could sleep right next to the U.S. Naval Academy. You see, I'm way ahead of you. I will have the captain investigate the options further. One benefit to this move is she will now be closer to the islands," he said with a grin. Sam, understanding the potentially temporary nature of this move, would do his best. The reality of the migratory life of journalists meant this position may only last a few years.

Natalia agreed, "We have so much to think about, after the race let's have our real estate manager for the states go over our options. We will need tight security in D.C."

For a hot minute, she thought maybe they should have foregone this race to search the real estate market over the weekend. But in the next hour, these logistics would be a fleeting fancy, with only the wind flowing through her mind. Just now, her brain had entered daydream mode, as her imagination conjured up a fresh breeze blowing across her face, riding like an eagle with each gust carrying her spirit higher. There would never be a substitute for the zen that sailing provided for her soul.

As they arrived at Baltimore harbor, they could easily identify the tall, wooden, double-masted schooners all docked and moored in the bay to show off their old-world splendor. Their masts towered over many of the buildings in majestic prowess. They would be hitching a ride on a 77-foot schooner with two wooden masts, six sails, and a crew of sixteen, and from the sleek looks of her, she certainly was a beauty. The race would take them from Baltimore harbor down the full length of Chesapeake Bay to Norfolk and with the winds forecasted to be quite breezy, with all blessings from the wind gods, they would be in Norfolk harbor by nightfall. If the winds died, it could conceivably stretch to 24 to 36 hours to make it that far, as there were no motors allowed.

Chip, Natalia, and Sam strolled out onto the dock just as the first crew arrived, just in time to help load the provisions, rig the sails, and prepare for the day of sailing on this exquisite yacht. The wooden carvings on the bowsprit and the blue-green oxidized brass steering wheel made it seem like they were stepping back 200 years into the past. There was nothing on the boat that was not constructed of wood - even the pulleys and blocks were mostly wooden with brass bearings. Within thirty minutes, the yacht was regatta-ready. The sails were lashed to the masts and booms with their halyards, and all of the lines were so clean it seemed like they were brand new. It was obvious this vessel had the care of loving hands over the years.

As the owner of the boat arrived, there were handshakes all around as Chip and Natalia were treated like celebrities once again, as revered America's Cup Champions. Natalia, never the shy one, complimented the owner on his choice of nautical transportation, "How long has this sexy lady been under your care? She looks beautiful! I understand she is a replica of the famous yacht for harbor pilots that once carried her name?"

The owner blushed, "Beautiful, that she is! She is a spry eighteen years young this year. My son and I commissioned her and brought her to life right here in Norfolk. Correction! Pardon my error. Christened in Newport News of Hampton Roads, the shipbuilding capital of the world. She moors and sleeps in Norfolk."

The three honored guests had a profound interest in historic tall ships with magnificent polygonal sails. The logistics arm of Merlin Commerce owned a few and held them on display at their shipyards in Portsmouth. As antique replicas of Sir Francis Drake's ships, they were under the protection of a covered dry haul and museum but were brought out on parade annually for a sail around Portsmouth Harbor during the Royal Naval Freedom Day festivities.

Natalia could feel the excitement of the crew building to get underway for the start. "Well, I can't wait to see how we can bring her up out of the water in these winds! That's going to be a lot of sail!"

"Yes, we may have to dial it back a little bit. She's very stable with a heavy keel, but she's faster than a normal heavy keelboat. You'll see! She does fourteen knots in a breeze."

As they motored out of the harbor, the crew began to ready the sails. Hoisting each of them required the herculean effort of six crew on each side of the ship, while the others prepared the other five for eventual hoisting. The captain, beaming with pride, stood behind the green brass wheel in a steady, firm stance.

Natalia and Chip took their positions on starboard and Sam on the port side to hoist the sails. Six on each side aligned with each mast, utilizing the ropes and pulleys to raise each sail one by one. Each of the fifteen wooden hoops one by one carried the sails up the mast.

As it turned out, they would need all sixteen of these crew members, because hoisting and maintaining all of these sails, with manual riggings and wooden hoops, raising the sails on the masts would prove difficult in these winds. The process was very different from the electric winches and pulleys of modern boats, especially the AC75 that Natalia and Chip had crewed on during the America's Cup, what seemed like just a few months ago. With a whole new level of technology, the Wizard II was a different type of schooner, as the whole mast was turned on a pedestal instead of having to move the sails around on booms.

By the time they reached historic Fort McHenry, they

had raised all of the sails, and the owner, during a short break in the activity, shared the story of Francis Scott Key writing the Star-Spangled Banner from a vantage point near Fort McHenry as the fort was bombarded by the British in the War of 1812.

It was quite a spectacle to witness, all of the festive schooners, each with hundreds of yards of sails lifted and billowing in the wind. The awestruck passengers felt like they were transported back to 1812, minus the bombardments. They could feel the momentum the wind was creating by the minute and as they rounded the first point and passed under the last bridge before the official starting line, they caught a glimpse of a large concrete structure in the middle of the channel. A boat positioned a few hundred yards from it served as the starting line.

In a break in the action just after the start, Natalia positioned herself near the captain to inquire about the history, "That must be another fort? They had a lot of protection for this harbor." She looked toward Sam and Chip, "Those Brits were quite the pests back in the day, weren't they."

The owner chimed in again, as he was accustomed to playing tour guide for all sorts of educational groups aboard the schooner. "Baltimore and Norfolk and every point in between have always been immensely important harbors, not to mention the Potomac River, going back to the days of the Revolutionary War, due to the shipbuilding that took place in these waters and the capital beyond, in my opinion far more important than Boston or New York. Many forts dot the coastline of Chesapeake Bay. This fort, Fort Carroll, was designed by Robert E. Lee before he turned coats. At one time it was used for a lighthouse but never saw any use as a fort. It is in quite a state of disrepair. Do you see all of the cannon ports? Can't imagine why they never commissioned it as a fort. Nobody is quite sure to tell you the truth. Off to our starboard is an old, abandoned fort called Fort Armistead. Haunted to this day by the tortured souls of her past."

The forecast was accurate, and a steady westerly wind kept them at a beam reach most of the way to Norfolk. There were several lighthouse sightings, which excited those who were visitors among the crew. The wind didn't shift much, so they didn't have to change sail angles much during the 14-hour cruise. It was early evening, with magnificent indigo twilight skies, when they rounded Fort Monroe and headed for the home stretch. Natalia gazed at the first stars as they became evident, mostly hidden by the bright full moon barely peeking over the eastern horizon and the bridge across the entrance to the Chesapeake Bay.

The bright lights of Newport to the north and Norfolk to the south were a spectacular display to behold. The naval base at Norfolk was especially lit up, with patrol boats protecting the waters as they entered the Elizabeth River to dock at the Norfolk harbor. This historic schooner was once again the winner of their division, and while it was not as prestigious as some of the races they had partaken in over the years, as far as Natalia and Chip were concerned, the idyllic setting and beautiful yacht were the perfect backdrop for the beginning of this new chapter in their lives.

The cruise into the harbor was relaxing with the night breeze beginning to switch to an easterly direction, bringing in the salt air off the Atlantic Ocean. Sam staked out a position on the bow so that he could inspect the marinas for possible resting places for the Wizard II. Chip and Natalia once again stood behind the captain to monitor the smooth docking operation. They also reveled in the sights of the Navy and Coast Guard ships along the harbor. The crew doused the sails and lashed them to the booms for the night. Once the ship was fully secured at the pier, the jubilant crew gathered for a social hour and celebration of their victory on the deck.

Natalia glanced over at Chip, with her brunette locks still flowing in the breeze, and asked, nay commanded, "Let's take a day to take in the scenery of Norfolk. I love shipbuilding and Naval history."

The captain, overhearing the conversation, contributed, "There is a great Navy museum near where we are moored and you can see right there, the spectacular World War Two battleship, the U.S.S. Wisconsin that we could tour. She was active in the Pacific fleet during the Second World War and assisted with the liberation of the Philippines. I will arrange a personal presentation with the curator of the museum. He will be excited to meet the stars of the America's Cup. He sailed aboard the Wisconsin and is an avid sailor."

The two Brits' imaginations were also piqued at the thought of a day of walking through the history of shipbuilding and Naval warfare. Chip's family business, Merlin Commerce, had made a miraculous transition into the modern age during World War Two, participating in the war efforts for the Allied forces. Of course, none of the three had been born yet. That era of transformation of the company belonged to both of their grandfathers on the Isle of Wight and Portsmouth, which were an integral part of the Allied submarine warfare. As the three guests reveled in the history of the era as told by the captain, they could now identify the outlines of the battleship as the decorative lights on the gun turrets created a magnificent display.

The next day flew by in a whirlwind of introductions to the amazing people of Norfolk and a stroll through the nautical antiquities of yesteryear. This quaint seafaring yet industrial town reminded Sam and Chip of their old stomping grounds of Portsmouth so much that they felt quite at home among the inhabitants they met that day. As they stood on the pier looking out into the harbor before departure, the three gathered for a picture with the schooner in the background. All of their smiles were genuinely bursting with joy on their faces for the photo.

"This place gets my vote for the new home of Wizard II," Chip offered enthusiastically.

Sam acknowledged, "She does feel like home, doesn't she? It is a good jaunt from D.C., though. Would be nice to be able to take her out from Annapolis on weekends. Let's check that out before we make any hasty decisions. I think you will equally be impressed by the Naval Academy at Annapolis and some of the museums there."

Natalia, for her part, concurred regarding the convenience of Annapolis, "We can always cruise down the Chesapeake to this magnificent port on our way to the islands."

The last few weeks had been the most blissful times she could remember. She hoped these joyous, relaxing days would never end.

—·≫ ≪·—

CHAPTER 7: INTERN

—·≫ ≪·—

This momentous Monday was the first day of orientation at Georgetown and the door to Natalia's office did not even have a nameplate yet, which necessitated a quick document print in 32 font: NATALIA VOLKOV. As she cut out and taped the makeshift sign to the frosted window in her door, she thought whimsically at her audacity to inscribe her name in all caps. She typed and printed it so quickly that she forgot to include her title or her department. The office was just down the hall from the Dean's office and as she peered down at the same athletic fields that she had gazed upon just last week, she thought to herself, "It's official. There can be no reversing our decision now. Onward and upward."

As with every monumental shift she had made to this point in her life, this transition was no small affair. As the newly minted Professor contemplated the decor of her office, she pondered the similarities of this move to her relocation just a few years ago from London to New York. Natalia was not the usual assistant professor moving into some tiny apartment on the outskirts of town or perhaps across the historic Potomac River in Virginia. Natalia's (and Chip's) family money afforded her the luxury of never having to worry about rental trucks, tiny apartments, or even small houses in the suburbs. The fateful pair had settled on a reddish-brown brick classic that was built in 1832, next door to a Supreme Court Justice and across the street from the ambassador of Germany. Most countries could not afford to pay cash and close on a real estate deal this quickly, this close to Georgetown and in the middle of Embassy Row, let alone a newly hired professor of business and journalism.

The upside of the hasty purchase was the security that would be ever-present in the posh neighborhood. The location met with wholehearted approval from the security-minded Sam for this reason alone. The basement, guest house, and spacious patio with a pool would be perfect for a security detail. For Natalia, the setting was ideal for traveling as it was fifteen minutes from the airport, and she could become accustomed to having a yard and open spaces with landscaping after high-rise living in New York. She envisioned herself, laptop open under the gazebo in the afternoon sun, researching the earnings ratios of small Malaysian tech companies.

The large, wooded ravine in the back of the property was well-cased out by the US Marshals for the security of their principal, who was in line to be Chief Justice. Sam had already reached out to the head of the US Marshals detail for communication and cooperation. Not that they were that agreeable, for security details of important figures were not fodder for sharing, even with multibillionaires. Nevertheless, it was some comfort knowing your flank was covered by 24-hour security professionals with badges. And with a Russian national next door, the Marshals were sure to keep a close eye on this suspicious domicile.

Aside from the new digs, Merlin Commerce had maintained, for decades, a bonafide presence in the District. Their clients, which included certain un-named heads of state, would need robust security when they were visiting the capital city. The company's security division retained an office and hangar space at the private jet port at Washington Reagan Airport and another conference center located on the top floor of a secure office building directly on K Street.

The office was complete with a helipad if they chose to use it. Chip intended to continue working for the Times newspaper remotely, and this same conference center would grant him (and Sam) a comfortable office from which to work.

Despite the fact her appointment had not yet been announced, word on campus got around that the celebrity business journalist had accepted the position and had settled in. In a few days, they were due to have an official recognition ceremony for not only Natalia but all of the new faculty in the School of Business.

Natalia, it seemed, would never break her habit of drifting off into daydreams while gazing at picturesque views, and the subject was always about connecting the past with the future. She appreciated her transcendence from the immature European prep-school athlete in Switzerland to the academic, power-house journalist that she was at this stage of her life. Each step along the way, there were obstacles to overcome, prejudices to conquer, and adversaries to defeat. In addition to neutralizing the negatives, she had learned to harness her strengths, utilize the energy of her mentors, and radiate a positive, boundless love toward the world.

This was the secret to her success she believed in her heart. Having been raised in Russia and Switzerland, she was not indoctrinated into any one religion and therefore gravitated toward Buddhism and Daoism for inspiration. She practiced yoga and meditation frequently in her primary and secondary years in Geneva at a lab overlooking the harbor of Lac Lemán. The yoga master there taught her to extract only the positive energy from the world around her. Leaving your disciplined mind open to these positive visions relegated the negative as moot. Yet at the same time, she was tough as nails and would stop at nothing to achieve her dreams.

Taking in the bright blue vibes of the late summer sky, she breathed it all in and could feel the strength of her ancestors before the positive energies entered her consciousness and knew in her heart that they approved of her path and not that of her uncle. How high that path would carry her, she knew depended on her courage and fortitude to battle against uncertainty. In the distance, she could see the Washington Monument, and metaphorically she visualized the top of the mountain to gain and shifted her focus from the broad view of the landscape to the solitary point at the pinnacle of the monument. Breathe out. Move on. Move up. She felt an overwhelming contentment with her continued success and the journey from Russia and Switzerland to Oxford, New York, and now D.C., growing along the way. She heeded her ancestors' guidance of her spirit, as enduring lights in the fog that was today's adversarial world.

Her profound reminiscence was interrupted by Dean Smythe casually half-entering the office, leaning with one hand posted on the door jam, almost peeking around the corner. As she gently tapped on the frosted glass door, she inquired, "How was the move?"

It took Natalia a few seconds to descend from the stratosphere back to Earth with a deep breath outward. She replayed the dean's words in her mind like a recording to comprehend and finally replied as she leaned on the window sill, looking back toward the door, "Oh, a little nerve-wracking but I am having it done professionally. I found a cute little brownstone just a few blocks from here. We shall host a few people for dinner there soon if you would care to join us."

Natalia's humble description of their new mansion was not lost on the dean for she knew the specifics of her purchase already. Real estate acquisitions of this size were fodder for gossip in the Beltway, not only about the esteemed buyer but also the identity of the seller, who was a retired billionaire senator, who had just lost an election for the first time in over forty years to a young, idealistic upstart from Georgia.

Dean Smythe apologized for intruding on her first day, "My husband and I will definitely take you up on the dinner invitation! But, first, there is someone I would like you to meet. If you approve, she would be your first intern and office assistant, fully funded by the Washington Chronicle as she is already interning there as well. This is Samantha. She is our star Merit scholar in the journalism program and is a

John Quincy Adams Scholar in our business college."

Sheepishly stepping out from behind the dean, the studious sophomore with a blonde single braid on her left temple that merged into a ponytail, held out her left hand in a waving motion while flashing a confident smile. "Ms. Volkov, I am excited to work with you if you think I can contribute in a meaningful way to your research. I have been following your work for over a year in my Developing Economies class."

Natalia uncharacteristically felt an instant trust in her new charge. "Why yes, come in, both of you. Sit down. I have new comfortable chairs already, as you can see."

As the two visitors settled into the deep leather chairs, it became immediately obvious they were not a standard academic issue.

Natalia pointed to the chairs, "Those were a gift from my partner, Chip, who is also a journalist, as you probably already know."

Partner. Natalia thought the title fitting. It was better than boyfriend, husband, or any other descriptive title. Partner incorporated all of the positives of having a relationship as equals who supported each other unequivocally, which was the way it should be in these modern times. How could there be any other way?

"How do you like Georgetown?" Samantha asked, searching for common ground.

"I love it! It's just like my old stomping grounds at Oxford. Same old-world charm. Same old-world air conditioning!" It was well known that the air could become a little stuffy in the building. It seemed the solid stone building did not keep out the humidity of the summer. "How did you come to specialize in Developing Economies already by sophomore year?"

"I am majoring in International Business. Oh, and I would have loved to study at Oxford. Maybe I can study abroad there for one semester soon." Samantha said, looking over at Dean Smythe with an inquisitive grin.

"We do have great study abroad opportunities here. It is one of our hallmarks," was the vague answer.

"You know, Samantha, I have also been thinking of setting up a research program studying the developing economies of the industrial Midwest, steel country, and the deep South. These are fast becoming the forgotten economy of the US. Of course, I will always focus most of my energy on Africa and Asia if that is more your interest."

This, at first appearance, did not seem as romantic and fascinating for a young international business major, but Samantha was wise beyond her years. "Do you think it is the technology gap, or do you think it is more rooted in educational decline?"

"That's why they call it research. I think it is all of the above. Infrastructure, teacher pay, manufacturing loss, the opioid epidemic, etc. Samantha, let's see if we can learn where the investment opportunities are. The automobile companies capitalized on this in the deep South years ago, but that investment has declined. Michigan and Indiana have lost a lot of industry over the years which subsequently led to educational declines. Even in the West, where technology has been booming for decades, the prosperity of the Nineties has not reached the rural areas. If you tackle this, I will also let you work with me on an anti-BRIC project."

The Dean, patiently listening to the back and forth for a few minutes, decided to change the subject. "What do you think of the Chronicle? Have you been to their offices yet?"

Natalia, indeed, had not yet made her way to the gargantuan office building that housed the Washington Chronicle in its ivory towers. Embarrassed, she answered, "No I have not. I have it first on my agenda."

Before Dean Smythe could respond, Samantha exclaimed, "I can take you there! My sponsor is the editor of the online business section."

Natalia needed to cross this off her to-do list and the short trek across campus would give her a chance to get to know Samantha. The headquarters of the Chronicle was just down K Street toward the White House, an avenue of influence where the most powerful attorneys and lobbyists resided in D.C.

Samantha was equally excited to get this opportunity. Pulling her phone out of her back pocket, she enthusiastically blurted out, while simultaneously dialing, "Let me call the editor's secretary to set up a meeting right now. I was heading there this afternoon to meet with her and to do some line editing, so I know she and the team are there."

"Excellent! Let's begin this journey right away! I have heard the team there is a truly progressive, enlightened organization, with creativity and integrity at the forefront. How do you like it there?" Natalia asked.

"I love it! I feel like I am already appreciated there as a newbie! It's the..." Samantha interrupted herself, talking with the secretary succinctly. "It's all set. We can head over there whenever you are ready," she continued. "It's the most coveted internship on campus. I'm incredibly lucky."

"Let's go now," Natalia said, standing up at her desk and packing her tablet into her backpack. "I have heard we can walk there in just minutes. Are you ready? Do you have your walking shoes? You will need to keep up. I learned to walk fast in New York. You get trampled if you don't."

It took no time at all to exit the building, and as the two new friends descended the now familiar worn marble steps, they began chatting about their backgrounds. Since Natalia's family background was public knowledge and the subject of back page news, the first several minutes were spent explaining the non-public story. For Natalia, over the past few years, it had finally become cathartic talking about her family and her struggles to break free from the hold they had on her. The catharsis was brought about by framing the struggle in a positive light, showcasing how she constantly grew despite her uncle's thumb on the scale.

As they exited the black wrought-iron gate that was the entrance to the hallowed learning grounds of Georgetown, the blue sky again seemed to focus her mind on the positive. She sequentially took three deep breaths of the positive blue sky and exhaled the negativity that was her family. "This is how I survived this negative situation, by accentuating the positive aspects in my life and limiting the exposure to negativity," she explained.

"Tell me where you are from. What's your background?" Natalia asked, changing the subject so that she could learn about her new intern.

"I'm from Virginia, just across the river, but I've lived all over because my father is in the military. I was born in Colorado and lived in Germany for a while," she responded.

"Oh, really? Which branch?" asked Natalia.

"He is in the Air Force. Now, he works in the Pentagon. Pretty high up. Brigadier General. He was a fighter pilot prior to joining the Pentagon."

Natalia was impressed. "You must have some great experiences living in Germany."

"My mother and I traveled a lot through Europe and Africa and sometimes my father would join us. By that time my dad was already a colonel. Being a military officer's family, we were privileged to experience the culture in ways most couldn't. I witnessed firsthand the poverty and some of the oppression, in these third-world countries, which is why I became interested in developing economies."

"Yes, also being a journalist gives you some license to delve deeper into the details of business and corruption. We have to be careful, though, because the unscrupulous in Africa do not value human life the way we do. Asia is a little better. Have you traveled to Asia much?

"Only once and only briefly. I'm looking forward to the prospect of experiencing Vietnamese and Thai culture."

On this subject, Natalia was an expert. "The Vietnamese and Thai are a deeply spiritual people. There are varying degrees of similarity to the Buddhist religion amongst the several religions and quasi-religions of the countries of Asia. They live their lives to please their ancestors and most do not worship a deity, just an overarching philosophy of life. As with any religion, that philosophy can be twisted to serve one's purposes, but that corruption of values is rarer than in Western society."

"I am taking Comparative Religions of the World this semester. I can't wait to learn more."

"A few semesters abroad and you will become an expert," Natalia added.

The conversation continued along this vein until the two suddenly found themselves at the front entrance to the towers of the Washington Chronicle, that bastion of honest journalism the two revered. The pair ascended the elevators to the editorial offices where Natalia hoped to consummate a productive research relationship with her new editor. The editorial conference room was full, much like that conference room at Georgetown a few weeks ago. Full of the brightest journalists, from political to business specialists, they were all there. It seemed that in the fifteen minutes that it took to walk from Georgetown to this building, someone had notified the entire building, perhaps by overhead page, that she would be arriving today. An introduction to her editor was all she wished to accomplish, but it was plain to see that was not all that was in the cards for today. She and Samantha would be treated to a hero's welcome that she took very humbly, blushing all the while.

The accolades flowed forth and Natalia was embarrassed by all of the attention. She found herself wishing she could continue the conversation she was having with Samantha. There was just something remarkably mature about her that she could tell would serve her well. When the introductory meeting was over, and all of the commotion dissipated, it was just Samantha, the editor and herself present. She decided to try to commandeer Samantha for her research at the Chronicle also. The editor relented and a deal was made and a team was fashioned for a series of articles on the Midwestern economic decline along with the usual BRIC research.

That was easy, Natalia thought as the morning was getting away from them, with lunchtime fast approaching. "Let's grab a salad on the way back to campus. I need to tackle some logistics this afternoon and it's going to be a long day."

After her inspiring visit to the offices of the Washington Chronicle, both Natalia and Samantha indeed had time for a brief lunch. They chose a restaurant on M Street which, from the outside seemed to be a small pub, but on the inside opened into a beautiful sunlit room with ancient brick walls. This classic eatery became an instant favorite of Natalia's. The atmosphere and decorations showcased the history of the area as a respite for educational thought. And it was a perfect excuse for Natalia to get to know Samantha even better. They spent the greater part of an hour hashing out the first few projects. While consuming the healthy fare of the café, they agreed to a few goals for the year and also a schedule and duties for Samantha to adhere to. Samantha's first assignment would be to present more detailed goals and produce a plan to attain them.

Natalia needed to finish a list of proposals for the coming semester and Samantha was obligated to return to Georgetown for some meetings with her advisors before commencing her studies for the term. With that, they parted in opposite directions with a heartfelt hug on the sidewalk in front of Natalia's now-favorite restaurant.

—⋅⟫⟨⋅—

CHAPTER 8: MISSING FRIEND

—⋅⟫⟨⋅—

The text seemed like any other nightly text: "Going out for sushi. Txt when I return."

Samantha had responded to her best friend in Atlanta several times overnight but had received no response. This was not like the incredibly organized hyper-texter Mía, which was short for Maria Gonzalez. The friend she knew invariably sent dozens of texts per night to all of her friends while she was eating her usual Spicy Eel roll. Even if her phone had died, certainly she would have charged it by morning. If she had lost her phone, Mía was the type that would have texted from her computer and then sprinted to the store to buy a new phone by morning. Samantha thought to herself she knew dozens of classmates who couldn't keep track of their phone or charging level, but that was not Mía. In fact, Mía was the exact opposite, and that worried Samantha so much that she contemplated skipping class for the first time in her college career to investigate.

Instead, during her first two classes, Samantha busily texted their friends in common and checked her online profiles and could find no selfies and no sushi pics, only a share of a story on women's rights earlier in the day. A few months ago,

Mía had begun an internship with the Atlanta Sentinel and already earned her first byline with some of the protests that had been occurring across the country. Recently, she proudly informed Samantha that she had begun an investigative piece on the elections and politics in Georgia.

Samantha was incredibly impressed by the soon-to-be accomplished author and journalist that her favorite college friend was becoming. Mía was a senior on the staff of the Georgetown student newspaper when Samantha was a newbie freshman trying to earn her spot on the staff. Mía took Samantha under her wing and helped her with some of her stories, becoming her go-to copy editor before she submitted them to the actual editor. There was an ease in her prose that Samantha found almost lyrical. Even in factual documentary news pieces the rhythm of her writing made the news enjoyable to read.

Nearly a hundred direct messages to every mutual acquaintance she could think of, including one of their mutual friends now living in Atlanta, unfortunately, had come up empty. She even tried to track her on a messaging app that could show your location to your friends, and even that turned up empty. Nobody had heard a peep from Mía since last night before dinner. She dared not skip her 11:00 am quiz in her International Relations class so, right before she entered the lecture hall, she sent a message to Mía's mother to see if she had heard from her. The quiz would not go well, as she was distracted thinking about all the possibilities running through her mind. Samantha normally was not a worry wart, but she knew the statistics all too well regarding the percentage of women who experienced violence during their college years.

While putting forth her most valiant effort on the quiz, she had several flashbacks of different milestone moments of the past year where her mentor Mía had helped elevate her mood when she was down, celebrated her many successes, and provided a shoulder for her to cry on at least a few times. She was there when Samantha failed her first quiz but proved Mía right when she not only passed the class but received an A. Mía was by her side when she broke up with her first serious boyfriend. And she celebrated with her when a story Samantha wrote was taken up for national distribution.

Miraculously, with her anxious mind distracting her memory of Buddhist leaders, she was able to finish the quiz, but no one was allowed to leave until the end of the hour. The clock on the wall, a classic black and white one with a red second hand, moved in single-second ticks that seemed to take hours. There was no worse feeling in the world than being held back before being able to take action, she thought, with her spinning mind racing ahead.

As everyone stood up synchronously on the loud click of all three of the clock hands to twelve, Mía immediately reached for her phone in her book bag. As she exited the room, she quickly flipped to the messages app only to see that her friend's mother had replied no to the same question she had posed to several dozen others. She knew her friend was not that close to her parents so it would not be so unusual on a weekday for her not to be in touch with her parents. Nonetheless, something was not right and in Samantha's estimation could be dreadfully wrong.

Luckily, Old North Hall was less than a hundred meters away from her dormitory flat where she knew her roommates would have already returned from their classes. She immediately made a beeline and crossed the street diagonally, not waiting for the crosswalk. She was now running, not walking, and cut across the grass to the entrance. With a lump in her throat and pressure welling up in her chest, she rushed up the steps, skipping every other step.

"Has anyone heard? What about Sage? I've been texting everyone I know all day." she shouted from the doorway before the solid-oak door had even opened halfway.

Her suitemates looked up from their phones with exasperated looks. They also had been texting and calling everyone they knew in common with Mía, including Sage, who had been Mía's longtime partner, at least longtime as far as college girlfriends could be. Sage and Samantha had not been very close, due to some small amount of jealousy of

Mía's mentorship of Samantha. For this reason, Samantha left these texts to her suitemates.

"It's time for Jennifer in Atlanta to physically go over to her apartment. And we need to call the police in Atlanta. Should we lie and tell them it's been more than 24 hours?" Samantha had already rehearsed a multitude of times since her quiz started what the next steps would be.

"Yes, probably by the time they get to her apartment, it will have been 24 hours anyway. So, yes, definitely we tell them it was yesterday noon that anyone heard from her," one of her roommates agreed.

"Okay, I am calling Jenny now," announced Samantha. Jennifer was also a graduate of Georgetown and had been in Atlanta working for the same newspaper as Mía for over a year. She scrolled through her phone and pressed the call button, first putting the phone up to her ear, then decided to turn on the external speaker so all could hear. The phone only rang once. "Jenny? This is Samantha, Mía's friend. We still have not heard from her. Can you go to her apartment?"

There was hardly a half-second pause before the exasperated reply erupted from the phone. "Yes, I'm already on my way. I don't live very close but I'm almost there. She usually texts me a few times a day and she hasn't texted at all since yesterday. She was going to a sushi restaurant that is not far from her apartment. I don't get it, she lives in a nice neighborhood, so you would think she would be safe. I also called her boss. She didn't show up for work today."

It was going to be a few minutes, so Samantha put the phone down on the table, with the speaker still on. As they discussed some of the possibilities with Jenny, they could hear her driving, then a few jostling noises, a few beeps from the car, and finally what sounded like the door opening and closing. "OK, I'm here. Nothing out of the ordinary yet. I will try to ring the door buzzer for her apartment." Several seconds passed. "Nothing yet. I will look around and head to the sushi restaurant to inquire. I will call you back."

"While we are waiting can someone please look up the

Atlanta police non-emergency number?" Samantha, as one of the newest reporters at the school newspaper, also knew the director of the Georgetown University Police. The freshmen wanna-be reporters all got the low-end on the totem pole assignments, including campus crime. After this scare, she would be more than ready to hand it off to the new freshmen for the year. "Then I will call the director here. Better yet, I am going to his office right now." The office of the campus police was less than a hundred yards from their luxurious dormitory apartments that overlooked the Potomac and the Lincoln Memorial.

As Samantha ran down the steps, all of the horrific possibilities continued to run through her mind like a movie trailer for a B-movie horror film. She felt like she was running slowly but in fact, she carried on a dead sprint to the Campus Security office. As she swung open the door, she startled the student employee sitting at the front desk. Samantha only then noticed how out of breath she was from the 100-yard dash. She caught herself in mid-inspiration and held her breath for a second so that she could talk. She could see the director in his office who was peering around the doorframe to see what the commotion was all about. "Hi, director," she struggled again to breathe. "I have a problem to run by you."

"Yes, come on in, Samantha. I haven't seen you in a while. You seem distressed!"

"I am! Do you remember Mía? She is in Atlanta on an internship and she has disappeared, and hasn't contacted anyone in 24 hours. She always contacts us and hasn't answered multiple texts and calls from her friends, parents, or her partner."

The director put his hand up to his chin, while still sitting at his desk, and, with his other hand, motioned toward a chair across from him. "Come. Sit down," he offered. "That indeed is concerning. She was always on her phone. You know, I still get texts from her occasionally when she has a legal question. Both of you are among the best reporters I have seen come through this school. Let me see if I can help. I have a friend in the Atlanta PD. We can file a missing person report, and send someone over for a wellness check..."

Samantha interrupted, "We sent a coworker over to her apartment and she was not there. She had possibly gone out for sushi last night about the time she disappeared."

"Let's send someone over there and start an investigation. Remember not to disturb anything if you do gain access to the apartment. Let the police make the first entrance to preserve any evidence." The director then picked up the phone and after a few minutes into the conversation, which began with the usual formalities, the exchange quickly morphed into an official back-and-forth exchange of information. The necessary facts, address, cellular phone number, height, weight, and hair and eye color were all provided by Samantha to relay to the officer on the other end.

"Alright, Samantha. We have some action that will happen right away. As luck will have it, my friend is a detective in the same precinct where Mía lives. He is going to personally perform the wellness check with a uniformed officer."

Samantha felt relieved to only the tiniest degree. Her investigative journalistic instincts were kicking in, as she felt she needed to be there, physically in Atlanta. There was no comfort in the arrangement of other people's actions as her control-oriented personality compelled her to be in charge of the gathering of evidence. As she headed back to her dorm room, she began to hatch a plan to get to Atlanta, in between her classes, without anyone knowing, though she knew that would be next to impossible.

If only she was a superhero, able to protect all of her female friends from the threats that existed out there in today's society. There was no shortage of freaks, stalkers, rapists, and murderers in the world, and she wished she didn't have to worry about them constantly. The only thing she knew to do was to expose the truth to the world. Maybe that was what was needed for her friend Mía, though the thought of what that truth could be in Mía's case brought a cold-chilled shudder from her neck down to her shoulders on this warm, late afternoon day.

As she bounded up the black metal steps, she burst

through the doorway and into the dorm suite and blurted out to the assembled crowd, "We have a contact with the Atlanta PD who is going to do a wellness check on Mía's apartment. I know everyone is feeling this, but it seems we can and must do more. I wish we could hack into the security cams like in the movies."

Samantha suddenly realized there were now a dozen more classmates who had gathered in the small confines of the common area of their dorm suite for the crisis. The now overcrowded room contained two couches, two tables with chairs, a ping pong table, and a large-screen television. A floor-to-ceiling window let in the afternoon sun over the trees of the Potomac, lighting up the few Georgetown Hoyas banners hanging on the walls.

Having nowhere to sit, she stood in the open doorway and glanced around at all of Mía's supportive friends. From the looks on their faces, she could tell that there was still no miraculous news to report, but she asked anyway. "Is there any news? Any?"

One of the friends relayed with an exasperated, sullen voice, "Nothing!" as she fought back gushing tears.

Samantha was pleasantly surprised to see Mía's girlfriend Sage had joined them in the dorm suite for the investigation. She looked distraught but by all appearances looked like she was holding it together as best she could. Sage looked up from her phone toward Samantha and delivered an awkward expression of acknowledgment.

Sage, with a cracked voice of distress, gave some words of encouragement to the group, "Thanks, Samantha for all you are doing, and everyone else. It means a lot to me, and to Mía, that you are going so over the top trying to find her. And, yes, Samantha, it would be nice to find a hacker to hack into the security cameras and maybe even hack into her cell phone account for the Find My Phone feature. But the fact her location isn't even available on Snap suggests that wouldn't be helpful at all."

They spent the afternoon and evening exhaustively calling, texting, and messaging on social media to all that they could think of. A social media group was formed to share information and get the word out. They found out from Jennifer that Mía had been at the sushi restaurant with a female friend, and she felt she was close to finding out the identity. Samantha could tell that Sage, who was a little bit of a jealous type, was more than anxious about that information.

Not one iota of information could be gleaned from the Atlanta police detective. They had gained access to the apartment and there were no signs of foul play, only a few hungry cats that Jenny was able to coax into a small pet carrier to take to her apartment temporarily. Her small car, a nondescript silver Mazda 3, still was not located. They had not been able to interview many of her neighbors as yet, because few were at home during that time of day. Their friend was hoping that would soon change as the clock inched toward evening.

After all of this, how could it be that the police had so little information? To all involved, the investigation seemed to be moving too slowly. The overwhelming feeling of helplessness from everyone in the suite was so painfully apparent with every minute that went by with no news. The participants in this sad vigil took turns passing the tissue box from person to person. The gloomy mood of the crowd was worsening in direct relation to the darkening late afternoon light as twilight inched toward enveloping them in its tight embrace.

Sage was slowly becoming nauseated by the inaction and lack of results and was on the verge of outrage. So much so that she began to arrange to travel in the next few days to Atlanta and became totally engrossed in her own search through mutual friends. Late in the evening, as the group was disbanding, Samantha approached Sage and offered to travel with her to Atlanta to join the search. Remarkably, Sage took this very well, and, in the end, they left it at an open-ended offer. Sage was the last to leave and the two exchanged a heartfelt embrace.

Samantha tried to boost her spirits with a repeat of her offer, "I will help you. You will see, we will find her. Girl power can defeat the negative in this world."

As it would turn out, they and many others would be

expending a lot of girl power in this endeavor to find Mía.

—❧❦—

CHAPTER 9: FIELD TRIP

—❧❦—

Her freshman year at Georgetown, having passed so splendidly, could not have passed the torch to her sophomore year in a worse fashion. Classes were on the cusp of beginning for the fall semester and Samantha had barely sunk her teeth into the new internship. This week was supposed to be the beginning of this dream internship with her idol and all hell was breaking loose. She felt like she was losing her mind as she found that she could not even complete simple tasks like brushing her teeth that morning. She barely managed to remove the cap from the toothpaste, dropped it on the floor, and then clumsily stepped on the tube, resulting in a shot of gooey green across her dormitory bathroom. On any other day she might have laughed at the predicament but not today as she ended up in tears sitting on the cold tile floor. She felt she could be losing her best friend in the whole world and, as with everything else that was going oh so wrong in this godforsaken world, she felt responsible and helpless to boot.

She had not slept a wink the night before, but woke up early, ostensibly because of the adrenaline still coursing in her veins. She knew that she needed to get to Atlanta, but she didn't know how to do it with all the different responsibilities she needed to manage. Classes, homework, internship, friends - her entire life's work was occupying a smaller and smaller space inside her brain at the moment. She had barely managed to recite and copy the goals that she and Natalia had discussed a few days before. With Herculean effort, she finally made it out the door, late for the first day of her new internship.

As her eyes adjusted to the light of the bright morning, she made her way down the gray concrete steps of her dormitory flat. Normally she would have taken a keen interest in the squirrels tending to the acorns on the ground, the myriad of flowers blooming in full force, and grand statues lining the groomed pathways that Georgetown was famous for. But not today, as her eyes were swollen and fixated on the ground as she continued to fight back the tears of guilt and helplessness.

As she raced up the steps of the business building, she thought for the first time that she needed to confide in her new mentor. Maybe she would have some advice. She had just saved the world from an outside invader, using her investigative journalistic instincts. She had only met Natalia once, but she already trusted her mentor's intuition. Perhaps she would have an idea as to how to proceed to find Mía. At the very least, she would have an unclouded judgment, being an unbiased observer. Samantha was acutely aware that in the last few days, her reasoning and rationality had gone out the window.

As she rounded the top floor of the steps and into the hallway, she could see that Natalia's door was open. Thank goodness, she is in her office, thought Samantha as she, for the second time, suddenly realized how out of breath she was. She wasn't even going to be able to talk this time. She slowed down and stopped to catch her breath, as she exhaled forcefully against pursed lips to clear her lungs. She had not stopped rushing from one place to the next since yesterday, in full fight-or-flight mode like Forrest Gump, running just to keep running, with no particular aim.

As she calmed her nerves with her deep breathing exercises, she advanced through the doorway to spy Natalia sitting at her desk, peering out the window at the Georgetown campus, daydreaming yet again. Natalia, half-startled, looked up quickly at Samantha. It was immediately apparent to Natalia that something was disturbingly wrong.

"Samantha, what is wrong, my sweet child? You look like the devil himself is chasing after you with a pitchfork from hell!"

Samantha sputtered, suddenly out of breath again it seemed, "Ms. Volkov, I fear something awful may have happened to a friend of mine. She is in Atlanta, so far away. And I feel like I am powerless to do anything about it. I feel like I need to go straight to Atlanta to rescue her. What do you think I should do?"

"Alright, calm yourself. Breathe. Tell me. Who is it, what is the situation, and what do you think we need to do to rectify whatever this situation is?" Natalia asked with bated breath. Exactly like Samantha, her predisposition compelled her to immediately fix whatever was wrong.

Samantha sank down into the luxurious leather chair and desperately tried to gather her thoughts as she stared out the window into the blue summer sky, the clouds blurred by her tears. It took a few seconds to squint her eyes and wipe the salty fluid on the new white blouse she had purchased for her first day. She slowly began, "It's my friend Mía," pausing again to wipe her cheeks dry. Her thoughts were picking up speed, "who is doing an internship in Atlanta. She texted two nights ago but has not responded to any of our texts since then. We have checked her apartment and her car is gone. I want to personally go down there to find her. I need some advice to figure out what to do next."

"Well, let's think about this logically. Who do we have in Atlanta already working with us? You said someone checked her apartment?"

"We have two people working on it, a detective who is friends with the director of our campus police, and a mutual friend, a Georgetown graduate. They both stopped by her apartment, and the detective was able to enter the apartment.

That's all I know of so far. Mía has a girlfriend here on campus who is also freaking out." Samantha tried her best to fight the tears from welling up in her eyes, but to no avail, as they flowed down her cheeks.

"Do you want me to get involved? We may be able to provide a whole host of resources to investigate this. Let's call my partner, Chip. I'm not sure if you are aware of the details, but both of our families own security operations. Chip's company, Merlin Commerce, is second to none. They have former FBI agents and have contacts with the FBI that could help."

Samantha somehow had overlooked this connection, and the possibilities flew through her mind. FBI! Their thinking hadn't even progressed to that level yet. They seemed to be getting nowhere with the Atlanta police, and yet she had no idea what any of this even meant. Maybe they should have called the FBI in the first place. Hopefully, Natalia's friends were just as good. It was surely worth a shot. "Oh my god, yes! Anything that will save our Mía!"

Natalia set her phone on the desk, pushed the quick-dial button to Chip, and waited for the answer. "Chip, you are on speakerphone. I have my intern, Samantha, here with me. She has a friend, an intern in Atlanta, who is missing. We may need some guidance from our Atlanta division. Is Sam there with you?"

"Yes, he is. We can get our guys there to investigate. What is the status so far? How long has she been missing?"

Natalia answered, "I'll let Samantha give us the update on her friend. Samantha is a sophomore here at Georgetown and is the new intern I told you about. She just confided in me about this, and all of her friends are quite concerned."

Samantha took a deep swallow to try to clear her parched mouth and throat. She was so amped up with the speculations of bringing in this newfound assistance that she could barely contain herself. "Hi, Chip, this is Samantha. My friend Mía Gonzalez is an intern with the Atlanta Sentinel. She lives in an apartment in the midtown area of Atlanta. She went out for sushi two nights ago and hasn't been seen since. She was there with an unknown friend and left the restaurant toward home. We know her car is missing. Our campus police have a friend with the Atlanta PD who is investigating and has conducted a wellness check. Nothing in the apartment that suggests foul play, other than the missing car."

After a long pause, Sam, who was also on speaker phone on Chip's end, asked, "Samantha, this is Sam, I am the security director at Merlin Commerce. I will feed some information to our security team. But first I need some basics. What is her height, weight, eye color, hair color, and some bio info, date of birth, address, make and model of car?"

Samantha provided a relatively brief sketch of her best friend in the world. At the end of the few minutes of bland facts, Samantha knew there were dozens of characteristics and qualities she left out, so she gave some extraneous biographical information. She paused, thinking she needed to go over more about her writing and her hobbies. "I think what I'm trying to say is, she is passionate about women's and minority rights, and she wrote vociferously and eloquently in the furtherance of their causes."

With the information becoming interesting but superfluous, Sam stopped her there, yet tried not to sound cold. "Excellent information, Samantha. While you are continuing to talk with Chip, I am going to do a little searching. I have some of the best investigators that could assist with this."

Chip began to ask some more questions about her background, parents, friends, and prior partners. "Have there been any arguments or fights with any of her current or prior partners? Any inkling regarding anyone new in Atlanta?"

"Well, we just learned she was last seen with a female acquaintance having sushi. We think it could have been a neighbor."

Natalia suggested the obvious, "Let's do an internet search of the apartment building for known occupants so that we can narrow the identity of this person."

"Right," Chip answered. "I think the team is pursuing a query on some deep web chat rooms, too. They have had some success with this tactic with prior kidnappings."

Several minutes of discussion ensued. Then Natalia could hear some chatter in the background as it was apparent Sam and Chip were having a video conference call with their investigators. After a short silence on the other end, Sam interjected, "Natalia, do you have time to accompany us to Atlanta? We can drop everything here in D.C. and leave today. Samantha?"

This surprised Natalia, but maybe nothing should shock her in this new partnership. There must have been something impressive Sam or his investigators uncovered in their research that they were not divulging. Certainly, Sam was normally all business and not the type to chase mysteries and investigations. Perhaps he was becoming a softie in his old age.

It took but a second for Samantha to respond. "Thank you so much! And your answer is undeniably yes. Can we bring her girlfriend, Sage, along?"

Chip answered resoundingly, "Samantha, we have plenty of room. We will assemble a team and file a flight plan. Plus, we already have a team on the ground in Atlanta. We have the perfect lad who is flying in to head this investigation. They have no assignments this week. Can you guys make the arrangements on your end? Let's meet at Reagan in an hour. I will send two cars to get you now."

Natalia answered, "Yes, agreed to plan. I will text you when we are on our way. You sure are full of surprises lately."

Samantha texted Sage, who was undoubtedly already making travel plans of her own. Within a minute, her phone rang and it was Sage.

"Hello, Sage. You'll never believe this development. You remember that we have a new professor in the business college, that is Natalia Volkov, who broke open the whole financial crime of the century several months ago? Well, she has a security company that employs former FBI agents and has a gazillion connections that could help find Mía."

Natalia overheard Sage screaming with some exclamations of surprise.

Samantha answered, "Can you meet us at my dorm room? Fifteen minutes? We need to pack and I am sure Ms. Volkov needs to pack too."

Samantha hung up the phone and made plans with Natalia to meet at her dorm room in fifteen minutes. "Ms. Volkov, I can never thank you enough. We have been beside ourselves for two days now. I am afraid we may be too late."

"For one, call me Natalia. Two. Do not even think about thanks at this point. Our only thought needs to be finding your friend. Three. Let's not waste time with worry and shift our energy to what we can control. Let's get going. I will have the dean take care of your classes and responsibilities. I will also text the Chronicle supervisors. This will be a journalistic and investigative field trip."

Natalia locked the door on their way out and paused as she turned and faced a teary-eyed Samantha. "Come on, everything will be alright, Sam." They hugged briefly, and, with a look down at her watch, Natalia gasped at the time, and they were off.

What followed was a whirlwind of packing mixed with emotions as the drivers met them at the Georgetown dormitories and whisked them away to Natalia's domicile. The fact Natalia had not even completely unpacked necessitated emptying a large suitcase of clothes onto the bed so that she could repack. It would seem impossible, but she was entirely packed again in less than ten minutes. That gave them fifteen minutes to make it to Reagan National Airport in the allotted hour, which was entirely conceivable when arriving at the private jet hangar. Three women, packed separately in thirty minutes was likely a world record though, Natalia mused to herself.

She briefly lamented how this was now her new normal in her ever more treacherous life. Maybe she was destined to become a detective or private investigator, she thought with a wry smile as she gazed out at the passing greenery. She caught herself mid-thought and visualized the negativity creeping in. During the short ride through the scenic wooded drive along the Potomac River, she observed the other two were also lost in their apprehensive subconsciousness. She tried to resist conjuring up the myriad scenarios that could ultimately play out on this new adventure. Natalia momentarily replayed the antecedent affair involving her family in her mind, believing there would not be a re-enactment of those harrowing events. While she knew her life ultimately was always in danger from her family's connections in Russia, she felt safer recently, each passing month of normalcy bringing peace to her mind. She reminded herself to reframe the negative into the affirmative safety she felt.

She focused on the best possible outcome and the impact that their efforts could have on multiple lives if it came to pass. She contrasted this with the immense torment she sensed in the eyes and facial expressions of her fellow passengers. The aura of the back seat of that car could be summed up as the torture of an unknown fate. Suddenly, she felt the need to soothe the pain she saw, as worry could be their worst enemy if it clouded their judgment.

"You know, we shouldn't open our umbrella until it starts raining. Worry only clouds our thinking and restricts our thought processes." Natalia took a deep breath, slowly let it out, and decided that, for the next minute, peace was going to be their friend. "Okay, breathe with me. I want you to take three deep breaths to release the guilt, regret, and hate. Okay, first breathe in and exhale all of your guilt. Guilt is an external force placed upon you by others, you control your destiny."

Natalia breathed in, held it, and exhaled with a willful force. "Now, regret. Exhale your regret. You cannot change the past, only the future." With renewed vigor, she continued after the long respiration, "Now, let out all your hate. Tame your demons. Bring into focus our task and all the mental concentration it will take to succeed."

Samantha, upon finishing her third exhalation, felt a modicum of relief. "That helped immensely. I need to focus on Mía and bringing her home and quit worrying about the past and any expectations that are placed on me artificially."

102

The rest of the brief journey to the airport was spent discussing Mía and her life, all of her friends, and her hopes and dreams. Samantha and Sage recounted where she grew up, her rocky relationship with her parents, and her new life relocating temporarily to Atlanta. Sage relayed to Natalia that Mía was working on an election piece regarding the divisions in the deep South.

"That is some good information. We need to keep that in the back of our minds. Does Mía keep her notes and stories on an online drive?" Natalia queried.

"I believe so, and there are only a few possibilities through her email account and her school account," Sage answered.

That juicy morsel of information sent Natalia's investigative mind into overdrive. The airport frontage roads and hangars were now coming into view as they crossed the Potomac River into the hills of Virginia. "That needs to be one of our first targets for information. She may have some interview notes."

As they approached their designated hangar, she could see that Guinevere was already in departure formation outside on the tarmac, as her gargantuan body, wings, and tail were unmistakable even in the busy airport. "Is everybody ready to meet Guinevere? She is a magnificent sight."

"That's our airplane? I was thinking small jet. It looks like a cargo plane. There aren't many windows." Samantha was in awe.

"The main area over the wings and the cockpit are armor reinforced and each has its own safe rooms that are impenetrable. The belly of the plane carries its own armory. It is used to transport kings, princes, and Presidents all around the world. We are lucky to have her right now with all of the strife in the world." Natalia recognized Merlin Logistics had surpassed her own family's company years ago and was proud to lend her expertise to the new partnership.

The fuselage was painted a dazzling white with blue accents, with the centerpiece being a depiction of Merlin's wand and stars as if he was casting a spell to make the plane fly. The jetway stairs were deployed to the side of the plane, which, as they came closer, towered into the sky above them. Natalia flashed back to the only time she had seen the armored underbelly stairs deployed and the firefight that ensued. As her mind slowly returned to the present, she felt an aura of security fall over her that she knew to cultivate.

"Get ready to meet my family, my partner Chip, and our best friend Sam."

As the three Suburbans in their convoy rolled out onto the tarmac, the three other Suburbans were just vacating the area, and Chip and Sam were already halfway up the stairs, waving to the new arrivals as they ascended. The boarding and takeoff procedure was complete within minutes, proving to be a quick exodus from the capital city southward bound on another new venture.

CHAPTER 10: ARIZONA PAIGE

The dream assignment was the very first internship responsibility given to Paige Etienne and she continued to painstakingly labor over it even today. Those two years had flown by like a desert bald eagle since her debut with this formerly small-town Phoenix newspaper. For the last decade, the Arizona Post had been rising in stature and readership with all manner of political drama emanating from rogue sheriffs and conspiracy theorists, which seemed to proliferate in the desert air like cockroaches in these divisive times. Following a series of exposés and partnerships with the New York Journal and the Washington Chronicle, and several infusions of cash by liberal think tanks, there was a sudden air of confidence in the newsroom that piqued Paige's level of interest following her relatively boring first year of internship.

Gone overnight were the days of painfully sitting through a daily briefing with mundane discussions regarding the heat, airport parking, and infrastructure. The current mode of discourse replaced the written verse with a more interactive newsroom, with video boards mimicking the online experience of the modern information digest. During the first year of her internship, Paige dreaded the monotonous task of listening to everyone's story of the day, surviving only through a constant infusion of ice-cold caffeine and passion fruit teas. These days, however, Paige had become a consistent contributor to everyone's stories using the sharing video screen set up in the room for just this purpose.

Following a productive second year of her internship, what had started as a temporary move from the comfort of her liberal stomping grounds at Columbia University in New York City had become an unexpectedly semi-permanent career when the Post gave her a generous offer to remain as a full-time journalist. With the fresh influx of talent, Paige surprisingly found herself garnering the respect of her more seasoned colleagues who had recently joined the staff from established liberal press organizations.

Notwithstanding the fresh increase in job satisfaction and the comfort of finally earning a paycheck, the ultimate goal remained to move back to Manhattan after her internship was finished. However, frustratingly, she was unable to secure a position yet. "Patience," she coached herself, as something great would come her way eventually. Multiple interviews with big city newspapers, television stations, and online news outlets and Paige had come up empty-handed thus far. She was beginning to lose faith in her destiny, but at least she secured this position for the time being, and she really had begun to enjoy the inspiration that the elevated morale of the bright contemporary newsroom had brought to the position. Then, as always, fate intervened to complicate her life, as a position opened up with the Journal that could change everything.

Despite her love of her current position, her preferred specialty was financial reporting since she also had an international business and finance degree from Columbia University. A star pupil from her hometown of Massapequa, New York, Paige had earned a National Merit Scholarship which was impressive, as her parents were first-generation immigrants from Haiti. She could speak English, French, and Chinese and scored a perfect 1600 on the SAT, sealing admission to any number of Ivy League schools. Never a doubt in her mind; once accepted, she of course chose Columbia to remain close to home with her parents, with whom she shared a special relationship.

She had never been away from her parents for more than a few weeks during her studies abroad and she now found herself regularly becoming homesick for her mother's cooking and her father's inspirational pep talks. Her father was trained as an electrician but was constantly tinkering with new inventions at the kitchen table in their humble apartment. He and her mother were fluent in multiple languages and by custom, the dinner fare and conversation revolved around a new culture every night. An incessant worrier, she was also concerned about her parents' financial status, now that they were empty-nesters. Her father had endeavored to hide it from Paige, but his health was not the best, having had heart troubles in recent years. From two thousand miles away, she spent considerable effort concocting reasons to pack up and head home, but that choice was something she knew her father would not approve of.

That's not to say she wasn't savoring her life here in Arizona. She was settling in, becoming comfortable with the Southwest lifestyle, hiking canyons in the spring and fall, contending with snowbirds crowding the city in the winter, and hiding indoors in the summer. The winter festivals in this Western oasis celebrated the desert life and she was getting a charge out of the distinctive music scene. She also appreciated the casual support of feminist and LGBTQ groups, which, in this area were a little more relaxed than in the Big Apple. Despite missing her old life in New York, she sometimes didn't appreciate feeling compelled to conform to the internally set expectations and rigid fashion of the alternative social scenes. She didn't experience any of those pressures in Phoenix, which she welcomed for a change.

There was, however, a noticeable transformation developing insidiously in this winter haven for northerners. The Hispanic heritage was gradually being replaced by those who migrated from the North. In the antecedent, immigrants and native Americans built and shaped this town in the image of their unique culture, emerging from the sands of the desert in harmony. Today, though, there was a decidedly anti-immigration and anti-native shift in the political landscape. While the politics of the area had always been slightly conservative, recently a nationalistic extremist upwelling was occurring within the ranks of the right wing. She was not alone in harboring these feelings of fear for her fellow immigrants. For this reason, she frequently volunteered in support of immigrant relief organizations in the city and connected with the other volunteers.

At least once monthly, she reported on the Hispanic and Native American businesses that were struggling to maintain their foothold in the new business landscape, creating multimedia presentations that were consistently among the highest click counts on the Post website. She was also given some latitude to report on international business news stories, which she explained to her editor was necessary to maintain her global economic journalism skills.

On this sunny, sweltering afternoon, she was waiting at her favorite vegan coffee shop, Namé Namé, gazing out of the window from her customary corner booth at the orange and brown hues of the barren mountains in the distance. Her source for the breakthrough story was overdue for a meeting today to feed her some information on a right-wing extremist who had shown increasing volatility. Her informant had just texted that she would be late. Her cup of spearmint tea sat empty on the table, and she had long finished her vegan cookie dough pastry. It had only been two short weeks, but the memory of a momentous weekend at home was already fading, given the explosive developments of the past few days. She attempted to jog her memory to keep herself focused on the future, for that weekend in New York could change her life if she just let it happen. She needed to fight the negative energy with the positive. The spearmint lingered in her sinuses, clearing them as she drew in a deep breath and closed her eyes to bring back the positive energy of that weekend.

It was during a particularly stressful week of deadlines when the potentially fateful call occurred. She was excited to learn of a recent opening for a staff writer in the developing economies section of the Journal. One of the lead journalists in the section was on sabbatical and they were seeking a research writer, therefore she had submitted her résumé the week before. Having followed the career of Natalia Volkov, the reporter she could ultimately replace, she knew she had gigantic shoes to fill if her candidacy was successful. She was taking a hiatus from the Post during her lunch hour, viewing a landscape exhibit at the Phoenix Art Museum, sitting in a half-empty food court. It was summer, after all, and the snowbirds had all but disappeared, and indoor activities were the name of the game in the oppressive heat. Her cell phone, sitting on the wooden bench beside her, rang with an unknown number from the 212 area code and she immediately picked up. Barely concealing her excitement from the human resource officer, the lengthy informal interview that day sealed her invitation to visit in person.

She took the next Friday off and flew home to the comfort of the family apartment in Massapequa. She arrived late on a Thursday night and her parents greeted her with her favorite rice and beans with poule en sauce. The simple joy the meal brought to her tastebuds evoked so many memories that carried her back to her childhood in this centuries-old barrio of Long Island. To rekindle the tradition, during this meal, the discourse was exclusively in contemporary French, which Paige welcomed as she realized that she was out of practice. Late nights of her adolescence were devoted to teaching her parents to speak better English, while they helped her learn Creole and French and the whole family experimented with Spanish and Chinese.

"What a homecoming this would be if I could land this job," she sighed to her mother immediately upon finishing the simple, yet delectable flavors of home. She found herself gazing out the window at the lights of the city streets that were decidedly different from the pale lights of Phoenix. As Paige turned her head back to the dinner table, her mother was peering at her with a spoon of the poule en sauce held up to her lips to cool.

"This does seem perfect for you and your writing talents and maybe we could finally move uptown. You will need someone to housesit while you are traveling the world," her mother replied. Moving back to New York would be the answer to Paige's almost constant prayers and wishes and undoubtedly those of her mother as well.

"Right, Mama! I have already cataloged and categorized every country in my brain that I would be researching," Paige remarked and listed several locations and storylines as she cleared the dishes to the sink, washed them, and set them in the teak drying rack.

Her interview process went smoothly with the Journal. First, a series of meetings with human resources and a few writers on Friday allowed her to display her talents, and she was invited back on Saturday morning. Over the long weekend, it was one meeting after another with what seemed like every financial reporter on staff, which culminated in the official meeting with the financial editor Saturday night. Her stellar performance in these sessions sealed the deal for an in-person Sunday brunch with the editor-in-chief. Word on the street had it that if you interviewed with the chief, the position was yours.

She didn't sleep a wink Saturday night. As she drifted in and out of nirvana, she speculated which part of Manhattan she would live in. "No way is this dream coming true," she thought as she stared up at the ceiling of her childhood bedroom, "if I could land this opportunity, I would never need another job." But then her practical side countered, "Don't get premature, now!" Characteristically her optimistic personality took over again as she began to contemplate which stories and locations she would concentrate on first. Her imagination conjured up images of her future travels to Asia and Africa investigating developing companies and other business news stories.

Her final day in the big city was a whirlwind and while there was no definitive job offer yet, she picked up on very genuine positive vibes from her potential future editor-in-chief. She was told in no uncertain terms that she would hear from them within two weeks. The sleepless weekend was followed by five hours of shuteye on the plane in coach despite multiple crying babies surrounding her. She awoke to an almost empty plane and a rather annoyed stewardess as she had passed out next to the window. After sleepily walking through the quiet Phoenix International Airport, Paige groggily made her way back to her desert abode in the late-night heat.

That following Monday morning would prove to be a rude awakening. Having just returned from the excitement and expectations of her lofty future prospects, the productive thoughts of her destiny were swiftly replaced by the realities of modern journalism. Early that day, in a meeting with her editor, she learned that this assignment she had been working on for years would not pan out for publication. This frustrated Paige to no end, as the assignment had brought in so much investigative information, and at any other newspaper, she could have gleaned several breaking stories already if it wasn't for her editor. Paige was not sure if the stories were being killed politically but it didn't matter in the grand scheme of her résumé building. She was earning plenty of by-lines as her editor had handed her so many premium business assignments over the past year that could have gone to other more experienced journalists.

Fortuitously, even during this hectic past year as a staff journalist, she had allowed herself extra allotments of time to continue to work on the leads of this now rapidly developing storyline on the societal turn against immigrants in Arizona and Nevada. As a child of immigrants, the story possessed a special, personal meaning. The underlying racial proclivities of the bigoted dragged even third- and fourth-generation Hispanic Americans into the lumped category of immigrants due to their skin color and family names. Her extensive research uncovered many examples of systematic bias in government and business-to-business dealings that, if discovered in the Northeast, would have been revealed and corrected long ago. Professionally, her work on this story could mean being branded a radical liberal among some of the local population if she was branded as protecting illegal immigrants. Lately, though, the story was garnering some new leads in a different, more ominous direction, uncovering the burgeoning extremist movement and a group intent on stoking a more dangerous racial and anti-immigrant bias.

Today, quite unexpectedly, before she made her way to the Namé Namé coffeeshop, her editor pulled her aside after the morning staff meeting and gave her a lead on the disappearance of a local small-time activist for immigrants. Not usually known for taking crime stories, Paige, at first was taken aback until she heard who the potential victim was. María Gonzalez was not a leader of any particular immigrant relief group, but Paige had met her many times. What she was known for was being a tireless champion for immigrants, working at homeless shelters and local food pantries. She probably spent sixty hours per week in these efforts and worked part-time in a Mexican bakery.

"Now you keep to this story. I don't think that the other one is going to be a good one, especially with the political climate out here right now. This person who disappeared, herself an immigrant, she is not very popular right now, trying to create sanctuary cities here in Phoenix. Not well known enough though, maybe that's what got her. Or could it have been a robbery gone bad? From what they tell me, thus far, the police have no leads."

Paige always felt powerless in this position to speak her mind, but this story was different. "But I have a lot of great information on some pretty unsavory folk coming down from Las Vegas and Utah meddling in the elections and intimidating people who are fighting for immigrants' rights. Something bad is going to happen soon, mark my word."

"Well, just be careful. You can keep working on it for your own personal purposes but know that, at this time, there is no plan to publish. Just check this one out, too. It's right up the same alley, so to speak." Her editor gave her a cursory, almost insulting pat on the back and a wry look of concern

"You are so right. Maybe this is the tip of the iceberg." That moment of clarity once again brought to the surface her fears for all of the immigrants in the area. While she clandestinely continued work on the story for the past two weeks, she was just given permission by her editor to continue to do so.

As she regained her focus on the present at the café, she noticed a young Hispanic couple entering the shop. They were a cute pair, couldn't have been more than sixteen. "Young love," she thought as she covertly observed their conspicuously amorous caresses from afar. After they politely ordered their agave lemonades, they settled into a corner booth opposite Paige, staring into each other's eyes. She then began to think about the subject of her new assignment, María, the kindest soul and now apparently a new member of the Desaparecidos. The term conjured up memories of Central American and South American countries where these kinds of disappearances occurred on a regular basis. She came to the abrupt realization that perhaps she and any of her sources would also need to be careful not to become part of the same statistic.

She had just begun to consider the precautions she should take when the glass door opened with a chime and her source materialized out of the bright rays of sunshine. Paige motioned toward the booth with her hand and the woman looked furtively around the room, and since the only other souls in the shop were the Latin lovers, a look of relief appeared on her face. She sat down with an apprehensive look toward Paige and introductions were exchanged as this was the first time they had spoken face to face.

"Where should I start?" her new source asked. "There are some new faces in town that I have never seen before. Let me start with this. My husband is part of a group of conservative supporters of President Zorin. I should say former President Zorin, which is a sore subject for my husband. He is a member of the city council of Sand Butte. There are some new people from Utah and Idaho that he has been talking on the phone with that have scared me a little. Ok, maybe a lot. My husband likes using speaker phones in his office and it echoes throughout the house. I have heard quite a bit and last year's events pale in comparison. Conspiracy theories, plots, framing, murders, you name it. I think my husband is getting in too deep for his britches. He's not the same man I married."

"Do you have any names of these people?" Paige jotted down the name of the town, though she already knew exactly who this woman's husband was from reverse number look-ups that she had performed.

"I have some information. First names, which may be pseudonyms for all I know. They keep talking about a leader called Action Man, or something like that. I don't think he has been here, but there is a guy, Ben, who has been here and is snooping all over the place. Ben keeps talking about a target list. And it sounds like the target list is pretty long. Like in the thousands. Says it will take a year to complete the elimination. Elimination is his word. He also talks about preparing for the disposals."

"Wow, this is a bombshell. And you are sure it's real? Not just talk?" All capital letters, "ACTION MAN" was underlined twice in the middle of Paige's white notebook. She drew three more lines, encasing it in a box, making it unmistakenly important for her notes. The name Ben was also emphasized in a similar vein.

"Yes, I'm one hundred percent sure it's real. Last week they talked about the trial run. And I think it is this week. This Ben guy said, 'She's just an immigrant. No one will miss her.' That was when I realized it was real."

Not-so-pleasant thoughts began to swirl around Paige's mind about the congruence between these two stories that were coming together like two railroad tracks merging. The gravity and urgency of this calamity in the making were unfathomable. The storyline was just escalating too quickly for Paige to grasp. If the subject of her new assignment was the victim, the erroneous label from this interloper named Ben was not lost on her, for María Gonzalez was a third-generation American.

"Have you thought about going to the police? I think that's where we need to take this. Probably more like the FBI." Paige didn't want to divulge yet about the missing ac-

114

quaintance.

"Yes, but then I heard through our mutual friend about your work for immigrants and the story you had been working on."

Paige was not aware that the report she had been working on had been anywhere near public knowledge yet, though her new source was right, their mutual friend was fully aware of the assignment. Combined with the disappearance, this information only intensified her intuition that she needed to be attentive to her surroundings and interactions going forward with this investigation.

"Well, let me start to get some background information on some possible Ben's from Utah, and let's see if this passes the test to go to the FBI."

"Okay, let me know if you need anything more."

"Yes, we should stay in touch regularly. But probably not here. I take it you are not vegan or involved with any alternative lifestyle. What I'm saying is this is not a place you would normally be seen. We need to meet at a place that you frequent on a regular basis. Some place without windows in the front of the store. Do you go to a mall frequently and where would that be?"

"I go to the Sandy Road Mall often. There's a coffee shop inside. Very segregated from the rest of the mall."

"Let's meet there every Monday at noon. At the center fountain, when you see me, don't acknowledge me, then follow me to the best location which will be different every time. Could be the coffee shop, could be another location. And Margaret? I am assuming I don't need to say, 'Be careful'. People like this are serious. Sound good?"

"Yes, agreed."

With that simple affirmation, they proceeded with trepidation to a future that neither of them could have imagined.

—•❥❥❦❦•—

CHAPTER 11: FINDING CLAIRE

—•❥❥❦❦•—

Guinevere touched down in Atlanta before the conversations among the passengers could even get off the ground regarding the strategy for finding Mía in this unfamiliar metropolis of Atlanta. As they were taxiing to the private jet terminal, the realization that they still did not have a plan slowly began to sink in. There were only three connections to pursue at this point: the police detective, the coworker, and the woman with whom Mía ate sushi. The five newly branded investigators at that moment were already standing, seemingly in a catapult for the door, ready to launch as soon as the plane came to a stop. At that moment, they quickly agreed to dispense with a comprehensive strategy and tackle their three meager leads in that order, from the known to the unknown. They had experience on their side, having two seasoned journalists and a security expert to follow where the trail went cold. In no time at all, their lead investigator would arrive from London with more technical assistance.

Natalia took the lead as they bounded down the jet stairs onto the tarmac and the familiar, awaiting Suburbans below. When they were all settled into the plush confines of the armored vehicle, the flood let loose. Samantha, who had remained quiet during the plane ride, felt more comfortable speaking her mind now that they were in the car on terra firma. She felt intimidated by the luxury and ostentatiousness of Guinevere. Naturally, even those who had flown in private jets before were awestruck by the opulence during their first voyage aboard her. Equally impressive yet disquieting to her first-time passengers was the overwhelming security and armor on board. It often begged the question, "Why would all of this be necessary?" which was always followed by the scary realization regarding the violent world in which they lived.

The answer to that question was unfathomable stateside until the events of the Manchurian Markets. The moniker was publicly known now as the codename of the CIA operation that was indeed primarily undertaken by Merlin Commercial Logistics' security division. Everyone in the entire world had heard of and seen the cell phone video taken through the porthole window of Guinevere a mere two years ago of rocket-propelled grenades bouncing off the tarmac of Teterboro airport and of the Secret Service airplanes limping to take off after being partially disabled by Merlin security ops. It had ten million views on YouTube alone. Regardless of the stories of stalwart Guinevere's past heroics, Samantha felt safer on the ground.

"I feel like we are already days behind in being able to find her. Whoever has done anything nefarious with our Mía is seven steps ahead. They could be halfway across the country for all we know!" Samantha let out a sigh as Sage interrupted her.

"You are right. I hope and pray there is nothing nefarious." Sage let out an even deeper sigh.

"Hope is our friend," Natalia encouraged the discussion. "Sam, did you call the detective with whom Samantha and Sage have talked?"

Sam answered from the front seat, "Yes, I just scheduled a meeting at his station office. We are on our way there first. I have dangled some information to get him to agree to the meeting. God knows how much or how little information the detective will divulge from the investigation. At this point, it is barely a missing person investigation and he probably has no manpower assigned to this. After we meet with him, let's get our geographical bearings about us. We should proceed first to the sushi restaurant where we will be greeted by her coworker, then retrace Mía's steps to her apartment. This is where we hope to identify our first clues to get to the bottom of this disappearance. By that time, Huy should be on the ground and the headquarters should be well on the way to being set up."

Sam paused for a few seconds, with his finger in the air and an indecisive look on his face, then, upon deciding the correct wording, "This may be bigger than this one person, Mía. Before we even began this odyssey, I took the liberty of sending the information regarding Mía, her location, and her cell phone number to our investigation unit in England. I am not sure what information they pinged off the airwaves. Whatever that is, it has piqued their interest beyond all measure, that's for certain."

Natalia quickly interjected, "What does that mean, 'piqued their interest'? I'm confused. Did they not tell you what they found?" Natalia's journalist mind wanted facts, and these were not facts.

"Sorry to keep you in the dark, but Chip and I have taken the liberty of inviting all of our private investigation units to Atlanta. We have the command unit from London, but we also have multiple units stateside. Some team members are already on site. We are setting up a command center in a conference room in our hotel. It will be functional in about an hour."

Natalia had not witnessed this aspect of Merlin before. "Well, this ought to be better than operating out of the conference room of Guinevere on a tarmac with missiles being fired upon us!"

"These guys are every bit as capable as the FBI and can work around the rules. Hackers, you might call them, but we will procure secure communication channels, and the whole works. It will be like having a whole unit of FBI agents at our disposal. They coordinate and interact with our protection units. Satellites, drones, and everything. We use this unit for investigating threats and safe passage routes for heads of state who do not have their own Secret Service. This is an unpublicized unit that works behind the scenes for the safety of ultra-high-net-worth individuals. Andddd... as luck would have it, none of the Saudi princes are traveling right now for safety reasons."

Chip, noticing the tell-tale signs of an older police precinct building, sat forward in his seat, pointing to the parking garage, "We are almost there, let's see what information we can obtain on the first pass with this guy. Sam, I am looking to you to lead this." Chip, who had been mostly silent until now, was out of his element. He was accustomed to performing economic research and accounting investigations. At least the prior adventure contained some of these financial components that necessitated his input. The present situation demanded an entirely new mindset. This focused criminal investigation regarding a missing person would test his mettle and that of the whole team. "Sam, can you better inform Natalia and me what experience our investigative guys have for missing persons?"

"Well, actually quite extensive. We have been hired for high-profile kidnappings all over the world. This is an up-and-coming sector for Merlin, because our men provide more meaningful results than police and mere small-time private investigators, especially in countries where the police and even investigators are corrupt. The technology and the security personnel that they bring to bear are almost like bringing a mercenary army for protection and investigation."

Natalia interrupted, "But Sam, this is the US. Do you think this is a good idea? The police in this country are easily offended by people taking things into their own hands."

"Don't get me wrong, they ruffle feathers and sometimes get under the skin of the established law enforcement investigators. However, the resources that the average police department can work with are limited by laws and budget deficits. And we journey into a lot rougher places than Atlanta, Georgia." Sam paused as the driver found a parking spot, and then turned back toward the backseat passengers. "Here we are. Let's get a baseline on this investigation. Samantha, Sage, remember to keep calm in talking to this guy. At this point, I don't want to give away that we will have an investigative unit coming in. And I am not picking on you, I always have to remind myself the same thing."

Though the downtown area of Atlanta was hip and modern, the police precinct station spoke of decades gone by as the stark, stone building stood dwarfed by the convention center and modern hotels. The motley crew bounded up the gray granite steps, leaving their security detail behind. Upon entering the building, they counted no less than ten police personnel, none of whom could direct them to their contact's office. They finally found one helpful octogenarian Southern lady, with glasses attached to crystal chains who led them to a nondescript door with a frosted glass window on the second floor, hidden in the dingy labyrinth.

The next hour was not exactly a waste of time, but close to it. The only information they wanted to glean from this meeting was the name of the neighbor that Mía had met for dinner and the information on her automobile. As it would turn out, the main investigative team, which was still airborne on approach to Atlanta, already possessed this information and more. The one salient piece of intelligence obtained during the meeting was that the detective was able to search one traffic camera and was able to place Mía's car driving toward the apartment parking lot after dinner that night. They also learned there was nothing unusual in the apartment and no signs of a struggle there.

At the end of the discussion, Sam stood up from the chair to shake hands with the detective, extending his hand across the desk. Immediately the detective rose from his desk as well, but instead of shaking hands, walked around behind his guests to open the door of his office. The slight was the kind of power play that Sam was accustomed to witnessing in third-world countries but was not altogether surprised to find in this locale.

Sam, always looking toward diplomacy, placated the officer, "All of us, including Mía's best friends Samantha and Sage here, appreciate your assistance in finding this promising young journalist."

Sage, who up until this time let Sam take the lead, expounded on that thought, "Sir, thank you from the bottom of our hearts, and if you need anything or any further information, don't hesitate to call us. We will be here all week waiting for word on your investigation. She is our best friend and she means the world to us."

Natalia, feeling that was the perfect closure to the meeting, did not add anything further. The wording could not have been more demure, deferring to the expertise of the detective, allowing him to presume control of this investigation was still his.

As they left the precinct station, the disheartening news hit them that there was not a lot of evidence developed as yet by the professionals. It did not appear that the detective had even met with the dinner date or the owner of the restaurant, nor had he even identified the dinner date, and he did not offer a single reason why. The next item on the investigative agenda was to drive to the sushi restaurant, located in a quaint reddish-orange brick building tucked into a residential neighborhood just off the main road, where they would meet their friend, Jennifer. As they arrived, they waited a few seconds for their escorts to park and exit their vehicles. Sometimes it seemed to Chip and Natalia they were always waiting for their security to get into position, but through past events and recognition of her family's security situation, she long ago had succumbed to her fate that it would always be a necessary delay.

Outside the restaurant, from the parking lot, they spied a studious-appearing female pacing in front of the building. She certainly looked the part of a journalist, and Natalia surmised this was the coworker that they were meeting. The overgrown vines that lined the several red brick buildings in the area lent a decidedly old-world feel to the neighborhood. The streets were well-lit and the homes and apartment buildings immaculate. No professional kidnapper would ever dare

122

make his move here. The restaurant was the lone building whitewashed, obscuring the decades-old red clay brick, yet it still displayed years of jasmine overgrowth, trimmed neatly.

As the group approached the restaurant, Natalia began to feel a twinge of hunger as she could smell the lunch fare still being prepared. It was well past lunchtime and she had barely snacked on the plane, let alone taken the time for a meal. Moreover, upon leaving her new house this morning, she regretted not eating at least a muffin or granola for breakfast before leaving for campus, instead grabbing a quick java on the go in the cafe on the first floor of her new office.

"Maybe we should partake in some of this sushi while we investigate. I think the owner will be more responsive to paying customers," Natalia suggested, trying to hide her ulterior motive, her hands covering her vociferously growling stomach.

Chip, sensing her reasoning and his own appetite craving some sustenance, replied, "I think you are right, Natalia. Sushi chefs usually make quick work of it and the restaurant does not look busy at this time."

They cautiously approached Mía's shy coworker, still pacing with her hands in the pockets of her white capri corduroy pants. Her gaze barely left the ground as they exchanged greetings, but she gave a few hugs to Sage and Samantha as fellow Hoyas would. Without much further ado, they proceeded toward the entrance, with Sam courteously holding the door for the ladies.

The troupe quietly made their way into the quaint eatery and filled a large corner table inside the restaurant away from the windows. While orders were being placed, they asked the owner, who incidentally was also their waitress, about their friend Mía, showing her a picture on Sage's phone. A diminutive, Japanese-American woman with sharp features, she peered at each of her guests over her reading glasses, coincidentally also attached to her neck with a crystal chain. Seemingly sizing up her inquisitors, an expression of trust suddenly alit on her face after her inspection. Ostensibly, in the owner's estimation, the men in the group appeared to be non-threatening and the younger women must have adequately passed as good friends of Mía.

She spoke quickly with pressured speech, "Well, my Mía. She's new here. Nice girl. You say she's missing? Shame. Not a dangerous area here. Can't say the same about a few blocks in that direction though." She pointed across the street toward the freeway and the expression of trust gave way to some disdain toward some invisible forces in that direction.

Sam asked her if there were any surveillance cameras either outside or inside the restaurant. Interestingly enough, she had kept a copy of the footage and was able to provide both inside and outside video to them. Not only that, she provided them with some information on both of the participants of the dinner that night. Both were frequent diners at the location. This other guest, Claire, she remembered, had dined there for the past four months, Mía had only been there for the past month or two, and only a few times did they dine together.

Not much of a consolation, but that was a relief to Sage, who had been a trifle worried about the faithfulness of her one-and-only love Mía. Sage was not holding it together well inside, but outwardly, expressively, held her stoic ground. There were still so many unanswered questions as she feared they were slowly growing apart in the short few months Mía was away. Such was the insecurity of long-distance relationships.

As the search party left the restaurant for their final destination for the day, the daunting task before them felt overwhelming. There could easily be hundreds of cameras between the restaurant and the apartment. Each of these cameras had a finite amount of hard drive space that was being overwritten as often as every twenty-four hours. Luckily many cameras had thirty days or more of recording space. That would be their first target for evidence. If there were other suspects they would surely present themselves on one of these camera snippets.

Each of them kept an eye out during the short drive for

each of the locations along the way that could harbor a camera. Sam easily spotted the traffic camera at a lighted intersection a block away from the condo building. This was likely the one the detective had easy access to but was too far away to provide any meaningful recognition of faces, cars, or license plates in the parking lot. Unfortunately, the supposition was that the official investigation probably stopped there, since the restaurant footage had not even been requested by the police.

As they approached the condo building, all eyes were fixated on multiple two-flats across the street, at least two of which had doorbell cameras pointed directly into the apartment building parking lot. As they slowly, methodically drove up the block, next to the parking lot there were at least two more cameras. They suspected that the detective had not as yet accessed any footage from these four cameras and that the ideal vantage points of these cameras would provide the start to the investigation they desperately needed at this juncture.

The third and fourth cameras didn't provide a direct view of the parking lot, but they did provide superb views of the exits from the parking lot. As they pulled into the drive and parked, there were few residents' cars present on this late afternoon. Two of the Suburbans maneuvered into the lot and one remained out on the street as the advance security exited onto the sidewalks, drivers remaining in the vehicles.

Scanning the area, Chip nudged Natalia, as he noticed the cover of the many live oak trees lining the brick roads, "These trees may obscure our views a little, but I'm confident that one of these will give us some information. What do you think Sam?"

Sam looked outside his front passenger door, then turned around to look over his shoulder, placing his hand on the driver's seat. "With four cameras, I should think so. That will be one of the first items on our list."

Natalia felt her investigative instincts kicking in. As the crew disembarked from their cars, Natalia walked toward the apartment building, then turned away toward the parking area and waved her hand in a broad motion through the lot toward the houses across the street, and began, "We have a lot of work cut out for us. Whatever happened, happened between that traffic camera and here. We need a week's worth of footage from all of the cameras. And, first of all, we need this neighbor. Let's find her apartment and see if anyone is home. And, sooner rather than later, let's canvass the neighborhood."

Of course, at the apartment of their chief witness, there was no one at home. There was one polite, older African-American woman on the second floor, who opened her front door only a crack with the security chain in place. While she could not provide much, the information she did contribute was that her neighbor, Claire, was out of town for the weekend on an assignment and she worked for WNN. That employment and assignment information would be easy to track down. And the weekend would be over before they knew it so hopefully, their chief witness would return soon.

After walking the neighborhood, they found no one at home at any of the houses across the street. With that failure, they made the difficult decision to head to the hotel to meet the team that Sam had assembled. Not one of them wanted to leave the potential crime scene without at least an important clue being found. The drive was short, and the conversation had become more animated as all the participants were now in full investigative mode. Before they knew it, they were entering the parking garage across the street from their accommodations for the foreseeable future.

The Sybaritean Collection Hotel was a swank new boutique hotel in the heart of Midtown Atlanta. They crossed the skywalk and ascended an escalator to the lobby of a third-floor conference center which was opulently decorated. At a table outside the conference room sat an administrative assistant to the team and two armed security personnel managing the entrance to the area. The administrative assistant led them through a doorway to a jaw-dropping sight, even to Chip, who was conspicuously unaware of the advanced capabilities of his own company.

126

As they walked into this expansive conference room, they realized it was not just one conference room, but the team had managed to commandeer the entire floor and what they thought was going to be a conference room was more of a ballroom with space for 50 workstations. Twenty 120-inch television screens were installed one above the other and many slightly smaller ones were sitting on the ground ready to be positioned at the long end of the room and dozens of workstations had been assembled throughout the room facing the wall of video. This marvel-of-a-setup made the typical CIA situation room in the movies look like a cramped New York hotel room.

In another smaller conference suite across the hall, they met the commander of the team who had just arrived, a boisterous Vietnamese-British national whose smile would not stop, though his British accent surely adjured the respect it deserved. The workstation in front of him was his office, with his own set of monitors and computers at two conference tables set up in an L-formation. On the wall in front of him were another four ten-foot screens set up in a two-by-two formation. A video gaming chair with speakers in the headrest and his separate thin headset microphone gave notice of his hacking credentials.

"Hello, everyone, my name is Huy. Welcome to the Merlin Investigative Headquarters," He laughed a hearty laugh, with his serious smile manifest. "We are almost ready to go live here. I have our forty field investigators split into four teams ready to hit the trail and get out into the action. Each team member has body cameras and everything they do will be fed into these monitors and recorded. We then have paired four teams of inside investigators communicating with them and a team of twenty digital source investigators under me in the command center performing our electronic investigations here. We have encrypted satellite communication at all times among us. So tell me, what did you find out today and where do we need to start, other than the obvious?"

Chip began, "Impressive, then we have our security

teams also communicating. I believe we will have two sets of ground security ops and one helicopter. Sam just informed me we have two drone pilots on their way and will be set up in two of these rooms. They can accompany whichever teams need drones. Do you need more assets?"

Sage and Samantha were speechless. After witnessing the low-tech police detective's office and the little information he could provide after being on the case for at least two days, they were disappointed and discouraged, to say the least. This development gave both a glimmer of hope. A big glowing smile crept across their faces as their jaws remained open and their eyes widened in surprise. Simultaneously, they looked at each other and mouthed the word, "Wow," to each other.

Natalia finally answered the commander's questions. "I'll tell you the first thing we need is to pour over the footage from every security camera between the sushi restaurant and everywhere near the condo building where Mía was last seen. We have found four cameras that could be helpful. Then we need to find this woman Claire and find out what she knows. She is on assignment somewhere for WNN."

"We are right on it. Field Team One is on its way to the area now. They should be in place in a few minutes to access neighborhood videos. Any video they obtain will be sent directly here. Then each inside investigator will review the footage. My digital investigators will be able to access traffic and other public cameras in real time to also track. Every hour, we will have a five-minute update on the results. I promise to you now, we will have substantial results in less than 24 hours."

Chip interrupted him, "That is fantastic, but it's getting late already. The only positive factor going for our Field Team One is that the residents of those apartments and houses will be getting home from work any minute now."

Huy retorted, "Trust me, our digital teams are already gathering some electronic intelligence on the area. We already have a database of owners of properties, telephone numbers, sexual offender databases, criminal databases, and background checks of every target individual and location we develop. We already have information on Claire Taub, who is the neighbor of whom you speak. She is clean. Hippie type, but no drugs, barely drinks alcohol, no priors, very creative, writing and performance art. Has two cats that could be vicious though." The only hint of the last statement of dry humor that was evident on his face, was a slight upturn of the right corner of his mouth and an even more subtle raise of his right eyebrow. To Natalia, it was reminiscent of the dry wit and comedic delivery of Steven Wright from decades before.

Natalia reminded him, ignoring the humor, "Yes, and the video. Let's get the recordings in here now. Priority number one."

Just then, four body cam feeds pixelated and then came into sharper view on one large monitor in the upper right of the wall. "There is Field Team One, on the scene," noted their new acquaintance. Commander Huy spoke into his headset, "Video Feed, Check. Test Audio, Check." After four different audio checks, the neighborhood that they had just visited was apparent from four different vantage points of the four team members. "Okay, proceed. There are at least four doorbell cams in the neighborhood. First priority is to attain the video from these feeds. Then canvass the neighborhood. Remember, hand out cards with the main number for information and reward."

"We are offering rewards too?" Samantha asked. "How can we ever repay you?"

Huy answered, "This is standard ops. Always offer rewards. Adds to legitimacy. Cards and security investigation company credentials also add to our authority for information. Also in our favor? Missing girl or child. Everyone stops what they are doing and helps right away. And remember we have our former FBI darling, Torey Severin on his way. He will be part of one of the Field Teams or one of the Security Teams, I haven't decided yet. He has extensive experience with missing persons."

Just then, Huy brought his hand to his ear, paused for

a few seconds, and chattered into his headset. "Yes. Really? How did we get it that fast? That's great. Access it now. Bring it up." He then turned to the group, "One of the houses has an unsecured router, username for the admin is 'admin' and the password? You guessed it, 'admin'." He held up two fingers on both hands for emphasis of his verbal quotations. "Field Team One is accessing the video feeds now. No need to even knock on the door. We will have a week of video downloading soon. They have a networked recording device."

Natalia chimed in, "Wow, that is amazing. Thirty seconds on the scene. And Torey will be here? That's awesome. He is by the book, no fine detail overlooked. I can't wait to see him again. Saved my life. If it wasn't for him, I would have walked right into a trap last year. I mean, I am usually pretty security conscious, though I have always had a security team to look out for me. But he recognized the small things that I was not aware of at first. Could have been disastrous."

Chip brought up the obvious, "What about the FBI? Shouldn't this have risen to FBI missing persons yet? This is a journalist, even if she is only an intern. Natalia says she was working on a political piece. I wonder if they are aware?"

Huy agreed, "I have a feeling they will be in on this before long. Torey arrives within the hour. Tomorrow, I will have him reach out to his friends with the bureau."

—◦❭❬◦—

CHAPTER 12: PING

—◦❭❬◦—

The non-descript day began as quietly as any other, as Stamos and Point had only just begun their new routine which, with their new offices and server lab close by, would start early at the Q Café in Quantico. That was after, of course, Stamos' ritual pre-dawn run and kayak workout around and on the base reservoir with some of the more eager FBI cadets. Hanson, as his assistant, and their other new team member James, joined him begrudgingly. Hanson figured he could use this opportunity to slim down and get back into the shape of his youth.

They were now on Stamos' home turf and he was in his element here in Q Town, where he always recovered and trained when he returned from overseas missions. With his daily workouts, he could not help but absorb the palpable energy of all the younger FBI and U.S. Marines recruits in the area. As he dismounted from the colossal Ducati superbike outside the Q Café and set his helmet on the tank, he watched as Point exited his black Cadillac CT5 sedan. Nice car, thought Stamos as he sized his new partner up with new respect. "Nice ride! Did you just buy that?"

"Yes, been saving up. And I got a steal. Besides, I now

have a black car to match my black suit and black tie." Point removed his black Ray-Bans, setting them on the center console, and looked over the roof of the sleek sedan at Stamos.

"Moving on up. That's not government-issue, I can tell you that. You are rolling with the kicks. Look at those twenties." Stamos just smiled and motioned toward the door, "Come on, let's jumpstart the day."

Following closely behind, Hanson and James exited Hanson's Black Audi A6 and strolled through the door hastily. "Stamos, remember what we talked about? I always go in first. James walks in after."

"Oh right. How far behind you?" Stamos asked, with a wry smile.

Hanson retorted, looking "Far enough for the door to shut."

"Right, but if we get two assistants each, then this is going to get crowded real quick." At this point, Stamos was only slightly irritated.

After grabbing their mission-kickstarting caffeinated concoctions, they paused to sit briefly inside the café. As they sat down at a corner table, it was difficult to ignore the TV on the other side of the shop with news headlines flashing on the screen some violence erupting in a few cities ahead of the election. Stamos just stared incredulously while sipping through the white lid of his coffee. For a few minutes, the reporting continued to elaborate on the various threats that elected officials were facing in locations from Michigan to Arizona.

Most in the café were paying the news no mind. However, the significance was not lost on this duo, the newest protectors of democracy for the FBI. Point remarked in disbelief as he rose from his seat, "This country is like a tinderbox. Could go up in flames any minute if we aren't careful. There are some on both sides with gasoline cans just waiting for another spark so they can throw them into the flames. It's months before the midterm elections, practically years before the next one, what are these crazies doing?"

Stamos barely acknowledged the television as he stood

up to leave. "Unbelievable how a small, vocal, violent minority of the population is demeaning our country," Stamos added as they walked out the door into the sunny Virginia morning. He had a job to do, and it needed to get done. He grabbed the grip of the handlebar, tilted the bike, and swung his leg over. Flipping his helmet up in front of his chest, he looked at Point with that familiar look prior to intense battlefield engagement. "We've got our work cut out for us against this adversary. It's go time, Point. I'll see you at the lab."

The Superleggera growled its approval several times before Stamos let go of the reins. The smooth suspension would not allow him to feel any imperfection in the road as he rounded the corner out of the parking lot. He was out of sight before Point could even open the door to his car. With this partner, he could already tell this assignment would be an interesting adventure to say the least. Point looked over at Hanson, who was struggling, just now opening his car door to follow in pursuit. Security was sure to be an issue to be ironed out.

Both Point and Stamos were pretty moderate right when it came to law and order and moderate left when it came to the rights of citizens. Though they were both moderate, they grew up in very conservative families and towns. Stamos' hometown in Maine was a boat-building, logging town along the coast while Point emanated from the tough Boston suburbs. Both of these localities possessed strong traditional values of right and wrong and the American way.

To Point, what was happening in the United States over the past few decades was a gradual, systematic deterioration of the political system, devolving into tribalism. The transformation of the normal civilized debate of ideas into the political violence of today did not happen overnight. Politics had always been a dirty game for centuries before the birth of modern democracy in the United States and France in the 18th century.

Steven Point always deemed himself a student of history and knew full well that even in the nascent infancy of democracy there was acrimony in the backroom deals that would cement slavery as an institution for more than a century. What followed the wild, untamed violence that saw duels and the first assassination of an American President, was an enlightened decorum in the mid-twentieth-century halls of government. Compromise became a celebrated, integral component of American politics. It was in the setting of those mores that Nixon and Agnew shocked even those in their own party regarding the dirty tricks of the times. Since then, little by little, the decency of men had been tested by the derogatory actions of opponents with ulterior motives.

Breaking out of his daydream, he finally shifted the CT5 into drive and, with its growl imitating the superbike, gave chase out of the parking lot, albeit a few minutes behind.

Steven Point's migration from the SEC to the FBI and DNI was natural as the SEC was too stodgy for his type A personality. He had bristled at all of the red tape and delays that, had Point not pushed ahead with the launch of ARTI without approval, ultimately could have caused the downfall of the United States economy just last year. He was already feeling the palpable freedom of their new digs in the newly created division.

There was very little control from above after the initial approval of manpower and that suited these two just fine. With the DNI, Stamos was used to maintaining operational control of all of his assignments from the get-go. He would not have taken this job without that supreme authority and autonomy and, following his lead, neither would Point.

Waiting alongside the Ducati when the Cadillac pulled up and backed into a shaded spot at the front of the lot, Stamos smiled again at the ostentatiousness of the black suit and black tie emerging from the shiny black sedan. He mouthed the words, "You rock!" as his new partner swaggered up the sidewalk, straightening his suit and tie.

As they joined together and walked up the pavement to the monolithic two-story building, Point stopped and turned toward Stamos. The architecture of their new home looked like someone had thrown a hundred limestone cubes down randomly and inserted dark glass windows and doors in some of them. To both Point and Stamos, it had a beautiful symmetry combined with the randomness that mimicked both of their logical mindsets with attention deficit tendencies.

"Let's get to the lab so we can attach the Russian server surveillance to ARTI again. We just have to activate the malware." Point felt like a sprinter standing at the starting blocks, muscles already firing before even getting set into position. It was almost 9 am and he felt like he was hours late to the starting gun.

Stamos flashed his serious look at his new partner, followed by the thinnest of smiles. "Right. Let's get this party started. We also need to fine-tune our investigative targets to the ones we can glean the most information from. ARTI is helping already but we need real information and I don't think we are going to get that from already-known sources. Also, we may need to get into the field again."

Not entirely comfortable with field work, Steven Point was more at home in the server room. Having missiles launched at them last year was not his idea of a good time. "I thought you might say that. I thought we were done with all of that dirty dangerous stuff after your last brushes with death."

Stamos held the door and gestured for Point to enter before him. "You can't force a pit bull into a poodle costume. Hopefully, some of the younger agents will be closer to the fire and they can take some of the heat off me."

That was wishful thinking, thought Point. He had only known Stamos for a little over a year and there was no sugarcoating the action-hungry attack-dog personality of his new partner. Maybe he was more like a lion than a pit bull with his nine lives. Or more. As they walked into the lab, Sebastian, who had just joined the team from New York, greeted them with an awkward, sheepish grin. The computer hacker, who had been the first, along with Natalia and his since-deceased partner Jignesh, to uncover the prior Russian plot, possessed a new-found confidence in his abilities.

Now it appeared that confidence might be overflowing, "You guys are late. I've already begun to IP-locate and possibly even geo-locate the target server. There are multiple fire-walls and VPNs present that it is hiding behind now. They have fortified their defenses but they still don't know we are there. I have set it to only send us information when it is active so they won't be able to track our activity. It's not very active."

Point was visibly disappointed, raising his palm to his forehead with a palm bump. "So, what you are telling me is we won't get information from it very often. When you say it's not very active, how NOT active is it?

"Well, it has barely even pinged the network once in the past three hours. No other communication. So other than IP-locating it by allowing it to ping our server, that is all that I have accomplished. It's only a matter of time before I geo-locate it though."

Point turned to face Stamos, "While we are waiting on that, let's set up our war room. We need to strategize and prioritize our surveillance. Who is most likely to break their cover? I mean most of these extremists are not very intelligent. Someone will slip up and reveal their true intentions. We need to have a dossier on all potential bad actors by the moment we crack this server."

Stamos' heart skipped a beat. He thought to himself, "When would they break through on this server? It couldn't come soon enough. They needed intel and they needed it now. What were the Russians up to?" He sensed a momentous operation afoot. Their opponent's server was quiet for a reason. "OK, Point. Let's prioritize these white nationalist groups now. Anyone who has probable cause that we can target. We need to get some intelligence on the ground. We need informants. With these groups, that isn't going to be easy. These guys are like the mafia, you don't turn on them if you want to continue to live your life in these small towns. We are going to have to be stealthy when and if we go into the field in these locations."

As the three team leaders entered the conference room that served as the server lab control room, they noticed all of the chairs were taken except three. "Maybe we are late,"

Point thought, as their team was already waiting for them. As he surveyed the room, Point agreed, "We need a breakthrough before this powder keg explodes. Let's get our regional offices operational so that we can be there if and when informants come forward."

Point walked to the front of the room. On the whiteboard, taking a play from Stamos' playbook, he neatly printed the words, "In It To Win It!" in capital letters in red marker. Under those five words, Point traced a relatively accurate drawing of the lower 48 states. "We know that there are roughly four divisions we need to cover with our regional offices. The Southeast is obvious. Upper Midwest, obvious. West Obvious. Southwest, a new frontier. We are going to commandeer some headquarters office space in each of these locations. Atlanta, Salt Lake City, Phoenix, Detroit, Pittsburgh. The extreme left is easy to target, they reside in the inner cities and they like to geolocate close to the extreme right."

Stamos voiced his approval, "We need to get boots on the ground. No operation worth its salt ever sat at a computer screen and waited for the information to come piling in. It just won't happen. There are networks out there already formed to carry out the bidding of extremist leaders. In the past, these networks were loosely organized. I think that is about to change. They are reorganizing. And they will prove difficult to investigate."

Stamos already had ideas on who was going to lead each division. "Hanson and I are going to Atlanta tomorrow to begin setting up our operations there." He pointed out the rest of the division leaders and gave their marching orders. "Hanson here will assist in commandeering the space we need. Our assistant will handle travel and lodging. Any questions?"

Hanson and James, appearing out of breath, had quietly entered the room just a few seconds after Stamos and Point, and had assumed their positions at the table. Hanson stood up and motioned toward their office assistant who was no stranger to logistics. "We want this mission to be up and running within twenty-four hours. This is not a wait-and-see mission. This is a mission-critical, division-defining setup. The enemy is already in operation, we need to be too."

Point nodded his agreement, then turned toward Sebastian, "Sebastian and I and the AI team will remain here, working on retooling ARTI for this surveillance. We are close, so close to learning a Russian connection to something big. Something bigger than any of us can imagine, I am betting. And we will be feeding your information into ARTI also. Each day at 4 pm I expect a SCIF video conference with all divisions attending.".

Stamos stepped away from the whiteboard toward the window, and turned to the group, "Great job everyone. We have our work cut out for us, but this operation is shaping up nicely. It won't be long now for them to slip up and cough the ball up in the scrum. They're not going to like getting popped in the nose in the scrum. They're not used to it. They are bullies and bullies cry when they get popped for the first time. But then they regroup and strike back, hard. So don't let your guard down," Stamos was trying to channel his inner Rudy. He had become accustomed to rallying troops during setbacks on his assignments. The key to preparation was to predict the failures, even if you couldn't entirely prevent them, so you could plan your response to the breakdown to minimize your losses. Getting back on your feet swiftly was the key.

Stamos, Hanson, and Point stood up to shake the hands of all of the agents on their way out the door. When they were alone, Stamos turned toward the whiteboard, pointed to the words, and spoke slowly, "We are IN IT, to WIN IT." They held back briefly and Stamos put his arms on both of his partners' shoulders and reiterated, "In it to win it. I love it, Point! When we are in, we are all in. This is our lives for the foreseeable future. No distractions. Distractions kill."

Hanson took the pause as an invitation to speak, "We need all of these four divisions acting like paramilitary units. These backwoods areas and inner cities will not be easy to infiltrate. I came from small-town America and for the last decade have known the inner city. If they don't know you and you are snooping around, they will discover who you are."

Stamos agreed, "Right. Wouldn't it be nice to get some drones into some of these areas? That might not fly well with the Director."

There was no sugarcoating the difficulties they could encounter in these investigations. Point reminded them. "Well, you know we already have some targets in each of these divisions that have active cases against them with subpoenas. We already have access to their files and to their ongoing surveillance. Perhaps we will glean something from them. Get on down to Atlanta and set things up and I will use ARTI to obtain some information on these few targets we have there for you to start in on. Everyone else, I will have your orders within the next hour."

"Okay," Stamos was halfway out the door when he remembered he had an assistant again. He gestured toward the exit and said to the man almost twice his age, "Come on young man. Is James coming with us too? You know that A6 is pretty swift, you must have the V6."

Hanson nodded as he trailed Stamos out the door, "Of course. Too bad we won't have our fast cars in Atlanta."

—◦≫ ≪◦—

CHAPTER 13: MISSING WOMAN

—◦≫ ≪◦—

In an ever-expanding operation, Natalia, Chip, Samantha, and Sage found themselves sitting in a second conference room outfitted with similar monitors to the other room, now numbering forty here, Natalia counted. But this space was outfitted with no desks, but a single long coffee table and three oversized leather couches facing toward the video bank. On the other end of the room was another set of televisions with ongoing local and national news coverage. While the exact function of this room was not clear, Natalia surmised that, with the comfortable couches, it was meant for guests such as themselves to view the action.

As the Merlin investigative team steadfastly continued their setup in Atlanta, Natalia spent the better side of an hour on the phone with WNN trying to locate a supervisor in Claire's department so they could locate her. They couldn't afford to wait until she returned from whatever assignment she was on. She name-dropped every Journal editor she could think of from New York and was feeling like she was hitting nothing but roadblocks when suddenly she reached a real person with real information.

"Hello? This is Natalia Volkov from the New York

Journal." Natalia mistakenly name-dropped her old employer. "Are you in the Culture Section? I am trying to reach Claire Taub, one of your esteemed journalists." The rest of the group could scarcely hear intermittent, unintelligible noises on the other end of the line.

"Yes, I understand she is on assignment. I was wondering if you would be so kind as to either send an urgent message to her to contact me or provide me with her contact information. It is really, truly a life and death matter. I can give you my editor's phone number to confirm my identity." She considered name-dropping the FBI, but journalists sometimes clammed up with the mention of the Feds.

Natalia's eyes lit up, her mouth flew wide open in a gasp as she commandeered a pen and paper and scribbled some numbers. "Oh my god, you are a lifesaver. I appreciate your assistance. I will be calling her right away. Thank you!"

Natalia turned to the other four before disconnecting the call and exclaimed, "I got her phone number! I need to think of the questions I will ask first."

Before she could formulate a single question in her head, an incredible sight caught her attention from the corner of her eye. On one of the local news channels, the headline flashed at the bottom of the screen, "Missing Woman". An astounding development to be sure as she wondered who could have called the story in to the press. They had not even discussed a press strategy yet, though she was sure Huy already had one. "Turn up the audio on that TV!" she exclaimed.

It took a few seconds to ascertain which remote controlled the appropriate television, and when they did manage to increase the volume, the story was already half over. However, it was readily obvious from the pictures on the screen that this was not their Mía. It was, though, someone who was a young female in Atlanta. The reporter went on to say she had disappeared less than a week ago. That was merely a few days before Mía disappeared.

"Maybe these two are related. We need to get Huy in on this. Someone grab him."

As the visibly out-of-breath commander rushed into the room, Natalia had already brought up the search on her phone for a missing woman in Atlanta and showed him the news story. "This is breaking news about another woman here in Atlanta. We need to connect the dots here if there is a connection."

"Yes, we already know about this. This is one of the reasons we accepted this assignment. There was something suspicious in the air in Atlanta. As a matter of fact, we are seeing something suspicious that has just begun to occur across the country but we haven't connected anything yet. We will connect the same camera and digital work for both of these women."

"Aha, I will do what I can to dig up some information too. Do you have an office with computers we can use?" Natalia again felt her investigative instincts kicking into high gear as she compiled dozens of avenues of inquiry in her mind.

"Most definitely, right in here," Huy led them across the hall to his command center, "Make yourself at home."

"I also just found out Claire Taub's cell phone number. She is in Denver and will likely be back on Sunday!"

"Okay, let's put her on speakerphone in the main conference center so we can all ask questions."

With that, the group huddled around Huy's command center and proceeded to open the dialer on Huy's massive computer control board. He switched on the speaker connection and Natalia dialed the number. With just one ring, the phone clicked over to voicemail.

Frustrated, Natalia looked at Huy and exclaimed, "Damn! they did say she was covering an event. I'll leave the voicemail. It might sound better coming from a woman."

The greeting finished rather quickly, catching Natalia off guard. Hastily, she left a brief message to call. She sensed the tone of her message came across as a tad bit edgy. Maybe the message was too abrupt, but there was no option to re-record. Oh well, she hoped Claire would grasp the urgency of the matter. They hung up the dialer and within just a few seconds, there was an incoming call from the same number.

"Thank goodness!" Natalia blurted out before hastily pushing the green answer button on the dialer since her extended index finger was still close to the touchscreen.

There was a lot of noise in the background, but a female voice answered, "Hello, someone just called from this number?"

Natalia began, "Yes, this is Natalia Volkov. I am here with a few friends of Mía Gonzalez. We understand you are her neighbor in Atlanta."

"Yes, I can barely hear you but, yes, I know Mía. What's the matter? Is she okay?"

"That's what we are trying to find out. She hasn't answered her phone since the other night after you and she had sushi. She's not answering her phone or texts. We wanted to see if you had any clues to help us."

"Oh my god! Well, she left the restaurant just before me. I went straight to the apartment. I didn't see anything wrong when I got home. But wait, I have seen for several nights in a row, a suspicious car at the far end of the parking lot. I think it was a black Toyota. She also told me she was working on something that seemed to me a little dangerous for an intern, something in a rural area, something political. I will see if I can recollect anything more. I will come right home tonight after this next set. There's not much more going on with tomorrow's headliners and I will leave my producer here to get some video. I can be home in just a few hours."

"That would be great, we are going to need all the help we can get. Anything more to add or that you can remember, this is our friend Huy's phone. I will text you my number also."

As she hung up the dialer, Natalia spied that Huy was receiving a message that the video was ready for viewing from the digital team. Even before they managed to read the whole text, there was some commotion in the hallway outside as they could hear a hearty laugh and some shouting. They didn't have to wait long to learn the culprit of the clamor. Like a warm summer gust of wind preceding the storm, Torey Severin, the self-appointed U.S. Commander sauntered into the room and set a large duffle bag on the ground just inside the doorway.

Huy stood up and the two old friends embraced, "Torey, old chap, long time no see. You are just in time. I think we are about to break this case wide open. Your guys are good."

"Well, they better be, they are all professionals." Torey turned to Natalia, putting his hand on her shoulder as a greeting, "Field Team Two commander is my old boss at the bureau. He was with us in Teterboro." Then he turned back toward Huy, "Shall I will turn my attention to the Field Teams to make sure they are properly equipped and pre-pared?"

Huy acknowledged him with a nod, "We have the first video coming up. We will view it at first sight now, then share it with all the field teams. We are looking for this suspicious, black car that Claire just told us about. I will time-lapse for-ward starting with the hour before Mía would have arrived, then we can look over the whole file. I understand we will be receiving some more footage soon."

On the ten-foot screen in front of them, the video ap-peared. Fast-forward moving cars and people walking to and from apartments could be seen. One dark blue or black car remained stationary the whole time, and they could almost make out a shape in the passenger seat. Mía's car came into view and the only spot available was to the left of the suspi-cious car. As she exited her car, the entire incident played out in full view in the video, albeit slightly grainy in the eve-ning light. The footage was difficult to watch for the entire crew.

Mía did everything right as all women were instructed by their mothers at an early age. She already had her keys in her hand. She appeared to put up a pretty good fight and even managed to use her keys to her advantage, but the size of the man brought her into the back seat of the black car with relative ease. There was no audio to ascertain the verbal exchange. For such an early time in the evening, it seemed unlucky happenstance there were no other people in the parking lot at the time.

The motivated investigators now had their target to track. Piecing together the footprints in the sand to find this perpetrator would take a feat of investigative prowess. Huy first calmed the group as they were all visibly shaken after witnessing the event unfold like a crime documentary on television. The whole lot of them were still holding their hands up to their faces in aghast astonishment as the video was now emblazoned in their minds. He then assured the crew they would have the past and future paths of this car outlined soon, utilizing Atlanta's increasingly ubiquitous traffic cameras.

"Claire was right. That black car. I will have the digital team work on this path. I can guarantee you, within the hour we will identify the full path of this car and maybe even have plates. These guys will make quick work of this." Huy's confidence was reassuring. They were fighting time now. He spoke with the digital team on the comm clarifying the target to track. "Before we identify the path, I will also send this to the police. Better to maintain contact with them so they can put some official stamp on this and do their own parallel investigation."

Natalia summed up the mood, "That scene is every woman's worst nightmare. Parking lots can be so scary because you don't know who is in the cars you are walking by, especially with the tinting on cars these days." With lips pursed, she looked toward Samantha and Sage, and continued, "The only feeling I have right now is rage, to the core of my being. We will find this horrible person and we will find Mía."

Samantha and Sage both blurted out in unison, "I know, right!" They looked at each other, both with tears welling up in their eyes, letting a nervous laugh escape their tense lungs. As she noticed Sage sobbing uncontrollably, collapsing her head into her hands, Samantha reached over to console her.

Sage gathered her composure and looked up, then with a steely expression contributed, "Having observed the awesome capabilities that you are bringing to bear for Mía, I can tell you this. This person will not escape the long arms of our justice. And even before that, you know what? There's no doubt in my mind that she gouged his eyes out with her

146

keys. I hope he's still bleeding from his eyeballs right now." There were no more tears in her eyes, only an injection of red-hot anger.

If there was one thing that Huy had learned in his prior investigations, he always kept the victims' families at arm's length through the entire process. Having emotions enter the case always clouded judgment and objectivity. Having two best friends of the victim along for the ride would complicate things, but at the same time, Huy thought the added pressure could serve some purpose. Because of the possible wider conspiracy, he was already more emotionally invested in this search than at any other point in his life. Like a previously caged bird, objectivity had flown out the window a long time ago. The entire team was working these leads so fervently as if their own sister was abducted in that car.

Huy briefed Torey a little more since he had missed the last few hourly updates, "In a few minutes, we should have some info from Field Team Two and Digital Team Two on the second woman. You can see from the body cams on that screen over there that they are already at the scene. Let's walk over to their command center to get a bird's eye view." As they walked next door, the brighter lights in this room took a little getting used to. This digital team worked with the lights on. "Where are we on this?"

One of the resident hackers cleared his throat as he finished typing something onto his keyboard with an emphasis on the last stroke. "Well, we have an identification and we have quite a bit of background. Apparently, she is a lower-level political volunteer for a local candidate here in the Northeast outskirts of Atlanta. Works a retail job for a clothing store out there too but lives in the city. Very active on social media. Originally from a smaller town even farther to the Northeast, in the same general area where Mía was doing her political story. That might be our connection."

This piqued Torey's curiosity, "Interesting, any video yet?"

"I think we are close. We have already identified some traffic cameras that will be useful and also a few store cameras that will help. There weren't very many homes in the area of this apartment complex. We are engaged with some apartment company to attain the apartment complex security camera footage but the police already have these. That video is already out in the public domain and there is not much there except a possible suspect in black clothes seen in the area. Looks pretty similar in size to Team One's suspect. No black car as yet."

Huy skipped the pleasantries, as he desired more direct information from Field Team Two. "Field Team Two, report please?"

The commander of this team was an older FBI agent who was still on active duty but was allowed sabbaticals for community support, for which this apparently qualified. As Torey's former boss, the pair had led multiple high-level investigations. He was as tough as they came. Paving the way for Torey, he was also a former Army Ranger, with multiple tours in Iraq. Torey had left the FBI first to join Merlin, and he recruited his former boss to lead some of the brightest they could steal away from the various military and bureau teams.

The commander reported, "We are just now getting our bearings. I have three men heading to those stores over there for camera footage. The apartment has only two entrances. The stores have good views of this area and are open so it shouldn't be long. This is a poorer neighborhood so there might be some distrust. We will try to get some interviews."

Torey interrupted, "Do we have a target location for the abduction? I heard the videos don't have any concrete evidence."

The commander responded, "DT 2 has given us some information from what the police have publicly relayed, and that is that it was somewhere within the outside perimeter of this block. There is one video that shows her leaving the building to go to her car which was not within the surveillance area of that camera. We think that is right over here within full view of these stores."

Another voice responded, "We have all three stores giving us their video. No police have asked for it yet, incredibly. I told them to take it to them directly. The managers said they will send someone to the station today. I will have it in a few minutes. Our guys are reviewing it now online inside the stores. They will download as much as they can, and then send it on to you."

On the body cams they could see at least three of the field team agents in some sort of back room of each of the stores talking with a manager. On one screen you could see a computer screen with video being played back. On another, there seemed to be some distrust by the barely college-age manager, who was looking a little perturbed at the interruption in his quiet evening.

Chip was getting a little perturbed himself, "Someone put that manager on the phone. He doesn't seem to get it. And how in the bloody hell have the police not obtained these films yet?"

All Sam could do was just shake his head, "Same reason they don't have the video that we just obtained of Mía's abduction."

"I can't wait to see this video. If it's the same guy, or even if it's not, we can track him just like we are tracking Mía's attacker. Huy and Torey, can we get facial identification on him?" Natalia knew Merlin possessed that capability but was more than curious as to how much.

Huy replied, "We can if we get a good enough video. Has to have a good view of the face. Do you guys have anything on that?"

As the new video was downloaded and scrutinized, it was apparent that it was not a Toyota, thus scratching the idea that it was the same perpetrator. The footage was, however, much clearer and detailed with at least a face. Huy immediately interrupted, "Someone get on that face, please!"

The digital team member again cleared his throat, "I understand Digital Team One is working on it, but we are not likely to have the information quickly. The video is too grainy on the first video. This video is better. Sending to Digital Team Two now."

Huy figured as much, "Okay, we have a few tasks to labor on. I expect the video will give us some more information on our attacker or attackers. I anticipate it will not be the same guy, but I do think they are related. And I predict that they are both from this area Northeast of here. Digital Team One, what do you have for me? Digital Team Two, backtrack and forward track this vehicle, please."

As he was waiting for the reply, Huy motioned for the others to follow and turned to walk out the door, returning to his command center, every few seconds inserting an "Okay" into the one-sided conversation. And finally, "Okay, let me know as soon as you have it." He was already sitting in his gaming chair, and as he looked back at the group following him. "They have some tracking and will have both a forward and backtrack in the next thirty minutes. We will see what we accomplish on this track. I think it is going to be earth-shattering."

Natalia was getting antsy, "Torey, can we get out in the field? I feel helpless here. I am not sure how we can contribute but I feel like we should be doing more."

Torey glanced over at the three passionate women, then brought his hand to his chin in a thoughtful pose. "It's not good to expose yourself to danger when you are overcome with too much emotion. Too dangerous. Soon, when we have more concrete information to investigate, At some point, I will let you work with one of the field teams. But only from within the confines of the armored car. I know you are well-trained in combat and self-defense, but it is unsafe right now. We need you here doing digital work. That's your specialty."

Sam agreed, "We will get in on the action soon enough. Let's see who we are dealing with first. The real combat professionals will handle this. If there is one thing I have learned, and you know well enough from last year, they are working this at light speed and we will not add anything to the play."

Natalia sighed, she still had her gun in her bag and it was loaded and ready to go, "I know you are right but we will contribute to bringing these criminals down."

All in attendance nodded in affirmation as they eager-ly awaited the results of this promised tracking of the black Toyota. Waiting was nobody's specialty.

—•≻≺•—

CHAPTER 14: EL DESAPARECIDO

—•≻≺•—

As was her usual weekend routine, Paige had planned for this Saturday to be her usual bland work holiday, starting at her favorite organic pastry shop. She ordinarily would start the day with a few hours of writing, working on her journal and on copy for each of her work assignments. She also had some personal works that would bubble to the surface as poetry, a novel, and a children's book for immigrants she was working on. Certainly, her work situation was not ideal, but Paige appreciated that she was still allowed to continue to develop this story concerning the denigration of immigrants in the Southwest. She was certain this new kidnapping back-page article would intersect with it in some twisted way. The Phoenix police were not forthcoming with information for the press, as a matter of course.

Now armed with this fresh information regarding her informant's husband, whose full name was Franc Koenig, and an out-of-towner named Ben, she availed herself of internet search engines, delving deeper into the seedy underworld of white supremacists in the Western enclaves of Utah, Idaho, Nevada, and Arizona. Deep down, she knew that following the parallel tracks of these men and her desaparecido, María

Gonzalez, would lead to some sort of revelation. In the highest hopes she could imagine, perhaps she could even find the connection in time to save her acquaintance. She was now devoting almost all of her time to this endeavor, finding no need for sleep, and running on pure adrenaline, as she did not need to dig deep to find motivation.

The dining area of Namé Namé was slightly crowded early this Saturday morning as she glanced furtively at all the regulars that she recognized only by face but not by name. She staked out her usual booth facing the door and kept her computer screen facing away from all of the other customers. Her research findings on the husband certainly were cringeworthy, to put it lightly, and finding the information was easy pickings. There was no shortage of online social media posts, blog entries, and chatroom threads to paint a broad picture of his racist, misogynist persona.

Long ago she had created outrageous fake accounts on social media and in the most popular right-wing chatrooms she had followed and at times even contributed to the vitriol to gain access to this sleazy underworld. Those painstaking efforts were now paying handsome dividends in this investigation. She shuddered at some of the overtly racist statements that had earned him a ripe reputation in the more rural area surrounding Phoenix. He had designs on a run for a seat in Congress and those aspirations were inspiring even more outlandish proclamations against immigrants. But those public comments paled in comparison to his more private conversations that were easily uncovered in these chatrooms.

In stark contrast, the search for a man named Ben from Utah would prove the most difficult needle in a haystack pursuit of her short career, and the breakthrough would come from an unexpected source soon enough. She had never led a probe of an active criminal enterprise before but knew full well the danger to journalists investigating the mafia in New York City. In the back of her mind, she was aware of the peril her public exposure could be placing on her safety. The mere fact the wife of this politician could find her based on reputation meant she needed to take extreme precautions

154

from this point forward. In a bid to minimize the risks she faced, she just yesterday increased the security of her surroundings, purchasing security cameras for her apartment and a dash cam for her car. However, there was only so much protection she could afford on her meager salary.

Owing it all to her investigative journalism professor at Columbia, who was also an expert in exposé works for the New York Journal, Paige possessed quite a knack for internet research. The term "internet research" had such a negative connotation and in ordinary parlance encompassed the process of entering a name in a search browser. The more apt term, digital research, was the bread and butter of journalists and other professional investigators. True professionals utilized various commercial websites that culled databases of names, addresses, land ownership, insurance policies, and voter rolls. The fruits of slaving over her laptop screen for a few sleepless nights created an extensive spreadsheet containing a few thousand Bens and Benjamins from Utah so far. She was able to eliminate about a hundred who were registered liberals, which unfortunately for these purposes was rare in Utah

The growing spreadsheet now included pictures, social media accounts, and occupations that would come in handy the closer she came to Ben's identification. She cross-referenced Ben and Franc to no avail and, on the surface, there was no discernible connection. Paige thought to herself how nice it would be if cell phone providers still tabulated phone calls on bills that her informant could provide. At this stage of the game, it would be too risky to ask her to request the information anyway.

Paige knew that this assignment ultimately might require some covert espionage on the informant's husband, one Franc Koenig from Sand Butte. The fortuitous aspect of this sleazy man was the peculiar spelling of his name, which stood out in Arizona. Due to the highly unusual ethnic name, it would prove easy to find genealogy and other historical information. The further she examined his history, she discovered that his parents immigrated to the United States under a special East German asylum during the 1950s. His father was not a skilled worker, so it was not clear how he had made his way not just to West Berlin, but all the way to America. Once he made it to America he settled in Boston and ultimately moved to Arizona with his wife and children, Franc and Anna.

What he was lacking in education, Franc made up for with his persuasive charm and wit, probably a result of his profound narcissism. Despite living in a small desert town, it appeared from the outside that he was quite successful. However, to the contrary, both he and his father had been involved in some fraud involving real estate and rentals a decade ago. Escaping with just a slap on the wrist, he had established a small real estate agency in this dusty area of Arizona and also owned a small tract of ranch land with cattle. The quiet town sat next in line for expansion and suburban sprawl so if he played his cards right the ranch land could be quite valuable. How ironic and fitting it was that he had been convicted of fraud and was himself an immigrant. As per his own rants about other immigrants, he would be deportation candidate number one, having not been born in the United States.

Her next course of action was to pay a visit to Sand Butte. Her next meeting with her informant required travel to these suburbs to the Sandy Road Mall anyway. With a few clicks on a travel site, a hotel reservation was made for Sunday night at a small local hotel in Sand Butte for there were no major hotel chains in these parts as yet. But the deeper she looked, the other many business establishments likewise were devoid of the usual national chains, with the exception of one McDonalds. This suburb definitely did not fit her concept of what it should look like, for it ceased evolving after the 1950s. There were larger suburbs another thirty miles farther from the city center that were much more developed even though Sand Butte had the advantage of a major highway running through it. The land around the perimeter of this town was owned by just a few families, including the Koenigs.

The one gasoline station had a name she was not familiar

with, and, not surprisingly, the only real estate agency in town was that of her target. What's more, the town government looked like it would fit in well in Georgia or Alabama with its all-white makeup. On her visit to this small, dated hamlet, the name of the game would be to tread lightly, as this certainly was not a location where she could blend in easily. She thought better of it and canceled the reservation and instead found a national chain near the mall thirty miles away. Better to be safe. Who knows what she would find in this homogeneous locale? Taking a short break from it all, she scheduled herself to volunteer for some immigrant relief organizations that could also provide her with information regarding her acquaintance.

She closed her laptop and looked around at the usual Saturday crowd, whose sweat-soaked clothes quickly dried once inside. It was now late morning, and this weekend was going to be an especially hot one, as the crowd was lingering a few minutes longer after finishing their organic pastries in temporary reprieve from the oppressive heat. She cherished this one place, with its diversity and friendly atmosphere, where she felt one with those who cared about their health and the environment. She had met several of her fellow immigration crusaders here over the past few years. She chatted with the owner and a couple at the counter for a few minutes before striking out on her investigative adventure.

One of the relief organizations she chose today was tucked in the corner of a strip mall just west of the city. As she entered the front door, she immediately sensed the somber mood in the front lobby. As she joined the condolences and commiseration, the consensus seemed to be very morbid, with a grim outlook for finding their friend. María had been abducted in a destitute industrial area of Phoenix and her car was found on a dimly lit side road with doors unlocked and no evidence of a crime. The gathered crowd collectively wondered why María was alone late at night in this area in the first place, unless it was to help someone she thought was in trouble.

The group traveled two hours east to a small suburb closer to the Apache Native American reservation to assist with a consignment store that doubled as a soup kitchen in the evenings. Paige carpooled with another member of the group she trusted who was also an immigration attorney. The conversation was lively and informative as he was a staunch supporter of immigrant rights, and he had been an invaluable source for an earlier personal project. He relayed some intelligence that he was hearing regarding these white supremacist organizations making inroads from up North. When Paige asked him vaguely about the groups, he responded presciently that some type of violence would be coming soon.

On the return trip, Paige stared morosely at the cacti passing by her window at a high speed, and lamented, "Do you think María's disappearance could be related to these groups you spoke about before?"

His answer was not surprising, "It certainly seems likely. Even if it isn't related, some type of violence is bound to happen soon."

The two-hour ride back was just as fruitful as he provided details about several groups from Idaho that were setting up shop in the area, though he did not know of anyone named Ben. A promise to investigate this mysterious shadow of a man was forthcoming and appreciated. He was, however, all too familiar with the city council member Koenig and his brand of politics, which he regretted was becoming more common these days. Paige did not divulge the information she knew about either one, nor did she divulge her source, as she never trusted any source, no matter how well connected.

It was late in the evening when they returned and Paige had an intense next few days cut out for her, so she bid adieu to her fellow volunteers. That night as she drifted into her short-lived dreams, she thought how productive, yet disturbing the last few days had been. For anyone else, the new knowledge would cause nightmares, but Paige's courage was only matched by her ease at falling asleep, and so, Sunday morning she awoke early with only a few hours' rest, refreshed and ready for a few days of sleuthing.

It didn't take long to leave the city limits in her small

Toyota, as she planned her attack. With the skyscrapers far behind her yet still visible in the distance, the major highway suddenly slowed down to 35 miles per hour through the sleepy town of Sand Butte. This would be an easy speed trap, she thought, and it probably was, though no hidden police car was evident. One stop light and a coffee shop lined the main street that was just off the highway. The gas station seemed to be the only market in town and was bustling with a few local residents. She passed the Koenig Real Estate Agency which appeared to consist of a set of three buildings, with lights off and no cars parked anywhere in sight. It was Sunday after all, so not unexpected. There was a xeriscaped central courtyard nestled among the three buildings with various cacti growing seemingly wild and the shrubbery was overgrown. At the end of the main street, she turned around and decided to start with the coffee shop and then fill up with gas and check out the only other local action.

There were only a few cars parked in front, but the coffee shop was quite nicely decorated, with several customers lounging at a few tables and one older gentleman sitting alone at a small bar with several antique vinyl-covered bar stools. She sat at the end of the bar and surreptitiously watched the reaction of her fellow patrons as most of them followed her every move. She knew that none of them was Mr. Koenig, but she had not memorized the few thousand pictures of Utah Bens that she had collected in her database to ascertain if he was in present company.

Long ago she had learned to feel confident in the presence of fearful white folk. It was their problem, she had trained her mind to think subconsciously. The barista was busy cleaning a coffee maker, but Paige, after about a minute, caught his eye and ordered an iced coffee. In this heat, was there any other way to order coffee?

While there was not much chatter while she sipped on the refreshing drink, she did gather the name of the barista. She relayed her rehearsed story that she was on her way from Phoenix to Las Vegas and needed a coffee to wake her up that Sunday morning. She placed a reminder in her brain to be sure to turn left on the main highway toward Las Vegas when she left town. She did not sense an opportunity to make conversation with the rest of the clientele, so she paid cash so as not to leave a trail, thanked the young man, and left the little shop on her way to fill up her car with gas at the market.

The gas station was more of the same. She was only able to say, "Hello," and "How do you do?" to the attendant. They also served coffee and had quite an array of snacks, so she loaded up on these for the hotel stay later which was closer to Phoenix near the mall. She turned left on the main highway and exited the town, where she passed the only hotel, which was more of a motel with only two cars in the parking lot. She surmised that, in the dark desert night, it might manifest perfectly as a horror film location. That sight and the subsequent gruesome concoctions invented by her imagination made her thankful that she had canceled that reservation.

She hastily turned the car around to head back toward civilization. As she gazed out at the desert landscape for the second time in two days, she noticed the ranch land that existed here was not fenced in whatsoever. Her mind began to race through the possible scenarios of the disappearance of the missing María. She needed to press her informant for more information, especially possible locations where they could take someone, or as the informant had eerily said, "dispose of" someone. Paige had also learned from her investigative journalism professor that immersing yourself in your subject always brought forth creative juices to enhance the success of the mission. That lesson couldn't have been more true here, as she regained fresh vigor to delve deeper into this case. Her instincts were screaming in her ear the connection to this case lay somewhere in that town or at least nearby.

That night passed with a rapid succession of posting fake posts in chatrooms to attract comments from the peanut gallery of nutcases out there. She made sure to geolocate her posts in Phoenix and Las Vegas so she could attract local comments. It didn't take long for dozens of comments

160

to appear with some pretty egregious content. She recognized most of them from previous threads, but they seemed to multiply tonight and were increasing in their severity and cruelty toward immigrants. If only they knew her status and probably that of law enforcement who she only hoped would be monitoring these threads.

She also continued to narrow her list of Utah Bens and started to come up with some likely candidates. As far as she could tell, none of their online identities were screaming out flagrantly as her suspect. What she wished she could do was to truly geolocate each of these posters' IP addresses to better identify them. Just as she was about to call it quits for the night, a few comments popped up that unnerved her. One of the commenters asked her to join a private chatroom on an app called Anti Sosh. Finally! This was the type of chatroom where she had hoped to end up tonight.

What she wasn't expecting were the direct invitations that were coming into her direct messaging inbox that night to physically join whatever group or groups were out there in Arizona. She accepted the invitations but told them she was busy this week so that she could better plan any investigations. Wisely, she made a decision that night, that after she met her informant again tomorrow, she would take some information to the Phoenix police so that they could investigate alongside her. She would also take some of this intelligence to her immigration attorney source to get some advice. And the FBI, she forgot about the FBI. She had made a connection with the FBI here in Phoenix that she had developed through her crime storylines.

The next morning, she found herself more nervous than usual. These online conversations were starting to set off alarm bells in her head. She skipped the free continental breakfast and decided to scout out the Sandy Road Mall for good locations for a rendezvous with her informant. She left her little Toyota near the least used exit with a direct link to the highway. As she parked herself on the dark blue tile of the fountain in the center of the mall, she sipped on another iced latte and took in the sights to calm herself. She had a few hours to familiarize herself with the different stores and exits, but it was a pretty large mall so it might possibly take that long. She found the coffee shop that her informant had mentioned, but it was not a good fit as it was too exposed. As she explored the mall, she found that luckily one of the department stores also had its own coffee shop and restaurant in the women's department. That could come in handy, she thought. She had frequented these in other cities and there were very few men who would even think of entering into that den of estrogen.

With her location decided with thirty minutes to spare, she headed back to the fountain area to wait. It wouldn't even be that long, as her informant was fifteen minutes early. Mrs. Koenig followed directions well, and the two made their way to the department store coffee shop without acknowledging each other. What came next would change her life forever.

As they sat down together at a table in the back, her informant started quickly without taking a breath, "Do I have some information for you. I know Ben is here in Phoenix now. And I know the locations of everything, every place in Utah, Nevada, Idaho, and Arizona. And this whole plot is going down now. They have kidnapped two people in a short time span, and they are aiming for something bigger, I can feel it." She let out a breath as though she had been holding it, and the information for hours.

"Two, are you sure?" Paige could not just feel, but hear her heart pounding in her chest.

"Yes, the one you wrote about and another immigrant activist. I will tell you where they took them, but I need somewhere to go. I can't stay there anymore. I suspect he knows I know."

"I can take you to a safe house, but you must leave your car here. You can't trust that you are not being tracked. You need to take everything out of your purse and wallet that you don't need and we will leave the purse here in the mall. I haven't heard of another desaparecido. Sorry, that's a term used in Hispanic circles for a kidnapped person."

162

The answer came immediately as if she had made her decision beforehand. "Okay. I am ready. I can tell you on the way."

"First, we will stop at the FBI headquarters here in Phoenix. This is their expertise. This is out of my league. I have a connection there that can help us navigate." As her informant opened her purse and removed her wallet, Paige continued, "Only credit cards and IDs, that's all you need. And don't use the credit cards unless in an emergency. Write down any phone numbers you need, back up your phone to the cloud, and we will ditch your phone."

"Really, my phone? That's severe. But I get it. This is big, organized, dangerous even. I need to collect my thoughts, but you are right. Let me just figure out what numbers I might need." Paige reached into her backpack and handed her a small blank notebook to use, and the painstaking process began with a few scribbled names and numbers. She paused after the first few entries and stared across the restaurant for more than a few minutes with a blank look. The waitress walked by, asking if they needed anything, which interrupted her apparent daydream.

She looked back down at the screen of her phone, which had timed out, unlocked it, and restarted the entries. After several minutes went by, she had filled two full pages of the notebook. As she wrote down more numbers from her phone, Paige sensed her informant was visibly flustered, "There are just so many numbers I might need. I give up." She ripped the pages from the notebook and put it in her pocket.

Paige reassured her, "It's okay, you aren't going to lose these numbers forever. Now, you are going to back up your phone to the cloud. We will help you recapture the phone after everything gets back to normal, I promise."

Unlike manual copying, the phone backup took a mere few minutes to start and finish. There must not have been that much data after all, as most phones would take a few hours. The mall Wi-Fi was quite fast for this purpose.

As the unlikely duo reluctantly arose from the table,

Paige put her hand on her informant's shoulder, "You're doing the right thing. What needs to be done, needs to be done. You are so brave. And you will save so many lives. Now erase the phone with a factory reset. I will show you how."

Her new life about to commence in earnest, her informant reset the phone and turned it off. The phone flashed a warning and then the screen went black. With the finality of the blank screen before her, the tears finally burst forth and she held her face in her hands, then pulled her head back, and reached up to wipe them off her face. Then she stood tall, and with a few more wipes, there were no more tears. She is strong, thought Paige. Paige took the purse and dropped her informant's phone within it, and, when no one was looking, placed it deep into a garbage can at the back of the restaurant.

The two women walked out of the department store separately, as though nothing had happened, and met at Paige's car at the rear of the mall. Predictably there were not many patrons in this lot which was fortuitous. As they both entered the car, for the first time, Paige addressed her informant by her first name, "Beata, let's get on with this. You will have my full support through all of this. Tell me more about what you have found out. Do you mind if I record?" In the moment, Paige was careful not to call her Mrs. Koenig, as she suspected this would have the potential to do more harm than good thus impacting the flow of information. They had already spent the better part of an hour in the restaurant which was far too long for Paige's comfort. Luckily, during that hour, not even a single man entered the area, let alone any white supremacists. If they had, the sight of Mr Koenig's wife sitting at a table with a Haitian immigrant would have sent whoever it was over the top, Paige surmised. She set her phone on record mode and set it down on the center console between them.

As Paige suspected was the case, Beata Koenig turned out to be a very intelligent woman. The ride to the FBI office was a never-ending stream of consciousness of everything this woman had overheard in the past week or more. She was able to recount every conversation her husband had, down to the most minute detail, including names, addresses, and phone numbers. This Franc Koenig was not particularly sharp and had severely underestimated his wife, to say the least. Paige thought about the audacity to have such conversations on a speakerphone, not to mention the idiocy. Beata still was not finished reciting the information when the three-story stucco building with the FBI emblem at its pinnacle appeared on their right, at the front of a complex of federal government offices.

As they turned into the parking garage behind the FBI regional headquarters, the guard at the gate asked for identification, which they provided. As they reached the rather sparse lobby, Paige's contact met them and guided them to a conference room on the first floor. The security was tight, they were required to leave cell phones outside and were searched a second time. A few minutes later, as Beata was recounting the story, the agent suddenly excused himself, "I just met a new director, who flew in from D.C. yesterday, who would want to hear this. I'll be right back."

He left them alone for what seemed like thirty minutes before returning with a tall agent who looked a bit nubile to have such a title, fully twenty years younger than her contact. "Ladies, can you start from the beginning? This is the new regional director of domestic counterterrorism. Did I get that title right?" He looked over at the director, who nodded his approval with a stern look. "It's a new division of the FBI and they are just getting their feet wet here in Phoenix."

The process of recounting the tale would take up the rest of the afternoon and into the evening, with a phone call being placed to Quantico and Atlanta to bring the whole team in on the story. Stamos, Point, and Hanson would soon catapult the investigation here onto equal footing with the Georgia inquiry. The FBI now potentially had two leaders of this conspiracy square in the middle of their crosshairs. With the informant's cooperation and testimony, they could easily obtain an ex parte sealed warrant against this fellow and his compatriots.

With new information soon gleaned, perhaps even FISA warrants.

CHAPTER 15: STAMOS CHASED

It felt liberating to be in the field again. Stamos knew he missed that element of excitement and intimate involvement in his missions, on the road, like a rolling stone. While deep down he recognized the limitations that his battered body placed on his abilities, he also realized that, in many ways, he was like an aging professional ball player who could not hang up his cleats as easily as he thought. Finding himself on the rural outskirts of Atlanta with a small team, he couldn't fathom exactly how he would accomplish this surveillance. He argued with his own sensibilities that he was only supervising the surveillance, as he and Hanson decided, against their initial judgments, that they simply needed a cursory introduction to the small towns of rural Georgia.

As he and Hanson stared out of the window with "Coffee Shop" hand-painted on its surface, he thought this main street with its red brick, historic buildings eerily reminded him of his own hometown in Maine. This aspect of this investigation was not compatible with his life ethos. He was used to tracking espionage and criminal suspects through European and Asian cities. Rarely was he expected to remain exposed, out from under the cover of city buildings and parks. And, for the first time in his law enforcement career, he perceived the enemy to be just like him, American and passionately patriotic. However misguided and violent they were, they were shaped by the same communities that he and Hanson had grown up in. And now these suspects were unknowingly, or possibly knowingly, being misled by a foreign power intent on the destruction of the American way of life.

Furtively he looked around the room to be sure no one was listening, and with a sullen look, he turned toward Hanson, "Does this remind you of your hometown as much it does me of mine?"

"Absolutely, to a T. But I think times and motivations are a-changing. These are not the same people we grew up with. They have changed. There is no longer a sense of building America for everyone. It's more of building up your tribe in competition with another perceived tribe that is against you. And if they are, knowingly or unknowingly, following a fascist movement, it is still just that, fascism. And that movement in and of itself is un-American, especially if it is turning violent."

"Where do we begin? This reconnaissance is a good wake-up call to how difficult this will be." Stamos was limited as to what he could say in public, so he stopped short while glancing over toward the few clientele that were several tables away. He then thought silently to himself, continuing to stare out at the empty sidewalk, "Small towns won't be a great environment to surveil. We can't just buy or rent a building like in Kyiv without being noticed. And when we are noticed, what is our cover? These are the things that bother me.

They stood up to approach the counter to pay for their bill and noticed the looks from around the room turning their way. If Stamos looked the part of an All-American athlete turned businessman blending in, Hanson unfortunately carried himself with all the awkward demeanor of a fed. He might as well put his badge on his belt. There was no undercover with this guy.

The two strolled out the door into the warm sunshine and walked down the street toward their rental car which had

168

Texas plates to blend in as a business rental car. The car even had rental car no-smoking stickers on the side windows as part of the cover. What was not part of the cover were the two other agents, James and another junior agent who were in another car across the street. As Hanson started up the car, they collectively decided to first pay a visit to the local gas station to fill up their cars with fuel. Hanson always had security in mind because you never wanted to be caught without fuel in your car, for they had used more than half a tank to get here from Atlanta. From there, they had several predetermined locations to simply drive by to get the lay of the land.

"You know, Hanson, you blend in for undercover operations like a pink flamingo. We are going to have to change your outfit for these missions. You look like a classic cop from something like Dragnet."

"Yes, you are probably right. Been working the desk too much, too. I'm afraid I won't be too useful in a chase. I'm getting better, though. The last week of training in the morning with you has helped. At least we have James with us. I picked him because he was a boxer in the Army before the Academy and knows how to shoot."

"He is a good guy to have around for sure. Green as a sapling, though."

As of now, the small force had no designs on any full surveillance or espionage. There was one criminal target already under federal surveillance in this town close to the border of South Carolina so they didn't need to establish any new operation here. By cell phone, they were in constant contact with the other two fellow agents. The next stop was to visit the local police station and sheriff's office, which was at the very end of the main drag. The meeting would be billed as an outreach from the Atlanta office of the FBI to local law enforcement. They had cards introducing themselves as FBI agents, with fake names and without any mention of the division they were in, which in these parts might not be perceived well.

As the four agents climbed the steps and entered the station, they noticed two older patrol cars in the parking lot to the side. The worn brick facade and granite steps along with the cornerstone with a date that could barely be read but was clearly in the early 1880s declared the history of this small town which had been in existence since the beginning of the eighteenth century. Inside, Hanson introduced himself as a community outreach liaison.

The older, rotund policeman with a bushy mustache at the back of the expansive room with white pillars spoke first and introduced himself, "I'm Chief Stewart. If you need anything you have to go through me or my counterpart over here, Sheriff Watson. We're cousins and our family has been in this town for the better part of two centuries." The sheriff had his feet propped up on a corner desk, staring at a large brown tablet, that he had connected to a larger monitor. The two simultaneously stood up and walked toward the counter with a swing door. The obviously younger and taller of the two spit into a spittoon on the ground by his desk and put his hand on his holster. He was on the taller side of six feet four but seemed even more gargantuan due to his barrel chest and full beard.

"Glad to meet you. Nothing much happening in these parts except a few drunks needing to sober up." His voice boomed and echoed off the vaulted ceilings of the historic building. "But if you need us, don't hesitate to call." The sheriff had a much more open demeanor than his cousin for sure. He handed his card over the counter to Hanson's outstretched hand.

Hanson gave a hearty Midwestern thank you and shook his hand in return. The conversation was short and abruptly ended when the chief announced he had a meeting with the mayor to attend. The four agents made their way back down the granite steps into the humid Georgia air.

"Well, they were cordial but useless." Hanson offered as he opened the driver's side door and peered over at Stamos across the roof of the car.

Stamos agreed, "I'll bet these two could be sitting in the police stations of every small town from Maine to California and we wouldn't be able to tell the difference. Local law enforcement probably has inherent biases that we at the federal level will never fully understand. Did you see the jail cell from where you were standing?"

"Yes, one drunk was all I could see. Not regulation for sure."

While the station did not appear to garner much activity in these parts, the lockup could be seen through an open door, and there appeared to be at least one prisoner asleep on a cot in the only cell visible. Clearly, this was not a jail operated under modern regulations, which would require multiple impediments to entry and egress. No wonder there were still jailbreaks that the FBI had to assist local jurisdictions with all over this country.

The next stop was lunch at a diner and mingling with some of the locals there, attempting to not identify themselves as FBI agents. They relayed to the waitress they were just stopping through on their way to Atlanta. The menu was chock full of good old home-cooked nourishment with plenty of gravy. The waitress inquired with great interest as to what part of Atlanta they were going and when they mentioned Midtown, her eyes lit up as she raved about the shopping at the Midtown Mall. One of the other customers looked at her with an unapproving glare as if to say, "How could you complement Atlanta in any way."

As the agents scraped the last bit of country gravy from their plates and licked their forks clean, they quickly learned that in these parts you shouldn't mention Atlanta. Maybe Savannah or Macon would be best to mention, but not the big city.

Immediately afterward, they stopped at the small, green central park, which was lined with maple trees and benches, and walked to the central fountain. Towering over the fountain and at each of the four corners of the park were statues of Civil War heroes of these parts, the largest of which was the revered Robert E. Lee on a majestic stallion. This was the one place in town where the four agents could talk without being heard.

"Well, I think we have established the local geography and local law enforcement. Let's get back to Atlanta to set up some further information gathering. I wish we had some informants in these areas. That would make things easier. Who knows who our adversaries are or where their head-quarters are located? They won't be in plain sight, that's for sure." Stamos was disappointed, but he wasn't expecting any breakthroughs on this outing for sure. He looked toward the police station across the street and could still see the two patrol cars they had seen previously. "I don't think local law enforcement will be much help, maybe even a hindrance."

Hanson and the other agents nodded in agreement. Hanson directed the other car to exit the town behind them by several blocks.

They walked away from the fountain toward their car and were halfway across the grassy area away from the police station when two large, lifted pickups pulled up next to their cars. Without warning, the sound of gunfire erupted and the first two shots ricocheted off a park bench several feet to their left.

"Take cover!" yelled Stamos.

Luckily, two large maple trees shaded either side of the sidewalk which gave cover to the agents. Thin, undercover Kevlar may only help so much in this firefight, thought Stamos. They were caught in the open and would need more firepower than they presently possessed. As he dove behind the tree, Stamos felt the familiar sting in his side, that in his rugby years could have been a simple rib injury, but painful past experience told him otherwise.

He had helped Hanson to the tree and, by the look on Hanson's face, he had been hit even worse. They were safe for the time being, but as Stamos brought out his Glock he could see that James was already returning fire from behind the other tree. Luckily the two trucks were not triangulating the two trees and with a roar of their big block engines, both moved to the left, away from the agents' cars to the corner of the park.

"Get to the cars, both of you cover on the run. I have

to help Hanson!" Stamos exclaimed. "Reload now. Go on ten," he commanded as the agents counted down from ten and reloaded their firearms

Hanson was a load to assist, but he was able to carry most of his own weight. Despite the cover shots from the other agents, incoming gunshots were still raining in. Luckily, the accuracy of their adversaries was not passable, and the four fleeing agents piled into their cars. Both undercover cars had run-flats and protected engine compartments but the windows were not bullet-proof. They both made U-turns to the opposite side of the park toward the main road.

With the trucks soon trailing them, they could hear a few more gunshots glancing off the roof of the cars. They were far enough ahead of them now that Stamos did not feel the need to try to fire back. Their car was in the lead of the two, and all he could think about was getting back to Atlanta and civilized society. He hoped the other car was not damaged by any of the last few shots since they were more in the line of fire.

As they turned on the main road toward Atlanta, Stamos spied the police cars still stationary in the same lot and announced over the cellular connection, "Let's get to the cover of the city. We can outrun these guys and their oversized tires. Hanson, you okay?"

"Yes, I can make it." was the faint response.

"Have we lost them? Do you guys see anything behind you?" Stamos asked the other agents.

The connection was slightly garbled, but the answer was an obvious, "No, I don't see anything. They turned around about a mile ago."

From the driver's seat, Stamos inspected his and Hanson's injuries, handing a bandage to his partner that he extracted from the center console. From the looks of them and the location, not life-threatening. His own was just a flesh wound. Hanson's, however, was a bit deeper in the torso, but off to the side. Not much bleeding. On-the-job training from various witnessed bullet wounds, to himself and others over the years, informed him that they had at least a few hours.

Stamos spoke over the cellular comm to his fellow agents to call ahead to the Atlanta office and to D.C. to report the situation and to have agents meet them at Grady Memorial Hospital.

"How are you feeling buddy?"

"I'm fine, just fine. Just burns a little. I've been shot before. Not to worry. This is nothing. I don't think it is near anything vital. Exit wound is just a few inches around the back. How is yours?"

Stamos winced a little as he responded, "All the same, continue to hold pressure on that bandage. Mine is nothing. Barely even stings. Something tells me, I think we were not welcome in those parts. Unfortunately, this will call attention to the area. The chief and sheriff didn't even pop their heads out the window. Hopefully, they don't shut down whatever operation they have going. I want to get these guys now."

"We need different tactics. There is no way we will be able to have boots on the ground anywhere near these guys from now on, without a combat team and extraction team. Good Lord. Now I have some idea what you guys go through in the field overseas." Hanson's voice trailed off a little as he closed his eyes.

Stamos could tell this was not the ominous closing of the eyes he had seen so many times before. "Yes, we can either operate under the cover of darkness or continue with electronic surveillance. You know, this area is heavily forested outside of town which could provide some cover. But if we are caught, there is nowhere to run but through the woods, and these guys know the area better than we do."

Hanson concurred on that point, "It is what it is. Let's regroup after we get back to headquarters."

"Buddy, we are going straight to the hospital, and we are staying there until you are cleared. And I am certain that both the director and the medical director are going to be involved in that clearance. I can see the headlines now, 'New Director of Domestic Counterintelligence Shot by Rednecks in Georgia.'"

Something deep in his bones had been troubling Stamos ever since they landed in Atlanta on this current mission. He had an inkling there could be trouble with the rural locals. Why didn't he trust his instincts and better protect his men? Could have been even more disastrous if those good ole boys were better shots. Maybe they weren't aiming to kill, just scaring the intruders off. Either way, they weren't very good with guns, either they aimed to kill and missed, or they aimed to scare and missed. Regardless, it almost seemed like his team was allowed to escape in the end. The trucks moving the way they did, away from their cars, allowed his men an escape route they otherwise did not have.

It was an excruciating thirty minutes before the towering buildings of downtown Atlanta came into view on the horizon. Soon enough they would pull into the Emergency Room entrance of one of the finest hospitals for trauma that existed. They were in good hands here, Stamos reassured himself. Just a flesh wound. Hopefully out of here in an hour, right? He knew better.

For the second time, the thought crossed his mind to contact his old friend here in Atlanta. How would he explain this? He suddenly found himself on a stretcher being wheeled in alongside Hanson. The other agents were assisting with the triage.

"No, really. I don't need a stretcher. I'm fine. James, tell her," he told the nurse, who curtly informed him who was in charge here.

James, who was pushing from the foot of the stretcher near Stamos' feet, yelled over the din, "I'm not arguing with her, man. You need to listen to her. You might get hurt worse. I don't think you can take her."

Stamos just shut his eyes for a moment to clear his mind. Let the process play out. There wasn't anything they could do now but wait for clearance and let the nurses and doctors do their job. He hoped Hanson's injury was as superficial as he thought it was. He was certain his own was. Might be sore in the morning after the usual adrenaline wore off.

That same adrenaline wearing off from the gunshot

wound must have set off a chain reaction in his mind of the usual mental exercise of examining the failures. What went wrong? What should he have recognized before the event? Just as in Kyiv, there were warning signs present that he did not heed. Snippets of the last few hours flashed through his mind. What he thought were curious looks of the fellow coffee shop patrons, were they actually menacing stares? The chief of police and sheriff in hindsight now had a more intimidating, aggressive posture toward his team.

The waitress was the only non-threatening person making an appearance in his post-failure dream. As the images of the inquisitive smile on her face and the disapproving glares from her customers revisited his subconscious mind, he briefly wondered whether she too was actually in danger. From his deepening sleep, he left a mental note to his awake self to inquire about her if the opportunity presented itself, for she seemed different from the rest, an object in the picture that surely did not belong. As he drifted further into his exhaustion-fueled nirvana, he slowly forgot the blame that he had heaped upon his own shoulders and started to move on to the next phase of processing, plotting his return.

He wouldn't wake up for at least an hour, but the short-lived sleep was as refreshing as any he had experienced in recent memory. Upon rousing, with a sweat-soaked gown, he sat up in his hospital bed with a jolt and the blurred outlines of his hospital room came into better focus. The squiggly green lines and numbers on a monitor were the first objects that he could make out. Then slowly a whiteboard with the name Doe,Alpha and today's date came into view. It took another whole minute to recognize James and another younger agent from his detail standing inside the doorway. Now fully conscious, he felt reinvigorated with fresh designs on revenge, though some measure of pain in his side that had other ideas.

CHAPTER 16: DIGITAL TEAM 5

It was a rare moment of downtime in the nascent inquiry at the Merlin Investigation Unit's makeshift command center. While Sam and Chip joined Field Team One chasing down leads in Midtown Atlanta, Claire had now joined the three other self-appointed female private investigators in their quest to find Mía. The four of them were plotting strategy in the sofa room as it was starting to be called, catching Claire up on the events while probing her for any further information she could remember. Huy's team had now tracked the target vehicle all the way to the Emory Hills neighborhood as it exited the freeway and ducked into the small tree-lined community. With the assistance of local doorbell cameras, they were closing in on at least a secondary location, a vehicle swap, or at a minimum a venue they could monitor.

On the same news network they had watched earlier, came a news story about the murder rates in the nation's cities skyrocketing this year. It seemed a redundant story that played out year after year across the nation. The populace of these cities was becoming more worried than ever about safety. This great, free nation was becoming a less safe place to live, breathe, and raise children. The numbing news had transformed from shocking to ordinary, in the course of everyday business.

As the story was ending, a simultaneous deep breath in and slow breath out from the depths of their lungs, commenced and ended with a few exclamations of empowerment.

"There is safety in numbers you know. We do outnumber these creeps two to one!" Natalia proclaimed, channeling her best inspirational tone. The inflection was amplified by a slight echo in this cavernous conference room, partially due to the tall ceilings. She swept her wavy, dark hair behind her ear in a powerful gesture. "We have the leverage of the majority, the stronger sex, therefore we hold the advantage!"

"However, in this moment, I still feel pretty powerless," Sage offered. "Even with all of this equipment, I feel like we could be doing more."

"You're right," Samantha agreed, rising from the sofa with her hands on her hips and pacing behind the others. "But what CAN we do?"

Natalia had an answer, "Why don't we form our own full digital team? We are every bit as capable in the research department. You guys are students, but in reality, experts of the digital and social media age, and Claire and I have extensive journalism experience with a lot of resources at our disposal. We could use this room as our base."

Claire responded, "True. We can be Digital Team 5. Where do we start? I am a cultural journalist. I don't think I have the experience you do, Natalia."

"We can start with all disappearances in the Southeast. Huy said there are other, more sinister plans from these bad actors. Let's keep our ears open on the airwaves or news channels, so to speak. Keep track of all newsworthy stories."

In a heartbeat, Sage's eyes morphed from disconsolate to fiery terminator mode. She rocketed off the couch and twirled around to face the others. "Every local newspaper and television station in the Southeast has an online edition. We might miss what doesn't percolate up to the national news if we don't pay attention to these sources. We can compile all

180

of the stories from various sources and correlate them with Huy's database of sexual predators and violent offenders."

Samantha scooted forward to the edge of her seat, "Great idea! Let's get in on this action. We will still participate in the briefings, but we can bring our own expertise to the table. We may not be hackers, but every journalist is as close to a hacker as you can get in reality."

The four women sat down at the nearest workstations in front of the monitors that continued to display body camera footage and maps tracking the movement of the teams. "We apparently need logins. Someone get Huy's assistant in here." Natalia pointed toward Claire, who jumped up from her chair. In no time, they were gathering articles and vignettes on crime from every local news outlet they could find.

Natalia began with the Atlanta area news stations and newspapers which were dominated by reports of their known case, so she changed tactics. Frustratedly, she slammed down on the table the pen that she had been holding in her mouth like a cigarette, as she announced, "That's not helping. Let's concentrate our efforts first northeast of Atlanta and into these rural parts of North and South Carolina."

Within seconds, Claire was the first to report a finding, "A shooting in a small town northeast of here just earlier today. According to reports, there was an attempted robbery and vandalism of Civil War statues, and some vigilantes chased them off before the police even got there. It says here the perpetrators got away, heading back toward Atlanta. Probably not related, but it's a start. I'll enter it just in case."

Natalia pulled up the same story, "In broad daylight, no injuries. Well, keep looking. Search for all arrests. Anything newsworthy."

Samantha proclaimed her first noteworthy discovery, "Nothing much on this site, someone arrested for child pornography. Another was charged with perpetrating fraud, a waitress stealing money from a restaurant. All in the same county as your shooting."

"Put the names and dates in this shared spreadsheet on the shared drive. I have also sent you my login for the AP portal if you students don't have one."

"Huy thought these guys might try other tactics, like framing people for crimes or leaking damaging information about businesses. Maybe there is something to the arrests and other salacious news stories. What if the guy who is charged with child pornography is also a victim of this? Hard to fathom, but may be true."

"Claire, you have a point. Definitely put them in the spreadsheet and we can sort it out later." Natalia had already logged a few entries into the sheet and noticed that Sage already had a few as well. "Great Sage! Let's do a rundown of all new stories in our own briefing every thirty minutes or so."

Just then, they noticed the time and took a break from their productive beginnings to participate in the unit briefings. Natalia turned up the volume on the comm-link that was at her desk. As they listened to each unit's input to the briefing, it was apparent they were closing in on the perpetrators' hideout. In one short hour, the amount of detail that was becoming available was mind-blowing.

At the end of the briefing, when there was a brief pause in the communique, Natalia spoke up, "This is Digital Team 5, we have begun some investigation and would like to join the evidence-gathering efforts."

Huy sounded ecstatic at the other end of the line, "Yes, you guys have decades of experience and can provide a much-needed perspective. We need all the help we can get. You have the floor."

Natalia started off with a brief summary that they were researching all news stories related to disappearances and arrests. Following the introduction, Natalia pointed to Sage to fill in the details. Sage brushed her hair to the side, which was slightly disheveled in a not-so-unbecoming way due to her recent, involuntary insomnia. She cleared her throat and then found her confidence and relayed the findings so far, "Well, we have only just begun within the last 15 minutes, but here is what we have. There is a shooting, a child pornography arrest, a fraud arrest, and a waitress arrested for stealing, all in a small town northeast of here. Maybe they are related.

Seems like a lot for a town of less than a thousand people. We will be starting with this area and broadening our search to all of the Southeast."

Huy responded, "Great work! Maybe they are related. I am sure these guys aren't just going to kidnap everyone with a different viewpoint. That would be too obvious. All other digital teams, pay attention to this tactic."

"We are compiling this data on a spreadsheet in the shared drive that I am sending to you now." Natalia sent the link to the team. She held her breath and clicked the share button as the link was sent through the server links to all of the participants.

Torey, with his voice booming like a sergeant on a platoon hike, joined in, "Okay, Natalia and Digitial Team 5, you guys rock! We look forward to your contributions! Outstanding work team! In the next hour, I have no doubt we will have our targets' names and some surveillance starting. Field teams get ready, stand ready for combat action. And, starting now, watch your backs. We are now entering into the target's territory and at any point, they could engage. We cannot be too careful. At all times, we need a covering team member aware of surroundings. Combat Level 2 gear required. That means Combat Level 2 body armor for all field team members."

That announcement changed the tone of the room immediately as Natalia nervously looked over at Samantha, who was also looking around at the other three women for reassurance. "Here we go again," Natalia thought to herself. Things were about to get serious. She found it necessary to calm those nerves, remembering from previous events the importance of confidence in breeding success. She then provided the comfort the other three were subconsciously asking for, "No worries here. These guys are professionals. Torey does everything by the book. Confidence. Steel yourselves."

Samantha answered her with uneasy laughter, "I'm not nervous for us. I'm nervous for them. They are putting themselves in harm's way for us. That announcement brings these dangers into focus. And we wanted to be out in the field."

Natalia pushed her chair back from the table and stood for emphasis, pulling her dark, curly hair into a long ponytail. Stretching her arms to the sky, she stood exceptionally tall, even extending to stand on her toes. She flexed her calves and brought her arms into a show of strength and muscle. "They cannot hide. They will not win. Our strength lies within us."

Sage didn't hesitate a second to respond, "Let's get back to work. I feel it. We are going to find our Mía soon."

Samantha, pointing to the partially filled spreadsheet on the large screen, also responded, "Yes, in less than thirty minutes, we already contributed some useful information that will benefit this search. I believe there will be some associations to tie this all together from this data. If there is some sort of conspiracy it will become evident if we can manage to connect the dots."

As Natalia reclaimed her position in front of her workstation, she renewed her pursuit with a few keystrokes, followed by a pause and a few loud clicks of her mouse as if it were a precision weapon. "Look at this county on the border of South Carolina that is not far from the place you just found. Multiple arrests today in some sort of conspiracy to commit fraud. Today has been a busy crime day in Northeast Georgia. The arrest warrant doesn't specify the details."

Claire, having just reached a similar result, reacted with, "Good find. It hasn't even been reported on yet. Some of these disappearances or arrests may not have reached the news yet if the location is remote enough. This area of Georgia seems to be the epicenter of something big." She slid back in her seat, away from the computer screen, and straightened her rasta-patterned power dress, pondering the possible inferences of these persons being arrested for some nefarious reasons. "Were they framed? Were they guilty?"

The rest of the afternoon only produced a smattering of results, nothing to denote a common thread and no further disappearances. None of the arrested individuals seemed to have any link to the press or any political organization. But

184

the potential implications of what they were finding furnished them with plenty of inspiration to continue their work.

"It's getting close to the next briefing. And it looks like from the body cameras, that there is something important developing. See that car they are tracking? Let's listen in to their comms for a minute."

Within the hour, the tide would change tremendously as the investigation would be augmented by an advanced technology that heretofore only armies had access to, which would give them a decisive advantage in the war.

—·❧ ❧·—

Chapter 17: Breakthrough

—·❧ ❧·—

Stamos was still in shock. Against the wishes of the nurses and the assistants posted inside his hospital room, he perched himself on a chair with a vantage point of the lights of Atlanta. His mind had not seen a minute of sleep tonight as the day's events continued to weigh on his conscience. As an FBI agent with dark features in the Northeast, he had never felt out of place, unwanted, or unsafe even in the roughest neighborhoods of Boston, Washington, D.C., and New York City. Indeed, on every continent and in all corners of this dangerous world, he could blend in with local populations, from South America to the Middle East, even in Asia. As a matter of fact, in most places, the natives would flock to him if he chose to divulge his American origin. The poise with which he carried himself had always exuded confidence that commanded respect.

A hefty portion of that fearlessness arose from representing the strong arm of the United States of America, or maybe it was derived from the weapons he carried. Brashness could also be a liability in the wrong place, he thought, and at this moment he had made a mistake. He let his guard down in this little hamlet in rural Georgia. He almost lost a senior agent here because of his cavalier attitude regarding safety. The country was in a different state of mind than the last time he patrolled stateside, and he had lost his edge, his advantage.

As he felt a twinge of discomfort in his newly sutured wound, it was also becoming painfully obvious that there were some on the extremes of both sides of the country's divide that believed the mantra, "If you're not with me, you're against me". Their creed apparently now included political violence. Two-thirds of the country was caught in the middle of the culture wars of our times. Increasingly, despite their obsession with law and order, the political zealots were endorsing violence against the police. The FBI was finding themselves in the crosshairs of a third of this country, combining one-sixth of the country on each extreme side of the political spectrum. Threats and attempts to kill and maim the feds at the bureau were becoming all too common.

It was this divide and the importance of protecting the average law-abiding citizen that now drove Stamos. This near-catastrophic event reinforced his resolve to never see this happen to any of his agents or any citizen standing up for their rights against these extremists. Making some rough calculations in his head, he decisively appraised his needs for junior agents on his team and decided to obtain approval for a substantial increase in manpower. This request, if authorized, would make the Office of Domestic Counterintelligence the third largest division of the FBI, but he was not going to take no for an answer. He called the office of the director, whose assistant had proven responsive in the past, even after-hours, and requested a callback, purportedly to report on the events of today.

Not surprisingly, the return call came within only a few minutes, from the director himself. The director was somewhat of a political hack, but he still was an FBI man through and through. The safety of his agents was paramount, and the incident likely left him rattled.

"Stamos, I hear you guys got in a little skirmish down

there in Georgia. Those rednecks are feisty. Anything you can report to me? Is everyone alright? We are hearing the official police report sounds like you guys were labeled the aggressors, criminal mischiefs, vandals even."

"Yes, sir, I am worried about one of our agents. Hanson, you know him, but both he and I are expected to be out of the hospital by tomorrow. Just flesh wounds as the saying goes. More hurt to the pride than anything. I don't think I was prepared for such an ambush before we even got started. And the police chief and sheriff were within a hundred yards and didn't move a muscle."

"Well, looks like you need to pretend you are in your old haunts of Ukraine at all times and watch your back a little better. I am sending the assistant director and the medical director down there tonight to meet with you and assess your needs. Do you need some time?"

Stamos paused as he stood up from his chair, still gazing at the lights of the big city. "Resolve," he thought to himself as he summoned the words. Where to start? Were his requests reasonable? He went with his gut and brought forth steely courage. "No, sir. I am ready to get back out in the field tomorrow. I would be out of here tonight if it wasn't for the doctors here. But, sir, I need to ask. I know I have only been at the helm of this new division for less than two weeks. But Point and I are thinking we already see a large movement here that we think we need more manpower to investigate."

"What do you think you need? We do have a pretty large class coming out of Quantico that is already pre-qualified and cleared. Within reason, I will give you what you want.... I think."

Stamos turned sharply away from the window as the nurse entered the room. The bed alarm was going off to alert the nurses to a roaming patient and he didn't even hear it. She started to say something, but James shooed her away. The view from the fifteenth floor gave him a wide view beyond the skyscrapers northward toward Midtown. For a brief moment, he knew who he should call next after this phone call. He had felt close and even missed her before, but this was different. She was his base, his grounding when he needed it, going all the way back to childhood. Distraction.

"Well, sir, I am looking for manpower and I need it in four offices. Atlanta, Detroit, Phoenix, and Salt Lake. Forty more agents each on top of our present central command. Hanson has already commandeered the office space and infrastructure to support the agents. You won't be disappointed in what we bring home."

"Holy toledo, that's more than half the graduating class. Hell, half of them want to be in the Foreign Counterintelligence, not Domestic. I'll see what I can do. They just graduated and haven't even been given their assignments. There's going to be a lot of disappointed cadets."

"I won't disappoint them. We need these guys. Let's meet this week and I will discuss our findings that require this manpower. Or we can SCIF now, but I am in up to my neck with this thing. You saw what happened. This is serious and you will take all the credit for breaking up the crime of the century. This is foreign and domestic terrorism, I can feel it. We are also going to need a liaison between us and Foreign Counterintelligence."

"I will get you what you need. Don't worry."

Stamos set the phone down on the arm of the chair and continued to gaze out at the city lights, with a reflection of James barely visible, standing behind him across the room, his eyes wide with surprise and respect.

Stamos pictured the director sitting on the corner of his desk staring blankly out at the D.C. skyline, hopefully not with his fingers crossed. In reality, in the same pose, he was perched on his home desk, with a Scotch in his hand, staring out toward a folded flag on the wall across the office from where he sat. Stamos knew that political appointees had a habit of speaking out of both sides of their mouths and saying yes to anything until the appropriations request was on their desk. That was when the red DENIED stamp came out of the drawer. However, Stamos sensed some base morality with this one that he had not seen in a director before. He would set up an appointment as soon as he returned to D.C.

With his statement to the director, he was promising something he could not yet deliver. If he was hoping for a breakthrough, he was about to get it. Still in a dream-like state, he didn't notice his phone was ringing until too late. It was Point, whom he had not talked to since the new development. He touched the answer button but it was too late. Damn. He desperately needed to talk to his more pragmatic partner. Thankfully, a half second later, the phone rang again.

"Point. Thank God. I need to talk to you, buddy. This was not the start that I was looking for to kick off this mission."

"Stamos, first things first. How are you and Hanson?"

"Well, we are ok. Hanson's injuries are a little worse than mine. I have only a flesh wound. All sewed up and good as new. I've had much worse. Hanson is out of surgery and is already awake and walking."

"Thank goodness for that. What do you think provoked this response? I know there is a lot of rhetoric nationally against the FBI for a lot of reasons. Do you think that is it? Do you think we already touched too close to home on these extremists? We don't want to reveal our hand too prematurely."

"I think some combination thereof. As soon as I am out of this hospital room. I am girding myself for a fight. Point, I just got off the phone with the director. I just requested 160 new agents. He seemed to approve it preliminarily. Can you believe it?"

"Maybe this development jarred his sense of responsibility to his agents. We probably went in there too unprepared and outmanned. A dozen agents in each division is too few."

"True, that was my point to him. I sort of promised him some results to back up the request. I'm worried I won't be able to deliver that to him."

"Well, hold on to your hat because we have two major breakthrough developments. I will brief you when you get back here. It requires clearance. How soon can you be at the SCIF in the Atlanta office?"

Stamos knew what that meant. There was something on the server that he couldn't talk about without secure communication and Stamos did not have a SCIF vehicle in Atlanta presently. That needed to change. His heart was suddenly beating rapidly and that never happened. What was it?

"You're working the heck out of it, right? Did you call the full ARTI team in for tonight to work on this? Now I want to check out of this hospital tonight."

"We are all over this like gravy on biscuits, buddy. Just hang tight until tomorrow morning."

"Okay, Point. Gravy on biscuits? Since when have you talked like that? Are you wanting to come down here to Georgia too with that Southern slang?"

"Been working on my colloquialisms so I can relate to my junior agents here. These guys are a little different from my SEC officers. Different breed. They are teaching me some new tricks."

"Well, isn't that nice? Don't go too hogwild with that. I don't think it fits your persona. Don't you ever go changing your tie. We won't recognize you. Next thing you know you'll be wearing overalls and a Bubba hat." Both Stamos and Point had a good chuckle with that one. "With that, it's getting late. I am going to get an hour of shut-eye in this hospital. The assistant director is bringing the medical director to spring me out of here early tomorrow morning. I will hopefully be in the office in the morning before 9."

"Well then, it's good you are staying until morning. Meet with the assistant director. Maybe the sympathy card will help us obtain the manpower we need so that we can be anywhere and everywhere these extremists run. Play it up. Wince and grunt in pain."

With that Stamos directed James to call to request the appointment with the medical director be as early as possible at 6 am.

Sleep came relatively easy for Stamos after the two momentous conversations, if only for an hour or two. Not surprising, for Stamos never had trouble clearing his mind for sleep even in the most intense situations. His best friend since childhood had taught him meditation and mindfulness which came in handy in all sorts of situations. Even with the pain of the injury, the immediate calm of his breathing and thought control brought his heart rate down and cleared his mind for sleep. He never needed more than a few hours to refresh and recharge. He would be awake by 4 am and ready to begin the next phase and hopefully soon after, the takedown phase of this operation.

That morning's meeting with the assistant director went well. The sun had not yet risen on the Eastern horizon when the two were knee-deep in the back and forth of bureaucratic bullshit. But reason and Stamos' will won the day. In the end, the assistant director could only shake his head in defeat. More than two hundred young men working on what two weeks ago was thought to be a dead-end mission. The two shook hands just as the medical director walked in the door.

The medical director approached Stamos, inspected his wound, and was about to begin his physical exam. The assistant director took a few steps toward the door, before turning around to face Stamos once again. "Are you certain this is going to land some big fish?"

"I am not a betting man, but this mission has the smoking gun already, literally. And we have some digital breakthroughs that I need to be briefed on back at Quantico. The Russians are up to something and they are communicating to someone on this end. By the way, how quickly can your pilots turn the plane around? Point has some sensitive data for me."

"The engines are probably still warm. I always have four pilots and so does the director."

Stamos responded with jealousy, "Wow, how do you rate?"

"Well, I am almost always flying multiple stops each day and returning to D.C. If the medical director can clear you, then let's get back up north."

The flight back on the assistant director's plane was quicker than he thought it would be. He managed to talk the medical director into skipping much of the exam and approving his and Hanson's redeployment. And rather than wait for the call from the SCIF, why not just get to D.C. sooner rather than later? He, Hanson, and his two assistants were even dropped off in Quantico via the assistant director's security detail at the computer lab. Steven Point was waiting for him, thin black tie and all, in the parking lot. This ought to be good, he thought. Stamos sensed the assistant director wanted to be briefed also.

As he exited the vehicle, Point assisted Stamos out of the vehicle.

"I'm not that injured," Stamos began, resisting the support. "It barely grazed my arm and flank."

Point, realizing the assistant director was joining them, quickly assumed a professional posture.

"You're never going to believe this. We are finding some incredible data that will shake you in your boots." Point was beginning to have a flair for the dramatics.

"Not in a million years. But I'll bet you are going to tell me. Let's get inside." Stamos said, his good arm grasping James' shoulder on the way in

For the next hour in the SCIF conference room, Sebastian and Steven Point elaborated on some data findings from ARTI in a very vague way, being careful not to tip too much to the assistant director, who left halfway through the briefing.

"Well, he couldn't leave soon enough," Point said. "Okay, so here is what we have. The Russians are sending and receiving pings from about 30 different devices spread out across the U.S. They are also receiving some pings from a satellite in geostationary orbit. Not much information transferred thus far, but with the pings, we are getting IP addresses and should have some approximate locations soon."

"How long will that take?" asked Stamos.

"Each one will take about an hour to run some diagnostics. We already have a few locations. They all seem to be using satellite communications, which makes it more difficult. But the signal, though encrypted, can be intercepted by our satellites. We have to run this through signals with our brothers at Counterintelligence. They even have the encryption key for the satellite that these two devices communicate with. All told, maybe a day or two. And the location down to within a mile."

"That's great. I would bet they are mobile." Stamos thought of the thick brown tablet immediately. "Where are the first two?"

"That is the amazing thing! Do you know the town where you were just shot at? Literally within a mile of your central park."

"That sheriff had a tablet he was engrossed in when we walked in the door. No way! That could be the clincher for that story!"

"Well, Stamos. I've got to hand it to you. You have a knack for finding your way right into a hornet's nest."

Stamos was deep in thought but interrupted his trance with a summary, "Alright, thirty tablets that we have to find, and we just found one of them. Where is the other?"

Sebastian spoke up, "Some small town outside of Phoenix. Nondescript, we don't have as good of location data on that one."

"Okay, let's start with those. You know we have that development in Arizona. Could be related. We need to drill down on that too. We are about to be on the receiving end of a whole platoon full of agents who can investigate this. Let's get on it. Hanson, you ready to travel again?"

The three commiserated briefly about Stamos' injury and told a few jokes at Stamos's expense. "Point, why don't you come with us down to Atlanta, and let's start some surveillance on this town. You said you have another breakthrough?"

Point surprisingly agreed, "Well, we think we also may have a mole in Georgia trying to communicate with us. We are sending it through the usual fake channels so as not to give any sense of an investigation. We can check that out while we are there."

"All the more reason to get back to Atlanta." Stamos was glad Hanson ordered their plane to return to Quantico with them, but they would have to wait a few hours for the crew to be ready to fly again after such a short turnaround.

—⋗⋘—

CHAPTER 18: THE MOLE

—⋗⋘—

Earth-shatteringly, the nascent Office of Domestic Counterintelligence team had uncovered the Russian's method of communication and was working directly with Foreign Counterintelligence, which had even better tools at their disposal for satellite espionage. While Signals was working on verifying the correct satellite for direct satellite-to-satellite surveillance, which would take a day or two, Stamos and Point, began their trek back down to Georgia, which was the epicenter of all they knew so far. Within a few days, the new additions to the team from the FBI Academy would receive their assignments and begin to fan out to the four predetermined locations. With any luck, the extra manpower would flush out any relevant facts.

They received the go-ahead to take 24 recruits immediately to Georgia and the majority of them were already on their way to Atlanta. All of these junior agents already possessed the necessary security clearance to begin work right away. The others would take a day or two to receive top-secret clearance. To Stamos and Point, it was not ideal to have inexperienced agents, but in some ways it might work better, considering the mission. Having men with less preconceived notions about the operations of the FBI suited Stamos just fine.

"Point, let's further investigate this informant you were telling me about, and see what he knows. Ricky Burns. That's his name, right? I can meet with him tomorrow if need be."

"Yes, he is a relatively new member of the Georgia Militia. Story seems to check out. Doesn't seem to fit the true Good Ole Boy stereotype so I'm not sure how he made their roster. He went to college at Georgia Tech, Computer Science. Returned home to work for the family business. Family goes back generations to before the Civil War. Maybe that's how he fits."

"Maybe that's how he doesn't fit and why he's coming to us. An idealistic college kid comes home and realizes something isn't quite right with the family business. I know if I had returned home to Maine, there were some things I would not have put up with after I experienced the real world outside the sticks." Stamos had come from small beginnings in small-town Maine where boat building and logging were the expected local careers after high school unless you broke free and went off to college.

"After this last week, we will have to be careful and let him come to us in Atlanta where he has plenty of anonymity. In the communication, it said he would be in touch this week. Hopefully, that is tomorrow. Hanson, do we have a plane ready for us to jump on?"

"Yes, sir. We can turn around in an hour. We will be there before 1600. And I will arrange for the new agents to arrive tomorrow."

"Alright, file a 5 am flight plan for our new recruits to travel to our Atlanta base. Let's get our new recruits cracking on this. Are you going to stay here with ARTI, Sebastian?" Stamos turned to their assistant for that rhetorical question. Sebastian, who was busy taking notes, nodded in agreement. Stamos noted for clarity, "Hanson, send messages to everyone to meet at the Marine Base at 430 am."

Stamos strode through the double doors on his way out

of the Toppled Tower of Cubes as he and Point had begun to call their headquarters. It felt like they were in a futurama movie at a space base on planet Earth. Then Stamos caught a glimpse of her out of the corner of his eye. There she was. He had not seen her in a few days, "Point, you didn't. You brought her here to me? Hanson, meet me at my house so I can give her a proper goodbye before heading back to Atlanta."

He was going to miss being based in D.C. so he could spend more time carving out the roads between Quantico and the big city. As he opened the door, he slid softly into the black refinished leather of the vintage 1968 911. She just fit perfectly. Now that he lived only a few minutes away, he would have to be satisfied with taking her to Pat's, which was his favorite hangout for one Guinness and a dozen hot parmesan garlic wings. He had one hour which gave him not a minute to spare.

The engine started with that characteristic Porsche whine, then as he put her in gear the power of the big cat came to life in his hands. Not coincidentally, the sound system, as if on cue, immediately began with the solo guitar of the beginning of "Take It Easy" as he backed her out of her new workplace. Not as protected from the elements as the Hoover FBI building parking garage but every bit as secure. She seemed to be happy with her new digs. The Polo Red classic screamed out of the parking lot and onto the country road that led into town. As he shifted through the progression of gears, it only took a few minutes to reach the tiny pub owned by one of his good friends, a retired, very decorated, Marine general.

Along the way, he thought of home back in Maine, and what kind of reception he would get if he came home after all this time. He didn't travel back there often these days since his father was gone. He still communicated with some friends online but the only connection was the old times of high school. Would he be able to relate or would he realize all too quickly the trap that it was? The last time he returned several years ago, the local pub hosted several of his friends' old habits on a nightly basis. He couldn't really fathom what they saw in that life of work, nightly drinking, and stumbling home. While they did not seem overtly racist growing up, he knew their leanings were not to accept outsiders easily into their hometown, and these times had changed even the most open-minded Mainers.

Pulling the sporty car into the lot, he found a shady spot that looked lonely enough and backed her in slowly. Once again, due to the excitement of the smooth ride, he forgot about his assistants. He knew that Hanson would soon resume his old role, but James was still on the job, following him relatively closely behind, with Hanson in the passenger seat. Stamos waited patiently for a few minutes while James parked a few spots away.

James, flashing his smile, exited his government-issue Ford and joined Stamos as they walked across the lot. "You know, you need to keep your cover in sight at all times. We are here to protect you. The safety of a director is number one and we almost lost you on day one. So, from now on, don't exceed your cover. The longer you are in this job, you will see. There will soon be more threats than you even know about. Hanson is going to stay in the car for a few minutes. We are only here for a few minutes, right?"

"You're right. I'll behave. By the way, can you pick me up at home before we leave? I am going to leave her in the garage. This Virginia sun is not good for her skin." Then he pointed to the sign over the door, "Have you ever been here? Best wings in town. I am vegan ninety percent of the time, but I need some wings to calm my nerves."

"No, I have not. But it looks like they can get pretty busy on the weekends." Luckily, the parking lot was not as crowded today as the two men strolled through the glass door. "Patrick! Great to see you, my friend! Meet my friend James. He's my shadow for the week. Looks like you could use some company for lunch!"

The stout but muscular man with closely cut red hair and beard smiled from across the bar and immediately made his way over from the cash register. Two hearty handshakes later the stories started to fall one by one about the old days. Patrick had been through the ranks of the Marines on his path toward retirement as a bartender and bar owner. His federal pension made the financial decision easier.

"How's your new gig going, Seanie boy?"

"Well, it's had an eventful start. We are learning the job on the fly."

"I know you'll do great, lad! There's no stopping you when you have them in your sights. You're like a pit bull with a steak in its mouth!"

Stamos only spent about thirty minutes talking small talk with Pat, but he thoroughly enjoyed his wings and the ginger ale that was served in place of the usual Guinness. He knew that wheels would be up all too soon, and he really needed to get back to at least a semblance of a run even with his injuries. If he was going to survive any further adventures, he needed to stay in shape.

"Okay, Pat. I will see you when I return." As Stamos turned to walk out the door, he turned to James, "Let's get back down to Atlanta. Point is coming with us. We are looking into a possible mole in one of these organizations. And we need to see how Hanson is doing."

An hour later, as they met Point at the Quantico marine base, there were more than a few fresh faces to join their crew in the Southeast. The jump flight was short but it was rather crowded and seats were at a premium on this C-130 heading to Dobbins Air Base. Stamos had become spoiled traveling in the comfort of the CIA jets around the world. He decided to get a short workout in at the center of the belly of the plane. The pushups, dips, and situps were a much-needed diversion, and his wound was only slightly sore as he massaged the surrounding bruising. The stitches were still fresh and sometimes caught on his shirt, but it was more of a nuisance than anything painful.

Later, as he stood between Hanson and James, holding on to a strap hanging from the padded wall, the dimly lit surroundings were not conducive to staying awake. He drifted into and out of a half-sleep, watching the lights on the ground below meld with the burnt-orange western horizon and the indigo night sky to the east. All of this was so mesmerizing, it quickly brought him back to his younger years with the DNI and CIA. In those days his eyes would have been wide open at this stage of a six-hour flight overseas, but today he was content with getting a few minutes of sleep before touch-down of the short jaunt.

The jolt and high-pitched tire screech sent him forward a few feet into James, standing in front of him and the casual bump directly into his gunshot wound also sent a few gallons of adrenaline straight into his heart. That certainly would jump-start his adventure here in Atlanta. Maybe, he hoped beyond all hope, that he would finally get to see his long-lost friend.

He and Point, along with Hanson, James, and Point's new assistant, then embarked on a mission to find this mole, while the others set out to find their southern headquarters. The call from the mole came in as expected and was routed through multiple agents to Point's phone, who answered with a vague, "Investigation unit, Point speaking."

Stamos could not stand being on the outside of an important telephone conversation looking in, without hearing the other end of the exchange. Today's transportation was austere, a tinted FBI-issued Suburban with a driver, so it was crowded and a tad noisy. Every once in a while, he could make out a few words but had to wait until the phone call was over to learn the details. It reminded Stamos of a simpler time in his career, before his deep dive undercover, when he first joined the agency. These Suburbans were part of an ever-aging fleet he didn't miss one bit.

"Well, we have a meeting," Point said when he hung up, gazing out the window with a pensive look at the passing cars. A long, worried frown came over his face, "We need to be careful with this guy and this guy needs to be careful with us. He could easily get made by his outfit. We are meeting him on the campus of Georgia Tech. We should be able to blend in. I look like a computer science professor and Stamos, you look like a football coach. From pictures of this guy, he fits

202

the nerd stereotype. Let's get him a burner phone."

"Agreed," Stamos said. "Let's call ahead to the campus security to gain access to the buildings. We need to meet this guy in a computer science building where nobody will be able to follow him. And set up our own tail to make sure he isn't being followed."

It didn't take long to set up the clandestine meeting situation and the access was easy enough. They painstakingly took care not to allow the campus security director in on their plans for the encounter, under the auspices of meeting with an IT expert Point knew from college. They assigned the official team to one location within the labyrinthine building, while Point and Stamos would meet with their mole in an unannounced room with no cameras. Trust no one and there will be no failures. They arrived one hour prior and met the security director at the entrance to set up their mock session and proceeded to scout secondary locations. Upon finding a satisfactory room nearby, the team felt comfortable with the conditions in place.

"Make the call!" Stamos commanded Point. He realized he sounded dictatorial just then. "Do you want to meet him outside on the pathway behind the building?" That was better, and less overbearing.

"Yes," was all Point could say before the mole answered. Operation Mole Meet was going smoothly so far.

With one security team planted outside on the main road and one behind the building, the setting was secure enough. Point rendezvoused with their man for only a few seconds, making it look like he was asking for directions. Aside from the expected extreme nervousness of this young man, he looked young enough to be in high school. Then, like an old pro at espionage, Point, the newly anointed spy, pointed the mole in the right direction to follow Stamos, who stood at the entrance of the building. All was rolling along smoothly.

Soon the three were face to face in a small alcove on the third floor, down the hall from their compatriots who were providing cover in addition to the diversion for the security director. Stamos sized this young man up from head to toe and affirmed his suspicion of him as a naive computer nerd who had not yet grown up. He was still dressed in clothes you would expect to see a college freshman wearing.

However, the fact he was here in the first place spoke highly of his evolving maturity. Stamos spoke first, "So, are you sure nobody suspects you are an informant?"

"Yes, so far. I am continuing to participate in their meetings and activities. I have lived in the South for over twenty years. I know how to blend in. Unfortunately, you have to just to survive. I am going all in to bolster my credentials. They are targeting people who have connections to Atlanta. Which is a slight problem for me coming back to Tech. At the same time, it is wrong what they have planned, and I will help you monitor what they are doing."

Point was more than curious. "Can you tell us some of their plans?"

With that question, a serious look fell over the diminutive man's boyish face as he looked down at the stark white floor of the room. "Where do I start? It is quite extensive and I haven't seen any full outline yet, but they are about to receive some sort of master plan from above. There are only a few leaders and I don't know who they are. They use a special tablet to communicate. It looks to be a specially-made device. I have never seen this type of tablet anywhere and it has no brand markings. And I think it communicates with satellite technology, not cellular."

Stamos pressed for more information, "Can you give us names and their locations?"

"Yes, I can get you what I know so far and will keep you informed."

"These men could be dangerous. We have reason to believe they won't play nice if they discover you are informing us. And I am talking life-and-death serious. We are going to give you this phone. Keep it turned off at all times until you need to call us because they can track cell signals. When you call us, do so from somewhere where there are no other electronic devices within at least fifty yards."

The man outlined as best he could all names and locations while Point looked on incredulously as he entered the information in their shared database. The information was spectacularly detailed with names, phone numbers, and exact addresses. He could tell that while this man might not look particularly sharp, his memory was photographic. His first thought was that it might play to his advantage if his relatives in the organization thought he was not capable of becoming an informant.

As the men were about to depart. Stamos placed his hand on their informant's shoulder and thanked him, "You're doing the right thing. Be careful though! The people your brother is working with can monitor your every communication. For this reason, I am asking you now, if we granted you a safe harbor, would you take it? That means we will give you a safe place to live and all expenses paid for a temporary length of time."

"I appreciate it but I think I would be more useful in my hometown."

This warning would prove insufficient to prevent a surreal tragedy in this young man's life. But the information he would provide the means to save many others.

CHAPTER 19: EYES IN THE SKY

Presciently, during the last decade, Merlin Commercial Logistics had a vested interest in tracking threats and defending its fleet of cargo ships worldwide. Always at the forefront of the technology of coordinating and monitoring their container ships, Chip Merlin and Sam Steed had formed an offshoot of the company to develop drone surveillance, at first with defensive capabilities and subsequently adding offensive military technology. The burgeoning drone technology sector was a lucrative addition to the rapidly diversifying portfolio of Merlin Logistics. The company was a relative newcomer to the military-industrial complex but quickly found its niche developing the technology for the myriad of private mercenary companies around the world.

Keeping the technology out of the wrong hands proved a difficult proposition, however. Vetting their customers was already a key part of their executive security business plan to ensure they always found themselves on the right side of wrong. However, this new level of technology required its own elevated clearance which was especially onerous but necessary. They exclusively onboarded clients who utilized only the defensive capabilities of the drones and reserved the offensive capabilities for their own fleet's protection in the dangerous waters off Africa and the Middle East. Developing the robotics and satellite control capability for the drones required outfitting their already blossoming satellite network with highly encrypted communications for their drones in the air.

It was a natural progression of this venture into their executive security division, with the added satellite communications, to aid their dozens of mercenary-like paramilitary divisions around the world. The company by now operated more drones with offensive technology than almost all of the countries in the world. They recruited former drone pilots from the military of the UK and US to be part of their security divisions to operate them.

After witnessing the successes of drones in the open sea, protecting their ocean fleet, the newest utilization of unmanned aerial vehicles for Merlin had only just begun for this investigative arm of the security division. These vehicles could stay aloft for up to 18 hours at a time and were charged in less than a few hours. They had a combination of fixed-wing and hover technology and possessed small missile and artillery capabilities.

In a small room without windows at the Sybaritean Collection Hotel conference center, sat a newbie just discharged from the Royal Air Force. Noah Smith was one of the most adept drone pilots in the world and had seen action in Iraq, Afghanistan, and multiple other clandestine operations which he could not name. From the Royal Air Force, he was farmed out to the US military Central Command in Tampa, Florida on a regular basis as he had the reputation for maintaining structural integrity in some of the most intense situations.

In other words, he didn't crash the damn drones. And with the price tag of each of Merlin's drones in the upper seven figures, that fact was an important asset. It was not unusual for a military drone pilot to have multiple splashdowns in their career. Winds, enemy fire, satellite miscommunication, and even birds caused some crashes, but Noah had never impacted a single drone with the ground. That's not to say he hadn't had some near misses and a rare, partially-damaged limp back home to whatever base or ship his drone was supposed to return to. Now he would be trusted with even more missions with a different payload.

Behind him stood Torey Severin, the former Army Ranger and FBI agent who was in charge of the US Security division of the enterprise. Of utmost importance for mission success, Torey had already established in his mind that his handpicked drone commander would dominate this aerial stakeout. This surveillance required stealth only visually from the ground as it would be highly unlikely for any of their targets to possess radar of any sort.

Torey put his hands on his pilot's shoulders, and gave some words of encouragement, "Okay, what we needed to accomplish is a forward and reverse tracking of whatever vehicle we can connect to the intermediary base in this neighborhood. The dire circumstances demand immediate results. We need to find this young lady fast. Her life may depend on it, you know."

Torey paused, realizing he was stating the obvious, but Noah nodded his head as he used both joysticks and foot pedals just like a manned airplane pilot, performing his preflight checks. "On the surface, this appears to be the easiest mission I have performed without any armed enemies in the air. Yet the stakes seem even higher here with possible unidentified victims and unrecognized locations. We normally send our drones in with targets already pinpointed by GPS or laser targeting."

They already had a team in this suburban Atlanta neighborhood with eyes on the ground, but to be able to follow vehicles was easier with eyes in the sky. Whoever was operating out of this neighborhood, was counting on the anonymity that the partially-constructed houses afforded, since most of the houses were uninhabited. The consensus was it must be an intermediary site to prevent being followed.

As luck would have it, the same small airport at which Merlin maintained a hangar was within only a few miles from this neighborhood and possessed long runways and a helipad Charlie that offered perfect proximity to their hangar. Satellite communication was established with the ground crew and the drone at the Dekalb Airport, and Drone Commander Noah requested permission for takeoff from the tower. These extremists did not stand a chance now with the applied robotics of Merlin Commerce. The second drone would soon also be airborne, commanded from another room and a second pilot. They would overlap by 6 hours to maintain full twenty-four-hour coverage of the area.

Noah went through the progression of his pre-flight checks and video checks. The ground crew checked focusing parameters of the 16K cameras and the targeting systems were also inspected. No missiles were loaded but the small caliber artillery rifle was armed. No mission was ever commenced without the small arms outfitted for defensive capabilities, but at this stage of the mission, they didn't want to risk flying the drone by the tower with missiles under her wings.

"We are next in line for takeoff," Noah commented to Torey.

"Excellent, that was a quick flight turnaround time. Make sure you thank our ground crew," Torey reminded him.

"In due time, let's get airborne first." Noah was OCD regarding his preflight order of operations, perhaps part of the reason for his flight performance ratings in the military. "In this area of Atlanta, we have a ceiling of 1200 feet in the immediate vicinity and areas east and northeast of Emory Hills according to the waiver notice we applied for and received from the FAA. Our target area is only minimally in the flight path of the short runway, Runway 9, which won't be in operation for the next week. I am going to circle around and approach from the East. We can maintain noise cover from the interstate on that side of the area."

Torey countered, "Yes, but then let's drop down to 400 feet if we have that kind of noise cover. Besides, any suspicion should be limited as anyone who spots our drones may think it is a helicopter monitoring traffic on the interstate. I want to get a visual of all license plates in and out of this neighborhood for the next 48 hours. I will have Digital Team Three cross-reference all of them."

"Affirmative, sir," Noah answered, then opened his comms. "Approach to runway 16 from Helipad Charlie 1, request takeoff clearance. Liftoff commenced. Taxiing to Runway 16. From Helipad Charlie 1. " A short pause. "Tower, altitude twenty, ceiling 400, bank to 90 degrees. Target max ceiling 1200. Takeoff commenced, Runway 16." He was sure this was the first unmanned aerial vehicle this airport had ever encountered. The tower would be fully aware by the end of this mission regarding the capabilities of the Merlin MR-16 UAV. Inevitably, at some point, someone was going to notice their offensive capabilities, however. They would have to cross that bridge when the time came.

On the six screens, the ground and runway quickly gave way to trees and commercial buildings surrounding the airport. The forward camera and instrument panel in the center tilted the rotors and wings leftward to 90 degrees heading as Noah guided the drone to her destination. It only took about 2 minutes for the interstate to slowly come into view, above which the drone now hovered and rotated 180 degrees to face westward into the target area. He slowly brought her down to 400 feet and hovered there. All of the neighborhood could be seen from this vantage point. There were no cars on the residential roads at this time. Noah rotated all three auxiliary cameras forward to focus on the streets and houses below.

Now came the tedious part, logging the cars to pass the information along to digital team three. A few hours passed, and Torey became tired of the inaction. He hated this part of the mission. He was not a very patient man and could not sit still for long. He needed to stretch and was itching to get back into the field with the other teams. As it was, Noah also could not bear having Torey pace back and forth behind him much longer. Torey exited the room and joined Huy in the command room.

Like a watched pot that was left unattended, the water immediately started to boil. A few minutes after he left the room, Noah paged him on the comm. That was more like it. Maybe it was the proverbial watched pot, but this escalation developed more quickly than he thought it would. Sometimes these investigations stretched for days.

"This is suspicious," Noah noted to Torey as he entered the room. "Look at this. This vehicle enters the neighborhood, and parks in the garage of this partially built house. Then the driver exits and walks across the street to this house. Then he or someone exits that garage in this vehicle. Neither of them matches our target vehicle. But there is a similar vehicle also in that same garage."

Torey performed a little fist pump and quickly paced a few times behind Noah before saying, "Let's circle around a bit to get a good look at both garages and license plates when you are able. You are right, that is suspicious enough. Stay out of sight though so you don't break cover. I will send the information to Field Team Three. I think we may have our location. I am going to head there now."

Before exiting the drone command room, Torey switched on his comm to the field teams, "Field Team Three, I think we may have something. Two houses, one partially built. At 18 and 17 Emory Circle. So far three vehicles, maybe more. One vehicle just entered one garage at 18 and the driver proceeded across the street to 17 and exited that garage in a different vehicle. Both houses have three-car garages. One may match our target but we don't have a clear view yet. We will have plates in a few minutes. Get the dog out now, just in case. Suspect car is exiting the neighborhood now. Field Team 3, mobilize to track a gray Toyota pickup with plate XYR 316 passing your location now. Drone Team 2 how quickly can you be airborne?"

Field Team 3 had a search dog, which would also serve as a good cover dog as one of the team members would walk by the target houses with the dog. As a relatively new neighborhood, the residents would not expect to recognize every person walking their dog. Earlier in the day, the team was able to train it in on Mía's scent with some clothing that the detective provided them. Drone Team 2 responded they

212

could be airborne in 15 minutes.

Huy came on the comm, "Let's reverse track that first vehicle please."

Torey responded, "Agreed, Digital Team 3, do you copy? Obtain the video. Let's at least get an idea of the direction from which it came. Then reverse track it from our available traffic cameras from there."

Digital Team 3 responded on the comm, "We have the video, tracking through serial traffic cameras. He came from I-285. The video is still adequate from there. The vehicle appears to come from I-85 Southbound. That's as good as we have so far. Will reverse track from there. It will take us some time along the interstate because we have the state feed backlogged for some reason. The connection just slowed. We now have the tracking on the plate. It comes from Rabun County, far Northeast. Owner Claborne, Jesse."

Torey congratulated the team profusely, "Great job guys! Hold your position on those houses. This investigation is heating up! I know we have a missing girl in the balance, but we surely don't want to tip our hand too early!"

Sam then brought up the obvious, "You know, we already suspected an intermediary location, but this is turning out to be a conspiracy, not just a lone disappearance. Digital Team 2, how is it going with the new disappearance? Short answer only so as not to interrupt this pursuit, please."

A new voice came across the line, "We are getting somewhere, albeit slowly. We don't have the initial leads we had with Claire and the restaurant. Getting video feeds soon. Will let you know on the hourly update."

Several minutes later, Drone Team 2 finished their pre-checks, and a minute later had approval for takeoff. The rotors could be seen in the video feed, starting up and the cameras lifted off the ground, hovering at first, then moving forward on the monitor.

"Drone Team 2, track the Toyota, now southbound on I-285 toward the city. Field Team 3 is four cars back, sending you its track. Remember from Claire's description and the video that the perp was casing Mía's location for a few days.

He could be just casing another location or for that matter, he could be heading to another intermediary location. Field Team 3, anything from the dogs?

"Field Team 3 responding. Negative. No affirmative response. Just walked them pretty close to each house and up and down the neighborhood. Also, remember there is a lot of digging and new construction here. I am going to walk the entire neighborhood with our old faithful, Duke. Hold that thought, gentlemen. Another car just emerged from the garage of house number 2. Ready for pursuit and tracking? We are going to need another Field Team here."

Huy commanded Field Teams 1 and 2 to split up to form another Field Team temporarily. "Drone Team 1, pursue that vehicle and we will leave this location without drone surveillance for now."

Sam joined in, "Torey, we are going to need two more drone teams. How quickly can we get them here from Miami? We need to activate all Field, Digital, and Drone teams nationally to be on standby. This is nuts!"

"We are already on it. Miami will be here in three hours. We have two full Field and Digital teams on call there. We have sixteen more full teams nationally on standby in addition to what we have already scrambled. I will activate all of them from standby. And remember we are hearing rumblings of a nationwide network of this same kind of shit!" Torey couldn't believe how quickly this had escalated from very little information to activating half of the US division and the entire Field and Digital team contingent. "Sam and Chip, you know we have the Combat Teams also. Our Field Teams are not ready for anything like what we encountered last year. It might be good to have full teams with more military and combat experience if we face hostile actors."

Sam sensed the urgency, "I agree, Torey. Bring in the D.C. team. They performed flawlessly last time. I want them here immediately. How many troops can we have on standby for the other locations?"

The D.C. group was now listening to the same comms information from the sofa room that now was the headquarters for Digitial Team 5. The four women in the room could hardly grasp the enormity of the situation, with combat teams now being called up in reserve. Natalia knew that the Field Teams were more than capable at combat since many were ex-special forces soldiers, and she had seen first-hand the combat team's success on the tarmac at Teterboro airport in New Jersey. In direct comparison, the Field Teams carried SWAT team gear, but the Combat Teams wielded heavy infantry gear with armored humvees.

She asked, half-expecting a crazy answer, "What is our maximum capability? Are we going to be spread too thin? Wait, did you say nationwide conspiracy?" She readied herself for Sam to tell her that they had 100,000 troops or something insane like that.

"Can we bring some teams in from Europe or South America?" Chip interrupted.

"If we need four or five divisions each with eight Field Teams, eight Digital Teams, and one Combat Team, then we have that capability. It also depends on how nationwide we are going to go with this. We do not have the ability to operate more than five divisions simultaneously," Sam answered. "Of course, we can expand that if we need to. And the nationwide conspiracy thing. That can wait. Let's get Mía first!"

On one of the monitors, Drone Team 1 was alone in its pursuit of the second car. As its camera started to zoom in, everyone in the room immediately recognized it as the car that took Mía. This realization brought gasps to the lips of all in attendance and solidified the belief that they were hot on the heels of the perpetrators. The first thing that crossed Natalia's mind, she did not voice aloud, but she cringed as she thought, "Was Mía still in the car, in the trunk, or in that house?"

The zoom kept narrowing in on the license plate, but the feed was a little shaky. What they needed was a stoplight, which they were fast approaching. The drone settled in directly behind the target, still with one of the cameras zoned in on the plate. As the car came to a stop, the drone hovered, and the plate came into crystal clear view. Got it.

"Okay, do you have that, Digital Team 3? Take this plate and identify, please," Huy commanded again, now pacing back and forth as if he was the one chasing after the car.

When the light turned green, the car seemed to speed up beyond the speed limit and was turning erratically, as though it thought it was being followed. It took a circuitous route, doubled back and forth several times, and finally entered the interstate heading north. The drone tracked it all the way to its destination, what appeared to be a farmstead in a rural, wooded area. It increased altitude to avoid detection, but zoomed in at the same time, as two male perpetrators exited the car and went inside the barn, opened the door, and the driver backed the car in slowly. From this vantage point, they could almost make out faces on two of them as they walked into the barn. Huy noted to the group that it was probably not enough to get facial recognition, but enough to identify them later.

As expected, Huy then instructed though he really didn't have to, "Okay, identify this property, Digital Team 3."

Quicker to the punch, Digital Team 5 had already zeroed in on this property as soon as their target pulled into the driveway. From the start of the pursuit, Natalia had her browser on the map of the area, tracking the progress. Then, she opened a second browser on the county appraiser's site and the ownership information flashed on her screen. But she would let the official Digital Team 3 identify and trace ownership for the record. On the map, she dropped pins on all of the target locations and added some from their own research on notable events that they had collected.

Interestingly, they were awfully close to the sleepy town where the random shooting had occurred earlier, not to mention the waitress charged with stealing. Was it possible to call this a busy week in what most would call a modest, insignificant slice of northeast Georgia? Anywhere else in the country, she wouldn't have batted an eye at this amount of crime, but here? She quickly searched the owner for other properties, performed a Lexis search, and gleaned an extensive legal and family history, even if they were just petty, small-claims lawsuits. Social media gleaned up-to-date pictures and more family pictures. Into the database he went.

While the first drone hovered in silent surveillance mode, the second drone followed the other car to another midtown Atlanta apartment building, where it remained for a few hours without much activity and then returned to the intermediary neighborhood again. Within a few minutes, a third vehicle, a gray larger pickup, emerged from the neighboring residence. Plates were made and matched to another individual, another database entry, and another pin on the map. This pickup appeared to have two men in the cab, and it made three stops along the way to its final destination about an hour away from the first. Three more pins on the map. What a productive day this turned out to be. They had developed quite a dossier on this organization, a lesson on how not to utilize an intermediary location.

At the next briefing, Digital Team 5 made a splash with all the information they had learned about this gang of perpetrators. Huy wasted no time placing a copy of her map of pins on one of their main, shared monitors. Despite being detail-oriented, DT-5 was also turning into the mile-high bird's-eye-view of the burgeoning investigation. But now, the collective thought process turned to how to use this information to find Mía.

Natalia, sensing the mood, proffered, "None of this does any good if we can't use it to find Mía. I think we need to move in on these people soon. Maybe not today, but we need to prioritize what is going on in these pinned locations."

Torey answered the collective nervous consciousness, "Where do we go from here? Into the field for surveillance will yield the most intelligence. Drones can't fly inside the buildings or listen to people unless they are closer to the subject. Digital Teams and Field Teams, dedicate one individual from each of your teams to study the safety and feasibility of casing any of the locations of each of these target pins. We need real operational surveillance. Also, Digital Teams, bring to bear all surveillance tools, illegal and legal, onto these individual targets. I want these perpetrators by the end of the week and most importantly, I want Mía by the end of the week."

Natalia thought to herself, "Could he possibly be right? Would they find her in time? However improbable the fight, Torey had overcome the odds last year, could he do it again?"

CHAPTER 20: REDEPLOYMENT

The day had heretofore presented a laundry list of challenges for Stamos and Hanson as they entered the lobby doors of their Atlanta FBI offices to get an eye on the transformation of this new regional facility. They spent a few hours on the phone with the Director's office, assessing the status of the investigation into the rural ambush, which was proceeding at a snail's pace, and had not even resulted in any interviews. All of this sat just alright with Stamos, as they did not need any information tipping off these small-town law enforcement officers that there were feds creeping around.

As the elevator doors opened to their suite, Stamos' eyes widened so much he had to shade his eyes. To say office space was a precious commodity in the FBI was a gross understatement, so Hanson must have performed a miracle of all miracles. This cavernous venue appeared to be a whole floor of the building and it was fully furnished. Some of the junior agents had already claimed some of the prized real estate of the available workstations. That central area of modern cubicles was surrounded by two dozen private offices. A large triple-sized office, with small, square blacked-out windows, was situated along one corner that would be perfect for a command center conference room, with enough room for all forty of their agents.

As they exited the elevator the next thing they spied to the left, appearing quite out of place, was an elongated black box, a room with black walls well away from all windows, that seemed to have been recently installed, as more than a mess of construction debris and wires were still scattered around the floor. Excellent, he thought, his requested SCIF was also in place and hopefully fully operational. And it was big enough for at least a long conference table and communication equipment. This would prove invaluable in communicating with Point and Sebastian back in Quantico.

"Hanson, you had this installed almost overnight? The last time we were here I thought we were only getting a few offices. Who did you have to bribe to get this? And this had to have been arranged before our unfortunate episode."

"Well, let's just say I know a few people in logistics and procurement." Hanson, while he had traveled to Quantico and back, had only been given the medical director's partial approval to redeploy, but continued to work regardless and was more than a bit industrious at real estate negotiations from his hospital room. Stamos appreciated the loyalty and the natural instinct to finish the mission.

"You know, Hanson, you should run the logistics of the entire FBI. You are like a pit bull. First, Quantico, now Atlanta. These offices have been set up and operational in what seems like just a few days. Any other assistant would have waited for approvals from the assistant director. And you know what they say about those who wait? Those who wait only get that which is left behind by the bold. You are bold with a capital B, my friend." As Stamos managed to loosen the grip of his surprise to move about, he patted a hand on Hanson's shoulder a few times, stepped forward, and held his hands aloft as he smiled from ear to ear.,

As they slowly made their way across the central room, taking stock of the capabilities of their new location, he quickly recognized his chosen regional commander, who, among all of the recruits, actually had the highest security clearance, having moved over from the CIA. He also had significant mission experience in espionage and investigation of threats overseas. Stamos walked over to him, smiling as he shook his hand, and patted him on the shoulder too, for good measure.

"Ready for this mission to succeed, Randy?"

"Yes, one hundred percent. We've got a great bunch of guys in this class. Newbies but overachievers."

"That is great. We have our work cut out for us and I think in the next few hours, this mission is going to be in full take-off mode. We have reason to believe our enemy is set to launch. We will be ready for them!"

He immediately called a meeting in the center of the office space and all of the others gathered around. There was some jostling by some of the younger men to see who could get the open chairs close by. Stamos got a chuckle out of his thought that this appeared similar to a middle school assembly. The excitement of his teenage-behaving agents was something to behold and would bring the energy they desperately needed right now. Energy to be harnessed against the enemy.

"Okay, first item on the agenda is, welcome to your new home for the next year or more. Again, men, our mission is called Operation Titan Realm in the Division of Domestic Counterintelligence. I know that for some of you this was a sudden change, but you are going to enjoy this mission. Over the next few days, you will notice a large influx of personnel. Our job is to protect law-abiding citizens from those who would do them harm in the name of sex, race, sexual orientation, politics, or any other bigoted thing you can think of. There are extremists from every angle of the political spectrum. This is not a political mission. We have some initial intel on some activities happening in multiple areas of the country and it appears Georgia is one of those districts. We are going to assign each of you a target, whether it be an individual, a location, a victim, or even a potential victim. These are not random targets. We will only investigate probable cause events. These present targets are being gleaned

221

from threats that are credible, emanating from a server that is directing unknown members of a hitherto unknown organization to harm others in the community. You will utilize whatever legal means you can to probe the target to scrutinize and prevent harm to our citizens."

Stamos paused and looked over to his new commander. He walked over and slowly placed his arm around his back. "This is Randy, he is your regional commander. He has more experience than anyone in this division, including myself. Every morning at 7 am you will have a meeting in the command center which will be the large conference room in that corner. There will be fifteen agents on duty on weekdays, five agents on call every night, and twenty agents on duty split into two shifts on weekends. All forty agents will be expected to attend the 7 am conference each and every day. Field surveillance will not only be encouraged, it will be expected. In some of these areas, you will need a cover. Randy here, who came to us from the CIA, is an expert in providing the necessary cover. Any questions?"

The room went silent for more than a few seconds. Then a few agents began to fidget in their seats followed by a few chuckles, yet the overall mood remained serious. All of the bright, fresh eyes were focused, determined. They had no idea what to expect.

"Okay, let's get to it. We will have our first mission conference now with Steven Point in the SCIF. Let's see if the communication protocols are operational. I think there will be enough room for all of us. I want all of you to hear what we have. All of you are familiar from your training what a SCIF is and what it means operationally. So, on your way in, hand your devices to the officer who will be stationed at the entrance at all times. Any deviations from protocol will require a downtime of several hours as they rescan the SCIF, and I don't want any downtime in case we need it urgently. No devices, no watches, no glasses, no wallets."

As they all filed into the SCIF to listen to Point's presentation, the atmosphere turned even more professional, even methodical, for it was the first experience handling or hearing classified material for many of their men. The joking and jostling that had previously resulted in nervous laughter amongst the recruits were now nonexistent. The presentation of new information didn't take long, and the entire cadre of young men could not believe their ears as it was relayed to them. So this was what it was like to hear credible top-secret information that the public probably would never hear about. Again, you could hear a pin drop as Sebastian finished up the report with the operational report on the server, the Russians, and possible co-conspirators, followed by ARTI and its capabilities.

Stamos stood at the front of the room at the end and directed the young men on their initial assignments. "Okay so let's get to it. It's getting late. Randy and I will lead the mission conference tomorrow morning at 7 am. I will see you then."

Stamos and Hanson exited the room together and rode the elevator down to the first floor. "How do you think that went? I didn't have my usual whiteboard. Can you make sure we have one installed in the command center and the SCIF?"

"Excellent pep talk. Every beginning of a successful mission needs a good pep talk to show who is boss, the mission objectives, and expectations. Your speech checked all three checkboxes. And yes, whiteboards are on the way." Hanson inquired if there was anything else missing from his usual operational routine as they made their way through security and across the white and gray marble lobby.

As they walked outside into the Southern humid night air, Stamos was quickly reminded by the large Grand Oaks lining the parking lot that they were in the suburbs of Atlanta and not the city. He disliked offices outside the city center. Less cover, less traffic, and less ability to egress without being noticed. Headquarters should always have a secure parking garage to conceal the identities of those arriving and departing. He felt the need to get back to his hotel closer to downtown Atlanta and to make amends for avoiding the long-overdue rendezvous with another partner of his from another era.

Stamos stopped suddenly, turned toward Hanson, put a hand on his shoulder, and stared deeply, sincerely into his partner's eyes, boring through to the truth, "Are you okay? Are you sure you are ready?" He knew the expected answer before it was uttered, so without hearing it completely, he continued on by force of habit of a lone agent, "Okay, I will see you back at the hotel later. I may have to go meet somebody. I'll text you where I am at all times, but I want you to get some more rest." Hanson understood the direct command and what it meant. He was supposed to be Stamos' assistant, which also meant protection for the senior director of the division. Directors were not to be without another agent at any time, ever.

Hanson replied, "Right now, here and now, it's either going to be me or we get you another agent if you think I'm not ready, Stamos. You know the protocol. This is not a new thing. You will not be left uncovered no matter where you are going, no matter who you are meeting."

Stamos threw his hands up in fake surrender, and with full emphasis from a familiar smile, capitulated, "Okay, I relent. But I'm driving alone. I need to clear my thoughts. And I need to reconnect with someone."

"Good, just let me know where you are headed, and I will try to stay out of sight."

With the rules defined, Stamos opened the driver's side door of the government-issue sedan and sat down in the uncomfortable seat. He let out a sigh of relief at being alone. Sometimes he craved detachment from others, connected only to himself and his favorite car or motorcycle. Even if this was a Ford Fusion and not either of his babies back home in Virginia, the small four-cylinder felt almost as comforting. At the same time, he needed this connection to last, and he feared that connection was in danger of being lost. He sat there, motionless, with the engine running, channeling his inner strength to do what he should have done long before. It's not that he didn't think about calling her while he was stuck in bed in the hospital for several hours. He did text her then, but at that time didn't want to let her know he had been injured because that would have meant a possible visit from her in the hospital and all kinds of unanswerable questions about how he was injured.

Call it pride, machismo, or whatever it was. He usually didn't like distractions during his missions, which was probably why he had never launched any other successful relationships recently. Solitary life suited him just fine. Besides, who could he trust with any information about what he did for a living? Now that he was out of the CIA and DNI, he found it difficult to change that mentality. Maybe he could change. Maybe he could let her in. Maybe she would let him in. They were so similar, just different means to an end.

"Hi, chica bella." the text began. Mesmerized by the majestic green foliage of the live oak trees in the distance, he spent an inordinate amount of time searching the humor department of his brain for something clever yet endearing to type into the miniature keyboard. Failing miserably to come up with it, he sighed nervously and, with an emphatic, defeated press of the thumb, he hit send, inadvertently adding an extra period at the end of the text with his oversized thumb. It was sent. Now for the waiting.

Within seconds, the chime was encouraging, even uplifting. But the text was noncommittal, "Hola, buenos noches."

"I am in Atlanta. Are you busy with the new assignment? How was Colorado?"

"Great, cut short, came home to take care of some friend troubles. In midtown now."

Stamos needed to see her. "Aha, do you have time to meet?" he typed and added a happy emoji. He then decided to add, "Miss you."

"Of course. I have to meet someone but you can go with me after we meet. Where?"

He already knew the answer to where. The planned location for this future event had been decided upon long ago by Stamos when she first moved to Atlanta, knowing he would visit at some point. Always a flare for dramatic meeting venues, atmosphere was everything to Stamos, especially for this critical encounter. It seemed cliche, and over the years, in a hundred different cities, with a hundred different friends, enemies, spies, and counter-spies around the world, he always returned to the same motif, a dimly lit jazz bar in a dark area of town. He had survived ambushes and surprise role reversals and always came out on top with this concept for operational cover in his long career. If he was going to propose a shift in their connection, he needed the same mojo as his prior successes. Maybe he was getting older but a rekindling of what they had seemed to be more enticing to him lately. Was he being presumptuous to think it might be to her as well?

For a moment, he envisioned a dossier full of information on him, kept by some foreign power. On the front page, he saw, in yellowed, faded paper, with smudged typing, "Always meets in dimly lit jazz bars. Cover the exits. Explosives planted at all exits." Then the next line, indented, "And next time, also cover the second-floor roof line." His imagination faded, and he did not get to read the next several sub-headings, as they too faded to grey.

He sincerely hoped these hundred-or-so great little jazz clubs recovered from his exploits, and something in his mind told him they did. Just a few months ago he saw a tourist video of Vienna, showing a side street with the familiar red neon "Jazz" sign of one of these clubs, proof that it was indeed still kicking despite the several incendiary devices he had utilized that night so many years ago.

He texted the location, and with a slight rev to the small four-cylinder engine, took off for the little Cool Fox Jazz Lounge that he had researched for so long, but had never even laid eyes upon. Hanson kept his distance but followed nonetheless as per protocol. The city's lights reflected upon his face off the dash in quick succession as he crossed over from the suburbs into Midtown. As they pulled into the small alleyway parking lot, the cobalt-blue lights outlined the entryway in a surreal way, backing into a nice spot farthest from the establishment. "Perfect," Stamos thought, "Even better than I envisioned."

226

No explosives would be necessary this time. Hanson pulled into a stall several cars away, closer to the neon-lighted entrance. Stamos took note of all the cars and people present. And as a matter of custom, also studied the egress pathways. Again, hopefully not necessary. He felt comfortable with the situation and made a quick change of clothes from the ready stache in the back seat into something darker, more avant-garde. Black leather cowboy boots completed the look, and he was now ready.

As Stamos walked past Hanson's car, he could see the quizzical look on his new friend's face, which was growing wrinkles by the minute due to worry. He could see that Hanson also had changed into less professional attire. He was learning the art of blending in. Reading the thought bubbles above Hanson's head could have been comical, but Stamos just kept passing by, with the blue neon reflecting off the dark sunglasses on his face as he stopped, turned around, and stood there, confidently inspecting the alleyway. His back against the brick wall, with ancient steel windows and blue-tinged honeysuckle vine behind him, it was now go-time.

Stamos had zero pictures stored on his phone and had never done so, but he suddenly felt the urge to snap a selfie. He chuckled at the absurd thought and turned to enter the dark mahogany door of the club. Once inside, the pungent, yet sublimely appealing scents of the bar conjured up a hundred memories of old as he adjusted his eyes to the dark, surveyed the room and its exits, and took his place at the far end, yet near the kitchen door. Old habits, but those habits were why he was alive and well today at this ripe age.

As he spied the auburn curls entering the door, he felt the usual fiery comfort of home surrounding him the way it always did. The rendezvous would turn out to be a resounding success but not for the reason he had in mind.

CHAPTER 21: COLLAB

The evening had proven quite eventful thus far for Digital Team 5. Huy and the Merlin Investigations units monitored all cars coming and going from these houses. It was getting crowded now, but Torey, Chip, Sam, Samantha, Sage, and Natalia huddled around the sofa room for a briefing from all of the units. Claire had departed for an unexpected, hastily arranged meeting but would return soon. The use of both drones and on-the-ground Field Teams to track these cars led them not to any single location, but several different rural residences, albeit all in the four-county area of Northeast Georgia. The names of the owners of these properties were in the process of being investigated, but so far no known connection to extremist groups could be found.

Sam was the first to state the obvious, "We now have one intermediary location and four rural residences. How are we going to be able to stake out all of these rural places? Our cover will be blown in five seconds. We need to create some diversions or maybe go in on foot when we know there is no one home."

Torey replied, "Let's knock them off one by one. We have Field Team 4 which has been less active so far. That's ten men, and I don't want to split them up. If their cover gets blown, I want them to be well protected. For now, we will continue electronic surveillance with drones. But we also need drones to monitor these cars and where they are going in Atlanta. I think the Atlanta police would be a possibility. We need to let them know our findings anyway."

Natalia looked toward Sam, "This seems like a major conspiracy happening, with multiple individuals, probably a whole organization. It should probably be the FBI that we notify, forget the local police. Local police from what we have already witnessed will be less than helpful. How many field and combat teams do we have worldwide?"

Torey circled the table to address the question, when bursting through the door would be the answer they desperately sought. Claire, desperately out of breath, excitedly blurted out, "Did you get my text?"

Natalia and Chip were about to answer that they had been too busy with the briefing when in unison they let out a loud, "Holy Mother of Jesus!" which was so synchronous it would have jinxed them both for life. Each and every face turned from shades of white to red with surprise in a matter of a half-second.

Sean Stamos, appearing out from behind Claire's auburn hair, also boisterously proclaimed his surprise with a resounding, "Hey, you troublemakers! Long time!" then as he looked around astonishingly at the technological set-up, "Oh my God! What is all this?"

Claire took a step back to allow all of those present, now old friends it seemed, to converge into a big group hug. Even Torey became involved in the affair, to his own surprise, possibly it was more of a sign of relief that there was more cavalry riding in. Natalia, Chip, and Sam were busy questioning how Stamos knew their new Atlanta acquaintance and suddenly realized that Samantha and Sage knew none of the back story to their knight in shining armor.

Still partially embraced, Natalia made the expedited introduction, "Samantha, Sage, this is FBI/CIA/DNI agent Sean Stamos. He was part of our investigative team last year and it was he who single-handedly saved the world. Along with Torey, Point, Chip, and Sam, of course."

"You're too much," Stamos blushed.

Natalia continued as she wiped a tear from her eye and sniffed the rest of the tears back in, to keep them at bay, "I think we may need your help saving the world again with what we have uncovered here. Did Claire tell you?"

As the circle broke up, Stamos continued, "No really, what is all this? This looks like a CIA command center. Even I don't have this kind of operational tech now that I am with the FBI." Stamos looked over at what appeared to be two different aerial footages on the one bank of monitors. "Drones? This is crazy. Okay, so Claire filled me in on what is probably only a fraction of this. And I will tell you that, once again, the multiple coincidences regarding my mission here and what is happening with you guys are uncanny! Natalia, I am not sure how you get yourself mixed up in these things, but thank God you have the resources you have because you could get in a lot of trouble. And I'm not talking legally. We were involved in a gun battle last week with some locals in the same area you are investigating."

Natalia took the lead since she felt she had the closest connection to Sean and Torey during the last mission, having been saved by both from her naiveté. "We were just talking about how we needed some help with this. Manpower actually. The issue is that we have multiple rural locations, and it is going to be very difficult to find out what happened to our friend Mía with all of these locations. The FBI did come up, not 30 seconds before you walked in, and we were contemplating our next move. You are a savior, Sean! But," Then she paused unexpectedly, and the proverbial light bulb flashed on for a brief second, "Wait a minute! Gun Battle? In Collier County? You were the vandals that were run off by some vigilantes?"

"Yes, that's what we hear. We are preparing our measured response. And when I say measured, I mean a heaping truck-full of whoop-ass!" Stamos stopped himself and contained his burgeoning excitement.

"Well, that answers a few of the mystery crimes. There was also a waitress and another individual charged with crimes this week in that county, among many others around the state."

"Waitress?" Stamos knew that girl was in trouble the way the others looked at her. "That wouldn't surprise me. Okay, fill me in on the whole briefing, from the beginning. I sense there is incredible overlap with my team's mission, but we will see."

When Stamos found out that the location of this intermediary house was within blocks of the FBI Atlanta headquarters of his team, he was astounded. It sounded to him like a kidnapping that the FBI should be involved with, and it sounded like multiple extremists might be at play. Maybe it was part of the same plot he was already getting wind of through their artificial intelligence program, ARTI. Developing this case was going to be a lot easier with a private investigative organization involved. "Organization" was not the right word. What would he call it? "Army" might be his best description of this outfit.

As Natalia and Huy filled Stamos, James, and Hanson in on the specifics of their findings, the three G-men were exchanging looks of incredulity. After just a few of the videos were replayed on the monitor before them, Hanson interjected, "And you didn't get any of this from the police? And as far as you know, until you give it to them, they had not even remotely obtained any of this? Not even traffic cameras?"

Huy answered, "We think they probably have a few snippets of traffic camera footage, but yes if they had any of the video showing the abduction and the car, you would think with traffic camera footage they would have some information by now."

Stamos immediately picked up his secure phone and dialed Steven Point. "Steven, have I got some news for you! Natalia, Chip, Sam, and Torey are here in Atlanta. They have locked onto something that is absolutely incredible here. It may dovetail with what we are investigating with the server connection we found near Atlanta. I suddenly wish you hadn't gone back to Quantico! When can you turn yourself around and get back down here so we can set up some surveillance? You need to see and hear what they have here for an organization and exactly what they have found so far. Yes, we will enter this info into ARTI. Whatever device is connected to that server, can we get some malware installed? Can you do that from the server yet?"

Stamos put the phone on speaker so all could hear Point's response, breaking operational protocol, "We can't risk too much activity from the server unless they become more active on that server. If they become more active, they won't be able to detect our activity, and we can upload another packet of malware through the same connection." Point was right. Still too risky, but the time was coming soon, he could feel it in his bones.

Natalia realized they had not caught Stamos up on what they planned to do next. "Sean, we were just talking about going in on foot to get some field surveillance."

"Natalia, that is really risky! What if you get caught out in the cotton fields of Georgia by a farmer with a gun? My partner and I just made that same mistake. I let my guard down. Didn't think some redneck would take offense to us just existing in a small Georgia town. And the local police are not very helpful, probably at least implicit, and I have a hunch intimately involved."

Chip answered the question, "Well, we will have to fight back. We have easily a hundred men here, and we can bring in a few more divisions. Sam is bringing in most of our worldwide divisions. These guys are battle-tested in some of the worst third-world situations. Not saying we are going to start a war. But we need manpower!"

Stamos agreed, "Everything in its measure. You are right we need manpower, but stealth is the key to finding your Mía."

Manpower was the theme of the conversation for the next few minutes, like a broken record. Chip commanded Sam to bring in all worldwide divisions. Visas would need to be worked out for their international divisions. Sam agreed to the plan and as he left the room to start the process, added, "We will need another division of command and control here at the hotel. I will book another block of conference rooms. We will use the same airport for staging those men. And each of those divisions has two more drones."

Stamos stopped Sam before he left, "You know, Chip, I have some manpower of my own in my division, but we need to be careful how we go about this. My agents will obtain surveillance subpoenas based on this information. There is also Russian involvement. If you can get me the footage of that car and that location and the cars that have left those premises to that small town, then we should be able to convince a FISA judge for probable cause and foreign interference. Hell, I could probably watch that house from my office window. I will get that first thing in the morning and we will give it 24 hours before we start knocking on doors the way you guys want. In the meantime, have your men draw up the plans and logistics for this field surveillance as you call it. Secondly, we are splitting our divisions up geographically in Arizona, Michigan, and other areas as we think there are multiple divisions to our enemy."

Sam halted in his tracks in the doorway.

"So, this is truly nationwide?" Natalia asked.

Stamos almost interrupted her, "Most definitely, we just received a phone call from our new Arizona office about a disappearance there, and from some classified information that you will learn soon enough, the answer is a resounding, yes. There is something big going down, and soon. We think these little happenings are some kind of practice runs."

Huy piped up from the control desk, "That's what I've been talking about. We had some rumblings in other areas of the country too. Our logistics team is already on the case regarding adding manpower, but Sam, light a fire under the arrangements. We will do as much as possible with the drones we have presently. More drones and more units on the way soon. I love it!"

"That is most encouraging," Stamos began. "The question is, what are these people up to and why would they take

Mía? She is a journalist. Maybe that is it. Maybe she ruf-
fled some feathers with a story. But what else are they doing
in Atlanta?" Stamos appeared to be posing with his hand
on his chin, GQ-style. But he was deep in thought. There
must be another way to get this information. "We have to
get into that server and find exactly with whom and to where
it is communicating. I think it is about time to ruffle some
feathers and get a little more up close and personal with these
rednecks who already sent us a not-so-subtle message to stay
away. They aren't going to like what happens to you when
you send nasty messages to the FBI."

"Can you tell us about this server?" Natalia asked. She
was more than just a little curious at the mention of servers.

"Okay, so we talked about clearances before. We are
going to have to have some pretty serious discussions about
federal investigation NDA and cooperation agreements.
Hanson, can you make that happen? What do you think,
Point?"

Point, who was taking all of this in quietly, answered,
"We might be able to make this work. Clearances can be
tricky."

Chip, for his part, couldn't contain his excitement, "You
know, there are divisions of Merlin Logistics that have top secret clearance with your department of defense. As a matter
of fact, Huy here, and I could see it on your face, as you were
about to respond, Huy. Huy has that clearance, maybe we
could bring ourselves in under that umbrella. It's a stretch,
but we could submit now for that clearance."

Stamos, deep in thought as he watched the live drone
and field team feeds on the monitors, fathomed that this
collaboration would be unavoidable and paramount to their
success. There was a real possibility that all of this could
blow up in their faces, and for a few seconds, he envisioned
the television news reporting on the congressional hearings
that would commence if the whole mission went south while
utilizing a British company and a Russian national to surveil
American citizens. But then again, he had the same exact
thoughts almost two years ago in New York.

Stamos broke his own train of thought and flashed-forward to the more likely success they would attain, "We have to do this collaboration, Point. I don't need to tell you how much I trust the Merlin Organization. Hanson, you are familiar with the history, can you make this happen?" He suddenly realized Hanson was the one he should trust with this FBI protocol-breaking assignment.

A concerned look flashed briefly on Hanson's face, but it was quickly replaced by an encouraging smile. "I'm not sure about the foreign agent angle, but everyone knows how instrumental Merlin was in saving America's ass. The director will have to be involved with this, and if he is on board, it will happen. Let's get him on the phone. Do you need help with commandeering space here? Maybe I can help with that. Can we get a SCIF in this location? Atlanta has one more portable full-room SCIF available.

Stamos put his arms around Chip's and Hanson's shoulders, scanning the rest of the group from between them, "This is going to be one eventful ride that is for sure! Let's get the clearances arranged and once that happens, we can fully integrate our briefings. We have a 7 am briefing on our end. If we can convince the director tonight, we will have our own mini-briefing at 6 am and you can attend our briefing. Agreed?"

Chip and Natalia both agreed, and the fateful private-public partnership was consummated for the second time in the brief two-year history of the Merlin-Stamos team.

Stamos began to negotiate the terms of this deal but was interrupted by a phone call. While he walked across the room, the mood turned from muted encouragement to wonderment as they all witnessed Stamos' animated gestures from across the room. They could not hear what he was saying, but from the look on his face, he was not having a casual conversation, to say the least. As he finished and rejoined the group, all waited with bated breath.

Chip beat everyone to the punch, "What is it? Something juicy I could tell. Can you tell us anything?"

Stamos relented, "Yes, it's something in Phoenix. Our

new guy hasn't been there but 24 hours and has uncovered some information regarding an organization throughout the West that may be quite extensive. This coupled with a second missing immigration advocate in the last week. The FBI is now officially involved in these cases and we have two informants, one of which is in protective custody. It reminds me slightly of Natalia here last year, breaking the story, as one of these informants is a journalist. Also, just like you three," he remembered, pointing to Claire, Samantha, and Sage. "And I think we need to get Phoenix up and running sooner rather than later. And when I say soon, I mean today. We have our regional director there and the rest will be there within a few days. We need to expand our footprint to find out who our adversaries are there. Sam, can Merlin set something up there that quickly also?"

"Hell yes!" Sam, still leaning against the doorway, excitedly interrupted Stamos before he could finish his question. "We can have a conference center and team there and ready with four field teams and four digital teams by tonight. More teams on standby. Just give me the location of your headquarters and I will have our assistant prepare a hotel and conference center nearby. We will fly Guinevere in with all of the equipment ASAP. We need an airport, and I will find hangar space also." Sam was suddenly glad he hadn't already left, but now felt he was a tad short of full marching orders, so he glanced with a questioning look toward Chip to be sure. Their subliminal communication was interrupted by Stamos, making his own orders.

"Point!" There was a pause before Point acknowledged Stamos, as he was still impatiently waiting on the other line, "Do you want to make a quick trip to Phoenix? And, Hanson, can you commandeer us a more readily available plane? Director status? We can be out there and back by tomorrow afternoon. I want to see the layout there first-hand and I want to meet these two brave informants. This journalist there that is on the front line has cultivated an informant who knows everything."

Sam, with no full approval yet from Chip, dispensing with

the visual hints with eyebrows, now walked over and stood shoulder to shoulder with Chip, and whispers were shared under their breath before he began, "I will make the trek out there also to oversee our response in the West. I will leave you guys in Torey and Huy's command. Sounds like these Russians have a silent backroom war on their hands again if they are going to attack us in broad daylight. They just won't learn, will they?"

Chip, knowing full well he would be without his right-hand man for the first time in years, nervously laughed, "Yes. Natalia and I will stay here to help Torey and Huy rescue our friend Mía. Sam, to be clear, I am authorizing a complete nationwide investigation no matter where this goes and a complete collaboration with the FBI."

That was the operational approval Sam was looking for. Everyone having agreed in the affirmative, this nascent Western Collab was now ready to launch.

—◈≫≪◈—

CHAPTER 22: INVESTIGATOR PAIGE

—◈≫≪◈—

Ambitiously and optimistically, on Paige's agenda early that day was to visit the offices of the same non-profit organization that this second missing person had helped found. With the sunrise barely lighting the badly broken concrete sidewalk as she walked up to the door, she encountered the door ajar, which was quite unusual for this heat in Arizona. She carefully opened the door, peering inside first, then closed it behind her. In the other room, she could hear some people talking. She politely yelled, "Hello." so as not to startle anyone.

Almost immediately, out from behind a front-office wall appeared a diminutive older Native American woman who greeted Paige, "You're Paige, right? We were just talking about Jyoti. I am worried sick about her. She has crossed a few people around these parts with the truth. And these people don't want to hear it." A teenager followed her into the waiting room, silently fidgeting with her pockets.

Paige turned quickly away from the woman, peered suspiciously out the door, and cleared her throat to speak, "I'm going to help in any way I can. Can you tell me as much information as you can about her and the work she was doing?

Do you mind if I record it on my phone?"

"Yes.... and no, I don't mind. Well, you certainly are aware of some of our work for immigrants, but it was not only that, she was working for the homeless, and women's rights. She isn't that well known yet, but she would have been soon because of her work, and now her disappearance is interrupting all of that."

"Do you have any information on any recent meetings she had or people she had spoken to? And who last saw her and where?"

"Jyoti was always back and forth between here and Vegas. She was in the process of moving here but still had connections in Vegas with this same organization. She helped start the Vegas branch, which was the first of its kind, several years ago. A few years ago, we started outreach to other areas in the Southwest. Phoenix, Reno, Tucson, Flagstaff, New Mexico, Utah. She was an integral part of starting the Phoenix office and wanted to be involved with all the other openings also. This organization combined the best of immigrant support with women's, LGBTQ, and voting rights."

"Yes, I am very familiar. Fantastic organization. Any meetings that you know about recently?"

"She was supposed to return to Vegas last week but delayed it because she was looking into that disappearance that you wrote about. Jyoti knew María because she had volunteered for us periodically. I don't know of any meetings. I last saw her Sunday here at the offices. She texted me Sunday night that she would head back to Vegas on Monday. She didn't show up in Vegas."

"Okay, so she was here at the offices Sunday night?"

"Yes, I think so."

"Do you know if there are security cameras?" Page asked, knowing the answer already.

"Yes, there are. The police never asked about them. There is one here in the front office area, another one in the small warehouse area, and one above the door on the exterior."

"Do you know where the footage is stored?"

240

"I don't know. She never told us." The woman clearly needed a lesson in security and self-awareness.

Paige had learned a thing or two about security cameras from her work on the crime beat the last few years, so she began to scrutinize the camera on the wall of the waiting room. Depending on the make and model, they could have a hard drive recording locally, online storage, or both. "Can I have a look around at the cameras?" There were now a few orange rays of sunlight entering the door, outlining the wires of the camera entering the wall behind the camera. As she traced the wires into the wall, Paige turned around to look for approval

"Go right ahead, sweetie." The woman motioned quietly for the younger girl to leave the room.

Paige always carried a flashlight in her pocket and with little effort discovered that the cameras were connected via cables to a hard drive in a large, locked closet just off the front office. Paige crossed her fingers that the hard drive was not password protected and was connected to a monitor. The assistants quickly located a key that fit the lock and they were in business. She found a chair, sat down at the makeshift table, and turned the power on the monitor which to her surprise, after a few pixelated seconds, was directly displaying the feed from four cameras, not just three. She surmised that one was hidden and from its field of view was able to locate the pinpoint hole in the clock on the wall of the back room.

The playback function was easy to find and, with a simple click on the rewind icon, it didn't take but a few minutes to locate the footage from Sunday night. It appeared from the video that a cot had been positioned in a corner of the back room. Her colleague indicated that she often slept overnight here to save money. Their friend fell asleep alone in the dark building, but that was not the concerning aspect of the video. Watching the video in fast-forward now, there was no activity for several hours except an occasional passing car on the exterior camera feed. Then, at about 4:00 am, outside in the parking lot, a dark-colored car paced back and forth a few times before parking in a dimly lit area down the street, just in front of Jyoti's car.

The two women were aghast at the audacity of these perpetrators as they loitered outside the car and smoked cigarettes, stalking their prey. The budding investigator inside her remarked upon the possible DNA evidence they might find from those cigarette butts. As the early morning light began to produce the first indigo-blue shadows in the street outside, they couldn't help ineffectually whispering, "No!" when Jyoti packed up her belongings and began to walk outside. They could not bear to watch as Jyoti's car was parked a mere few steps from the dark-colored car. The scene played out a good distance from the front door so there was no hope of recognition of the two perpetrators, who also subsequently absconded with her car.

As she located the USB port and reached into her bag for a USB drive, she remarked to her new acquaintance, "We need to copy this and immediately get this to the police. I know someone in the police department, and I also now know someone at the FBI who may be able to help."

She made a few copies and handed one to her new friend and planned her next stop at the FBI office that she had just visited yesterday. The new agent's card was still in her car. She would call after she was on her way.

"Do you have any plastic baggies?" Paige asked.

"Yes, we have some in the kitchenette at the end of that hall!"

Paige grabbed a handful of sealable bags, and as she rushed out the door, she reassured her nervous colleague, "Everything is going to be fine. We are going to find Jyoti. Are you okay? Do you need anything? Do you want to go with me?"

"No, I am going to stay behind and clean up a little. We have a thrift store event that needs to be arranged this week. Now that Jyoti is missing, the logistics will be a challenge for sure. She does everything."

"Well, lock the door for sure. Here is my card. If you see anything else suspicious let me know. And for your safety, be aware of your surroundings. Don't park near any other cars and only walk outside if there are other people around." Paige did not have time for the one-hour personal defense course this woman lacked

The glass door chimed with a small makeshift bell as the door closed. She realized that while it was good to know when someone was entering the little shop, it probably also alerted Jyoti's attackers that she was exiting that fateful night. With her phone on record, she hurried over to the other side of the street where their car was parked and, luckily enough, located several cigarette butts. She scooped each one into separate sealed bags. Seeing no more obvious evidence, other than some recent oil stains on the cement, she made her way to the dusty old Toyota sedan she had purchased used when she first moved to Arizona.

The next twenty minutes flew by in a heartbeat as she frantically raced to the FBI headquarters. On the way, she alerted her new-found federal agent friends to her impending arrival with the shocking evidence. She was greeted in the lobby once again and, exasperated at first, she calmed herself with focused breathing before relaying the timeline of Jyoti's tragic kidnapping to her new contact as they relocated to a small conference room that, with each passing minute filled with several more agents who entered the room with nods of quiet acknowledgment.

"And you are sure they forced her into the car?" asked the agent, redirecting the conversation after the most recent interruption.

"Yes, clear as can be. See for yourself," Paige said, producing one of the baggies that contained her USB drive. "Do you have a laptop we can bring in here? They must have taken her keys and then proceeded to steal her car also."

One of the men swiftly brought a laptop into the room, and within seconds after inserting the USB drive into the slot, the same sordid video was playing out the scene again.

"I have a hunch these cowards are part of the same group we just talked about yesterday." Paige rewound the video to pause on the moment the attackers absconded with Jyoti.

"Wow, this is incredible. And you are saying the police didn't even ask for this evidence?" The regional director of the Domestic Counterintelligence Office could not believe the luck he had stumbled into on his first two days on the job.

"Yes, the volunteers said they spent five minutes there, asking if they knew of any jilted lovers or jealous ex-husbands and left to go to some traffic accident."

One of the agents reassured her, "As luck would have it, our director is flying in this morning and should be here any minute with an entire cavalry to investigate." The statement proved timely, for no sooner had the words been spoken than one of his men opened the door to let in what seemed like the scouting party for a cavalry. Stamos, Point, and Sam walked in with several of their new agents filing in behind them, overflowing the room with more fresh young faces.

The regional director spoke first, "Mr. Stamos, you wouldn't believe what we have here. This is Paige, a local journalist with the Arizona Post. Paige has singlehandedly located an informant who is the wife of a local, rural city council member who seems to be at the center of a conspiracy. The informant is here, on property, right now, sir. And now, this second kidnapping that you don't know much about, Paige was just showing us on a security camera footage. The police here did not investigate at all."

"That is fantastic! Not the kidnapping, but the fact we have some major leads to go on. Paige, you are a brave woman! You are single-handedly saving America, do you know that? Can you help us catch these criminals?" Stamos stood ready and willing to utilize any and all assistance to solve this conspiracy, to the point of involving this young journalist in his investigation.

He stopped to gather his thoughts, as he felt he succeeded in his words to help this informant understand the gravity of her findings and the fact she could help bring these perpetrators to justice. What he had just offered was more of a deputizing than he could authorize, but he also knew that Merlin could yet again provide the cover they required.

"Definitely, I can and will assist with all my abilities," she boldly stated, her powerful brown eyes staring right back into Stamos' as if she had just taken the oath of a U.S. Marine.

"This man over here is Sam Steed, he is head of the security division of Merlin Commerce, which has an investigative unit coming in to help. I would like you to go with him and several of his men to be the eyes and ears, documenting and investigating this conspiracy. It doesn't make sense now, but when you see their setup, it will. All the while you will be under the protective custody of the FBI."

Sam just nodded his head and made his trademark British tip-of-the-hat gesture.

Stamos was more than curious about the new footage. "Who is the victim? Can you play the footage that you have for us?"

The regional director set his fingers in motion and rapidly cued up the relevant portion on the laptop and replayed the gruesome footage in front of them as the assembled crowd leaned in to get an adequate view of the grainy video.

Just as the video ended and all the normally stoic agents were displaying full open-mouthed gasps, in walked Paige's informant Beata Koenig, with a sheepish look on her face as she suddenly noticed all of the eyes that were intensely studying her every move.

The regional director interrupted the stares, "Beata, Beata. I would like you to meet the Director of Domestic Counterintelligence, Sean Stamos. Beata is the other bravest woman in the state of Arizona right now. The information she has given us is shocking and is the most detailed dossier I have ever obtained from an informant. She has a photographic memory and is now in protective custody with our office." He focused his gaze on her for a few seconds with a reassuring expression. "All of her family is safe. But her husband may be looking for her. And his organization may be in a state of alert that is for sure."

Sensing the nervous tension in the room, Stamos arose rapidly from his chair and stood at the front of the room. "Men and women, we have these guys just where we want them, they don't know where Beata is. For all they know she has been kidnapped. We need to capitalize on this information before they act any further and we need to find out who is involved here in the West. And we need to find these women. I would like to set up a SCIF video conference with Atlanta and Merlin to relay this information to them. Overnight, Hanson set up a SCIF in the Merlin facility in Atlanta and we are also setting up a SCIF in their facility here in Phoenix. I want Huy and the digital teams there to hear this. We have deputized most of their team, so to speak, and cleared them for classified compartmentalized information. Also, we are fanning out across the country to take this entire operation down. Our theory is they are merely practicing for a larger operation. Everyone in this room, I need to tell you the Russians are listening to our conversations so radio silence about this mission unless I okay it. That means no phone calls or electronic messaging or even talking about the case outside these rooms."

"What is our next play?" asked the regional director.

"Well, let's get Paige, Beata, and Sam over to their new headquarters. You will be staying at the Merlin headquarters hotel and Beata and Paige also will have accommodations there under guard 24 hours per day."

Sam sensed his turn to give his input on the play, like a lineman calling a secondary play in the huddle, "Our teams will be operational within the hour and fully staffed in the next six hours. First step, establish digital surveillance and drone surveillance within those six hours and reverse trace this car from our only lead. Second step, locate the crime scene from the first disappearance and attempt any tracing from there and field surveillance of any intermediary locations. Third step is to investigate our target local politician and set up surveillance of his location. It appears from Atlanta that their MO is to operate multiple intermediary locations, so we will assess this possibility here as well."

With these marching orders, the men and women excitedly departed for Merlin's second headquarters to supervise the buildout of their new headquarters. As promised, it was a short drive north from the FBI headquarters. Upon entering the hotel, which, as opposed to the swank Sybaritean Collection Hotel in Atlanta, was more of an adobe desert resort north of Phoenix, the group marveled at the rustic Old West opulence of the lobby. The investigators now commanded an entire building of a veritable desert compound with one huge ballroom divided into many rooms perfectly sized for each team.

The centrally located main command center was outfitted with a similar arrangement of monitors as its counterpart in Atlanta and a self-contained SCIF room was presently being erected by FBI workers in the middle of the cavernous ballroom. Paige immediately gravitated toward a set of computer workstations located next to what seemed very apparent to be reserved for the commander-in-charge. Before Sam settled into his commander's chair, which was identical to the gamer's chair that Huy coveted in Atlanta, he provided Paige with the necessary login information and a secure phone for communication. She logged in and glanced around the room at the professional men and women who were slowly filing in through the door. Paige noticed Beata as she peered through the door and, as Sam nodded approvingly, waved her in to join her at a second nearby workstation.

Sam, observing Paige's conspicuous trepidation, reassured her regarding her status on the team, "Both you and Beata are now enlisted to assist with this investigation. You are to have no communication with the outside world for at least the next 48 hours and likely longer. No parents, no siblings, no communication. You will be provided new clothes, no jewelry is allowed, no personal effects whatsoever. The most innocuous items could be bugged, pencils, notebooks, wallets, credit cards. The Russians will be scanning for any unusual calls or texts from anyone involved, especially Beata, and they will be monitoring all of your friends' and families' communications. In about twenty minutes, we will have a system-wide briefing with our Atlanta office, and by that time our SCIF will be set up and we will have our first briefing with the FBI. So, sit tight here, you can see the shared files on the server with Atlanta. Here is a spreadsheet that our journalist friends in Atlanta are compiling along with a map of Georgia, South Carolina, Alabama, and Florida. They were performing a news search of all missing persons and crimes committed and charged. There is some suspicion that these may be connected. Natalia Volkov is the lead of Digital Team 5 there and you will hear her speak during the briefing."

Paige could not believe her ears. "Natalia Volkov? Wow! She is my idol! I have been following her career for the past ten years in New York since I was in high school. She single-handedly saved America, you know. I was in New York just last week..." Paige interrupted herself and thought better of continuing on as she didn't feel appropriate to share that she had just interviewed for her old position with the Journal.

Sam smiled with a knowing grin, "Yes, she is an amazing woman and a talented writer! Keep in mind that all of your communications are set up with a secure VPN spoofed to a location in Sand Butte, Arizona. If you need to spoof any other IP address locations let me know."

As she settled in, Paige immediately began to connect the dots with all the information that Beata had provided, and identically to her counterparts in Atlanta, started a spreadsheet and a tactical map with all of the known Western target locations, beginning with the home and office of the rural Sand Butte city council member. She also imported the spreadsheet that she had already compiled on possible Bens and opened it on one of her screens, showing it to Beata.

Beata pointed to one of the not-so-obvious choices on the spreadsheet with a picture next to the name, "That's the one. The picture looks identical to the man I saw in our driveway the other day."

"That is spectacular, Beata! Hey, Sam!" Paige yelled across the room with regained confidence, "We have our Ben right here, who could be one of the ringleaders. Now we just have to find him and connect all of these dots. He has multiple wild social media aliases, and it will take some sleuthing to connect them to him. It won't take me long to find him though. It looks like he has limited family connections, especially in Idaho. He may be loosely connected to a white supremacist group called American Action Men. This organization makes the KKK look like a book club. It is run by the infamous Rodney Baylor. Let's make him target 3 and pinpoint any known locations on the map."

"We are going to share your map on that monitor up there right next to the Southeast map, so everyone can track the targets. In a few minutes, our drones are going to be airborne. We should begin with Mr. Koenig's home and business locations. In the meantime, find out all you can about this Ben. He may be the lynchpin."

Beata chimed in, "The lynchpin, as Paige knows is Action Man, that is probably Rodney Baylor. You know, they use this social media chat app called Anti Sosh to communicate. I have heard them talking about it."

Paige excitedly interjected, "Yes, I've been on this app. I have a fake persona that I created a few years ago to do some research. I've been looking for our Ben character and your pick was one of my top suspects.

Paige wasted no time bringing up the website. Huy turned to look over her shoulder. "That's a new one. I think we have that one in our database. Before you do anything else, let one of my hackers do some intel on it. We may need to spoof a different IP address before you log on."

Barely two minutes later Beata and Paige would be introduced to the high-tech world that was Merlin Investigations as two pilots marched into the room, exchanged a few words with their commander, and exited with serious soldier's demeanors, each to their own particular cockpit, which were two small offices connected to the command center. Simultaneously, two formerly blank monitors pixelated and focused, first on a patch of striated cement, and then, panning upward, on the inside of an airplane hangar. One by one, five other cameras on each monitor flickered, performing the same focusing exercise. The two pairs of wide eyes marveled at the clarity of the cameras as the drones exited the hangar and gained altitude in the early afternoon desert sky. The orange and tan hues of the landscape appeared different from this height, almost like an antique Western oil painting. Both drones diverged at that time, taking different routes to their targets.

The drone video signals both became a blur of action as they picked up speed over the desert, an occasional speck of green from a golf course or resort interrupting the brown xeriscaped neighborhoods and the vast expanse of North Phoenix. As it did so, Paige and Beata's attention returned to Sam's monitor as he was receiving information from one of the digital teams. From their research it seemed the app was safe but regardless the plan would be to continue to spoof their IP address location to the hometown of this Franc Koenig. With a few tweaks of the location information of their VPN from one of the team members, the two sleuths could now continue their search for their elusive Ben.

At their disposal, there were now four fully-staffed digital divisions in place to match four eager field divisions and the two drone divisions. Sam then set about entering operational commands to reverse-track these victims and any perpetrators they could flush out of the shadows. He commanded and fully trusted his soldiers would bring to him a breakthrough within two hours' time.

With the break in the drone action and some time left before the next briefing, Paige set about filling in the blanks in the life of their new target. With a little direction, Beata now became her talented assistant. Surprisingly, with little prior computer skills, she was learning Paige's internet research secrets quickly. Armed with IP addresses from the seedy alternative social media posts from this Ben character, she and Paige rapidly uncovered some new possible associations with other white supremacist nutcases.

Paige looked toward Beata from her workstation to provide some direction, but found herself learning something new, "I think you just opened up a whole new avenue for us. That user has connections to these other freaks over here."

Beata nodded, not even turning to acknowledge, for on her screen she could see exactly what Paige was talking about, "Right, look at this guy! Published a full manifesto on a pathway to Civil War here on Anti Sosh, overthrowing the government by systematically assassinating political leaders. Crazy stuff. And he is a gun dealer. I would think he would be on the radar as one of the ringleaders. Hopefully, the FBI already has him on theirs too. Then there's this guy. Always seems aloof, but then out of the blue sends some directions to some people. He may be an organizer of some sort. Looks like he is in Utah."

Sam was fascinated by the talent of his newly acquired Digital Team as he scooted his chair closer to the two and leaned over the desk to see their progress. "Yes, great work! Target numbers 4 and 5. But they are in Idaho and Utah. We will need one of these whole other divisions to track those."

It would take less than the two allotted hours to uncover a mountain more than they had discovered in Atlanta in several days.

—❖❖❖❖—

CHAPTER 23: THE FATHER

—❖❖❖❖—

Growing up on a sprawling, yet painfully boring cattle ranch in rural Idaho, Charlie Ritter always knew he would escape the small town and make the move to the big city. He always liked the lights of Las Vegas, the way they dazzled on television, illuminating the non-stop decadence, an oasis in the middle of the desert. With strumming fingers, a musical ear, and a classic rock voice, he was meant to entertain and loved the spotlight. He was not famous by any means, but he could play almost any instrument better than most of the so-called big-name musicians.

To his father's chagrin, while also working the cattle ranch during high school, he was active in his school's band, playing both jazz and orchestra. He mastered several instruments and could have been first chair in any one. While his favorite was the tenor saxophone, his real love was classic rock and, secondarily the blues. He could make guitar strings sing, playing one-man-band solos in monthly assignments for his music teacher, sometimes breaking out the sax for solos in between the riffs and vocals. The very minute he graduated, the old blue Monte Carlo with a white canvas top he had bought with his savings pointed South on Highway 95 and it didn't stop until he hit Reno. A few small gigs satisfied his musical itch in Reno for a time but soon decided not to let Vegas wait for his unique brand of music any longer.

After years of a non-stop schedule from margarita brunches and lunch-hour internet cafes to several-hour-long sets at various casinos and jazz clubs, Charlie had done well enough to afford a gigantic warehouse studio with a loft apartment just off Charleston Boulevard in the heart of the arts district of Vegas. This year, for the first time in his creative life, he chanced upon a set of soulmates he could collaborate with as a jazz band. In no small part due to his efforts, Vegas was becoming a melting pot of risk-taking individuals with creativity that could easily match that of Memphis and New Orleans. One of those kindred spirits was a muse that quickly became his confidante, a perfect puzzle piece dovetailing of his and her minds in a musical mesh of consciousness. From the moment of their introduction, he realized deep in his soul that his days of being a one-man band were officially over. Her melodious Trinidadian voice combined with her positive energy reeled him in like a siren on the open sands of this desert ocean. And his own grounded creative energy soothed her desperate need for a calming influence in this crazy town.

His life couldn't have been more perfectly in harmony with the underground creative scene in this eclectic Charleston Boulevard neighborhood. His studio had become the heart and soul of this community as the warehouse typically hosted a menagerie of characters each and every day. However, this unfortunate weekend, an unwelcome interruption in the harmony swept into town with menacing clouds of black aura. Uncharacteristically, Charlie's father was in town visiting on some supposed business excuse. It didn't seem to make much sense to Charlie, but his father had started to sell his cattle on the distant outskirts of Reno and Las Vegas instead of locally in Idaho.

Sitting on opposite velvet-red couches in the expansive loft with ultra-high ceilings, the two were locked in their prehistoric battle of wills. This unwelcome guest from Charlie's Paleozoic era, predating what seemed like eons from his childhood escape to freedom, stood once again as a resurrected antithesis to his newfound life. They had hardly spoken once or twice since his youth and Charlie was happy to keep it that way. Not many words had been spoken between them since his father's arrival at his door that week. Guitars, art-deco nudes, and the neon light outlines of cacti and desert frescoes lit up the room in pink, red, and yellow tones, hanging in stark contrast to the whitewashed brick walls and black cast-iron pipes and ducts in the ceiling. Charlie couldn't help but notice that the skin tone of his father seemed a little grotesque in this light, his reddened face a tincture of maybe Satan himself.

"I'll be here a few times this summer, and even more in the fall. It's costing me a pretty penny with gas prices the way they are, but my cattle from the northern lands can demand more money down here with the drought hitting heavy here and in California." His father was always trying to strike deals, but Charlie didn't believe it for a second. There was something not right about his father's new-found attraction to the city. In a now-distant past life in Idaho, he and his father had never agreed on most things existential, the latter placing undue importance on land over neighbors, race over humanity, intolerance over kindness, and physical work over intellectual thoughtfulness. Frankly, at the time he had become more and more embarrassed by his father, and this fateful evening in Vegas, the father-son conflict was heightened by the distance Charlie and his new life had evolved since those days. The almost elderly man, from a young age, had immersed himself in divisive local politics of immigration and government interference, which stood at odds with his son's creative, open mind. Charlie had not thought of it much since he took the liberating path out of his birthplace.

"Well, I guess there's one good thing coming from global warming. You can't sell your cattle to anyone, and you can't find them water. Even Vegas, the land of decadence, is rotating away from meat," Charlie sarcastically commented. "The only market for meat here is in the casinos. The price is not any better here."

"You know that's just a bunch of bull larkey. Been droughts for centuries in these parts. It's a desert for fuck's sake."

"Well, Lake Mead is dried up, and it's been full since the 1930s. Longer than you've been alive. There's no escaping the drought for your way of living."

Not to be outdone in the battle of intolerance, Mr. Ritter retorted, "It's all the Yankees flocking to Vegas and crowding this city that's using it all up. Using more water to water one lawn than a hundred head of cattle can drink. That's your problem here in these parts." His father's point was somewhat valid, but Charlie's will would not bend.

"So how long are you here this week? I have a string of shows coming up here and in Reno. Flying to L.A. next weekend to do some recording. Before that, I'm headlining a get-out-the-vote concert before the start of the election season."

"I imagine I won't be here but a few more days. I have bigger fish to fry. This election is the most important one in my lifetime. I will call you when I am back. You're not still hung up on democracy, are you? They keep stealing elections in this state. You should stop with your support of your so-called friends. They are dangerous."

"I have to do my part, since some of the powers that be are making it harder to vote, closing polling stations in the African American sections of town. Those are my true friends. But we have our volunteer buses to oppose the bigotry."

At this point, his father was staring blankly at the large monitor hanging on the white brick wall, overlooking the warehouse, which was playing random music videos. Charlie was not sure if he was daydreaming, but then something in the rap music video must have awakened his father's subconscious. Seemingly unprovoked, from the depths, out it came. It was never unexpected given his history of racist tomes and rants, but this time it was more direct than usual. He always had a knack for using the N-word as much as possible during casual conversation, but this was different. After his father said the sentence, Charlie repeated it a few times more in his mind, trying to edit the grotesque word out of the sentence and inserting the equally egregious abbreviation that he also would have expected from his father, "Well, they gotta keep those N-words down somehow." Repeating it with the abbreviated vulgarity did not diminish its horrible meaning.

As the shocking realization of what his father had just uttered sunk in, Charlie's heart sunk to the floor with a thud. He still had some vestigial respect for his father as the patriarch of the family and everything he and all of his siblings possessed growing up was directly the result of his grandfather's business success that started in the 1960s, and with one word, that was now erased for good. Certainly, Charlie had heard others in Idaho repeat the epithet, and both his parents had made racially insensitive comments before, but his father's racist bigotry clearly was hitting a crescendo of sorts. Memory was not his father's strong suit, or perhaps it was more of a convenient purposeful neglect to prevent the contradiction between his white bread ethos and his son's current chosen lifestyle. His father seemed to block out the entirety of Charlie's present and future reality. Charlie's muse, Jasmine, the love of his life, and Trinidadian inspiration, promoted more harmony in his life than any love of land, money, and power could, and perhaps that bothered his father beyond all imagination.

As if by divine providence, the door to the apartment opened, pouring illuminating rays of light from the hallway into the dimly lit room. Jasmine always did have a way of lighting up any room in Charlie's eyes, no matter the mood, and tonight was no different. As if shot from a cannon, Charlie leapt from his seat, almost tripping over the rug in his eagerness to greet the love of his life. She was the one thing that could shield him from the negativity invading this sanctuary. Craving a reprieve from his father, Charlie prayed this would be the clue for him to leave.

As if on cue, "Well, I had best be going, I have a long road ahead of me to get out of town." His father was never good at goodbyes. Charlie and Jasmine stood silently in a half-embrace, their light in stark contrast to the darkness on the other side of the room. Jasmine, her demure, yet resolute presence doing its best to combat the hostility, stood tall and girded her shoulders as if expecting a fight. Not even a side hug, just a cursory wave as he navigated his exit, stumbling his way around the guitars, piano, and couches. Just like that, the pitiful existence of a father was out the door.

As it shut with a metallic thud, Charlie stealthily made his way to the crack in the heavy steel opening to hear the elevator as it descended, then peered out the hallway window to be sure he had exited the courtyard. Upon re-entering, Charlie let out a deep sigh as he felt the remaining evil leave through the tilt windows set high on the brick walls. He sank deep down into the couch beside Jasmine. "Oh, my god. That man is living in the past. And the world is passing him by. He keeps lashing out as though someone is doing him wrong when he is making a good living. I just hope as he gets even older and more out of touch that he doesn't do something brash. He has so much anger pent up inside. I'm glad you weren't here to witness any of this."

"Well, I try to stay as far away from that man as I can, for my own balance. Ben Ritter is no good to nobody. I can't let that tortured soul's negativity invade my harmony. Discard these events and let's replace them with thoughts of tomorrow." Jasmine let out her own deep breath, releasing the negative air to be carried away on the night wind, while drawing her love closer to her neck, kissing his forehead gently.

Feeling secure in her thin, yet muscular arms, Charlie closed his eyes for a moment, drawing from her positive energy. "I don't blame you for doing what you are doing for your own health. Maintain your safe distance. I just can't figure out what he is doing here and why he has recently turned his attention to Phoenix. I don't trust him as far as I can throw him, and we need to set boundaries. No more unlocked doors, and I just installed security cameras for the first time ever here at the Muse Compendium. I am certain that he didn't even notice them. He has no personal awareness of his surroundings or the feelings of anyone around him.

He seems so self-involved. Turned inward, yet focused on some external perceived demons."

Jasmine looked up at the industrial ceiling and sighed, "There are rumors in our sphere that he is up to no good. Yesterday, Tommy said he thought he saw him on the news at that white supremacist rally, lurking in the background. I think he is recruiting and expanding his sleazy organization. Tommy even asked me if we wanted to have his friends in the FBI do some checking up on him."

"Maybe we should, if anything for our own safety and that of all our muses. We have a lot invested in this community and if he negatively impacts the sphere with his kind of hate, it could all fall apart. At the same time, just agreeing to the investigation introduces negativity." It was Charlie's turn to exhale the demons, replacing them with contemplation of self-merging with the universe.

Jasmine struck a conciliatory tone, "You know Tommy. I trust his aura enough to not allow the negative into the sphere. Let's trust in him and discard today. We can simultaneously avoid the negativity, yet still be prepared to defend our community."

Charlie agreed, "Okay, baby. Let's sleep on it. We have a busy day of music tomorrow." The two had planned an entire festival of sorts on their sound stage. No audience. Just participants. It was the beginning of an entire year of get-out-the-vote concerts around the city. A beautiful, full day of jamming creativity, overflowing with love yet infused with the necessary urgency and inspiration for a battle at the ballot against evil and hate. The day would be a dress rehearsal and inspirational retreat, combining their talents in defense of their rights. Thank goodness his father was leaving.

The couple continued their embrace for a few minutes longer, basking in the nurturing neon glow of their symbiotic sanctuary. Despite her words of encouragement, Jasmine was not entirely convinced the negativity would remain outside their sphere. However, she recognized the power of positive thinking could overcome evil if combined with a steely resolve.

"We got this, my love. Don't worry. The sphere will protect us, but we need to be vigilant. It's okay to build a wall, set boundaries, and then protect those boundaries. Physical force against us can be met with physical force in defense and still be positive. War can be met with war if that is what he is bringing to us and our kind."

The words penetrated Charlie's soul like a jackhammer, releasing a hidden element of his will. While his grit and determination were as strong as an ox regarding advancing his career and harnessing the musical talent of others, it was not used to fighting for those he loved. "True. I think Tommy and our entire community are ready. The events of the past few years have awakened our resolve against hate, and we now appreciate what that hate is capable of doing if we don't defend our own. We can mobilize kindness against hate, while at the same time marshaling our active resistance."

What they would soon discover would test their resolve and endanger their close-knit community. It would hit closer to home than either of them would have expected. Was their heretofore naive organization ready for the battles ahead?

—•}} {{•—

CHAPTER 24:
WITHIN | CONSPIRACY | WITHOUT

—•}} {{•—

The historical implications of the shocking revelations of the past 24 hours were not lost on any of the Merlin investigators or the FBI agents as they huddled into the four SCIFs at the two FBI offices, the Sybaritean Collection Hotel in midtown Atlanta and the Phoenix Sonoran Desert Resort in North Phoenix. Sean Stamos and Steven Point were careful not to divulge sources or intelligence from the server that could provide the breakthrough they needed any minute now. The most he would reveal was they had a source that could pinpoint their adversaries soon. As of yet, a few security clearances still needed to be obtained. Until this point, only the top leadership of Merlin was privy to more of this information.

Stamos sat at the head table of the Georgia FBI SCIF, his eyes analyzing those of his team, searching for any weaknesses in his team. An army was only as strong as its weakest link and the toughness of those links always needed to be assessed before battle. On the video screen was a view of the other three units, their focus appeared resolute.

"In due time folks. Hanson here says that we can be fully transparent about our source by this time tomorrow. In the meantime, we are working these sources and we just have to wait until they slip up. In addition, boots are hitting the ground for possible confrontation and close surveillance." Stamos stood up to address the men, for he had called this meeting about just that. "We need to know the strengths and weaknesses of our enemies. And we can't do that from afar or from four hundred feet in the air. But..." Stamos paused for more than just a few moments as he sternly looked each one of the men in the eye.

He was acutely and painfully aware of the methods that would be necessary to remedy the lack of physical evidence. The FBI Domestic Counterintelligence teams already had over 200 agents in four districts that would be fighting this fight. Bringing in the Criminal Division would bring that total to a much more comfortable number.

But what size of army would be necessary, God only knew. Were they standing at the precipice of a Civil War with the Russians aiding from afar? How many were their enemy? The full accounting of that number was key to defining their enemy and how extensive this battle would turn out to be. Before launching an entire counteroffensive, Stamos needed to know this numerator of the risk he was taking on. The Russian adversary was heavily armed and they had proven that they were willing to take down the entire United States based on their past attack on the financial system and on our elections before that. It also began to dawn on him that these many combatants were continuing to arm themselves and often quoted the Second Amendment not in terms of their ability to hunt or target practice but in their so-called overthrow of tyranny. However, the ancient quote in reverse held that one man's tyranny could be another man's liberty. If a man's sole definition of tyranny and the raison de guerre for overthrowing the government is another man's (or woman's) equal opportunity, then the first man is the true tyrant.

Stamos was not about to find out how far a Civil War would go without putting an end to the Russian tactics. However, an aggressive chess move by his team too early in the match against his fellow citizens could just provide moral justification to his enemy for that same Civil War. He surely would find it necessary to tread lightly and concentrate on the communications from the Russians until there was sufficient evidence of a conspiracy of illegal activity. It would not be enough just to show there were kidnappings, murders, and fraud occurring, but a full-on conspiracy to commit these crimes. Otherwise, the leaders of the adversary could use their favorite slogan, "Do Not Tread On Me" legitimately.

Stamos was pacing the front of the SCIF, waiting for the right words to reach his tongue, for this was the moment he relished. The call to arms, the inspirational launch, when a mission was on the brink of fruition, and all that was missing was the locomotion of a well-oiled machine. That was his specialty. He had always dubbed himself a leader of men in his past missions, though he had never led so many men on such a momentous mission. As the group settled in and the spark of command percolated to the fore of his mind, he wrote two words on the board at the front of the SCIF. The first "Within", the second "Conspiracy", and the third "Without", one above the other.

"Men, I don't think I need to tell you the incredible importance of getting this mission right from the get-go. There is absolutely no room for error." Stamos began as he pointed at the words with emphasis, underlined them, and then repeated the words over and over. "Within, Conspiracy, Without. It is not enough here that we find evidence of crimes. We believe that there are at least dozens if not hundreds of individuals working, with aid from and at the direction of the Russian government. We are THIS close to having that evidence. Communication of that aid and direction among any of these participants is what we await before tipping our hand. That is not to say when we find evidence of crimes and locations of any victims that we will not act. Far from it. If we find a location where they are holding even one individual, we will move in. We do have evidence that they may be aided by certain law enforcement individuals. We have an enemy from within and one from without acting in concert here. They appear to be loosely organized and careless but don't underestimate their proclivity for violence. We have already discovered this the hard way. But make no mistake, we will take them down."

With that, he crossed over to the other side of the room, held his arms to the side of this two-tone sport coat, and spoke once more. "We have an incredible team here assembled between the FBI and Merlin and we are going to use every means at our disposal to that end. We have incredible technology that we do not have on a daily basis. Thanks to Merlin, we are bringing drone tracking technology to this investigation as most of you already know."

"A month ago, I would never have imagined we would need such surveillance tactics on some of our own people to prevent them from attacking American citizens. I assure you that all safeguards will be taken so as not to spy on our own innocent citizens. I hold the Constitution close to my heart and with the highest regard. Only probable cause wins, and we will be obtaining warrants for all surveillance, if anyone sees any surveillance without probable cause or any abrogation of our enemy's Constitutional rights, let me know immediately. But you need to search your soul right now, whether you are ready for this battle. Are you prepared to meet your own citizens head-on in conflict to protect someone's rights? I see nodding and I see the strength in each of your wills. So now, let's get this started. Sam, I hear you have a lot of information for us from Phoenix."

Sam cleared his throat, adjusted the microphone on the desk of the SCIF conference room, and spoke, at first a little too loudly, with a little feedback on the line, "Understood. Thanks, everyone for all of your efforts, and we are thankful to the FBI for everything that you do. We are here today to discuss these new findings that appear to have taxed our present resources. This appears to be a much larger conspiracy than we first thought. And it clearly possesses international intrigue and national security implications. We both have our intrinsic strengths and weaknesses. Merlin has some technological capabilities currently that the FBI lacks, but we

264

are not a legal law enforcement entity, and the FBI possesses the all-important subpoena powers. The FBI, as a legal law enforcement entity, sometimes has its hands tied. This is why we think this partnership is a formidable one to fight this particular battle against internal and external foes just like almost two years ago in the financial crisis."

Sam could tell that Stamos was eager once again to put his two cents in at this point and paused to give him a chance to speak. Stamos had continued his pacing but halted and was facing the camera with his arms crossed. He released his right hand upward with his index pointed to the sky, with his head tilted downward in a deliberate gaze at those he commanded. "Indeed, what the Merlin units have discovered in a short time already eclipses what we could have uncovered in weeks. I love your drone units and your field units are comparable to our FBI units, maybe better because of the combat readiness some of your guys exhibit. Some of our FBI Academy recruits are just out of college and may be physically prepared, but they have bare minimum tactical training. But you have to be careful about the lack of legal authority. I think we need to tread lightly in this area. You can't get your nose too far over your feet in this endeavor."

Natalia interrupted from the Sybaritean Merlin headquarters. She and Chip and Huy sat at the head table, equal leaders of their team, and the camera zoomed in on her as she spoke, "Exactly, this is where we actually are superior in some ways before we have all the evidence. Chip, Sam, and I talked this morning, and we are willing to bring in almost all of our world security units that are idle. A total of 200 divisions of between 40 and 100 men each. We are going to need these men to investigate who is in harm's way and protect them. We need to be in Arizona, Nevada, Utah, Pennsylvania, Michigan, Wisconsin, Georgia, Florida, and beyond. We need to find these extremists now. If we don't stop them, they will kidnap, kill, and who knows what else to who knows how many people. We need something outside of the walls of government to investigate these people."

Stamos held his right hand to his chin, nodding, "Yes, I

agree. We have taken some of what we found to the police, and they have dismissed it. We will soon need to involve the President and the FBI Director. However, I think we need a little more proof of what is behind this and all of the actors. As you know we have some behind-the-scenes information that we cannot divulge, and we will in due time. We are waiting for this information to present itself more clearly. And Samantha, Sage, and Claire, we are not hiding something that would find any of our missing friends. It is the method of communication among some different groups that we haven't cracked yet completely but I assure you we are almost there. We think the threat and the communications are going to declare themselves in the next week. This mission has full approval of the director."

Sam pounded his fist on the table in Arizona. "So, it's decided. We have begun mobilizing our units. We are only involving US and UK citizens in this investigation to keep it clean. We are going to oversee four or five divisions at the start, expanding to eight by the end of the week. The second division is Phoenix, then Detroit, then Pennsylvania, Ohio, Las Vegas, Salt Lake City, and Miami. These will be set up in the next few days. We have enough drones right now for these first eight divisions. Another twenty divisions without drone support next week."

Claire, who was equally excited about the spread of the investigation to a national level, brought the lofty talk back down to ground level. "But we haven't found Mía yet. This is all well and good that we know what these people are up to, but we don't yet know where they have taken Mía. That needs to be first and foremost on our minds. Can we talk about this for a minute? We still haven't cracked this first organization in Georgia yet. Where do they meet? If they have Mía alive somewhere, where is it, and is it in one of these farmsteads? Maybe they have more than one intermediary house. Maybe they are communicating without meeting. On some social media channel perhaps."

Point, sensing the angst and anxiety, politely interrupted, "You are absolutely correct. And we have Arizona kidnap-

266

ping victims as well. We are using our electronic surveillance of messaging platforms and ARTI, which is our artificial intelligence surveillance algorithm, is picking up some chatter. We are moving forward with subpoenas to conduct more pointed surveillance of these messaging apps, which is I think where they are hiding. We have Sean's teams working on this and we can use subpoena power for this. All we are saying is that the large divisions that we at the FBI and Sam at Merlin have should be deployed as quickly as possible in as many places as possible to be ready for when we crack this code. They are planning something, and we need to be there to stop it. The people we are tracking on our end don't do anything small-time, they work on massive scales to impact whole countries. That's all I will say about that. We think that these few kidnappings are just practice rounds and are not yet at the direction of our old adversaries. We must uncover as much of their organization before the real plot begins."

He didn't need to say who he was talking about, as everyone in attendance knew the massive plot that Point and the present company succeeded in terminating only a few short years back.

Natalia rose from her table and put her arms on first Samantha's, then Sage's shoulders, and began slowly, "I agree, we will keep working as quickly as possible to find Mía. That is goal number one. We will find her shortly. In the next 48 hours, we will further activate the field units in Georgia along with these other locations and obtain some boots-on-the-ground surveillance to discover the hideouts and any victims they are holding."

Sage had not spoken a word in the past several hours with her face buried in her computer monitor, painstakingly sifting through pages and pages of news stories and helping to build a dossier on this organization. But, with Natalia's arm on her shoulder providing some encouragement, now was the time, "Yes, please. We need to find Mía. The answer is somewhere in these farms in these backwoods areas that we have found. We need to get more aggressive in the physical search of these locations. I understand it is likely a dangerous proposition."

Sam also sought to assuage the situation the best he could. "You are right, we will increase, right Torey? With the units I bring in this week, we will start our incursions. No more hiding at drone height. It's time to get in the trenches. We will find Mía, but we need to be careful and methodical in our quest."

Natalia brought up a good point, "Not to change the subject, but what I want to know also is where else in Georgia are they working? There could be other bases that are equally important. I am sure there are some pockets of this extremist group in the small towns near Savannah and Macon. In some of these places, the police will turn a blind eye even more than they are in Atlanta. At least the police in Atlanta were a little accommodating when we began the investigation."

The rest of the meeting would prove fruitful as the subject changed to a briefing of all that was known about every target, their victims, and tactics. The clear pattern emerging was certainly one of incompetence, yet if their adversaries perfected this modus operandi, it could be virtually indistinguishable from random kidnappings and murders. Fortunately for the rule of law, technology would not allow for this feigned randomness to go undetected.

"Our big break," Natalia started, paused, then restarted with emphasis, "THE breakthrough is coming soon. I can feel it. When you are looking for a needle in a haystack, it is much easier if there are dozens of needles and you have hundreds of people looking. Each of these needles will lead us to another needle and the needles to the tailor, the leader of this plot."

Stamos concurred, "Increased manpower, increased technology, and moving closer to the subject, getting in their faces will bring more to light shortly. This week. We will find Mía and we will find María and Jyoti. This week. So let's end this briefing and get back to work."

Natalia meandered to the back of the SCIF as if to get

a bigger perspective and clear her mind. There was by far more confidence in the outcome in this room than there was just a few days ago. She could not help but feel, though, that those needles they were looking for could also inflict damage to the inquisitors and others as their crimes were uncovered. Such were the consequences of warfare, which was where they were headed, right? She needed a break.

Everyone needed a stretch before putting their nose back to the grindstone. Torey, Chip, and Natalia stood up and exited the SCIF, each exhaling the stress as they glanced at each other with confident, yet anxious looks. Outside the conference center, at the end of the wide third-floor lobby, sunlight was streaming in hazy beams in a welcoming sight. The three made a beeline directly to the floor-to-ceiling window to soak up as much sunlight as possible. The crew at the Sybaritean had utilized this well-lit refuge as a place to stretch and release some anxiety that accumulated in the conference rooms inside. As they stopped to gaze up at the warming light, all in attendance knew that only vague generalities could be spoken here as the massive window provided a direct view of the parking garage on the other side of the street.

"This is going to be even more challenging than our last escapade for sure," Natalia whispered as she breathed in for measure, and slowly exhaled, stretching her arms above her head, almost touching the blue expanse above.

Torey agreed, "You are not wrong about that. We will need to tread lightly on the Constitution as we are not allowed to spy on our own unless they are committing a crime. We will have all the probable cause we need for every perpetrator soon." As Torey also finished a few stretches, he thought better of their open conversation. "Let's head back in and finish this job."

"Right. You can never be too careful, even with generalities." Natalia, in a slow circular motion, brought her hands around to her sides and clasped them behind her back in one last stretch under the illuminating sun.

As they re-entered their protective enclave within the Sybaritean Collection Hotel, Natalia felt more comfortable speaking her mind. The three joined Huy at his command post, and as they watched more drone footage unfolding live before them, there was a sense of accomplishment that washed over all of them. A few short days ago, they had nothing and now they were in full pursuit of multiple targets. The big picture was still haunting Natalia.

"Where is this headed? A full-scale proxy war on our own soil? They will be using our own citizens against us!" Natalia exclaimed.

Chip peered deep into the concern that was furrowing her eyebrow, and focused on her feelings, "That could be where this is headed. I would bet that will be what the Russian master plan dictates. I feel your concern. We need to be ready for this battle. You and I are entering this with our eyes wide open. It could get a whole lot messier than the last one though. With the team we have assembled, we will not fail."

"You are right. But, 'we will not fail' is in the negative. We need to refocus on the positive. We will succeed and win this battle! We are strong!"

CHAPTER 25: GEORGIA CLAY

The call appeared on the screen of Hanson's cell phone as he was sitting at the FBI command room in Atlanta talking with Randy and several of the junior agents. Sean Stamos was also conversing with some other junior agents in the central common area. Upon seeing the caller ID, he jumped up from his chair, placing the phone in the center of the conference table. He activated the recording device in the room. He answered, immediately switching the phone to speaker mode.

Hanson stood at the head of the table, and answered with a short one-word greeting, careful not to sound too much like the Fed that he was.

The response was muted, almost a whisper, "Can we meet in Atlanta? I have some information for you that could help your investigation."

"Wow," Hanson thought. He confirmed the voice was indeed Ricky, their informant in the Georgia Militia, calling from the burner phone they had given him. He must have something momentous to initiate contact. They weren't expecting this source to mature for a week or more. In the world of informants, as the saying went, it was like watching paint dry. These inside individuals usually were not motivated to give information unless they were in danger or the stakes were high.

Hanson immediately jumped up, ran to the door, and motioned almost frantically for Stamos to come into the conference room. Luckily, from where Stamos was standing, facing the conference room, he could see the commotion and had already begun to make his way toward the door.

As Stamos entered the room, Hanson stumbled to find his words, as he was not accustomed to talking with informants. "Why... yes, definitely. Where do you want to meet?"

"It will need to be somewhere private. I can't be too careful. I will need to park somewhere and leave my phone."

Stamos sensed the hesitancy. With the phone on mute, he directed, "Have him meet us at the Maker Hotel which is across the street from the Merlin command center hotel. There is a parking garage and shopping center nearby and we can talk in one of the conference rooms. We will have Torey and Natalia there to help." Natalia could provide the feminine touch to make their informant more comfortable.

Hanson began slowly, "Okay, we are thinking of the Maker Hotel. There is a shopping center and parking garage connected to the hotel. Leave your phone in the car, walk into the shopping center, then out the exit on the other side, cross the sky bridge into the hotel, and we will meet you on the second floor of the hotel at the top of the escalator."

The response was even more faint as Stamos strained to listen, turning up the volume on the speaker. "Okay, since tomorrow is Friday, I can get away as though I am going shopping. I will see you there at 1 pm."

"Perfect. Looking forward to hearing what you have for us. Turn the burner phone off and bring it with you to leave in your car too. You don't want someone finding it and then calling this number. Delete the number from the history as soon as you hang up."

"I will," was the short answer from their nervous source on the other end.

272

Hanson pressed the hang-up button on his phone and raised his eyebrows. "Wow, I can't wait to see what this is. We desperately need something to break in this case. And I mean NOW!"

"We can't be too desperate," Stamos could perceive the entire team was indeed desperate, but they could not compromise the entire operation for one informant. "Desperate is when preparation is overlooked, and big warning signs are missed. Don't be too eager. But, good Lord, do we have to wait until tomorrow? I am going to be pacing this building for the next 24 hours nonstop. He didn't give a hint as to what it was?"

"No, just said he had some information."

"I am going over to the Merlin headquarters. We need to be ready for tomorrow. I also want to monitor their surveillance and their field units for the first incursion tonight. Need to make sure this is not a trap. On the way over, can you arrange a room and a conference room there? We can also surveil this area from the Sybaritean and then we need to track this guy on his way in and after he leaves."

As Stamos and Hanson exited the FBI building that evening, he took a right into the Emory Hills neighborhood instead of going straight to the hotel. It was a 2-minute detour, past the target houses and out the other end. Pretty nondescript, partially built neighborhood. Pretty good cover for their adversary, he gave them that. At the other end of the neighborhood, they came to a main thoroughfare. Scanning the intersection, he spied the field team in a hotel parking lot, nestled among all the other cars facing toward the intersection. Even better cover. The only reason he knew they were the field team was that he knew exactly the make and model of their Suburbans and their approximate location.

Taking the long route through the tree-lined neighborhoods, the pair arrived at the Sybaritean Hotel as twilight was casting pink and purple shadows among the modern edifices of the bustling mini-metropolis known to the hip youngsters as midtown Atlanta. As he and Hanson entered the conference room area, they arrived just in time to catch the ladies, Natalia, Samantha, Sage, and Claire quickly entering the command center. Hastening his stride to catch up with them, he barely grasped the door handle before it closed.

His eyes caught Claire's and, as usual, his entire being melted like chocolate on an Atlanta sidewalk. As if suddenly transported back to his teenage years in Maine, he knew he could easily get lost in the mystique of her green eyes. Encouragingly, he sensed her eyes lighting up as soon as hers met his. She had such a positive vibe to her persona. And that smile. He knew that she still felt something for him. Maybe it was time to see if they still had that spark. He knew the answer, didn't he? But how to broach the subject? Then he looked up at the drone board and could see the dark indigo outline of a field and a farmstead in the North Georgia twilight. Don't be distracted. The mission.

Huy interrupted Stamos' thoughts just in time. "It's just about dark thirty. We've circled the entire property with the drone. No IR cameras. Not a person in the house. They seem to have been gone for quite some time. This is target number one. We are going to install some surveillance devices. Half the team is looking for any sign of Mía in the outbuildings. Your guys are embedded in our field team."

"We're just here to assist. Nothing to see here." Stamos played coy.

As the men entered the main house, the video feeds in green night vision flashed on the screens to the right with images of time-worn wooden steps with only a few remnants of white paint at the edges. A screen door in similar disrepair was met by an outstretched, black-gloved hand and promptly creaked open. In seconds all of the body cameras showed an interior devoid of furniture and any signs of occupancy. On the audio feed, they could hear, "No alarm system. No trips. No infrared signals. Three up, three down, three main. Weapons drawn." Three video feeds showed the progression of the upstairs and basement teams, showing a pretty bland scene without any findings. No electronic equipment to bug. By all appearances, this was a completely abandoned farmhouse.

Then the audio from another team, "Outbuilding A, large stone barn, two stories. A lot of digging equipment, shovels. Fresh red dirt. A few pickups, a tractor, and a backhoe. Tracks and red dirt leading to the rear door and outside."

Everyone's heart skipped a beat and then fell to the floor as they witnessed the same on the green bodycam video screen. Not what they wanted to hear at this stage of the game.

Huy turned on his comms, "Field Team 4 do you copy?"

"Field Team 4, Copy. Exiting the main house now."

Huy commanded, "After searching the main house, search behind the outbuildings. We need to look for digging sites. Follow the tracks from that backhoe."

After a few minutes of video of several men walking out the door of the house and down the old wooden steps, all of those at the command center observed the horrifying scene as they walked past the barn, which sat at the edge of a preserve of tall oak trees and thick brush leading down a steep ravine. They could not believe their eyes, as they saw some well-worn larger backhoe tracks leading into the ravine. Stamos, for his part, wished he was there in person to witness this spectacle. He glanced over at Claire and Sage, whose eyes could not have been wider in suspense to find out what was at the end of this path.

From the speakers, the commands continued, "Searching down this ravine. Two teams down, Two teams secure the egress. Weapons drawn. Everyone stay off the path in the brush to the side. No footprints."

The path into the ravine crossed a small stream and looked to enter a field beyond. Nothing sinister yet. As directed, the combat-trained soldiers were careful not to walk on the path to avoid making footprints. As they approached a clearing, they could see an expansive field planted with fully grown cotton and tire tracks leading along the edge of the wooded ravine. About fifty yards down, they came across what they had suspected they would find. Alongside a pile of torn-up brush was a large pile of red Georgia soil and a deep rectangular hole dug along the edge of the field, half-hidden by the trees. The twenty-foot-high pile of Georgia clay was relatively fresh and sticky.

From the field team, "This hole is approximately sixty feet long by 10 feet wide, ten feet deep. No other tire tracks lead from here. There are a lot of footprints inside the hole. It does not appear to have anything buried within it."

Huy swallowed hard, then, "Okay, make sure the area is secured then take lots of pictures. Take the next 30 seconds for pictures. Drone Team 4, I want IR pictures from above and I want a search along that entire field. I want to return here in the morning, and every evening and morning from now on and take drone pictures. I want to know about any changes to this hole. I want to know about anyone entering or leaving this ravine. I'm not sure how we missed this. It's tucked up against the forest edge, easy to hide in the foliage, I guess."

"Make no tracks in the dirt around the area. Don't step into the field. This is probably an abandoned farmstead that they have taken over for this purpose, but the cotton field is active. We need to find all other such locations. All teams on comms, take note of findings at our next incursion."

"Briefing in 30 minutes. We will egress in the next 10 minutes. Drone Team 4 you have 10 minutes to scan the fields in this 40 acres north of this ravine, which is the northern boundary of this farm. Then return to the egress point to secure the egress."

"Copy that."

Stamos turned towards Hanson, who was still standing at the back of the pack, "All we have is a large hole. That's not going to get us much. Who is the owner of this farm? Get as much information on all other properties owned by this individual and all individuals who own nearby farms."

It was still early in the evening, as the egress was accomplished uneventfully, the drone remained behind at 1200 feet in a hover.

"Good first incursion. Now we know what to look for.

They aren't going to be digging any holes out in the open where we can easily see them with drones or satellites." Huy began the briefing with the usual introductions between Atlanta and Arizona. "Later tonight and tomorrow evening we expand the incursions. We have a few more sites to visit tonight."

The next few hours flew by quickly as the field teams explored two other similarly situated abandoned farmsteads that surprisingly had no security, no cameras, and were not even locked. Each of these locations possessed almost identical equipment and dig sites, out of sight, away from the main road, except both of these excavations were created under the canopy of the forest instead of at the edge.

As the mission suspended for the night, Stamos let out a huge breath of relief that there were no new victims identified, but they still had not found Mía. He put his hand on Natalia's shoulder, "Well, it seems these perps are planning something big to have these sites. Imminent, I would say. No reason to dig these holes for some future use if summer rains would just wash them away within a few weeks."

"Correct, I can't even fathom how many victims those would even hold." Natalia's teeth clenched as her vivid imagination was running wild with the calculations.

His brow furrowing and a grimace appearing across his face, Stamos could. "I've seen something like this in Syria just a decade ago. Hundreds in each one, I would guess, out in the open though. Horrifying to see it here in this country."

"Hopefully we don't have to see it. We need to stop this before they can take even one more victim." Claire's disgust could not be hidden one bit as she stood up from her workstation and walked over to Sage, placing her hand on her shoulder.

"We will. We are hot on their trail. And they don't seem to have a lick of intelligence." Stamos paused, looking over at Claire, who was busy comforting Sage and Samantha. The mission. He turned back toward Natalia, "Well, we have an exciting day in store tomorrow. We have our informant coming in. He tells us he has some information.

277

Can't wait to see what it is. Hopefully, it breaks this investigation wide open. I need to get some shuteye so we can prep the operation in the morning."

"Okay, it is late. I'm exhausted," Claire briefly rubbed her eyes with her fingers, detecting the sleep that was soon coming and she desperately needed. Her curiosity about the informant finally rose to her consciousness. As she reopened her eyes, she caught her old friend gazing at her from across the table. "You are right. We need to be ready for that. Do you need any assistance with the meeting?"

Her inner self-awareness sensed her motivation could be construed as wishing, wanting to move closer to him. Was his motivation the same? They did make such a good team. She never knew a man more like her, more compatible with her needs. The mission.

Stamos had a brief flashback aboard a dinghy sailboat at twelve years of age, the two of them laughing hysterically as they rounded a point, beaching the boat amongst their friends, joining a drum circle. As he refocused on her eyes, he detected a glimmer of the spark again, but answered nonetheless, "Yes, we can use all the manpower we can get with this. This meeting has to come off flawlessly or all could go wrong."

"I can be your ears in the meeting. I can make a great interviewer, digging under the surface for any hidden agenda."

"Yes, you possess an uncanny sense of social awareness of people's motivations. And you have incredible control of your emotions. You have ever since I have known you. That is what makes you such a great journalist. It is also why I consider you my closest friend, even though we have been so far apart lately." Stamos turned toward Claire, giving her idea his full attention. She could be an asset but should he involve her in this, putting her in harm's way? But he also needed Natalia. Both of them could attend the meeting and Natalia could help him protect Claire.

"We are so much the same." Claire could not contain a happy tear from welling up in her left eye. She couldn't let it loose, but it was probably too late not to be detected by her soul mate. He knew her.

"We are. Let's regroup tomorrow morning at 0500."

Their connection would need to be put on hold for a little while longer. They both recognized the gravity of the situation and the absolute need for focus. Tomorrow would be consequential.

CHAPTER 26: BIG BREAK

The light of dawn was not even a thought yet when Claire, Stamos, and Hanson met at the top of the third-floor escalator to ready their conference room for the day's events at the Maker Hotel. Per Stamos' request, the meeting location had no windows and two entrances, one in the rear toward the kitchen. They had just held a briefing with their team, who would secure and monitor the route their informant would take that day.

Staring into the dimly lit lobby below, Claire couldn't stop thinking why she had never suspected the double life her best friend in the world had been leading. And right under her nose when she lived near him in DC, too. She knew he was mysterious, unavailable, and had a brooding personality at times, but so did most attorneys she knew. He obviously lived with more than just the usual legal stress on his mind. His cryptic personality truly was what she liked about him. She loved that they were both extremely independent and didn't need each other in the co-dependent way of other couples.

"What's your guess, Sean? Will we have trouble? I've never been involved with anything like this. And I had no idea..." Claire asked, slightly anxious regarding her first foray into spydom.

"I always expect it. In this line of work, there is no avoiding it." Stamos glanced over at her green eyes drilling inquisitively into his. He realized his error, sensing her unease, and now sought to allay her fears, "We will keep you safe. I have no doubt about that."

Hanson added his reassurance to the mix, "At all times, we have our teams that will protect you."

Stamos was becoming sensitized to Claire's present preoccupation with his previous line of work, so he added, "I'm sorry that I was not forthcoming with you in the past about what I do. It was unavoidable. I hope you understand."

"I do. I do. You don't have to explain yourself," Claire answered,

A few minutes later, Stamos and Hanson began to walk the same path twice to perfect the position of each member of the team for flawless execution. Claire and Natalia readied the layout of the conference room table to be closest to the rear entrance with the exact number of chairs necessary and no more. They also mapped out several egress routes for emergency purposes that they hopefully would not need.

Satisfied with the arrangements, they returned to their positions. The quartet stood basking in the late-morning sun which was pouring in almost exactly like at the Sybaritean Hotel where they were stretching the day before. While the layout was similar, this hotel had a decidedly Southern vibe, unlike the cubist modern style of their headquarters hotel. The two ornate couches, chairs, and tables with dark walnut finish in this sitting area would have been just as at home in a Georgia plantation home as they were here. They certainly appeared more comfortable and inviting, as Stamos was marking out the best vantage point of the third-floor lobby just above the direct entrance from the mall. This rather direct entrance from a public area made this hotel slightly less secure than theirs but they couldn't chance having this meeting at the Sybaritean, which could reveal the location of Merlin's headquarters.

"This couldn't be more perfect. I'm satisfied," Stamos remarked.

Claire agreed with a twisted smile, "I wholeheartedly approve as the amateur of the group."

For Hanson's part, "I want to walk the route one more time with the team in place. You guys stay here, and I will arrive from the entrance below."

The final walk-through was over in a flash, and all were now pleased with the arrangement. Claire had volunteered to procure snacks to hold them over since it was approaching lunchtime. When Stamos discovered the contents of his white paper bag, which contained a peach, salted whole peanuts, and candied pecans, he suddenly felt like a tourist.

"Have you become a Southern belle with your Georgia roots?" Stamos asked.

"Why, yes, sir! Y'all better eat those scrumptious treats, ya hear?" It was not her best Southern accent, but it would have to do.

He looked up from his treasure and flashed a smile and a chuckle toward the auburn belle as she and Natalia disappeared into the conference room for their own preparation.

Seemingly forever, Stamos was reading a newspaper on the third floor, at the set of couches, with a cup of java and the Southern snacks at his side on the side table. From here he had a straight visual aspect over the top of the escalator so he would be the first to see their honored guest arriving. He had already been informed of the informant's arrival at the parking garage, and then inside the mall. All was going as planned. As he saw the shape of his informant, Ricky, slowly appear from below, coming up the escalator, he slowly raised the paper covering his face, then slowly brought it back down again. It was unmistakably him. And he was alone. Now for the moment they had been waiting for all morning.

Stamos put down the paper, stood up, and walked tangentially away from the informant toward the conference rooms. As he reached the small conference room, he opened the door a crack, turned around, and motioned with his head for Ricky to follow. Ricky glanced furtively behind him down the escalator toward the sky bridge and complied.

Once inside, Stamos closed the door as Ricky looked

nervously across the room at Hanson, Natalia, and Claire. Hanson, not knowing he was displaying a closed posture, sat with his arms folded at the end of the table, while Claire and Natalia were positioned on the other side of the table in the middle. Hanson opened his arms and gave their new friend a reassuring look, inviting him to sit down in a chair that had already been pulled out from the table across from the women in the room.

"Welcome. We trust all is well?" Hanson queried the newcomer.

Stamos didn't wait for the answer as he hurriedly ushered Ricky into the room, "Yes, where shall we begin? We thank you for your assistance. I understand you have some information for us?"

Ricky sat down reluctantly, placing his elbows on the table with his hands covering his mouth and nose, before speaking. "Yes, I'm scared. I have a lot of information. Too much, as a matter of fact. Too much that I shouldn't know and my older brother is starting to act differently around me. I'm not sure if he knows."

"Well, we have the parking garage staked out and you have no followers if that is what you are worried about. I don't think they know you are with us now," Stamos reassured him.

Hanson agreed, "You are safe now. At any point, if you feel in danger, we can bring you in under protective custody. However, at all times, we need to keep our meetings short. Speaking of which, what information do you have for us?"

There were more furtive, paranoid glances around the room before Ricky moved his lips, stuttering at first, "A lot. The realm is still waiting for orders, but they are starting to meet more frequently in person and online and they have begun to make preparations for a large operation. They keep talking about their partners in the Russian government. The sheriff of a neighboring county and my brother have these unbranded tablets, communication devices from which they will obtain their orders. And soon I gather. In the past week, they have been rehearsing what appears to be kidnappings

284

and murders of those who are not aligned with them. And they have already kidnapped three women from Atlanta."

Stamos excitedly interjected, "Three? Do you know where they are or what they plan on doing with them?"

Ricky nervously looked up at the ceiling, pausing for more than a few moments, placing his hands behind his head. He closed his eyes tightly, and when he opened them, the look of doom could not be mistaken on his face.

Claire sought to reassure him, "You are in a safe place. We are here for you."

Otherwise motionless, his eyes met Claire's and a sudden calmness appeared across his face. "Yes, they are keeping them in a basement cell below the police station. They have arrested a few of our more vocal sympathizers, those who frequent the big city. That's what they call them, sympathizers. This harkens back to the sixties when those who helped black people vote, attend school, or march in protest were called sympathizers, albeit with some highly descriptive racist terms."

"Well, this confirms our suspicions. We know of two women who have disappeared. Somehow, I was hoping they were holding them in someone's house. This complicates things to know they are in a more formidable location. Do you know that they are alive? Do you have proof of any of this?" Stamos looked over at Hanson, who nodded in agreement.

"Yes, they are keeping them alive for now. I'm not sure for how long, though. And all I have is verbal confirmation. I have not been there. I have their names though. This was divulged in a meeting this week."

With some consternation, almost desperation, Stamos sat forward with his arms outstretched on the table, palms up as though Ricky was going to hand him the names, "Yes, we need those names. And we need any other names of those involved if you can. We are very concerned for these women. We are in touch with some of their relatives."

"I will give you everything you need. I know just about everyone involved in this realm. I am also peripherally aware of the other realms. But I think that I need to come in. I don't think I will have any further information for you and I am concerned that I may already be or will soon be labeled a sympathizer, especially since this is my second trip to Atlanta in just a few weeks. Nobody is allowed to travel to Atlanta unless it is on a mission. It's almost forbidden now. I'm in danger now, I'm telling you!"

Claire sought to comfort their new charge. "We can make that happen. We can house you in our facility and you will be safe here. And thank you. You are brave for coming to us. This really will make a difference. Now we just need to figure out how to locate and free these women. It's not going to be easy. Let's get everything you know written down first and then we can make some confirmations."

Stamos arose from his chair and walked around the table, extending his hand to shake the young man's hand. "We will protect you. You can be assured of that."

Hanson remained seated, but reclined in his chair, almost tipping over. "Wow, they have been at the police station all this time. How did we miss this transfer and how did we not see any activity emanating from the police station?" He stopped short, being careful not to divulge any further operational information.

Claire sensed there was more information he had not yet revealed, "Can you tell us a little about the organization? How do the realms communicate with each other?"

"I told you about the two leaders here and there is another leader outside of Macon and we have been in touch with some in Alabama, Florida, and South Carolina. We are separate from other areas of the country. They have their own operations. There are several other operations. Oh and another thing, they are communicating via Stealth Realm, a messaging app. I have an account and so does almost everyone else involved."

That was it, the whole reason Claire volunteered for this meeting. Two amazing breakthroughs and they were now oh so close to rescuing their friend Mía.

Stamos, who was now pacing the room and had just resigned himself to exiting the meeting soon, stopped dead in his tracks, and immediately sat back down, again with arms outstretched. "You're kidding me! Can you get us this login information? This will allow us to subpoena and may allow us to gain access to that police station if we have some proof."

"The app is downloaded not from an app store. It is sideloaded or directly downloaded from a secure Russian website. And they are IP-controlled so that nobody else can download the app. It is something that was given to them by the Russians. I can give you my phone but you will need to spoof your IP address so they cannot locate you."

"Yes, we can do that, no problem. Is your phone in your car?" Stamos immediately thought of Point and his team. Or Huy. Either one could arrange that in a heartbeat.

"Yes, it is. It's parked on the third floor of the parking garage. I also have my brother's password."

Stamos dialed Point, who picked up even before the first ring. "Point, I have access to a phone with their communication app. We need to spoof an IP address to access the app."

"We can do that. If you have the phone, turn the radio off, then the power off immediately and place it in a Faraday cage. Any true metal box. Huy should have access to one. Then bring it in and either of our teams should be able to jailbreak it," Point said, using the term for hacking into a phone's inner workings.

Stamos turned toward Ricky, "We know where your car is. You can remain here. If you give us your keys, we will retrieve the phone. We will turn it off first and later access the app, but we will need your passwords. And I thought you just gave us the motherload before. This is even more explosive."

Just then, both Stamos and Hanson reached for their ears simultaneously. On the comm, "There are two suspicious pickups parking on the same level as our informant."

Ricky, not privy to the communication, could sense the danger and sat up straight in his chair glancing around the room for the exits, with a frightful look, "Are they here?"

Hanson, also a bit apprehensive, walked around the table

and placed his hand on Ricky's shoulder. "Maybe. We'll investigate. Let's get you out the back door now. Do you have anything on your person? Anything that could be bugged? I knew we should have scanned him. Quickly, in this bag next to the door, is a change of clothes. I need you to ditch all of yours into the Kevlar bag inside, including underwear."

"Nothing, not even jewelry or a belt. I thought I took every precaution. Maybe my car is tracked," Ricky said as he was already half-undressed next to the back service door. The outfit given to him consisted of black jeans and a black shirt that would have blended in nicely in this hip area of Atlanta if it wasn't summer.

The egress from the kitchen was pre-planned as the four descended a stairway to the alley below. The short jump from the shipping dock was easily navigated and the route to the Sybaritean took them all of thirty seconds. The escape plan could not have been more perfectly executed as they entered the rear door that was secured by a passcode. Once inside they immediately made their way up a back stairway to Huy's desk in the conference room.

"Huy. The cover might be blown. Show us Field Team 2. We may need to neutralize those two individuals without them communicating. They cannot transmit a peep of anything they find."

"We could jam their communications. But we have to get close enough. I can jam a city block and at least four stories of a building. However, it will also jam any cameras." Huy rose from his gamer's chair and set about distributing a piece of equipment from his stash of electronics to a few of his men who just entered the room.

Stamos leaned over Huy's empty chair, peering at the monitors, and asked, "What are those two pickups doing now? We need that phone out of Ricky's car. He has access to their messaging app."

"They are just sitting there. They are probably waiting for him to emerge from the mall," Huy said as he pointed to the screen on the far right. He sank into the chair with a groan, "We have two men in the backseats of these cars at each end of that floor."

Stamos quickly recognized both of the lifted pickups as the ones who had fired upon them in the central square of that small town. Not a friendly bunch and well-armed.

Hanson offered a quick solution, "Should we have Ricky approach the car, and then we neutralize them if they make a move?"

Huy, pointing out the obvious, spoke softly, almost whispering his response to the untenable plan, "We will need a clean-up if so. Torey and his men could accomplish that. We also need a second field team in place. It will take me thirty minutes. We will send them up the stairwells from the second floor. I will have the jamming device in place on the floor below in ten."

Stamos glanced over at Ricky with a stern, questioning look, "Are you ready for this? We need to get that phone and we need for those men to disappear if they make any move on you. If they make any move on you, and we neutralize them, then they have to be disposed of. Do you understand?"

Ricky spoke in a surprisingly calm voice, belying his nervous eyes and wringing hands, "Yes. Agreed. Those two are the enforcers of the realm. If they are here, they are here for one purpose alone. Let's get it done and over with."

Huy added more logistics detail over the comm, "We also need to have no witnesses. Shoot to kill only if there is imminent danger. If they are neutralized, we dispose of them in the trunk of the Charger. Test the jamming before commencing the plan. Our own cameras and comms will be affected so we will have several minutes of radio silence. As soon as the plan is accomplished, turn off the jamming, but take care before and after jamming to not reveal yourselves to cameras. Is everyone ready? Field Team 5 is almost in position with the jammer."

Stamos checked his clips, then put his arm around Ricky, "Okay, I am going to walk with you to the mall and will follow behind you into the parking garage. I will have your back. This is personal to me. These guys wounded both me and Hanson just a week ago. They won't lay a hand on you. Trust me. Hanson, I want you stationed inside the mall behind us for cover on egress. Let's go now. Don't start the jamming until we are about to exit the mall, but let us know as soon as the jamming is operational."

It took several agonizing minutes, but as the operation unfolded on the screens above, Claire and Natalia stood anxiously behind Huy. Natalia, sensing Claire's unease, clasped her hand in hers. One of the field team members followed along with Stamos, Hanson, and Ricky so they could see the bodycam image. When they were on the third floor of the mall, the four of them paused. Four other members could be seen ascending the concrete stairwells of the parking structure.

Huy gave the signal over the comm, "Commence. Jamming in ten seconds."

As a very nervous, sweaty informant walked ahead of Stamos, the bodycams showed several men entering the third floor of the garage. Then all of the feeds changed to black and white snow, then to a vertical bar pattern.

When Ricky entered the garage from the large doorway, he walked swiftly on the left side of the lane toward his car. A few seconds later, Stamos exited the mall toward the right which, by the time Ricky arrived at his car, almost placed him between the two trucks and Ricky. The other team members effectively gave them a triangulation on both of the perpetrators.

As soon as the perps noticed Ricky nearing his car, Stamos could see the two men in black ballcaps simultaneously reach for their door handles, opening the driver's side doors. As the six men exited, they ducked down, which gave them cover for only a few seconds as they emerged with handguns drawn in gloved hands and pointed toward Ricky, idiotically in perfect side-by-side formation. That was enough. Stamos drew and fired six consecutive shots only. The other team members emerged a half-second later with weapons drawn, but another shot would not be necessary.

Stamos ran toward their informant's passenger door

where Ricky was crouched, trembling. He turned around in front of Ricky and knelt, gun still drawn and pointed in the direction of the pickups. He barked a few commands. "Check the vehicles and clear the area. Turn their phones off and place them in the boxes. Make sure they have no tracking devices on their persons."

The flurry of activity from the several team members who were scurrying around culminated in several shouts of "Clear!" from the area.

"Quickly, take them to the Charger. Ricky, get your phone. Put it in here." Stamos opened the backpack he carried and held out the metal box.

Ricky stood up quickly, fumbling with his keys. With a brief honk, the doors were unlocked and the phone was extracted. The pair turned quickly toward the mall entrance and, crouching at first, walked swiftly without looking back. They did not have a lot of time to make it out of the garage. The jamming would continue until all field teams were in their vehicles.

As they exited the parking structure, they were surprised to see that, despite the noise in the garage, people were unaware of anything untoward happening. They quickly realized why, as there was some loud music in the mall that must have camouflaged the operation. Hanson joined them from the bench he was sitting on as they made their way calmly through the crowd. Every other person they could see was staring incredulously at their phones, putting them up to their ears with exasperated looks. The jamming was obviously still working very well. Was there any doubt? They would soon find out how much or how little the perpetrators would have been able to communicate to their commanders via telephone.

Stamos could not wait to access these apps and the messages they contained.

CHAPTER 27: THE MESSAGING APP

The race to save Mía was hurtling toward the finish line, as Digital Team 4 spent the entire day and all night on the app, logged in as the informant's brother. Time was of the ultimate essence in this endeavor, success or failure depended on how quickly they could finalize the logistics for an eventual rescue. As soon as Ricky and his pursuers did not show up in his hometown tonight, the organization would become suspicious and delete Ricky's user information. They ditched all efforts at imitating the informant and concentrated on assuming the identity of the brother. The team was hoping beyond hope the Russians didn't know the brother's login information was compromised.

Being careful not to leave any traces of their search, they were able to copy all of his conversations and remain anonymous. They spoofed their IP address as the same IP address as the last known login IP of the brother, which interestingly did not change much for it appeared that he did not leave home often. The messaging app did not have any privacy controls, and the IP addresses of all posts were listed in the page code of the app. The sheer volume of incriminating evidence required several investigators to comb through it all. Screenshots were taken as much as possible. The team might soon have the entire Southeast portion of this organization uncovered.

As Natalia had suspected, half of these IP addresses pointed to locations within their initial target area, but there were others in Savannah, Macon, and various other locations around Georgia, South Carolina, and Florida. There were around a thousand of them altogether and only a few were hidden behind any kind of VPN or firewall. Not very bright, these guys. Had they not learned from any of the past few years of extremists getting caught communicating with each other in various plots? Were they that trusting of a Russian app, that it would not be compromised?

"A thousand adversaries? That doesn't sound like much, but there could be at least a few others for every user on this app," Hanson warned, pacing the floor while anxiously looking over the shoulders of the investigative team.

Sitting across from Huy in the command center, Stamos sat forward, with his hand on his chin, appearing to be in deep thought. He was busy rifling through prior missions in his head, going through his sordid past against the Russians to be sure he wasn't missing some false flag or decoy mission. He thought to himself, "Could they be trying to get us to spy on our own citizens without a real mission unfolding? If we are exposed before the real mission begins to play out, we could find ourselves in a real Civil War. All the Russians would need to do is publicize on social media what our two organizations had been up to."

As he snapped out of it, Hanson's words came to his consciousness, and he nodded in approval. "This operation uncovers the recruitment of a huge segment of our population. Even though several thousand perpetrators represent a small portion of the population of millions in the Southeast, there could be thousands more who would back them, especially if there is some sort of disinformation campaign by the Russians."

Hanson gave him a nod in return with his hands on his hips, "True that. Careful we need to be." It was no secret that Hanson was a little bit of a sci-fi nerd despite the tough federal agent exterior.

The whole group watched the monitor as names and addresses piled up in their database of actors in this scheme. On the map monitors on the left, the red dots on the map of Georgia suddenly widened to include the thousand dots in the four-state area.

"This is starting to look like a cellular coverage map," mused Claire as she was multi-tasking with some research on each of these new actors. "Some of these guys are well-connected. We have doctors, lawyers, and politicians working alongside common folk. Some of them own a lot of farmland around here. If we are looking for more burial sites, these farms are prime targets."

Stamos acknowledged Claire's work, then followed with a list of priorities, "Yes. Now to keep this legal let's get these to Hanson to file subpoenas with the FISA judge in DC. We will not serve these subpoenas, keep them under seal. Now we have some real work for the other Field Teams to capture some real-time data. Compile a list of priority sites for drone surveillance. I mention the next point last only because it will take some discussion." He paused and looked over at Sage, Samantha, and Claire who were only half-listening with their heads buried behind their computer screens. "Let's identify everyone who is on the same IP address as the sheriff. We can assume that IP address is the police station in that town. I want a priority team focusing on all of the actors that are in this town, their addresses, and their vehicle information. And I want a feasibility study and several action plans to rescue Mía and these two other women."

Simultaneously, all three women perked up and sat up straight at their desks. Sage wasted no time in offering with a slightly pressured speech, "I have already compiled a detailed map of the entire town. And I have the schematics of the police station building from the county appraiser's site. Pictures are hard to come by, but I have these few that I found from a private website. There is only one set of stairs to the basement cells and there are two entrances. Not a very fire-safe building."

Stamos walked over, and put his hands on her monitor, peering over it with a broad smile on his face, to place more focus on her for the moment. "Fantastic work, Sage. I was just going to assign this to one of the teams. Do you want to be part of this team? It will be one entire investigative team and one field team. We will have these action plans ready to go by tomorrow so that when we have the green light to take down the organization, our Mía will be our number one priority."

As the two commiserated over the risks inherent in this impossible plan, the Field Team 2 drone approached a small town that looked eerily familiar to Stamos, with the central town square slowly coming into view. There was not much activity on the streets, just a few cars driving down the main street. The police station sat relatively isolated on its own block, without any trees to serve as cover for ingress and egress. Across the street in the town square, those same trees and statues they utilized last week could prove useful again for cover. The parking lot was empty and there sat a white police car and two tan deputy SUVs parked in front of the building on the street.

"Can we see the heat signatures at this time of day? And Radar?" Stamos asked.

With a few commands to the pilot, the screen switched to infra-red which was very grainy with the heat of the day, but they could make out 4 individuals on the main floor and 2 individuals in cells on the second floor. As Huy switched to combination radar and IR, three more outlines could be seen below grade.

"Okay, map this with radar. If these are our three kidnapped individuals, then we know they are still alive at this time." Stamos pivoted back around toward the women in the room with a brief smile before turning his attention back toward the monitor.

At her desk, Sage buried her face in her hands with tears of joy streaming down her face, then actually laughed for the first time in days. Miraculously, they finally had more concrete proof of life, which promulgated a rolling sigh of relief around the room as each person could now fathom how close they were to their goal.

Interrupting the short inspirational moment, it was now briefing time, and all were eager to hear what the Investigative Team was finding on the app. As they prepared themselves for the breaking news, they had less than a minute for a brief break. As if everyone responded to the time cue like a whistle at work, they congregated for a few seconds at the coffee table near the entrance, which was adorned neatly with various beverages, snacks, and an ice bucket. Sage and Claire both gravitated toward the sparkling fruit water which appeared quite inviting given the intense heat outside.

"I just want to go in there right now with guns blazing like in the movies," Sage began. "I am definitely signing up for that operation. I will be the first one through the door, even before Iron Man."

Claire confirmed, "Maybe all four of us should sign up. We'd be like the Avengers, channeling the old movie she had only partially seen because they were so unbelievable, while at the same time boring to her."

Natalia and Samantha simultaneously, yet succinctly, could only offer the colloquialism, "Right?" They hugged each other with nervous laughter that lightened the mood at the refreshment table.

Stamos, who was also walking over with Huy, discussing the potential operation, overheard the conversation out of the side of his ear, and contributed, "I think that every one of us here is chomping at the bit to knock down the doors of that police station. That time will come soon. And all four of you ladies will be part of this operation. If you want to be there in person, we may even be able to arrange that. It depends on how much firepower we believe the other side possesses at this location. One thing we do know is they are minus six rednecks in two pickup trucks!"

"We are all there!" exclaimed Sage, as she put her arms around Samantha and Claire beside her in an act of solidarity as the entire group began to file into the SCIF.

At the very end of the bank of monitors, inside the

self-contained SCIF room, the connection to the FBI Atlanta SCIF and the two Phoenix SCIFs commenced, which signified the beginning of the briefing. Being caught absent from his desk, Huy scurried over to the red leather gaming chair to initiate the information exchange and then also proceeded to enter the SCIF.

The first item discussed was the status of the other team locations in Utah, Nevada, Michigan, Wisconsin, Pennsylvania, and Florida. It was revealed that the plans were ahead of schedule and would have headquarters and the first investigative and field teams active at all six sites by tomorrow morning. The gargantuan task of setting this up could only be appreciated by those who had seen the Atlanta and Phoenix sites through the process which had required several days to reach their present status.

"So, tomorrow morning the briefing monitors will triple, and you will see ten different feeds. We are consolidating the Merlin and FBI headquarters in these 6 sites into one site each. We will be working side by side in these locations. SCIFs will be set up and there will be co-commanders at each site." Huy, Chip, and Natalia could not be prouder of this crucial development.

One by one the four participant locations on this videoconference ticked off the rapidly expanding knowledge of the geographic and numerical enormity of their adversary. When the target map was expanded to show the entire United States, there were now twelve states represented and the joke about cellular coverage maps could soon be more and more accurate. If they could only uncover the other apps utilized by some of these other realms, the evidence gathering would increase exponentially.

The last teams to contribute were those tasked with monitoring the Stealth Realm app. Given there were a thousand distinct users and hundreds of threads of conversation on this app, they began with a caveat that they had only perused a third of the gleanable material. What they could relay were commands given for several locations, some of which were already known, that were termed disposition sites. Descriptions of the sites, the size of the holes, and the code names of these sites were given that matched the several sites they had already discovered. Gruesomely included in the disposition sites were two funeral homes that would also participate initially until these were overwhelmed.

"Funeral homes?!?" Stamos exclaimed in disbelief as the meeting was adjourned and everyone was filing out of the SCIF in Georgia. He could barely contain himself as the image of cremation being used in furtherance of this plot.

"That is shocking!" Natalia agreed. "Where will it all end?"

"Hopefully with a multitude of Georgians and Russians in jail. Don't do the crime," added Hanson.

Stamos felt the need to reassure all of his team members in Georgia. "It is important to remember these rednecks are not going to get anywhere close to any funeral homes. This plot of theirs is going nowhere. Positive thinking everyone!"

Natalia had positioned herself close to Sage and Samantha to emphasize that same point. She half-whispered into their ears, "The fact these women are in this police station speaks volumes as to their safety. They would not harm them in that location. If they even come close to moving them out of that location, we will stop it in their tracks! Right, Sean?" she asked rhetorically.

"Right!" Stamos sought to encourage the female team members, "Meanwhile, while we are preparing for the ground operation at the police station, keep gathering more information on this app and any logistics of any surrounding businesses. Soon, ladies, soon."

Sage resumed her excitement at the prospect of rescuing her longtime friend sooner rather than later, "We are free tomorrow! Tonight, I am going to investigate specifically this sheriff and police chief. And by tomorrow night we will meet them!"

Natalia, glancing sideways at Stamos, concurred, "Sean, we have the chance at this very hour to save three lives. We've found her so we need to act now."

Stamos relented, "I can't promise anything but let's involve Huy and Torey regarding feasibility. Let's see what they have to say about moving quickly on this location." This treacherous operation would demand a whole lot of soul-searching to reassure himself that involving these inexperienced civilians was the right path. While he trusted Natalia's combat readiness, he was not so sure about the other two much younger, inexperienced women. He envisioned that the developments in Arizona were coincidentally evolving into two additional rescues. Intestinal fortitude and plenty of antacids would be required over the next few days for sure.

The four of them walked hand-in-hand toward Huy's desk, where Torey also toiled behind the scenes. They were both barking out orders into their headsets to amorphous team members, drone pilots, and investigators. The myriad of moving parts was mind-boggling. In a pause in the action, Natalia put a hand on Huy's shoulder to get his attention for he didn't seem to notice their presence.

Huy pulled off his headset, growling, "So you want to go in now, guns blazing?"

"No," Natalia demurred, "we just want to hasten the operation. With three lives in the balance, we want to move quickly, before they do anything sinister to these women."

"I understand. I think we are so close. If not tonight, definitely by tomorrow. Keep working the logistics so we don't tip their hand."

That promise would not be kept, for none could have foreseen the shocking revelations and breakthroughs the next twenty-four hours would bring, on the most colossal scale imaginable.

CHAPTER 28:
ARIZONA SURVEILLANCE

From everyone's perspective, the newly anointed Phoenix Twins, Beata and Paige, were coming into their own with their new investigator gig, quietly flexing their keyboard might in tip-tap fashion. Over the past several hours, they had developed detailed profiles of several Western targets. Paige, for the first time in her life, felt the freedom she always dreamed of, where her true talents could flourish. There was no editor at this newfound outfit, no naysayer to quelch her spirit. Her rebel heart that so desired to help the downtrodden was unhindered to make the biggest difference. Where would her soul fly from here? She suddenly found herself hoping that she wouldn't get the job in New York, for in the hallowed towers of journalism, it seemed an editor's favorite pastime was to hold her back.

Inside the comfort of this adobe desert resort, the pair labored tirelessly in the command center, pretending to be extremists feigning interest in nefarious bigoted activities. They had established a presence in multiple chat rooms, uncovering vague coordinating commands from Ben, the Utah target, and Mr. Koenig. One of the most recent instructions seemed to be code words, but it was unquestionably related to their first planned victim. Similar to the Stealth Realm app, Koenig's IP address was publicly facing in the page code, which made cracking his location child's play. However, it was not shocking to see that his IP location could be narrowed to Sand Butte. Ben's IP was hosted by a dark web VPN, thus requiring a few more hours to pinpoint him. It would also prove much more difficult to locate the desaparecidos that they sought.

"We have a location of the Utah gentleman. He is presently in a law office in Utah. Mr. Koenig is at his home. Ben Ritter is somewhere in Nevada, we think. These IP logins are all recent, within the last hour." Paige looked up from her screen to an approving look from Sam, who smiled a knowing grin and pointed to the monitor overhead.

Beata looked up from her screen and suddenly recognized her former home and driveway on the feed from drone team number one. There were two vehicles in the driveway, which was one more than she would have expected. The camera zoomed in on the vehicles, capturing license plates from an incredible height. Somewhere, a digital team member had begun processing these plates immediately.

Another drone on a nearby screen similarly arrived at its target destination, a nondescript desert compound not far from Beata's former home. There were several brown steel buildings that blended in with the background and several large construction vehicles and dump trucks. There was a well-worn private road that seemed to stretch for miles toward mountains and canyons in the distance. She could just make out a quarry in the distance and then realized she had been there before.

"I know this place. It is the property of one of Franc's henchmen. He owns a lot of land and a construction company. In the distance is a quarry and beyond a deep canyon. If you are looking for a possible disposal site with no witnesses, that could be it."

Sam answered, "Yes, we tracked the kidnapping vehicle via traffic cameras to this general vicinity. It was last seen exiting the last major intersection near Sand Butte and it didn't appear at the next major intersection twenty miles away. This compound is the only logical stopping point."

Sam gave some commands to the pilot and the drone first painstakingly zoomed in one-by-one on the buildings and vehicles and their license plates before finally moving on toward the quarry. It took ten minutes to fly the length of the road, as it was several miles on a relatively straight path toward a magnificent deep burnt-orange canyon. There were no visible trails around the quarry that stood just yards before the canyon and no other roads in sight, making it a very desolate space.

Paige suddenly felt a sense of dread for her fellow immigrant champions' fates. That ten minutes proved very long indeed as she could suddenly visualize their potential gruesome endings at the end of this dirt path. Their initial fly-by of the azure blue quarry water found no outward signs of violence. There were fresh tracks from motor vehicles in the area, and with the camera zoomed in on the edge of the shore, they could see a few desert hares, but no human remains.

Meanwhile, from Drone One's feed at Beata's home, on the driveway, two men climbed into one of the pickup trucks that possessed a covered bed and oversized wheels. Huy commanded both pilots to switch to infra-red to assess the manpower or the presence of any live victims before deciding whether to track the departing vehicle. The accuracy of the infra-red images would be affected by the Arizona heat but that would change soon enough as dusk was not far away.

The answer over the comms was definitive, "No other persons at Target Location A."

"Drone Team Two?" Sam asked.

"No signs outside the quarry. Estimated ten minutes to return to the buildings at the highway," was the bland response.

Light was fading to dark quickly in the desert as was the temperature. As the investigators waited for the drone at the quarry to make its way back to its original Target Location B, the first drone continued to follow the pickup, which turned toward Sand Butte and then reversed direction to follow the highway to Phoenix. The desert darkness cast long shadows as cacti and the roadside brush disappeared except when illuminated by headlights. The lights of the passing cars obscured some of their green night sight view from above occasionally, but their target vehicle was not difficult to follow.

Paige could not contain her anticipation of the night's activities. "It will be evening by the time they arrive in Phoenix. Maybe they are headed to kidnap someone. Let's see how advanced in the plot they are. Are all of the field teams ready at the possible turning points?"

"Yes," Sam answered, confident at least in their preparation, yet wary of the uncertainty of their foe's intentions. "If we need any of our field teams, they are loaded and ready to pursue.

The second drone banked and made a move to hover over the multiple buildings at the construction compound and switched to infra-red again, this time revealing a multitude of persons inside each building.

Sam initiated new commands for his trusted pilots and digital teams, "Let's bring up the schematics on these buildings so there are no surprises inside. Any online photos?" Sam stood up to study the images more closely as the drone circled to get a few different perspectives on the scene. "They seem to be having some sort of meeting. But look at those two individuals there, who are awfully close to one another. Either there is some hanky-panky going on or those two are bound together. Zoom in on that! That's better. I see now. They appear to be both in chairs back-to-back and they are not moving. That could be our two, what did you call them, desaparecidos?"

Some much-needed relief fell over the room as Paige gained a smidgen of hope just then. "Yes, that's right. The history of the term comes from more than a century of oppression by various South and Central American dictators. And now, it seems, North American, as well."

Beata gave Paige some comfort, "They look like they are

alive for now. But we need to rescue them!"

Sam added unapologetically to the conversation, "In due time. There are far too many men in that building to go in now. In our next briefing, we will start planning a rescue." He then turned his gaze to the monitor again. "Drone Team Two, continue surveillance on this location. Can you pick up any audio? If there are no perpetrators outside you can decrease your ceiling to 200 feet to help with audio pickup. Digital Teams track and pre-track all vehicles in this location."

The drone slowly began to descend with its forward infrared video locked in on those inside the building. There appeared to be no stragglers outside. An audio feed opened, first to significant wind noise, which reduced the closer the drone came to the building. Now with a close-up vantage point, a few organizers could be seen standing at the front of the room talking to the crowd that had gathered, some of whom were sitting at tables.

"Yes, I bet you anything this is a planning meeting. This would make perfect sense. Remember the meeting I told you about?" Beata remembered attending a political meeting there once with her husband, who wielded his local power ruthlessly. "They have also utilized these buildings for hyperbolic political theater. I was there once."

Just then the audio focused and intensified as they could hear one man shouting and others cheering and carrying on.

"That's Franc!" Beata exclaimed and suddenly, embarrassingly sank down in her chair as she comprehended his racist words.

Some of the terms were difficult to discern but were captured by a speech-to-text generator on the screen, with a few seconds of delay. "We will be victorious," the text began. "With the backing of our friends, and the help of all our realms, the days of cowering our white skin inside the walls of our houses will be over! These two foreign enemies represent the tip of the iceberg in our lands! In the future that we take back from our enemies, we will take back our lands and our rightful country!"

The crowd erupted in boisterous cheers and chants, some of which included the name of the speaker, repeating over and over. To Sam, the political rantings were likely nothing new in these parts, but the two bound hostages marked a sinister development that required a response. Just then, however, he remembered Stamos' admonishment to seek proof before any incursion.

"That, sir, will be what you will get!" he boldly stated under his breath with gritted teeth. Aloud he shouted, "Drone Team 2, get in position for photographs through the door at an angle to identify those two hostages!"

The answer was crystal clear from the pilot, "That will be dangerously low but we can do so from a distance over the desert floor. We will drop down to 50 feet and focus on the door when they exit the building."

"Roger that, 50-foot, 5-0 foot ceiling approved," was Sam's curt reply.

From the looks of things, as the speech was wrapping up, it wouldn't be a long wait for the dispersal of these cult followers, as they quickly rose to leave. A few approached the leaders at the front of the room to congratulate them. Most were still clapping or chanting with their fists above their heads as they approached the door. They turned around when Franc Koenig started speaking again.

Sam added, "Remember also to try to get close-ups of all faces, please. Better focus please!"

While awaiting the evidence gathering, all attention turned toward the other screen where the first drone, tailing the pickup, had heretofore been a rather boring affair. The driver turned off a main road and slowed down to a crawl in a quaint neighborhood, at the end of which was a set of small office buildings. The truck turned its lights off while still moving and parked right behind a small hatchback next to one of the smallest buildings with a small light on.

Immediately Sam commanded, "Digital Teams, get me the names of every business and all employees in those offices, especially that one with the light. Drone Team One, check infrared for any occupants of those buildings, please!"

A set of answers to those questions began to emerge from the comms. Finally identified was the small office, which belonged to a social service agency. And, as suspected, a single occupant was typing away at a computer workstation.

"Can we get two field teams in there now on foot? I want one coming in from behind the office and one team on foot from behind this truck with two cars blocking both egress points. No communication jamming. I want to see the whole thing." Sam actually enjoyed this so much, he wished he could join these missions more often, which made him think, Who knows how long they might have to wait? Who were their intended targets tonight? He continued his queries of the digital and field teams, "Do we have any identification of these thugs? Notify me of any combat qualifications."

Again, responses to his queries were almost immediate, as the men's identities were uncovered a few minutes prior. No known military or law enforcement qualifications were evident, and it was painfully obvious by body habitus that the two individuals in this truck would be hard-pressed to run a hundred yards, though they were heavily armed, nonetheless. Outlines of two assault-style rifles were previously visualized mounted in the rear window of the truck, and earlier in the driveway, the drone had displayed to all that they each sported handguns holstered at the waist.

Paige and Beata fidgeted at their desk, exchanging brief nervous glances with eyes wide open, fighting back against the fear of what could occur next. It seemed like an eternity to the Phoenix Twins, but finally, the body cams were turned on above and the two field teams were exiting their vehicles and readying their weapons and tactical gear. Paige's computer screen displayed the satellite view of the area as she approximated the area of the two teams approaching the truck.

Simultaneously, at the compound, drone two was maintaining its view of the door, hovering in place. As the first participants slowly filed out of the buildings, the persons following them prevented a good view inside. A minute later the door slammed shut momentarily before a straggler opened the door. Fortuitously, he turned back toward the doorway to speak to someone remaining inside, all the while holding the door wide open. A quick zoom and focus of the optical camera and the proof they were looking for was in plain sight. Bound together and gagged were María and Jyoti, their unlucky desaparecidos. Several photos were taken from this vantage point.

Sam felt immensely proud of his drone pilots who were more accustomed to combat ops than photo ops. "We need to send these photos in a briefing to the others via SCIF immediately. The FBI needs to see these so we can finally take some action."

Most of the men exited the buildings except Mr. Koenig and a few others, who were still conversing at the front of the room. Audio was still being recorded, but no new information could be gleaned from the small talk about their rights and freedoms being abridged.

The next two hours went by uneventfully while the two teams waited in their strategic positions outside the undersized office of the social worker. Even if this new victim went near the pickup, the field teams were relaying their confidence they could prevent the crime from taking place. With few streetlights illuminated, the sheer darkness provided cover for the perpetrators, but it also allowed the field teams to approach them closely from two directions. The next few dizzying minutes had Paige and Beata at the edge of their seat as they strained for a better view of the green night sight body cam footage.

The first activity appeared on the infrared camera from the drone as the planned victim shut off the light and arose from her desk to leave. This prompted the two men in the truck to exit their vehicle quietly as they moved to crouch behind the tailgate. As the now visible short-statured older woman exited the building and turned to lock the door, the field teams held their ground until more activity was apparent.

"Hold steady," Sam demanded. "Don't bite yet!"

As she ambled down the sidewalk and neared her car, the two armed men broke their cover to engage with her.

They only heard inaudible voices in the background. Just as one of the men drew a weapon, a flurry of shouts emanating from behind the would-be-kidnappers and beside the building interrupted and surprised the men. Weapons drawn, several field team members in tactical gear surrounded the pair, without a shot fired. The two obese, older men immediately dropped to their knees and dropped their weapons. In some distress, the woman could be seen crouching, shaking beside the front tire of her car.

Two team members with yellow FBI emblems on the back of their jackets apprehended their suspects without incident.

"Now that is a relief! That could have ended much worse." Paige could not contain her joy as she jumped out of her chair and hugged Beata. "We have much more work to do though!" she exclaimed.

Sam likewise exploded from his table in elation, shouting, "Flawless! Great job everyone! That is how you execute a takedown!" He quickly regained his composure and sat back down, sending some orders to Drone One to continue aerial surveillance from a higher vantage point. He added, "Lock up their truck and leave it for the FBI evidence team."

"If only we could do a takedown of that desert compound just as smoothly and easily as that," Paige wished aloud.

Leaning back in his chair, with his hands cocked behind his head, Sam strained to look back at Beata and Paige. "With any luck, the FBI should be able to detain these perpetrators for 24 hours without communication. Then we can concentrate on the compound and rescuing our Desaparecidos."

This Western team of rescuers would have to wait an excruciatingly long time before witnessing the full takedown, all the while monitoring the activities of dozens of individuals from these compounds.

CHAPTER 29: SIGNALS

The proverbial pot finally produced those first few bubbles before boiling that day, but that was not a surprise to Steven Point. ARTI had been churning along that hectic day, sifting through all the signals from around the world, searching for connections that would either tie all the groups together into one cohesive conspiracy or predict the numerous small actors' next moves. ARTI was now connected to all clandestine and known surveillance methods. Sebastian, the hacker-in-residence of the new FBI artificial intelligence surveillance program, had also connected the Stealth Realm app information along with hundreds of targets the investigators had already identified.

Point, on a routine video conference briefing with Sebastian, remarked, "Steady as she goes. My grandmother used to say, 'It's like making cake, too much of just one ingredient, all you have is mousse.' As they were tweaking the inputs and algorithms, monitoring their progress on the output screens above, a series of what looked like lines of code scrolled down the screen. "That's what we want to see, now it's cooking, rising like a cake!"

Sebastian felt he was too new here to add his own dry wit,

holding back any dating references he otherwise would have added to the mix. Awkwardly, he kept his nose down on his keyboard, replying only with an occasional, "Yes, sir," as he continued typing.

Stamos, quietly taking in the banter between the two computer nerds, became impatient suddenly. "When do we get to taste this cake? It's been cooking for days!"

Point presciently retorted, "Be patient, any minute now. You'll see. Best chocolate souffle you've ever had. Sebastian, don't talk to us until you have something. And it had better be soon!" Point hung up the video conference line and paced toward the darkened windows of the conference room. The branches of the grand Southern Oak Trees outside meandered across the parking lots, dangerously close to the building like they were reaching out to catch every ray of Georgia sunshine. The result was a canopy that provided almost complete shade of the entire piece of government property. "Stamos," he started with a worried look on his face. He paused for a few seconds to collect his thoughts and rephrase what was really on his mind. "We had better get that breakthrough soon. I'm worried. Though I feel it in my bones, I'm not sure I am believing my bones right now."

"You and me both," was Stamos' curt reply as he quickly made his way out of the conference room to find someone who would talk him out of immediately driving to the small-town police station to raid it.

Not grasping the meaning of the abrupt exit, but also not seeing a pressing need to follow him, Point turned back toward the oak trees and swiftly became lost in thought.

Stamos and Point went a little stir-crazy in their headquarters in Atlanta that morning. Both impatient feds were marching around the office like they were possessed. The collaborative effort had mined copious amounts of information that was only quasi-actionable, prompting Stamos to ready his tactical gear and put his field boots on his feet, ready for the field. Rising toward the door, Stamos had enough. "As I've always said, "When the trail goes cold, only good old-fashioned on-the-ground surveillance will break the case."

Point, channeling his new hero persona, had even suggested half-jokingly that if nothing came in by sundown, they should dress in clown masks, break into the jail in the middle of the night, taser the sheriff and any of his accomplices, and free the girls in captivity. "Fuck it! Disguised, we can't get caught! Besides, what are they going to do? Charge us for freeing some people from jail who have never been charged?"

From the door, with his Kevlar duffle over his shoulder, Stamos glanced at Point, his head tilted to one side, eyes squinted, with a WTF look on his face. He didn't need to speak a word. Point rarely swore out loud and was making more of a habit of it today. If only Stamos knew how much he utilized four-letter words within his own internal dialogue since joining this outfit.

"Don't worry, Stamos! It's all rhetorical. I know the stakes. But damn, after all the data we fed it yesterday, why is ARTI not breaking this wide open?"

Stamos relaxed his contorted facial expression, "You are getting antsy. I'm telling you, we all just need to get out in the field."

Slamming his fist on the table for the umpteenth time, Point declared, "We need a breakthrough now, damn it! For these communication devices that are pinging, we need access to that server remotely. Now is the time. We need the location of these communicating devices before anyone dies!"

Point felt his phone buzz in his pocket and Stamos paused his exit. "I have to answer this. It's Sebastian. He never calls outside of briefings. Yes? Okay, I can get back to the SCIF. I will call you in 2 minutes."

He hung up the phone and pumped his fist, "This could be it!" He and Stamos looked at each other like two eagles who had just seen prey from up on their tree-top perch. They both sprang forth and flew to the other end of their command center where the SCIF sat waiting, for the moment empty and ready for this moment. With the almost-hourly briefings around the clock, it was seeing frequent use.

There was a guard stationed at a table next to the SCIF at all times. Point, Stamos, Hanson, Randy, and several top agents who could sense the activity was important, gave up their phones, and the guard scanned each participant prior to entry. The few-minute process seemed to take forever to complete, but it was protocol for these rooms. All four scanned their badges for entry and sat down at the long, wooden conference table. After everyone had entered, the door closed with a vacuum sealing sound behind them. The walls were thick and soundproofed, and you could hear the humming of the electronic apparatus that was randomly assigning noise-dampening vibrations to the walls. This one was a little louder than the usual SCIF but was far quieter than most portable SCIFs Stamos had encountered in far-away lands.

Point pushed the button on the dialer for the conference phone in the center of the table. With several commands through a central scheduler, he connected to their SCIF in Quantico. Sebastian, the now-famous ultra-talented hacker, who previously worked in Natalia's computer lab in New York, and who broke the Russian case wide open a few years ago with his programming skills and knowledge of AI, quickly picked up. The SCIF on his end was filled with men who dressed like Point to a T.

"Well, gentlemen here it is!" Sebastian exclaimed, a one-eighty from his previous demeanor. "There is a lot of data being sent from the Russian server as we speak. I just wanted you to be the first to know. It is being sent to all 30 of the devices through an encrypted connection, but since we are on the inside, we can see everything. And we are just now sending malware to each of the 30 devices. They won't notice a thing." Sebastian started to list some of the mechanisms of malware and their functions, geolocation and communication for example, which began to sound like a foreign language.

As he was listening to Sebastian, Stamos felt each beat of his heart send a jet of red-hot blood and adrenaline through his arteries. He could no longer sit down, he was so amped up. As he began to pace back and forth at the front of the room, he interrupted, "Wow, that's great! That's just the break we needed. We need to get that data sent to us here. We need to know what they are communicating. There is something sinister going on here and I think this is going to be the directive. As soon as you get the malware installed, I want the exact locations. How long until you can get that to us?"

Sebastian responded, "It should be a matter of only a few hours. To this point, we are getting some interesting data. It seems to be a list of names, addresses, and surveillance data like places of work, credit card data, and bank account data. The data is extensive on each of the names that are sent. There is a different packet that is being sent to each device. Probably location-specific information for each of these perpetrators."

Stamos, with hands interlocked behind his head, be-seeched Point, who was sitting beside him at the edge of his seat, "Between the messaging app communications and this, depending on how incriminating it is, we need to go to the director as soon as we analyze it. We can't wait any longer. This needs to be stopped before it gets off the ground. You saw all of these holes. They aren't planting trees out there. And we likely have some casualties we aren't even aware of, I would bet."

Point added, "We will hold a briefing as soon as we pos-sess all thirty packets, and let's send them to each team sep-arately to analyze while Sebastian and ARTI scrutinize the data en toto. I will invite the director to this briefing. Sebas-tian, would you say that in one hour we should have the data and in two hours you can have it all compiled?"

"I can have the data sooner than that, not sure about the analysis. I have estimated that if the packets are all the same size, the data transfers will be complete in thirty minutes, and we are compiling the data as each packet is completed. I will have everything in one hour. In two hours, it will be all uploaded into ARTI. In less than three hours I will have the first analysis."

Stamos clenched both fists in front of him as he turned toward the camera and Sebastian on the screen. "That is awesome! At 4:30 pm, then. Announce the special briefing. We need to defeat the enemy here in Georgia and Arizona, rescue our first victims, and then take down this organization. Now we just need to know who to protect. I am going to head to the Merlin headquarters. I want to help direct this effort on the ground. If we have a thousand actors in the Southeast and a thousand victims in the first week, how do we protect each and every one of these potential victims? We don't have a thousand drones! We might have a thousand men soon but that might not be enough! We are going to need all hands on deck in the field. This could turn into an epic battle!"

Hanson brought the high-flying spaceship back down to earth, "And that's just in the Southeast. We are not ready for this in all the other divisions. Half the SCIFs are not even set up yet. We will have to hold a briefing with these teams at FBI regional headquarters if the Merlin teams don't have SCIFs yet. I will do my best to work with Chip, Sam, and Huy to increase the readiness of the new teams."

"Agreed," Stamos, feet firmly planted on the ground, knew the next steps also. "Hanson, do you know the status of the action plan for the rescue of the girls?"

Hanson "All action plans are set. We will commence upon your direction. Drone surveillance of the station is ongoing. I would imagine that whatever packet is sent to the sheriff will set about a whole lot of commotion there and we may be able to take advantage of their confusion. Let's see if the sheriff, police, or any deputies are going to actively participate in their plot. If they do, then they are the first ones we take out. Here is the most exciting part of this! It elevates this most definitely to the FISA standing that we knew it deserved."

"The first ones we take out could tip off others. Should we jam their communications? How many electronic jamming devices do you suppose Huy has? And they were pretty weak. Do you think we can borrow some from our Marine buddies? Maybe I should ask...." Stamos trailed off as he could see Hanson, the logistics magician, was taking a deep breath as if he would explode.

"One step ahead of you, Captain!" Hanson exclaimed as he simultaneously exhaled. "I have commandeered electronic countermeasures from several bases around the country. These are military-grade and we will have communication devices that will function within the din. They are being delivered here and to each of our ten units. Three devices each. Just enough for each of the thirty communication devices they have. So at least we can take the leaders out of commission. I was so impressed with Huy's device, that I looked into it immediately. Learn new tricks this old man still can."

"Why didn't you tell me? That is so amazing! They won't see what's hit them until it's too late!" Stamos imagined dozens of takedowns going down simultaneously across the nation and was ready for it tonight.

"So, you approve?" Hanson's chest was bellowed out in pride.

"Make it so, ensign!" Stamos channeled the wrong sci-fi, for he was not much of a movie buff. No time for movies. Every action movie he had ever seen was so unrealistic that he could not watch for more than fifteen minutes before critiquing the military or stunt errors. Even so, he could not resist the silly play on words.

Loosening his tie, Point rolled his eyes in partial approval of the saying and added, "Here in Atlanta we have a distinct advantage with the app because I am certain they will disseminate these orders through it. We do not have access to this tool anywhere else, except for the app usage in the West. In all of these other areas, we will not have this advantage. These communication jamming devices will demonstrate their worth I am sure of it, but they will have their limitations."

"Right," Stamos affirmed. "We will need to use good old-fashioned surveillance and fieldwork, and hopefully with the geo-location of each of these devices, we can stay one step ahead. This will prove difficult. Let's get each of these other centers up to speed as quickly as possible. Countless lives could depend on it. Our men and Merlin's men are top-notch. Decapitating the leader with the device and incapacitating their communication may be the best we can do in some areas."

With that, the meeting adjourned with a quiet yet purposeful resolve in everyone's minds, for the next few hours of planning would prove pivotal to save the most lives possible. Hanson, who was still contemplating the ever-widening scope of their investigation, arose from his seat late to catch up with Point and Stamos. Stamos put his arms around both of his partners as they made their way toward the elevators. Stamos looked toward Hanson and smiled, "You know, where have you been for the past decade? I could have used you in Europe, Asia, Russia... just about everywhere I have ever been in trouble!"

Stamos turned toward Point at that moment and filed the ultimatum he had on his mind for the entire day, "Right now, I'm driving over to Merlin Headquarters. By the time I get there, I want the Southeast division of this outfit figured out and we will finalize plans to rescue these girls that are held in the basement of that police station."

"I get it. And we will work this information first," Point agreed.

Both Stamos and Hanson had packed their gear hours ago it seemed, making their exit a relatively nimble affair with few goodbyes. "Please tell me it's go-time," Stamos beseeched Hanson in the silent steel elevator.

"Yes, I believe it is," was Hanson's cold answer.

Unfortunately, the blockbuster lead could come too late for those potential victims who were not located near the two pre-positioned headquarters. The teams in Phoenix and Atlanta were well ahead of the game, but even they would be caught flat-footed as they had only begun their operations a mere few weeks before. Was their only hope in the other areas really just blocking the communications? They had to

318

do better than that if they planned on saving lives.

—◦❭❬◦—

Chapter 30: Belong In The USA

—◦❭❬◦—

The Vegas sun was blazing torrid heat down upon the pavement all too early this morning as the crowd gathered outside the Charleston Boulevard Muse Compendium, each with their various instruments strung across their backs. One of the group had begun to strum an unknown chord on his six-string acoustic guitar while a harmonica belted out an accompanying riff. Added to the voices and a lone bongo drum that started up in the background, the effect was a mesmerizing bluesy island feel to the morning collection of all the muses that Vegas could muster. The colorful musicians were subsisting that day on barely a few hours of sleep from whatever gigs they had the night before, but the mood was quite festive and the energy was building. Beaming from ear to ear, greeting his cadre with open arms, Charlie shoved the gargantuan iron door with all his might to the side to let them into the warehouse jamboree.

Giant cacti framed and lined either side of the opening along the entire length of the large, corrugated steel warehouse, which was adorned with a vibrant mural of a musical scene. You could almost hear each of the depicted musicians as they seemed to leap off the surface of the building. Above the door, a grandiose saxophonist with an Afro-weave was leaning over, with the bell of the sax pointed directly at those who were entering below. As if on cue, a lone alto at the back of the crowd provided the much-needed sound effect to round out the blues ensemble. A seemingly never-ending parade of dancing divas and rocking Rico Suaves filed through the metal archway.

Above the saxophonist, large balloon letters announced the name of the warehouse as the "Muse Compendium" with vibrating outlines illustrating the dynamic scene within. Bright colors of yellows, blues, and greens portrayed a tropical vibe, contradicting the desert locale. Most of their music, owing to Jasmine's influence carried a more Caribbean beat, but did occasionally incorporate the Native American local flavor also.

Situated conspicuously at the gate were the hosts of the day's festivities. At Charlie's side as always was Jasmine, who had embraced every person there a dozen times and then some outside on the sidewalk since dawn first broke. Now she did so a thirteenth time as the musicians and beat poets passed by toward the stage and practice area. The bright light outside contrasted with the dark, deep reds and purples inside the cavernous space. Just then an electric guitar erupted from within with a soulful tune as its owner had promptly attached it to an amplifier. The last of the creative souls to make their way in was a cute native Vegas couple that both Charlie and Jasmine just adored.

"Tommy and Isabella! So great to see you! How did the meeting go?" Jasmine exclaimed as she heard Charlie close the rusting, black iron gate behind them with a huge metallic slam. Now in the relative darkness, the four struggled to adjust their eyes so as not to bump into each other. As the two couples reached out to touch shoulders, finding their way through the indigo void, they constricted their pupils to pinpoints to accommodate their vision, and finally, the shapes of their friends came into focus.

Tommy Lightfoot was an impressive, imposing figure, standing almost 7 feet tall, carrying a bass guitar over his shoulder, bridge down without a case. He leaned over to hear her better, placing his long arm around her shoulder as

322

he did so. His Native American, curly black hair was fixed in a shoulder-length ponytail, and his neatly shaven goatee framed and accentuated his hearty smile. His contrasting, diminutive counterpart Isabella stood at his side, parting with his other arm to engage her host, clasping her hand in Jasmine's tightly. Smiles and laughter filled the air while the rest of the outfit tuned and warmed up their instruments. The chaotic sounds were becoming less disjointed to Jasmine's ears the longer they played.

Tommy brought his hands to his face, stroking his facial hair thoughtfully, before reluctantly offering, "Jasmine, we can talk more about this later. I don't want to interrupt the festive mood, but we are developing some information on your tip. I have some associates in our investigative community and also my friend in the FBI checking out leads on this group's activities here in Nevada. It seems most of them are not from around here. Utah and Idaho transplants, it appears. I will know more by tomorrow, but they tell me there may be something big in the works."

"It wouldn't surprise me that he would have brought some thugs with him. He doesn't seem the fighting type." Jasmine was right about the cowardice within the man.

"I just wanted to let you know we are working on it. Enough about that. Now let's start laying down some beats." Tommy swung his guitar around to his chest and he and Isabella walked off towards the stage, joining the assembling troupe under the lights. Tommy was always a leader of sorts whenever he felt a gathering of creativity, and he couldn't stop himself from conducting the orchestra now. He plugged in his bass and slapped a beat to bring all of the stray beats into line.

By now there were a dozen motley musical spirits on stage, and more were streaming up the metal corrugated stairs flanking each side of the black standard stage risers. Drum beats from two sets of drums prepositioned in the rear of the stage as well as several conga drums fell into a soulful crescendo-decrescendo blues bass line that Tommy held for them. Within a matter of seconds, the chaotic scene evolved into a well-organized melodic symphony of sound.

Overhead, a relatively modest laser array erupted into a vibrant light show which was automatically synchronized to the music by a system that Charlie proudly arranged just for this show and would be showcased for the upcoming get-out-the-vote concerts. The display bounced off the brick walls all over the place, accentuating the neon lights that were now dwarfed by the spectacle.

Charlie and Jasmine, who had made their way to center stage, marveled at the production. This was the pinnacle of his musical career, and that was saying something. He had credits, either songwriting, backup vocals, or guitar tracks on top ten hits galore over the years, but this was his own production, and he could not be prouder. On this first track, his role was more of a backup vocal to what would come next, for his creative partner and the center of his life sauntered up to the microphone, swaying to the beat as she awaited the cue to bring the house down with her sultry vocals. And that she did, as the entire expanse was filled and overflowing with her voice, line after line of sweet, deep caresses of the meaning of words. To Charlie and anyone with discerning ears, there was not a finer voice in the world.

The world over knew that soulful voice, but few knew her name, despite it being announced nightly at concerts all over the world, backing up the vocals of one of the most popular country singers in history. She could sense, however, that this endeavor was deeper and far more important than all of that success. As tears streamed down her ebony face, her entire body shook with each note. Lending all of her Caribbean vigor to everything she ever did, even to this practice session, she knew they would defeat the evil looming over Las Vegas, Nevada, and the country as a whole.

As song after song, mostly originals but some classic covers, flowed forth from the stage, the practice could not have flowed more perfectly from the stage to the mostly empty crowd. There were only about a dozen on-lookers, essentially family and a few local political leaders, who were each entranced by the show. There was not a dry eye on the floor,

324

and when it appeared the show was finished, the stage was quiet and dark, and only Jasmine stood in the spotlight, motionless and quiet at the microphone, with her eyes closed tightly and her head lifted, pointed to the sky.

Tommy stepped forward first, set the rhythm with a deep slow rhythm, and was soon joined by all of the drums in the outfit for the loudest simple beat Charlie had ever heard. The lasers flashed in unison with each beat, in a strobe-like effect sending forth brief explosions out into the darkness. In contrast to the Boss's version, that one-second beat was continued for a full fifteen seconds before the synthesizer joined in for one of the most recognizable keyboard riffs of all time.

Congruent with the beat, Jasmine lowered her head to the microphone and began to sing in a guttural tone with all of her might, "Born down in a dead man's town! The first kick I took was when I hit the ground!" She continued the classic lyrics with reckless abandon, inhaling deeply with a steely purpose at each pause. With each refrain, her voice became louder and louder with the altered words, "I Belong in the USA! I BE-Long in the USA!" and finally repeating over and over at the end, "Now I'm a cool VOT-ING mama in the USA!" which would be sure to bring the house down everywhere they played this summer and fall.

Tommy and Charlie, who were flanking Jasmine on either side of the spotlight, brought down the final beat with reverberating notes, which cued the lights to go completely dark for a few seconds. The house lighting came on, simulating the end of the concert, and Jasmine, exhausted from the herculean effort, fell against Charlie's shoulder.

"If that doesn't get every man, woman, child, and dead person to vote this year, I don't know what will!" exclaimed Tommy in his deep voice, as he swung his guitar around his shoulder, stumbled to the rear of the stage, and leaned it against a tall amplifier. "We can't go wrong with that set, inspirational as fuck!" He emphasized the four-letter word and said it again, "As Fuck!"

There were several "You got that right!" exclamations

from the small crowd of participants, who could not contain their excitement.

Tommy then moved to the microphone, announcing, "Alright everyone, two days until the first of the concert series which debuts at the Ellipse! We are going to rock the house like no other!"

As the several dozen musicians dispersed from the stage in the dream-like smoky, purple hues of the warehouse, the euphoria of the moment permeated the air, not unlike the blissful nirvana at the end of the night in a college dorm lit with lava lamps. The echoes from the amplifiers could still be heard in their brains reverberating chords of As and Gs and every note in between. Still weak in the knees from their musical menagerie, Charlie could barely support Jasmine in his embrace as they descended the side stairs to the floor of the warehouse.

At the bottom of the stairs sat a few oversized chairs, and a comfortable couch, into which Jasmine and Charlie promptly collapsed. With the weight off her feet, she began to come to, opening her eyes to several of her friends wishing her well, and congratulating her on her vocal masterpiece. Was there any mistake that she had found her people here in the City of Sin, the city where the dreams of its people were only as big as their minds could imagine? She hoped and prayed that the next few months would be as magical as this night, producing the desired motivational effect for the voters of Nevada and the Southwest.

As the evening came to a close, with only the glow of the neon lights illuminating the stage and the rest of the warehouse, with its many unique decorations, Jasmine was finally able to stand so that she could properly bid their guests adieu. So many of them expressed their appreciation for the creative venue that they all had come to know and love as their home, where they could express themselves without fear, without hate. Indeed, she thought the love floating on the wind that night was thick with gushing passion and oozing equality.

Characteristically, the last to leave that night was Tommy

and Isabella, who had taken up residence at the gate across from Jasmine and Charlie, bringing the perfect close to an evening full of strength in purpose and a vision for the future. These musicians were contributing a lion's share toward building this fine country that was under attack constantly. As each participant exited the large iron arch, the four leaders exchanged smiles and tears from their designated places in line, until there were no more ears to bend, no more cheeks to kiss, and no more shoulders to cry on.

Thus, the four partners in solidarity came together in a final circle of joy at the accomplishments of the last few months, now realizing their dreams had come to fruition. Jasmine spoke first, "You know, nothing can stop us now! The fascists had better watch out because we are going to defeat them with love and kindness. And if that doesn't work, we will do what we have to do."

Tommy finished the conversation, "Love is strong, love is brave, and above all, love is fighting for what you believe in."

The four walked through the arch, hand in hand, staring wistfully at the full moon overhead in the desert heat. Their collaborators were still quietly departing in cars, motorcycles, and scooters, magically disappearing into the brightly moonlit night. Tommy and Isabella followed suit, climbing into their blue stripped-down, jacked-up Jeep Wrangler. Jasmine and Charlie tracked every taillight as each red glow faded down Charleston Boulevard.

With a sigh, Jasmine turned toward her man, staring deep into his blue eyes, and professed, "This is what I was meant to do, this is my calling. I am so excited to see what tomorrow brings, and the next day, and the next... Two days and counting! I can't believe it is almost here!"

She fell into his arms, and they kissed a final kiss that night, as Charlie swept her into his arms and carried her off to bed.

—•◊► ◄◊•—

CHAPTER 31: RAMP UP

—•◊► ◄◊•—

As Stamos and Hanson strolled into the command center of the Merlin headquarters, sweat still dripping from their forehead from the already sweltering, humid Georgia afternoon, the immediate shock hit them like a ton of bricks. The video monitoring setup in the darkened command center had morphed drastically overnight, doubling in size to jaw-dropping proportions, looking a tad bit like the stage of a U2 concert. Stamos half-expected to see spotlights and incendiary devices hanging from the ceiling. What was previously a wall of monitors on one end of the 60-foot room with Huy in the center, now had Huy facing the room lengthwise with monitors running down both walls and the end wall. He had set up two desks, one at each end, so he could be closer to one end if need be.

The sheer number of video screens, which now numbered more than two hundred most certainly would be overwhelming to keep track of if it were not for large, printed labels now affixed to the top of each one. There were drone footages, body cameras, maps, and target lists strewn throughout the place. At one end was the local Georgia evidence gathering while the rest of the nine regional centers were each represented moving further west along the length of the room, ending with the Arizona and Utah contingent movements.

"Get a load of this!" Stamos exclaimed, as the three slowly made their way to the far end where Huy was busy sending commands to some unknown team. In Pennsylvania, a cadre of FBI agents and Merlin operatives had a rural farmhouse in their sights while a drone overhead was keeping track of what must have been some perpetrators they were following. On the next set of monitors, a black vehicle with a suspicious occupant was being observed by a drone outside an office building in suburban Detroit. On and on across the country the holders of brown tablets were continuously tracked from above.

Hanson couldn't manage a single word. He just walked along toward Huy's command center, mouth agape. In his many years of experience, he had never seen anything like it. Scanning the monitors, they eventually came to stand behind the desk where Huy sat, as he briefly, casually acknowledged them. It was almost like a carnival house of mirrors. The images and streaming monitors just kept going and going and going. When he finished what he was doing, Huy looked up at them with a wide smile that belied the seriousness of the hour.

"Well, what do you think? Now we ARE the CIA!" he exclaimed, as he reached for the headphones on his head.

As soon as Huy put down the headset, Stamos immediately brought the high-flying Englishman to the ground. "This looks great but are we going to be up and running soon enough to stop this plot in its entirety? I want to catch every one of these perps before they can lay one hand on our innocent civilians. I know. Wishful thinking, I know. But here is what I really need to know tonight. What do you have for me on this police station, Huy? And, can we begin our takedowns?"

"Here is what I have so far this afternoon. Point, Sebastian, and our teams have broken these documents' codes and much of each of the thirty documents is a roadmap for not only kidnapping and killing but the framing of individuals, some for crimes they have not committed. Then there is some evidence we are combing through that shows that some of these so-called victims actually did commit the crimes and the Russians intend to submit previously undiscovered evidence to the authorities. There are pedophiles, prostitutes, embezzlers, and tax evaders among this group."

"I'd hate to break up that part of the plan. So, as soon as they are convicted of a felony, they will no longer be able to vote. I see the motive now." Stamos scratched his chin with the mixed feelings in his brain that were battling it out about that development and probably would be for some time.

"In total, more than 20,000 hits are going down, and that's just here in Georgia. But it is not all at once, mind you. They are, however, dumping the evidence quite quickly over the next few weeks. Probably anonymously. IRS tips will likely be sent via tip lines and emails. The pedophiles will be easy prey. Just send the videos and pictures to the police."

"Well, we may not be able to stop those file dumps, but we can surely stop the murders and kidnappings, right?" Hanson asked with a sly grin.

"Right," Huy began, tenuously leaning back in his gaudy gaming chair. "The kidnappings and killings all seem to have a schedule. We couldn't have a better chance at stopping these. Everyone will be in place within a few days, and we can make our first move on that police station, for one. There are a dozen or so kidnappings planned for this week and we will be ready for them as well. We have begun to monitor a few of the potential victims here and elsewhere."

Stamos felt relieved. It seemed like only a matter of days before this whole scheme would be blown out into the open and the entire network exposed, hopefully before even one murder could be accomplished. The activity of each division was hitting a feverish pace to develop the evidence needed to bring down the entire network. The timing had to be just right to avoid any unnecessary harm to the public. Stamos knew full well the balancing act required in these conspiracy investigations from his time working in the banking world, where perpetrators could cover up their tracks quickly after the crime. Stamos did not want to tip their hand before all perpetrators could be held culpable.

This involved thoroughly identifying all 30 devices, their owners, and each of the numerous cells tied to each of those devices. The assistant director of the FBI and the entire criminal division would be brought into play to secure the subpoenas for each of the members of this plot, now numbering several thousand individuals. Stamos could not wait to present this evidence to the director. Downstream from the devices, there were numerous methods of communicating with the individual cells. Still, luckily, they involved only a few rogue messaging apps, Stealth Realm, that they already had access to. Otherwise, at times it seemed the less organized realms were using plain text messaging and a rudimentary code. Point's assistant Sebastian had set up a lab outside the mainstream to hack into the backend system of Stealth Realm to get the information without tipping off the administrators of these apps.

The security concern regarding this app was the Russian money and influence over this messaging app had likely tainted the entire organization. If they subpoenaed the information they needed too soon, the whole operation could be compromised. A FISA court ex parte subpoena for surveillance would be requested and obtained, thus legalizing Sebastian's hacking of Stealth Realm.

The exquisite planning and proper execution of the surveillance could not be more important for the later prosecution. Months down the line, during what would surely become a myriad of legal cases, further, more public subpoenas would ultimately be served, but for now, the data and evidence were just streaming in as fast as each of these rednecks could type with their thumbs. The investigators recognized there would be initial pushback from the companies that ran the apps and they could appeal the subpoenas, which would delay the outcome, but the evidence from the FISA warrant would already have been obtained. If there were any improper legal filings, invalidation of that evidence could occur.

With the investigations heating up on almost a dozen fronts, it was decided to split the leadership teams of both the FBI and Merlin into three divisions and three subdivisions each. Sam and Randy would head to Las Vegas where they would head the three subdivisions of Arizona, Nevada, and Utah. Chip and Torey would head to Michigan to head the three subdivisions of Michigan, Ohio, and Pennsylvania. Natalia, Huy, Hanson, and Stamos, along with Claire, Samantha, and Sage, would remain in Georgia to investigate the events in Georgia, South Carolina, and Florida. While this scheme would separate the three geographically, Natalia, Sam, and Chip promised there would be almost constant contact among them.

Each team divided the list of dozens of targets to investigate, prioritizing imminent kidnappings or murders. The hotels, conference rooms, and command centers, now numbering nine total, were being assembled with the Merlin conference rooms in Atlanta being converted into a master command center where they would all attend secure briefings electronically. With the impending victims of the plots being so specific even down to the location of the kidnappings, and potentially incriminating information being sent to law enforcement agencies, the background investigation was now essentially complete. The sheer volume of victims would prove difficult, for there were an estimated few hundred thousand victims identified in the communications from the server.

In addition to the perpetrators of the imminent violence, each of these victims would be tracked to guarantee their safety, thus requiring manpower in the thousands. The logistics to resolve the human resources nightmare were left to Hanson, of course. With a piecemeal plan in place, it was by no means foolproof but gave them the best chance of success.

Before running off to their respective command centers, the entire team gathered around a conference table in the Atlanta command center for a final send-off. Each of the teams still needed to plan more thorough surveillance and incursions. Through today and tonight, in parts of Georgia, South Carolina, and Florida, there would be drone and field team surveillance commencing, which Stamos, for one, could not wait to join. Huy was also busy briefing the teams on what they would expect to encounter at each of their centers. As they finished running through the processes of active surveillance, the group was milling about the SCIF, about to move back to the main command center.

Natalia queried the group, "There is something that I have found just amazing to me! If this entire data set of victims was just communicated to the perpetrators, and none of our present missing persons are on this list, then we were correct that this was not in the script and was just practicing. Was it just a grudge that they were acting on? If so, then their inept practice runs allowed their whole operation to be uncovered both here and in Arizona."

"Who knows, but by doing this, they picked on the wrong person with the wrong friends. They probably would have progressed a lot further along in their plot. Right, Sean?" Claire looked across the table at her new, yet old, most trusted friend in the world.

At that moment, Stamos had ceased paying attention to the presentation, and for good reason. He had just taken a phone call, and stood up from the table, walking toward the door. As he swung the heavy door open, he became visibly animated and agitated at the conversation. A silence fell over the group as they wondered the source of his angst.

Samantha sat back, noticing the awkward silence, and took stock of the situation in the void left in the room. Her mature beyond-her-years conscience had something to add to Natalia's point. She needed to lay thanks at the foot of those who needed to be appreciated. "You're right, Claire. If I had not linked up with Natalia's internship, and if she wasn't such a generous soul, none of this plot would have yet seen the light of day."

Natalia blushed as she stood arm-in-arm with Chip, deflecting the compliments with her own gratitude, "I am so
334

glad I took that hunch and called Chip. He, Sam, Torey, and Huy run the most selfless organization in the world. And not to mention Stamos, Point, and Hanson from the FBI. They all saved my life a few years ago, and they are not done yet."

Chip, from the beginning, had felt out of his element here in the massive investigation as there was not a single financial component to this evidence gathering. "I am just going with the flow from this gentle soul," he mused as he looked over at his partner.

Stamos returned in a flash, his face displaying every emotion all at once, and with every shade of red all at once. "I just got off the phone with Point and Sebastian. We are closing in on all of the devices. And get this, one of the devices in Utah is currently located in the private law offices of the attorney general of the state of Utah. And one of two devices in Michigan is currently located in or near the offices of the speaker of the state house of representatives of Michigan."

Natalia covered her mouth to block the audible gasp that was escaping, "Wow, they don't have any shame, do they? Why would they even risk this in Utah? They have a clear majority."

Hanson interrupted the thought, "Well, we thought there might be some high-profile characters ensnared in this dragnet. It is going to become quite crowded in the courtrooms by the time we are done. I know this guy. He is the most condescending individual I have ever known. What do you say we take a quick detour before we take this whole network down? I want to pay this guy a little visit. Just to document what he says." Hanson could be quite conniving when you were on his bad side.

The flustered look fled Stamos' face and was quickly replaced by an elated excitement, "Yes! Quick detour, no more than twenty-four hours. Then I want us back here for the takedown. Two separate planes. I want you to arrive first and preface my visit by a few hours. Pretend like you are already there investigating some amorphous right-wing individuals. Huy, are your field teams and drones in place there yet?"

Huy, who was intrigued by the sudden distraction, took off his headset again and leaned back. "They are. Up and running. Already performing surveillance as directed. One step ahead, they are presently tracking the device and target. Communications jamming equipment is also in place. Stamos, just a heads up, we are operating there as clandestinely as we can. We are cloaking our drones as hobby drones. Right now, they have no arms. If at any time while you are there, you see the need for protection, we will keep one drone on the ground, armed and ready to be deployed. Look at monitor 49 over there to the right. You don't even have to fly out there."

"No, I also want to look this guy in the eyes. Just like these guys in Georgia, I want to stir the pot. Draw their fire out into the open, so to speak. Not so much to tip..." Stamos paused mid-sentence to witness Hanson packing his tactical pack with gear, with a phone cradled between his shoulder and his ear, the wheels of the logistics machine in fast motion. "Before you go, let's attend this next briefing. I want to set a firm schedule for the next 48 hours. I want this entire operation in full gear by that deadline, with a full takedown commencing upon my return. I want the sheriff here in handcuffs by then and I want to be there. I want Mía freed by then. As before, If any danger exists, make the incursion without me."

That deadline was another delay but at least a definitive timeframe was finally known, a welcome change to the ears of the entire room. Now they were cooking. No turning back now. Less than 48 hours to revelation and truth. Sage, Samantha, and Claire simultaneously stood at their seats and collectively embraced upon hearing the good news. The revelation would prove to be the most uncomfortable saga in the nation's history, ripping the bandage from the deep wounds of the nation that hadn't seen the light of day and had not fully healed since the Civil War.

CHAPTER 32: UTAH

There was no doubt in his mind Hanson felt insecure, like a fish out of water in Utah. Originally from suburban Minneapolis, he was most certainly not the cowboy type and more at home in the Midwest or Northeast. Although he was recently injured in a shootout in Georgia, he somehow felt safer there than he did in Utah. He had only arrived in Provo a few hours previously and he already felt an eerie unease, as though he was being watched. He went about preparing for the meeting between Stamos and the Utah state attorney general there in Provo. The attorney general insisted that the meeting be in his hometown of Provo where one of his offices was located. As luck would have it, it was the same office that was under full drone surveillance by the Merlin Utah team.

Hanson stood silently outside his large SUV on the tarmac in front of a small hangar at this small regional airport, his mind racing, trying to keep straight all of the chess pieces that were on the board and threatening the republic for which he had sworn an oath to protect. He took that oath seriously and there were too many possible victims to protect realistically. His boss was due to land any minute at the airport in Provo and immediately they would depart for the meeting. Afterward, they would drive to Salt Lake City to surreptitiously inspect their operations headquarters prior to departure.

In the distance, through the sinewy waves of heat streaming up from the ground, he strained to see the small FBI jet landing at the far end of the runway. Less than a minute after the plane landed, he could see the plane taxi into the taxiway, aiming straight for the waiting SUV. The jet engines had not even cycled down when Stamos emerged from the plane and took the slow jog over to Hanson and the two black Suburbans waiting for him. The trademark was Stamos' signature move, a running arrival off a plane, with the stairs down while the jet was still moving. He was a man on the move, continually making haste, sprinting toward the SUV while crouching to avoid the jetwash.

"How was the flight?" Hanson queried.

"It went relatively quickly for the distance. I caught up on some phone calls that I should have taken care of over the past week. Still haven't reached the Director. I sense he is avoiding me. How is it here?"

"Well, I wish I could call it cordial. We have met with a bunch of stonewalling from the police. We have only told them we are aware of some extremists in the area, which is old news. As you know we have been very vague with our introduction regarding the subject of these extremists and their capabilities. I feel like at least in Georgia fifty percent of the population was open to other points of view. Here there is only one point of view, one demographic, and if you are a minority, you had better live with your head down with their domination of the laws."

Stamos agreed, "Well, these people have been living without much interference and without witnessing any other viewpoints for a long time. Looks like we will just have to inform them of the possibility of some vague criminal activity and tell them we are investigating. See what reaction that begets."

Hanson brought his right hand to his chin as he stared

out at the passing countryside, commenting his agreement in full, "True, these will be classified as hate crimes and national security and espionage crimes criminally, so they will be immediately advanced to the federal judiciary. I'm just glad our command center is in Salt Lake City where there is some tolerance. We are basing Merlin's drones at a hangar at a small airport in Ogden that has not much in the way of an air traffic control tower. It appears that the activity here is minimal and if anything, the perpetrators here and in Idaho are supporting the operations in Arizona and Nevada. When they do, we will watch them as they enter and leave the state. That, in and of itself, will create a federal case out of this."

In no time at all, they arrived at the understated two-story offices of this small-time attorney general. They pulled up with the two vehicles in tandem parked in front of the building. There was no security outside, which was odd for the offices of an AG of a relatively important state. He must feel pretty comfortable regarding any possible threats he may or may not face, Stamos thought. As they stepped down onto the sidewalk, the air was dry yet thick with a haziness that Stamos just couldn't put his finger on. Was it smog? Or was it just thick air? He strained to look down the street as the mountains in the distance on both the eastern and western horizons were barely visible, yet the few wispy clouds overhead revealed mostly blue sky.

"Alright let's get this over with. If they aren't going to be helpful, the less time we spend trying to convince them to protect their own people the better. I just want to stir the pot a little." Stamos removed his aviators and placed them in the front pocket of his gray suit jacket, as he rearranged his pressed white shirt collar against the glistening skin of his neck. He wiped his brow lightly before stepping down onto the dusty sidewalk. The first floor was mostly windows, which were mirror-coated, showing a perfect reflection of the two Suburbans back at Stamos as he squinted to see if he could view anyone inside. There were only two state police cars and one pickup parked along the side of the building if that was any indication regarding the number of individuals within.

They entered the glass doors and general formalities were exchanged with the secretary. The office was on the second floor, with an open, ornate stone stairway with red carpet leading them up to several offices upstairs. Two heavy dark oak double doors were opened by the secretary, allowing them into the antiquated office. As they entered, two tattooed, bald, yet bearded gentlemen who looked like they could be at home at a KKK rally exited the room. The stoic attorney general barely acknowledged them as he looked over some papers in a manila folder. He closed it as the pair approached the desk and sat down. Both Hanson and Stamos immediately spied a brown tablet sitting on the far edge of the desk that was thick, unlike any of the thin modern tablets that were so prevalent these days. Their host must have sensed their brief glances as he opened a drawer and placed it neatly under some folders.

The meeting was uneventful and the attorney general was genial enough, in a spaghetti western kind of way. Tough guy who just wanted to hear himself talk brand of hospitality. Stamos simply stuck to his guns, informed the attorney general about some possible criminal activity from extremists in his state, and left it at that. No need to tip his hand. But through the entire conversation, Stamos noted, these offices were obviously a front for something sinister. He had seen this type of behavior before, in Georgia perhaps, but also in the offices of every two-bit gangster in Eastern Europe. The aura and atmosphere were eerily exactly the same.

From the moment they entered the doorway of this man's office, from the greetings and salutations and formal handshake, the cold stare from under the shadow of the brim of this man's cowboy hat, to the steel handshake goodbye, Stamos felt something was hidden from view. Like they were on enemy territory. Like they were visiting a foreign land for peace talks while the enemy was plotting to invade. He also sensed they were under surveillance, though it would not be unusual for any law offices to have security cameras.

During the entire duration of the ten-minute conversation, two most comical, cartoon-like state troopers stood against the wall behind the attorney general's desk, flanking him on either side, staring straight ahead with mirrored sunglasses and their funny trooper hats. They did not make even the slightest move, such that Stamos almost thought they were wax figures. Stamos wondered whether the attorney general met everyone with these stoic figures standing behind him.

There appeared to be a closed door with a partially frosted window leading to a conference room on the left and a large dark closet to the right. There was some obvious activity happening in the conference room, with voices that could be heard yet not comprehended and a crowd scurrying about the place. Sure seemed like a lot of activity going on, Stamos thought as he rose to leave, extending his hand to shake the hand of the attorney general, who feigned sudden interest in a mostly blank pad of paper on his desk, writing some illegible words on it. At the top of the pad was written, in bold letters, "FBI"

As they entered the FBI issue SCIF Suburban for the hour drive to Salt Lake City, Stamos said, "Well, that was cordial, don't you think? In a cold, calculating way."

"Yeah, like a meeting with a mob boss before your demise." quipped Hanson, with a concerned look written across his face.

"Did you spy that brown tablet? And what do you make of those goons who walked out? Looked like some people we should probably look into. I assume Merlin is identifying and tracking everyone coming and going from there." Then he turned toward the driver. "I forgot to introduce myself by the way. Are you one of the new academy graduates?" Upon hearing the answer, he added, "Where are you from?"

The driver hesitated, "I'm from California, sir. Former police officer in Santa Clara." "That's great, we need to go over something. You guys are going to have to be careful as hell here. These locals are going to be watching you. I felt like we were being recorded in there. Something was not right. When you do any surveillance here you need double egress and double protection. This is going to be like operating in Ukraine under Russia's thumb, constantly needing to watch your back. You were right, Hanson, this IS going to be worse than Georgia. I thought the police in Atlanta were slow to respond, but you never had the sense they were on the other team. Even worse than the county sheriff."

"I heard about Georgia. Glad you guys escaped without too much injury. Being from California, we are fully aware of the backward state of affairs in Utah. Even white folks with a lot of money try to avoid these parts. Other than Park City that is. And Idaho? Forget that place."

"Hanson here got the worst of it. Seems like months ago now," Stamos paused, looking out at the brown desolate countryside between Provo and Salt Lake City. He couldn't believe that it was only a week ago. "I've decided, let's not visit the Merlin Command Center. Let's not even drive by it. Get the planes to SLC as soon as you can. Let's get back to Atlanta. We can video conference them in on our briefing. I feel like if we go even near the command center, we will draw attention to them. I like that they are flying under the radar so to speak. They need to get all of their drones operational. And I need to get back to Georgia before tonight. We need to make some headway in our surveillance and incursions. I get the sense that during the takedown I will be visiting either Phoenix or Las Vegas to participate there as well."

On the drive northward, Stamos stared out the window at the passing cacti and the rolling tumbleweeds. It appeared the winds were coming down out of the mountains to the west, stirring up the sands into a sand storm. A chinook of sorts, if that was the accurate term, Stamos thought. The brief jaunt through the arid, windy desert lands did not take long enough to merit a substantive conversation about the operations here, so Stamos took the time to make a phone call to the assistant director. He had not been able to reach him or the Director on the plane ride. As far as political appointees went, he trusted this man to be on the right side of history. The Director was another story. He thought back to

344

his last encounter with him, in his office. Not much emotion, not much trust was displayed, and the Director had spewed a whole heap of political skepticism regarding any possible organized extremist activity. He would need to tread lightly.

"Are you alone in your office? This is Top Secret, Special Intelligence. Ok, good," he started. "Sir, we have made a lot of headway all around the country. This organization is being directly commanded by a Russian server. Directions are being sent out from a central location within the US and we have intercepted them. The information that we have is quite grave and is actionable intelligence against a great number of American citizens. Highly illegal and involves murder, kidnapping, and entrapment. I would like further backing for the operation to take any and all action against the perps." He paused for a few moments, with a few Yes, sirs. "No, this goes far beyond hate speech. And it involves some law enforcement individuals all across the country."

Stamos fell silent, his jaw opening as though he was holding back, which he was. Hanson wished he could hear the political speech on the other end. It was not hard to fathom the content, though. Hanson had heard it all before. "Don't get too far over your head. Don't get caught spying on Americans without cause. Don't get caught, period." and the ending, "I don't want to be testifying before the Senate Intelligence Committee."

It turns out, it was far better than that. Stamos hung up the phone. "We have his full backing. It seems he has also heard from Point, and for some reason, he trusts Point even more than he trusts me. Point is as conservative as they come, and when something riles him up, he just sounds more convincing. He said we will bring the Director in on this soon."

"I want the planes ready, fueled up and jets running, and I want the pilots to put the afterburners on. Let's get home to where the action is."

As they approached the massive Salt Lake City airport with their awaiting jet barely visible through the sandstorm, the Suburban raced onto the tarmac, past suited FBI agents waving them through the gates. Stamos remarked to Hanson how uncannily similar the airport appeared compared to the Kabul International Airport where he had a similar hasty exit to rescue fallen comrades in Kandahar. He couldn't finish his sentence, flashing back to the searing sand slashing across his face like a blow torch, as he sprinted across the tarmac fully twenty years ago now, though at this moment it felt like just yesterday, the vision was so clear. His CIA commanding officer, an impressively tall, intimidating man who looked half-Russian, was yelling from the open door of the aging government-issue Learjet, telling him to get a move on. That day would live in infamy in his mind, as no one except he and the soldiers they saved knew the details of that day, and probably nobody ever would. The little Learjet stretched the limits of the little runway in Kandahar and evaded more than a few bullets in their escape that day.

Back in the present day, Stamos snapped out of it just as the Suburban came to a screeching halt just yards from their ride. In an almost reverse fashion to his entrance, Stamos grabbed Hanson by the arm, and with their suit jackets covering their eyes and mouths, they leapt up the steps of the much more modern G6 with no tail number visible. Hanson stumbled on the top step, leaning on Stamos, as the two almost crashed into the opposite wall. From the floor, Stamos peered into the cockpit at his favorite pilot, "Jimmy, get us home to Atlanta, quickly. We have some arrests to make and some girls to rescue."

—❧ ❧—

CHAPTER 33: GRUESOME FINDING

—❧ ❧—

Nearly a week had passed without the satisfaction he desired, and Stamos had broken promise after promise to himself regarding the timeframe he would rescue Mía. And while they were now miles closer to solving this mystery, he felt like he was not doing enough to protect this friend of his new friends. With this added self-pressure, he resolved then and there that into the field he must go to push things along. By now, this joint task force between the FBI and Merlin operated like a well-oiled machine even with the dozens of moving parts spread out across the country.

Stamos surmised he had wasted most of the day jetting to the mountains to help jump-start the operation there as they were meeting with resistance from the local and state governments. In the end, he was still quite bothered by his meeting with the Utah state attorney general though. He couldn't shake how it had disturbed his sense of right versus wrong, and that the AG there was not on the right side of history. There was something sinister about him. It was as though he was sitting across the desk from a Russian GRU officer and not a law enforcement officer in this country. With that memory, he reminded himself just then these men were the reason he pushed himself so hard.

As he strolled into the Atlanta Merlin command center with his best combat-ready team in tow, he stopped at the coffee shop in the lobby. The FBI agents looked quite out of place with the millennials crowded into this small space for a break in their shopping sprees in midtown Atlanta. At least they weren't in tactical gear, Stamos thought to himself. In the crowded coffee bar, the TV just happened to be tuned to a WNN news bulletin about political violence erupting with protests against the present administration's immigration policy. Protests with raucous fights were breaking out in D.C., Texas, Arizona, Florida, and elsewhere. In today's climate, it seemed if there was a protest, there were always counter-protesters there to clash over something about which our society used to compromise.

Shaking his head, he just let it slide off his shoulders as always. "Let's get this show on the road, gentlemen," Stamos said, with java juice in hand, as he corralled his men up the escalator.

They did not just casually ride the escalator but jogged up the moving stairs to the third floor, as they met their Merlin counterparts outside the command center. The difference between the groups was a particular contrast. The FBI guys were less-than-athletic federal agents, while the Merlin operatives were all young, fit ex-military special ops guys in tactical gear. The agents meanwhile wore khakis as though they were headed to a happy hour. Some of the Merlin men were even working out in a corner of the hallway outside the command center, stretching and exercising. There were a few jealous looks glancing sideways from the feds toward the Merlin teams, some of the older ones reminiscing about their younger, more athletic years, tightening their belts and sucking in their guts as they did so.

Hanson, noticing the contrast, looked toward his charges, and reassured them, "Don't worry guys, we brought our tacticals. They are in the truck being brought up to the command center as we speak. We'll be ready. I'm just so eager to investigate this new site, I didn't want to waste time getting all gussied up. Let's go over our briefing." Hanson cinched his belt and puffed out his chest in response to the competitive jousting going back and forth.

This location had been under periodic drone surveillance since being discovered several days ago. They would approach the farmstead from a mile away on foot from a more obscure drop-off site. Drone surveillance would ensure there were no perps in the location at the time of the incursion. The location consisted of an abandoned house and barns located at the rear of the property and a large area of woods behind the homestead. This choice of locations was made due to considerable activity that had occurred there as recently as today.

As both the FBI and Merlin teams prepared their gear, Stamos and Huy expressed their adamant warning that this incursion be handled with safety the ultimate objective. Any sign of perpetrators would be an automatic abandonment of mission. As a test run of civilians, Stamos had decided to allow Claire to ride along on this excursion, as she promised him she would remain in the armored Suburban. Talk about throwing safety out the window. He reasoned with Huy and the rest of the team that she did have some of the best gun safety training, having grown up in rural Maine. Realizing the slight he also promised the rest of the women they would participate in the live-action as well.

On the screen before them, Huy brought up the live feed of the drone in the daytime so they could see the layout of the house and buildings and the fields surrounding them.

"You will be egressing through either of these two routes, one team retracing your steps from the east and one south through the woods and circling back. You can see the field conditions after the short rain shower today. It is going to be humid and wet out there tonight. We will increase our incursions over the next few days to accelerate our timeline for discovery. Meanwhile, the Digital Teams are making new discoveries every day regarding each of these perpetrators and their locations. Next briefing on these developments is tomorrow morning. Any questions?". Huy readied the Merlin men with their safety gear for the night. Tactical gear was provided to Claire, Samantha, Sage, and Natalia, just in case. The four were surprised at the relative comfort they felt in the gear, despite the heavy payload.

With no questions, all tactical personnel were eager to get on the road and finish this. With the revelations from the previous few nights and the recent activity, an eerie anticipation of what they might find at this location crossed everyone's minds.

Stamos commented while the team was gathering their gear and getting changed, "Those woods look suspicious. We need to include a forensics inspection there in this incursion, alright, Randy?"

His best and most capable combat-ready team member also happened to be his division leader, Randy. Having experienced the most gruesome scenes of violence in Eastern Europe during the years following the breakup of the Soviet Union, he was also a seasoned evidence gatherer. Randy whispered in Stamos' ear his grim suspicions regarding tonight's outcome in only a few choice words and left it at that.

It would ultimately take them two hours to reach their rural destination that evening, arriving close to 10 pm. As if her heart couldn't beat any harder or faster, Claire could feel the rush of adrenaline settling into every fiber of her being. She glanced over at her best friend, and as their eyes locked in, she realized again that she should have known his true occupation all along. A silver steely shine in his eyes glimmered in the moonlight that looked like an alien predator on a hunt in some old science fiction movie. Her heart rate and her nerves calmed slowly as she felt safe in his presence, though she also felt a sudden capability in her own right. She had police training from her father long ago and could hold her own in martial arts competitions, even against men twice her size.

Their drop-off location was indeed a muddy mess as they quickly entered a mature cotton field from a dead-end road a mile from their target. The trek could take an hour through the muck by Stamos' estimate.

As they dismounted and camouflaged their trucks behind a few trees at a tractor entrance, they could see the growing cotton plants in the field with their headlights, which were now extinguished. Stamos was excited to be in the field, but wary about the condition of the red clay. He secured the Suburban so that Claire and the rest of the women would be safe with Hanson and the driver. She asked only once to participate, knowing the answer. It was all she could do to contain herself, but she watched anxiously anyway as he shut the door tightly, watching the locks engage.

Stamos turned around swiftly and began, "Team 1, Team 2 in position, drone team in position, request approval to proceed."

Huy answered emphatically from the command center, "Approved. Proceed. No activity detected."

In a mirror replica of the last incursion, the house appeared empty and the grove of trees behind the barn had identical fresh tracks leading deep into the forest. Stamos led the men in a beeline past grand oak trees, with Spanish moss draping off sprawling branches, again being careful to avoid the clay tracks. The late evening fog was setting in, and some dew and remnants of the earlier rain shower were dripping off the trees and moss. Then came the culmination of their worst fears in the sights of their night sight goggles.

Multiple small clearings were just now coming into view through the fog that consisted of deep pits dug into the forest floor radiating from one central area that must have previously been a picnic or fire pit site.

"Over here!" one of the agents shouted from the farthest pit from the clearing. As everyone dashed toward the sound, gasps of horror and a few "Oh my God!" verbalizations rang out from the remaining team members.

"How many are there?" asked Stamos as he slowly made his way through the wet underbrush.

"I think four or five. They're partially buried. It looks like they have gunshot wounds," was the answer.

The gruesome sight sickened some as the smell quickly overwhelmed all in attendance. Many of the men had seen combat action, and some had seen worse, but not in their own backyard. None were prepared for the sight of decaying flesh, despite having been advised earlier to expect the worst.

Stamos was equally unprepared. There was no adequate rehearsal to make anyone comfortable with this worst-case scenario. "Alright, I've seen enough. The killing has begun sooner than we thought. Let's move on the sheriff's office tonight. We've got to save who we know we can save."

He was interrupted by Huy over the comm, "About that, Stamos. There is some activity there at the police station. A few cars just showed up and the sheriff just exited with the communication device. We have split up Drone Three and Four. One will stay at the station and the other will track these cars. It appears they are headed out of town toward Atlanta."

"Looks like our sheriff is going to get in on this action himself, huh? Alright, a few pictures, please. It is takedown time. Everyone secure this site. Lights off during egress. I want anyone who enters this homestead to be apprehended, and I want communications jamming at this site for all such apprehensions."

"One more thing, Sean. You will get your first arrest sooner rather than later. There is a pickup truck approach-ing your position about a mile down the road. You have about two minutes to secure your egress. We have commu-nications jamming in about thirty seconds. You will still have your comms as requested."

"Okay, everyone. You heard him. Hightail it to the berm between the cotton fields. Egress now. Forget about the pictures. All lights extinguished."

The men scrambled back to the farmstead and beyond to the grass pathway between two fields leading north from the farmstead. Just as the last man reached the egress point, Stamos spied a beam of light coming down the road. Twenty seconds later, the headlights turned into the driveway and headed behind the barn.

Stamos broke silence into his comm, "Are you getting this? The pickup just went toward the burial site. See if the

352

drone can pick up the video in the forest, Huy."

"Roger that," was the only response.

"And after that, if they leave before we can arrest them, track them so that we can ID them. I think I know what they are about to dispose of." Stamos wanted so much to take this one down. "Move on them now!"

With that command, several FBI agents swarmed either side of the barn toward the vehicle, making an easy arrest of the unsuspecting perpetrator before he could shut the door of the pickup. Flashlight beams were bursting through the light fog like random strobe lights in the tops of the trees behind the barn. In the covered bed of the truck, one more victim was found to bring the accurate total to six.

"Ok. We got him. Put him in the back of the hummer. Lock it tight. Cease communication jamming. I want a team here all night. I want all comers apprehended. Resume jamming for all arrests. The rest of us, we are hightailing it out of here, guys!" Stamos was ready for the takedown now and could not wait for any new victims for further proof.

Once they made it back to their vehicles, the shock wore off and the men were ready for battle with whatever or whoever was behind this.

His concentration zeroed in like a laser sight finder, Stamos only had one thought process and could not think of anything else. "Huy, how many men are still at the station? And can you patch the drone surveillance footage into my phone?"

"Just two. And yes, I am sending you a secure link. This link is going to require a pass token that I am sending to your phone now in a second text message."

Once he opened the footage on his phone, Stamos propped the phone up in the seat-back pocket so that all in the back seat could see. The drone camera was already in IR mode so they could clearly visualize two red outlines on the main floor, along with the known prisoners.

"Okay, can you case all immediately nearby buildings to verify the total potential perps in the area?"

Within a minute, the drone camera zoomed in on several Main Street buildings and all of the buildings surrounding the town square, and the entire area was virtually empty at this time of night.

"Then we go in now. Let's move!" Stamos possessed all the seriousness of an infantry soldier readying himself in the back of a troop transport vehicle. He had that look again in his eyes.

Claire, Sage, Samantha, and Natalia were all beginning to feel uncomfortable in the tactical gear but didn't care one bit now that they knew the goal they had set for the last two weeks was finally in sight.

Stamos turned toward Hanson in the front seat, "We need to zero in on the sheriff's car and devote one field team to apprehending him if we can catch him in the act. We will need an FBI unit along with you for the takedown. Can you call that in, Hanson? In addition, we will need backup here at the station. One last thing, I want the two communication jamming devices in place if you can get near the sheriff's car and one to remain there at the station."

Several miles down the road, another pickup rounded a corner toward the homestead, and Stamos alerted the agents still present to be ready for another one. It seemed their foe was eager to begin killing. Then he would be too, he thought as he stared straight ahead. He did not notice Claire's gaze upon him from the back seat. His awareness was only tactical at this point. His sole focus was on taking down this sheriff and police chief to start what he only hoped would be a cascading fall of the whole conspiracy.

He struggled to put his feet in the shoes of his Russian counterparts, for what was it that he was missing? The answer seemed to be too simple, too easily revealed. His adversaries were famous for subterfuge and false-flag operations with surprise endings that were not expected even by the most die-hard experts in the intelligence community. And their operations on the surface were always designed to be blamed on either their victims or another easily blamed unwitting foe. These rednecks could easily be the false flag, but what was he really missing?

He stared out at the passing trees and cotton fields as he remembered his experiences in another Georgia in another time of his life. The Russians used the South Ossetians as a pretext for war to fully take over more territory. In assisting the Georgians, Stamos remembered all too well the many assassinations that occurred in the ethnic cleansing of Georgians in their homeland. Russian repetition, throughout Eastern Europe, Asia, and now the United States. How to stop it here? He hoped it would be easier in present-day Georgia than twenty years ago in his youth.

‒·✳‹‹·‒

CHAPTER 34: STATION SHOWDOWN

‒·✳‹‹·‒

The short drive on country roads to the once-sleepy hamlet in Northeast Georgia would take what seemed like only a few minutes. When they reached the city limits, Stamos recognized immediately that several black SUVs descending on this town could be met with some resistance even from those not involved in this plot. Stamos sat forward in his seat as Huy broke the silence on the comm, and all eyes, which had been fixated on the drone footage on his phone broke their trance and looked toward their leader.

"We have cover off each main road out of town. We have just infiltrated the two-story building diagonal from the station toward downtown, and four snipers are making their way to the roof. There is no security and no signs of perpetrators outside the police station. Pull over briefly as soon as you see the four SUVs. We have sixteen men there in addition to the twelve in your unit. Field Team One will be the incursion unit, and Team Stamos will come in as clean-up and rescue. We also have your SWAT tactical team trucks that are coming soon and I will hold them five minutes outside of town in case we need them."

The barely lit streets stood in spooky contrast to the neon

and halogen lights of Atlanta from whence they came. Not one of the businesses on the main street had a single light on, revealing an almost abandoned state of affairs at this time of night. That would suit this mission just fine, thought Stamos as he peered out the window into each building they passed, looking for any signs of life, in between glances at the footage still playing on his phone.

As the other field team's vehicles came into view, the mission hit the point of no return. It seemed they had only pulled over for a few seconds when the command arrived to commence jamming communications in one minute. Stamos quickly let everyone know, "There will only be secure unjammed communications from this point forward. Switch to that channel."

Huy's next commands set the trucks in motion, "Two vehicles in front of the station and two vehicles will be in the rear. The front formation will be cover one, three strikers on each. The cover one will be the decoy to confirm the front door is unlocked and he will announce as FBI, enter, and ask the two individuals about the prisoners. If he encounters resistance, he will then set off two smoke canisters. Then begin full frontal assault. At the mark of 60 the rear team will set the semtex to gain entry to the rear entrance. Begin jamming now. Wait for my mark for incursion."

"I can't believe we are here at this moment. I've been envisioning this day for two weeks, and we are here!" Sage exclaimed as they watched the lone tactical member walk up the steps of this small-town police station. Three fully outfitted team members flanked him, waiting crouched at the bottom of the steps beside the antique street light. The streets were eerily silent tonight in this little ghost town, as the cover one entered the glass doors.

"Set the mark now!" Huy proclaimed.

"We will begin our incursion after the second four exit their vehicle," Stamos informed the group just as they witnessed the three strikers bound up the steps. Gray smoke billowed out of the glass doors as they were opened. On cue, the four tactical team members exited the vehicle in front of them and approached the building in a wing formation.

"Oh my god, my adrenaline is pumping through my veins! I've never done anything remotely like this! Laser tag will never be the same!" Sage shouted from the back of the vehicle.

Claire and Samantha simultaneously placed their hands on Sage's shoulders from either side and proclaimed without words their wholehearted, serious agreement with that statement. The three young women were appreciative of the full tactical gear and helmets, and at this moment, they could not have appeared more ready for this mission than they did now.

"Alright, it's go-time for Mía. Everyone, follow Hanson and me and stay flanked following the two of us. That means stay in between us and two steps behind, I'll be right and Hanson left. Once inside, our job will be to find Mía. If at any time I tell you to egress, you immediately egress and don't go outside alone unless you are sure you are covered. That means that you have someone with a gun with you. If you lose us, stick with Natalia. She has a gun. You each have a gun, but don't unholster it unless absolutely necessary."

A loud explosion echoed through the streets and a cloud of smoke emanated from behind the building just as they exited the SUV. As they made their way toward the steps, they could hear the station was not secure yet, as evidenced by sporadic gunfire from inside the smoky confines. Stamos signaled for all to cease advance, shielded by the concrete light pillars at the base of the antique granite staircase, worn by more than two centuries of use. It would not be long now, with the teams surrounding the building.

A comforting silence now enveloped the area as they waited for a go-ahead from Stamos. One of their own cracked open the door, stuck their head out, and quietly confirmed the all-clear signal to the rest of the team. Stamos was the first one in and Hanson followed the ladies into the building. Just as he closed the door, he spied headlights coming down the street from downtown.

Huy broke radio silence, "Okay we have a single vehicle,

two men in an old Ford sedan driving by. As I said, they won't be able to communicate with anyone. This jamming device covers the entire town. They won't even get radio reception."

Once inside, the six would-be rescuers made a bee-line for the stairs in the rear of the building near the jail cells. They passed by the two neutralized individuals, who were unconscious or dead, which one was not readily apparent. But from the relative calm of the two team members crouching over them, perhaps the latter was more likely. As each of them passed the lifeless bodies, they kept a close eye on them anyway, just in case. Several tactical members were assessing the situation on the steps and near the jail cells, where two of the prisoners remained. Unfortunately, the windowless, steel door at the bottom of the steps was locked.

"Use the semtex, no time to find keys, Stamos commanded two of the men on the steps, as they each grabbed several objects out of their tactical bags. He then directed two other men with a wave of his index finger toward the glass door, "You two, guard the front door!"

They yelled at the occupants to initiate communication and commanded them to crouch in a corner as far from the door as possible. Several seconds passed before the explosives were set and the Merlin field team members yelled "All Clear! Fire in Five!"

Stamos ushered his fellow team members up the steps and around the corner with hands waving. "Back up the steps, cover your ears tightly," he directed the team. The heat emitted by the gray smoke canisters and flash-bang devices had all participants dripping with sweat. The explosion was louder than either of the younger women had imagined it would sound from the movies. Even though they all believed they were ready for it, when the shock wave hit them, they all jumped and crouched under the railing simultaneously, cringing as if expecting debris to rain down on them. Opening their eyes and seeing none, within seconds, Natalia, Sage, Samantha, and Claire bravely and brazenly sprinted down the steps and through the demolished door to where they wanted, no, needed to find their Mía.

Against their directions, they were the first through the door and into the hazy cell. Sage was the first to yell out, "Mía!" aimlessly through the smoky air. They could barely recognize the shapes of three people in the far corner of the room. Mía, who previously was seated on a bench, had crouched under it from all of the commotion and almost didn't recognize Sage in her tactical gear. Upon hearing the voice yelling at her, she excitedly yelled back and jumped up to an embrace beyond all embraces. Samantha, Claire, and Natalia joined in and as they did, they noticed the two other young women in the room that they had almost nearly neglected. Natalia motioned for them to rise and join the group of women rescuers. "Don't be afraid! We are the FBI. We are here to rescue you," Natalia declared in a very authentic-sounding law enforcement voice.

The two other women hesitated, then reluctantly joined the circle as they ascended the stairs into the smoke still emanating from the canisters lying at the top of the steps. Despite the murky air, their vision was better on the main floor once the overhead lights had been illuminated. The smoke was slowly clearing above them and they could begin to visualize the entire station with its tacky furnishings and decor. The combination of the dim side lighting and the bright halogens above created hazy, white rays of light illuminating the antique dark oak furniture, bright red gaudy carpeting, and the blood now pooling at the side of the two fallen officers. The scene created a surreal war-like atmosphere that slowly sank into those in the group not used to dead bodies lying about.

"Okay team, we need to secure the entire compound and indeed the entire town," Stamos spoke into the comm. "Huy, what do you have for me on the sheriff? The police chief here has been neutralized."

"Stamos, we have the sheriff's car in Atlanta, and they..." Huy paused for a second on the comm, trying to believe his own words, "Literally right in front of our field team, and in full view of the drone, kidnapped one of our known targets at gunpoint. The victim is in the trunk of their car. What do you want us to do?"

Events had escalated quickly in the matter of only a few hours here, proving those who stoop to criminal activity put little thought into doing it right. The entire Southeast realm would now go down like a lead balloon. "Take them down now. I'll file the warrants myself. Send in the FBI unit now for the takedown and later we can get the Atlanta police involved. Begin jamming the sheriff's communication as soon as you begin pursuit and during takedown. Huy, make no mistake, I want that device! Don't let him destroy it. Make sure we get our hands on it at all cost."

Exhausted from the excitement and the wild rollercoaster ride, the courageous women in the group made their way, arm-in-arm supporting one another, to two uncomfortable wooden benches situated in a small waiting area in a protected corner at the front of the building. They filled their newly freed captives in on some of the details surrounding the plot, which was met with incredulous disdain for the perpetrators and sincere appreciation for their rescue. Those emotions were soon followed by a resolve to assist in any way they could to terminate the sinister plot.

Stamos walked slowly toward the ladies with his phone to his ear and his eyes studying each for any signs of trepidation. He gestured emotionally with his hands while he was strategizing the next steps with Huy back at headquarters. He turned to Hanson emphatically, "After we see the sheriff, let's get these ladies back to Merlin headquarters for a briefing and then I want to be at the Federal Courthouse. Get me the US Attorney so we can get charging papers into the District Court. I want this under seal, and I want an entire Southeast takedown in the next twenty-four hours."

An entire Southeast takedown!?! Now that would prove more complicated than it sounded, he realized, but while he grappled with the enormity of the task, the ongoing killing had to stop. He hoped within a few hours after the findings of the incursion in Northeast Georgia, they would have precise locations of all other communication devices and the source of the mysterious pickup that was confirmed to carry two more bodies.

"That's going to take a lot of manpower but with the kingpin toppled and the brown tablet in our possession, it should be child's play. I'll call the director and the prosecutor so we can get full coordination of the evidence we have now. And we need to coordinate with the rest of the country too." Hanson's logistical mind was working overtime on what would be the largest operation to dismantle a criminal organization ever. He wrapped his head around the thousands of arrests of co-conspirators that would be required just in the Southeast.

Stamos could not fathom the cost of any delay, as he sternly relayed the risks, "Every day we delay, we could see dozens of deaths in each state. That could be hundreds of deaths daily. Let's conference in Point and the Director now. Good thing we brought the SCIF truck. Can you set up the call while we are on our way to see this Sheriff and the evidence we gathered there? I can't wait to see who it is they thought so important to kidnap that the sheriff himself participated personally. Must be some significant catch."

"What about the girls?" Hanson asked.

"Bring the women with us. The more the merrier. What did you find out about the identity of this other woman? Was it the waitress?"

"She is another journalist from Atlanta. No one knew she was missing as far as we know. We have not located the waitress. No sign of her. She was charged with theft so I would have thought she would have been in one of the cells."

"Okay, we have no time to waste. I want to see this sheriff." Stamos then reached his hands up to his comm to hear better, "Send me the coordinates to meet the Field Team. We will use lights and sirens and can be there in no time flat. But maintain official radio silence regardless. Huy, have them maintain communication jamming in this town for the foreseeable future."

As the team climbed into the armored SUV, Stamos introduced himself to the newcomer and she agreed to the terms of silence required. She had no cell phone and no belongings except an orange jumpsuit, so the risk of being followed was nil. With that formality out of the way, Hanson set up the SCIF call first with Point, who joined the call immediately, then with the Director's office. The Director was not presently in the SCIF, but the assistant director, the Director of Counterintelligence, and the Director of the Criminal Division were present.

"The Director will be here any minute. He is aware and in his office just down the hall," the assistant Director stated nonchalantly as he introduced everyone.

Stamos smirked angrily as he envisioned the Director sitting on the corner of his desk, phone to his ear, talking to some political donor or bigwig of some sort while staring out the window overlooking Pennsylvania Avenue. "Well, let's get started. As you may be only partially aware, we have uncovered a massive conspiracy involving the Russian government and thirty cells of extremists who have planned to kidnap, kill, and frame possibly tens of thousands of Americans. They are communicating through a direct server that we have infiltrated, and the commands have been sent out to each of thirty devices that we are currently locating and tracking." Just then the Director walked into the SCIF, and Stamos could hear the vacuum sealing of the door as he entered. "Sir, hello. Thanks for joining. I was just..."

The Director interjected, "Sorry, I was detained. I understand you have some big news for us. Let's hear it."

"Yes. I was just saying we have uncovered a plot to kidnap, kill, and frame possibly tens of thousands of Americans. There are thirty cells of extremists, and they are communicating with the Russians via a server we have infiltrated and thirty encrypted devices that we have also infiltrated with malware. We are presently locating and tracking these. One of these devices was geolocated to a police station north of Atlanta, and we have just freed two kidnapped journalists and a political worker from this police station, kidnapped by the chief of police. About an hour ago, the sheriff of that county was followed into Atlanta by drone, and they have just been apprehended after kidnapping another innocent American.

They accosted and just threw her in the trunk of a private vehicle. We also uncovered massive burial pits and we have so far seen with our own eyes, five bodies, and a sixth was dumped into the pit under drone surveillance, and then two more arrived after we left."

"These drones that you speak of. These are Merlin drones? I don't like the involvement of a British company. Can we be assured of their loyalty to the US? I mean, I know they helped uncover the financial plot before, but..."

Stamos interrupted, "Yes, sir. They are completely on our side. If it wasn't for them, we wouldn't have uncovered this plot. And we have cleared them from a security standpoint. We have both fanned out across the country to interrupt this plot and take them down."

"I am uncomfortable with this. Can you show me the proof?" Nothing could shock Stamos as he heard the words, and he had almost formulated his answer when he could see Point had jumped out of his chair to speak.

Point, from his server lab in Quantico, who previously was fidgeting in his chair and now stood with his face so close to the camera that you could see the veins on his temples protruding. He uncharacteristically loosened his tie and cleared his throat, "Sir, I am going to place onto the screen just one of the thirty documents sent out in the last twenty-four hours that shows the names, locations, and dates of what you can see from this column titled "Apprehension Date". Neither of our two rescued individuals appears on this list, but the person who was kidnapped this evening is listed on the spreadsheet with an apprehension date of tomorrow. It appears they started early. This document was propagated from a known Russian server that was used in the financial attack and on which we have maintained malware surveillance since then. This is the first time this server has been used since then to our knowledge. We are now in possession of the sheriff's device which received this document, and it will be sent here to Quantico for analysis."

"Wow, that is very brazen for a law enforcement official, a Sheriff and a Police Chief you say? Alright, you have my attention. This seems to be real, huh?"

Stamos answered almost before the question was asked, "Yes, sir. And we have evidence that this involves not only Georgia, but South Carolina, Florida, Nevada, Arizona, Utah, Idaho, Michigan, Pennsylvania, Ohio, and other areas. We have opened investigations in all of these locations."

"You have my approval. Proceed," was his curt response.

"What we need now, and we are proceeding, is the involvement of Criminal and all US Attorneys. We need all of their support for sealed warrants, indictments, and arrests under FISA jurisdiction. This is a rolling investigation. We are jamming communications of those areas where these devices are located so they cannot communicate with the Russians or others involved."

The Director was just now grasping the gravity of the situation, as he could now be seen wringing his hands tightly, looking around the table at his deputies, "When this shit hits publicly we will need PR involved. And we will notify the President tonight. I will call him personally. How soon until public notification hits?"

"I would say in one to two days, max." Stamos knew they didn't have much more time under the cloak of secrecy. They couldn't detain the sheriff indefinitely without him being afforded an attorney. "We just need some time to uncover the other plots and the perpetrators."

"Agreed. We can hold them under national security concern for as long as it takes. They have no rights as treasonous traitors," was the director's affirmative response.

With that, the full approval of a nationwide operation to round up the organization was given, almost too easily from Stamos' standpoint. He was pleasantly surprised at the little pushback from the political hack. That unrivaled success and approval was why he wouldn't play his full hand to the Director until they possessed the full proof they had now compiled.

"To accelerate the investigations in other locales would require multiple incursions each night," he thought aloud. "In Michigan, Chip and Torey command three divisions, using six drones north of Detroit, near Columbus, and north of Pittsburgh. For the incursions in the outskirts of Phoenix and just outside Vegas, Sam and Randy have been busy preparing that day at the command center in Vegas. After visiting the sheriff, let's get back to headquarters so we can direct the show."

He thought better of it for a second, then proceeded anyway, "And sir," Stamos paused for effect, "I am worried that there is some other false flag operation underway. It just doesn't make sense they are doing this just to silence opposition."

"Right. Well, keep on it. Let me know what you find out. The Russians usually telegraph their every move. You will find it buried in the subtext though." The director was right, thought Stamos.

"This is so outrageous it is hard to believe," Claire thought aloud to the nodding agreement of all present.

As Stamos stared through the tinted window at the passing dark void, under the watchful gaze of the whole vehicle, he knew one miscalculation due to the confusion could be disastrous. What was the endgame? What was it that he was missing? The endgame.

—⁌⁍—

CHAPTER 35: TAKEDOWN

—⁌⁍—

Deep in the bowels of the massive Federal Courthouse in Atlanta, interrogation rooms and a high-security jail were maintained for those who were arraigned within its walls. Stamos and Hanson were anxiously waiting, pacing the room outside the interrogation quarters, when two steel doors swung open from the opposite sides of two rooms separated by a soundproof wall. In the observation suite, two symmetrical mirrored windows and microphones gave the agents unfettered access to the action within. Stamos and Hanson watched with clenched fists as their two top-secret prisoners were led into the two separate rooms.

Stamos wanted his turn to interrogate the sheriff first, he was so smug during the last interaction with him that he couldn't wait to get his hands on him. His thoughts pivoted immediately to the restraint one should display given his lofty position in the FBI. That concept of civility evaporated as soon as he saw the sheriff and the police chief simultaneously trying to smile and joke with their handlers. In the stroke of a heartbeat, he slammed the two doors open in succession that separated him from the sheriff's room, surprising the agents within the cells. Hanson could only watch with trepidation from behind the thick panes of glass as Stamos slammed a chair across the room. The sheriff was handcuffed to the barren table with his arms and hands outstretched before him, staring down at his stainless steel reflection.

"So, tell me everything you know before it gets ugly for you," Stamos began.

"I know my rights. I want to talk with my attorney."

"You have no rights. You are an enemy combatant at the moment. Tell me why you think you are above the law. What did these women do to you?"

"They are the enemy. They deserve everything that they are getting. You can't stop this. It is already in motion. There are too many parts. And you can't stop the final play."

"Oh, we are stopping it alright. Right now, tonight! What final play is that?"

"You'll see it as it plays out. It's too late to stop it," came the reply.

Stamos now recognized what was needed. The tense exchange reminded him of Eastern Europe a decade ago, when chaos and anarchy still ruled the day. Torture was more commonplace than diplomacy in that bygone era to extract information from sources. A sudden brutal right cross caught the sheriff right in the ear, which began to flow with blood down the twisted neck of the once proud boy. That solid connection with a skull would on any other day cause a hefty dose of pain through his wrist, but the adrenaline coursing through his veins put an end to that. So satisfying.

"I'm not talking. You can't stop all of my partners in all of our realms," the sheriff blurted out, his mouth filled with blood. Despite the comical bloody look, he managed an evil smile that enraged Stamos to no end. However, Stamos knew the sheriff would not reveal much else.

"That is just what I intend to do. Your bigoted realms are powerless compared to all the hammers we will rain down upon you!" Stamos had had enough. "Get any and all information you can out of this piece of shit!" he commanded his FBI brethren from Criminal as he threw the chair against the wall. The police chief was not even worth his time. Probably did not know anything anyway. He needed to connect with Huy immediately.

"Final play, my ass," he thought to himself as he spun around, considering another round of punches. "That bit of intel was well worth the long drive all the way here. There WAS something more. A bigger play. What was it? And what was it about bad guys and their constant need to reveal clues to their interrogators about their crimes?"

The two doors seemed to open themselves Jedi-style as he exited with his focus and fury directed in a laser beam toward an unknown enemy. He fully recognized the immediate need to harness that energy and not let it get out of control. He corralled Hanson and the other agents to return to the Sybaritean Hotel. Sprinting up the sub-basement stairs to the ground floor, he skipped every other step and sometimes two. Mid-stride, Stamos looked down over the tubular metal railing, shouting from a half-flight above, "Did you hear what he said? Final Play? This is not the end game. There IS something bigger!"

Hanson remarked, fully out of breath now after only one flight, "Well if there is something bigger than this, we need to detect it now. The only thing bigger I can think of is nuclear."

"Let's notify the CIA and DNI sentinel alert system. They need to know. Other possibilities could be bioterrorism, attacks on our leaders, attacks on infrastructure, etc. The sentinel alert system will parse out the possibilities."

As they reached their vehicles in the police parking area, Stamos spied the stares from the impatiently waiting ladies who could not be privy to these dirty inner workings of the justice system and had no ID badges to clear through security anyway.

"Ladies," Stamos greeted them as he climbed into the back seat. The early morning light barely allowed him to see their faces through the window, but now he could clearly sense their restlessness in the confined space of the Suburban. "That was highly productive. We have some information about a bigger operation afoot. He threatened that we wouldn't be able to stop the 'final play', whatever that might be. We need to keep our eyes and ears open. Let's get Point and Huy on a secure line. Book it to the Merlin Headquarters!"

Stamos tried to hide his right hand, which had begun to swell, under his thigh, but it was too late as Claire immediately spied the grimace on his face. She grabbed his arm, inspecting the speck of blood and laceration, which Stamos shook off with a shrug of his shoulders. Undeterred, Claire motioned for Natalia to take a look. "Natalia, look at this! Stamos, are you okay?"

"It's nothing," Stamos motioned ahead with his left hand, thinking how lucky they were the courthouse and the Sybaritean were only minutes apart. "We're almost there. We need this strategy meeting to go smoothly. We can't have any distractions from that." He managed to avoid the subject for the remaining thirty-second trip through the parking garage. The run-flat tires of their rides screeched a horrendous chorus against the concrete floors until they reached their reserved parking next to the entrance.

In his storied past, if there was one thing that drove Stamos, it was the need for absolute victory over his adversaries, and no matter how successful he was in reality, his perfectionism would not allow him to declare victory, and, in fact, he always downplayed all achievements to the point of believing he was losing. That ethos pushed him to the brink each time, propelling him headlong into conflict with pulsing adrenaline and steely resolve. With each triumph, it was not until all battles were won that he could relax on any of his laurels. If his fellow teammates and his lifelong friend at his side had not seen this side of him yet, they were about to get a healthy dose of it as they observed him hastily leading the way headlong into the Merlin Headquarters.

Armed with the new intel, the nationwide team held a strategy briefing regarding the overarching mission, now concentrating on the Western front. After their success in Georgia, and their confidence soaring, they needed to tackle the uncertainties of the West and the unknowns of the "Final

Play."   All in attendance recognized the difficulties in pinning anything on their Utah and Idaho adversaries with their present evidence. The strategy they could not accept would be to wait too long, resulting in unnecessary deaths as the ultimate, disastrous outcome. The daunting challenge they were forced to accept was identifying all players to prevent any "Final Play" from succeeding.

"We require at a minimum direct evidence of these characters' involvement in the plot. And it cannot be just online posts on a social media platform. Sam, can we obtain that?" Stamos queried his Arizona lead.

Sam demurred slightly, "Well we are making a case for that online. I think since we now have one staging area and one disposal area, it is only a matter of time before the leaders slip up. And we have evidence of the two kidnapped persons still alive at the warehouse location in Arizona. It is Nevada, Utah, and Idaho I am worried about."

Point noted the new directives from the devices, "We actually have some potential future victims in Utah and Idaho, surprisingly. They appear to be mid-level operatives on the other side of the spectrum. And now that the directives are out, maybe direct commands will go out on the apps that we can track."

"We can't just sit here twiddling our thumbs!" Stamos stated emphatically. "We have several dozen innocent people in Arizona and Nevada who have imminent threats against them right now. And now a Final Play! Are you kidding me?"

"It's too many to surveil and protect with one hundred percent certainty, but we can make educated guesses as to their next moves. Say, I want you to take note of these notations. Some of these individuals have the word, 'Rustox' with the same date this weekend under the 'Apprehension' date. That's something new and sinister," Sam pointed on the screen to the first few victims. "They seem to be mostly in Nevada."

"I hope it's not what I think it is," Point, having some undergraduate experience in chemistry, did not recognize the full name, but any assassinations with the word tox in the name of the activity could signify that there could be chemical weapons involved.

Natalia immediately recognized the significance from painful experience, feeling a squeezing pain welling up from deep within her heart. "I know there is a Russian company called Genovrustox that makes some precursors to chemical weapons known colloquially as Novichok for the Russian agencies."

"That will be impossible to stop. Do we think these rednecks have any of these weapons?" Stamos could not believe his ears.

Sam proffered a vague response, "No idea, sir. I have not seen any reports from any of these apps or other communications that they do. As you know, Merlin protects many individuals who are assassination targets and nerve agents are only readily available to high-end, nation-state-level actors or I guess those who partner with them. I know that's no help."

"Jesus, extremists with nerve agents. They can make it look like the victim had a heart attack, seizure, or died in their sleep. They could release it in a crowd!" Stamos exclaimed, recognizing this new finding ratcheted up the urgency of their response to a national emergency. "We need to re-analyze all documents and immediately brief all teams." Stamos glanced at Huy with an exasperated expression, who reciprocated the aggravated look back at him in the dimly lit SCIF. Stamos continued, "Plan for a full briefing in fifteen minutes. I need Hanson to involve the AD again."

"Some good news by the way, our fourth drone in Arizona just came online, it will take off within the hour. Thank the good Lord, because we need it. And we have four drones that just lifted off in Vegas, and two each in Detroit, Cleveland, and Pittsburgh. All field teams and digital teams are on location and ready for action in these locations." Huy knew this morsel of good news paled in comparison to the bad outlook just revealed.

"They are all in Nevada?" Stamos asked of the Rustox entries. "Then we need to be in Vegas, baby!"

374

Natalia, Claire, Samantha, Sage, and their new teammate Mía to this point were quietly taking in the disturbing news. Natalia, for her part, had personal knowledge of the devastating effects that the Russian nerve toxins could have on dissidents both in and outside of the borders of Russia. "You know, one of my classmates in Geneva, lost both of her parents to what was widely believed to be Novichok, made by this same company. Then, within hours, she just disappeared. Nobody asked a single question. My father was sympathetic, but my uncle, now that I think about it, may have been involved. The event occurred immediately after my father visited me at school. In hindsight, he seemed to be casing the school to assess the risk to me. The one thing that I remember is that they were lax regarding the security of this substance. They didn't care who they gave it to, as long as it served their objective. The person who was suspected of slipping the Novichok into her parents' drinks was a servant in their home in London. And that servant was poisoned by the same agent. In the news, the story was probable carbon monoxide poisoning, but we all knew. And my friend was such a kind soul, a promising musician."

Stamos likewise had a more of a personal experience with the evil substance, having lost numerous agents and counter-agents to its deadly effects, with one episode being particularly harrowing as his own life was the real target. In the backstreets and alleyways of Prague, as was usual, he had just left a quaint jazz club along the riverfront, slipping away unnoticed after a clandestine meeting with an informant. However, in retrospect, it was perhaps not so unnoticed. After waiting a few minutes in the darkly lit alley, he spied his informant walking by across the street and rather innocently, a Middle Eastern woman with a hijab walking the other way. Moments later, Stamos noticed a change in the gait of his new friend. Stumbling toward Stamos now, he appeared sweaty, gray, and rather grotesque, with a contorted grimace on his face as if in the worst pain. Falling into his arms, the man could not speak, yet uttered the most guttural of sounds, as he frothed at the mouth, struggling to breathe. Stamos tried not to touch him, letting him fall to the ground, calling 911 on his burner phone.

Stamos knew full well there was nothing he could do for this man, but he felt responsible for his death. Since that fateful day, he had sworn himself to his soul to protect all of his team members during operations. Snapping out of the past, he now envisioned in vivid detail several present-day scenarios in succession about how they would use this weapon. Individually, serially, or dispersed in a crowd, those outcomes played out within seconds in his mind. Indeed, a combination of both could be possible. He then imagined Nevada and the sheer number of large crowd gatherings in casinos and popular shows. The risk there was unfathomable and would prove impossible to predict. Once again, they desperately needed boots on the ground.

As Stamos and Hanson exited the SCIF, Hanson notified his boss. "I just got off the phone with the AD's secretary. He is immediately available."

"Immediate action necessary. Tell him we will call him on the plane. Schedule another briefing in 15 minutes and I need the AD and Criminal on the call, and I want DNI and Homeland Security, with AD's approval of course. And arrange our flight to Vegas. ASAP!" Stamos readied his tactical duffle with his entire assortment of gear and slung it over his shoulder.

"Done," was all Hanson could think of to say in the moment as Stamos brushed past him, headed directly to the exit. Following close after him was his lifelong confidante.

Stamos walked quickly outside of the command center to the lobby area and down to the streets of Atlanta below. He looked to the left and to the right as the bustling crowds passed by in their hurry to get to where they were going. The people seemed to be talking loudly but he could not make out any words in English. It was as if he was on a sidewalk in Africa, one of the few places in the world where he had no ability to decipher at least some words in foreign language conversations. The lights gradually became brighter, overloading his senses as he remembered the Russian subterfuge

376

and decoy operations of the past, especially those involving the poisoning of their double agents in Eastern Europe. It had to be a decoy; they would make it look like a terrorist plot and the victims would be swept up into it. They always had one sleeper who remained quiet. That was who would have the nerve agents, quietly existing until the moment they were called upon. And they often used those who were not afraid to die and indeed expected to die in the operation, martyrs for the cause.

He felt a hand on his shoulder. Spinning around, he half-expected a double agent to collapse into his arms, foaming at the mouth. Instead, his eyes met the most calming green hues that he had loved all of his life.

"Sean, it's okay. We will win. You will see. Let me know what you need, Sean! I'm here for you!" Claire always had the most genuine smile that could light up his day, even when she was serious. She sensed his stress, his need for calm. It wasn't working well enough for him to relax today.

"Thank you, Claire," Stamos willed his heart rate below one hundred. Now, with a full breath in his lungs, he discarded this past negativity from his brain into his bloodstream and transferred it into the air collected within. His arms enveloped the smaller, yet strong-willed auburn spit-fire and exhaled the negative energy of that past forcefully, careful to propel it beyond their sphere.

She likewise exhaled her previously obstructing commitment issues and negativity, and felt herself becoming lighter, proclaiming, "Let's get going! I have a beat poet friend who is connected to the underground where we are going."

"You're right, let's get going! We need to find the decoys and the sleepers, but first, we need to activate the full force of the United States of America against this evil force!" he whispered, clenching his teeth. Checking himself from revealing to any listening foe, he pursed his lips and squeezed his friend harder, maybe to protect her from the lurking danger, perhaps instead to show her he needed her. He then thought to himself what he wanted to say to Claire, "We need to notify the rest of our clandestine services. We will hit the ground running when we get there. Thanks to Sam, we have an advance team in place. They have already begun to surveil this guy Ben, and it seems he has a son in Vegas which may be our entry point. Somewhere in this maze of Russian directives, there will be a decoy operation. I am sure of it!" Those green eyes that stared back into his own, if he ever gave up this madness, he could stare at them for the rest of his life. And this embrace was comforting for the moment. He felt deeply the overwhelming need to protect her. All the same, maybe she would be the one to shield him from his own doing.

"Well, that's what we need. Contacts in the right places to detect the decoys!" she displayed the confidence of an experienced agent in the heat of battle.

"There isn't time to waste, we will let someone else handle the roundup here in Atlanta that this Sheriff has unleashed," Stamos said to her as he released his embrace and shepherded her back into the building.

The updated briefing went down swiftly, alerting the complementary branches of the clandestine services to the risks to the country uncovered by the present operation. Stamos single-handedly willed the other directors into action and the sentinel alert system was activated against an unknown and unprecedented attack.

—•❧ ❧•—

CHAPTER 36: ROUND UP

—•❧ ❧•—

Surely the gig was up now. The FBI and Merlin were in possession of a mountain of evidence for arrests and any further delay risked countless lives. A race against time had commenced feverishly to determine if there was anyone who could procure nerve agents among these thirty cells across the country and who would have the balls to use them and how. While Stamos, Claire, and the rest of the team departed for Vegas, the official mechanism of justice spent the night in FISA court in Atlanta with the US Attorney and the Director of the FBI in attendance as they presented the evidence. The plan, if laid well enough and no interruptions presented themselves, would be to raid the more than two dozen locations tomorrow night to round up all of the present suspects. Subpoenas would also be filed secretly at the same time to officially access the Stealth Realm messaging app.

This meant that all locations across the nation had less than 24 hours to bring their evidence gathering up to speed. Each outfit's mandate was to avert any loss of life and not let any perpetrators slip back into the anonymity of society. Indeed, Utah and Idaho might not match the other divisions, solely due to the obstruction of local officials. In the Northeast, however, despite the lack of a communication app that they could track, the devices and many of the potential victims were under surveillance and in the process of being tracked. With a few attempts on the lives of victims there, the field teams and drones had begun to pin down multiple intermediary locations and targets. The Upper Midwest division, while behind on time, garnered many leads through the downloaded Russian directive.

The presentation to the federal judge was not an indication that the Georgia investigations were concluded. Far from it, to be certain, as the surveillance continued into the night, pursuing these criminal actors as they appeared to be casing each of the potential victims. Each field unit was instructed that if a single doubt remained in anyone's mind regarding the safety of any of these unfortunate, unknowing souls, there would be a coordinated takedown of that cell and others immediately. Some of the would-be kidnappers had not flinched as if waiting for a signal or perhaps they were working on the framing and snitching operations. And tonight, the field incursions would also go on as they had several key locations still to be investigated. For all of the operations, radio silence and communication jamming were still requisite.

Thus far a search of various locations, including the police station, had yielded nothing in the way of vials or canisters of any suspicious substances. While they had secured the police station, the police cars remained in the parking lot to maintain the appearance that nothing had happened, in case of satellite surveillance. One key target location, the home of an extremist, a thirty-minute drive north of the small town, had been under constant drone surveillance and the target in possession of one of these devices had not stepped out of the house even for a walk. Cars had come and gone from this remote cabin, and each had been tracked in the usual fashion and traced to South Carolina and various locations in Georgia.

They would soon come to realize through Stealth Realm, that the sheriff and police chief were not the leaders of this plot in the Southeast. While flying slightly under the radar, this extremist was well-known to hate monitoring organizations and the FBI due to his rise from anonymity to power in the newly formed realms. With a huge following on social media, he single-handedly commanded a large contingent of users on the Stealth Realm app. He must have been a recluse, however, as he rarely appeared in public. Indeed, there were conflicting accounts about his appearance, with the most recent accurate picture being from years ago. Through the best research they could manage, they knew, however, that he was a middle-aged Southern good-ole-boy, with family roots in these parts that went back to the Civil War. From the drone surveillance, they could discern that he possessed a noticeable limp and must have been a little under six feet, in comparison to his visitors.

Further research revealed that the Burns family was not wealthy by any means, but they participated in local politics extensively, including the burgeoning vigilantism movement. This hermit leader they had under surveillance had built a network of neighborhood patrols, some of which had ended with unfortunate and unintended consequences. When these "protectors" as they liked to call themselves made a mistake in identity or otherwise, and weapons were involved, the results were never pretty and always made the national news.

Ostensibly, his remote hillside cabin would be one of the first to be toppled in the upcoming round-up. Communication jamming would prove difficult here in this isolated area, as they would need to stealthily approach the cabin on foot to get close enough before being detected for the equipment to reliably work. The preparatory work had begun on the ingress and egress routes the field teams would take. The mission would require two full field teams as Huy and Stamos felt this high-value target was worth the expenditure of valuable personnel.

As it turned out, they would not get the chance to test their Smoky Mountain hiking abilities with the heavy mobile jamming equipment. Early that morning, before daybreak, a few guests came to call briefly, and the three individuals left together in a black Chevy Malibu. Due to the low light, they could not identify or even visualize their targets very well, but the drones were in hot pursuit as they headed south toward the suburbs of Atlanta. So much for a good raid on this hillbilly.

The loss of this mission did not diminish the predicted success of the capture of this reclusive leader. However, a notification went out to Stamos and the rest of the leadership given the surprise departure of their target. One benefit to this new development, within an hour they would begin to receive real-time pictures of the suspected ringleader and his compadres, especially if they leave their vehicle. A second benefit lay in the decreased risk to agents if he could have boobytrapped his home.

Either way, the takedown would soon begin in earnest, and that could not please Stamos more, as the more criminals they could bring into custody, the fewer opportunities the enemy would get to harm his fellow innocent Americans.

Stamos, staring out the tiny window of their borrowed unmarked CIA jet as it roared down the runway of the tree-lined southern airport, depleted and weary from the other night's findings, knew this was the right thing to do. The raids tomorrow would bring a large part of this criminal extremist infrastructure in the United States to a standstill. And to think they were in league with Russia knowingly, to in one way or another subrogate the rights of others to advance their own bigoted beliefs. His hero, Ronald Reagan, would be rolling over in his grave if he knew of the happenings of the last few years. These were the worst of the worst part of our society and Stamos was glad that he and the Merlin group were in charge of it. If this mission was in the hands of less capable investigators, or worse yet, in the hands of local police in Georgia, Arizona, and Utah, the outcome could be entirely different.

As he drifted into a brief nap, it was also clear to Stamos that he should help perpetuate this private investigative capability for the powerless in the future. Perhaps mercenary groups like Merlin were the dawning new age of law enforcement, which, if only in the hands of the rich, could be an unfortunate development because, though it might have succeeded this time for Mía, normally the defenseless would not have access to this powerful company and all the assets it had at its disposal.

The minutes-long cat nap was short but sweet, as he awoke during some turbulence with a start, reinvigorated anew for the critical mission. In a half-second, he went from slouching down in the undersized reclining chair to upright and suddenly ducking as he realized the ceiling was just inches above his head. The women in his charge, Claire, Natalia, Samantha, Sage, and Mía stared at him from the seats across the roaring jet with identical exasperated looks. The mood in the cabin appeared somber at first glance.

"What's the matter? Why so gloomy? What did I miss?" he asked, rubbing his bloodshot brown eyes, but it didn't help. Though his vision was blurry, he still could make out the frowns in the room. Stamos looked to Hanson, who just shrugged his shoulders in wonderment. The veins were protruding from his temples even more than usual in his present stressful state, and the daggers from around the salon of the older Gulfstream G-V.

Claire was the first to speak, "We have been talking, Sean. We have been feeling helpless there in the command center. Some of us want to participate in these incursions even more than we did last night."

"Specifically, me," Natalia began, "I, for one, have been trained in field operations in Switzerland and I feel that I would not be in the way. And I think it is only fair that the others get to at least participate in the logistics of this mission. We are capable and I will vouch for all of us."

Natalia could be quite convincing in any argument as her persuasive green eyes had always caught the attention of Stamos, but his gaze was fixated on Claire at the moment. His primary intention and ultimate goal right now for these involuntary assistants was to protect them at all costs. Claire, with an almost identical forceful expression to her brunette

Russian counterpart, just nodded in agreement during Natalia's compelling pitch for their involvement.

Stamos shook his head emphatically, "From the FBI standpoint, I don't agree. If the Merlin side agrees, then that is a different story." Stamos compromised, trying desperately to protect his less experienced friends, particularly the love of his life. Was he being too chauvinistic? "Hanson, can you bring Huy, Sam, and Chip online?

Huy, who had joined the video conference first, gave an immediate official response from Merlin, "Well, we can certainly outfit them at least with some tactical gear. You can ride along in the egress team vehicle. But you need to remain in the vehicle. And I would need to obtain approval from Chip, Sam, and Torey. If all three agree, then it's a go."

"Yes! We are ready!" Claire exclaimed first, followed by a chorus of cheers and high-fives from behind Stamos, who could only shake his head as he could sense what Sam's response would be. Natalia had trained them well, hadn't she?

Huy spent less than a minute bringing the three Merlin leaders into the video conference call and there was a reluctant, yet unanimous approval from the group. They had witnessed Natalia's ability to carry herself in New York and New Jersey and trusted her without a doubt in their mind.

Chip, from Detroit, reclining in a workstation chair in a small command center there, expressed his own confidence in his partner's abilities at the end of the call, "My sweet Natalia, you know my instructions as always. You can be over-zealous at times. Keep your feet under your nose. Don't overpower your sails. Don't get ahead of yourself, maintain a tactical advantage, and be careful my love." It sounded like sound sailing skipper advice.

"Well, it looks like we have a tentative approval for full participation in non-combat operations," Huy announced to a chorus of excitement for the day ahead.

Claire winked at Stamos, "We will leave the combat operations to this man, right?"

Having been outvoted, he faked a smile and turned his gaze toward the window and the passing clouds, fluffy white in the sunlit sky over middle America. "Can he speed this thing up?" he asked Hanson. "We need to be there now!"

"We are heavily fueled for the trip, but I will ask," was Hanson's timid response, sensing his boss's trepidation.

CHAPTER 37: VEGAS, BABY!

Over the years, Tommy and Isabella had become extremely OCD about their pre-concert routine, as had many of their other musician friends who were also superstitious regarding protecting their precious, overworked voices. The bedroom in their flat was blacked out, with thick blinds and drapes, which lent itself to sleeping late into the morning. With the adrenaline from the night before not worn off until almost six this morning, it was close to noon and the pair had just begun to rouse from their deep slumber. Unentangling their muscular naked legs and arms from each other was no small feat, as the pair slept as one every night. With the excitement brewing in each other's souls, all they could manage was a silly smile and a miniature laugh for the first few minutes of wakefulness and disentanglement. The day-of-performance ritual would start, as usual, with a cool shower, followed by yoga and stretching.

Nary a word was spoken during the yoga exercises, augmented by mindful ocean sounds from the surround speakers and the multi-level water feature in their shaded outdoor patio. Sitting on hemp mats with legs crossed, their gaze fixated on a multi-faceted crystal that hung from the middle of a cedar pergola that stretched from one end of their patio to the other with flowering jasmine hanging from each span. Two misting machines created a fog of humidity that dissipated quickly in the dry heat but kept the space moist for the hundreds of succulent plants that thrived in harmony with a collection of terra cotta pots and stones. Precious crystals and geodes were scattered among the pink and white flowers of desert roses and the towering gray and blue leaves of aloe and agave.

Tommy had imported much of their native culture into their routine, with face paint and quiet incantations that were whispered on the wind calling forth the spirits of his ancestors to bestow their blessings on his soul. Kokopelli, the Spirit of music and dance, was invoked to purify their rhythm, while they stroked a matching beat on tambourines and small hand-held drums. The presence of their guides could be felt more easily today than ever, surrounding their sanctuary with love and encouragement.

A full hour of stretching muscles, tendons, joints, and mind was followed by ten minutes of quiet motionless focus and relaxation. As with transcendental meditation, each muscle group was placed into complete flaccid relaxation in succession to focus the mind only on meditation breathing. As was the rule, upon standing, which took some effort to retrain each muscle to contract again, there was still no verbal communication. That was not to say their eyes and lips could not relay their burgeoning excitement with organic facial expressions. The moment they stepped foot inside the house from the sanctuary, they embraced to begin their day, with only whispers allowed from this point forward.

Now, finally in sync, balanced, and in rhythm with their forebears, their vocal cord regimen would start with a peppermint, ginger, cinnamon, and turmeric tea that was homemade with whole roots and leaves steeped in hot water. The glass pitcher of bright yellow steaming goodness sat half empty as Tommy raised his cup to his lips, blowing some cool air over its surface before sipping. "Ahhh," he smiled as he took a few more sips. His lips communicated silently, "Just a small detour from our day to meet these agents. Don't worry, it won't alter the energy of the collective."

"I hope you are right, baby! We cannot afford to allow any negative energy into this important event tonight. We will need to counteract with meditation immediately afterward. Let's visit our shaman." Isabella's voice was as quiet as a mouse even on normal voice days, therefore Tommy found it necessary to lean over to read her lips.

Tommy brought his crystal glass toward Isabella in a toast, as the two glasses clinked with a high-pitched harmonious sound that raised goosebumps on both of their arms. "Agreed," Tommy had barely intonated, with scarcely a sound escaping his lips. Over the past few years, with at least twice-weekly events and recording sessions, the pair had become proficient at lip-reading, which helped with communication on these frequent voiceless days.

Another embrace and their lips met in the perfect melding of their souls into one to go forth in the day, spreading their joy the only way they knew how, through music. "Shima," Tommy and Isabella simultaneously mouthed the Hopi word for love.

Having finished their mid-day concert preparations, Tommy and Isabella left the peaceful confines of their home in the Jeep, with windows down and only the bimini top deployed to shade themselves from the glaring sun. It was a short, sweltering drive from their Fremont Street townhome to the offices of the FBI, where they planned to meet with their private investigator friend and his federal agent contact. They parked in the visitor lot, and as they prepared to enter the building, Isabella stopped in her tracks, turning toward Tommy.

"Can we perform a shielding exercise now?" she mouthed, placing her hand on her heart.

"Yes, we should," Tommy started silently, also bringing his hands, clasped together, to his heart, as they both closed their eyes. In a few short, whispered vocalizations and motions of their hands, their hearts and minds were shielded from the chaos within this building. He was satisfied with the protection that his ancestors were providing to him and his partner, and he wanted to be sure she felt safe. Breaking protocol, he let his voice be heard this time, "That's better. Are you good?"

"Yes, thank you," was her slightly less vocal reply.

Through several layers of security, they passed quietly and purposefully, mindful of their breathing at the same time. Once inside the imposing structure, they were ushered to a waiting area outside of a nondescript conference room, where through the frosted window of the door they could see several waiting agents.

Little did they know, watching from a remote feed aboard their Gulfstream jet, Stamos and the rest of the crew, arriving soon from Atlanta, were keenly interested in their friend's knowledge and research on Charlie's father, too. For the past few days, there had not been a sighting of the elusive Ben Ritter. Stamos and the entire Criminal Division of the FBI had internal alerts circulating and had been combing various public-facing cameras for facial recognition of their quarry.

Everyone else on the plane was seated, listening intently to the barely audible stream of several men who were still filing into the small conference room, while Stamos paced back and forth. He hated the hard tan leather seats of these old CIA Gulfstreams anyway, but they were the only unmarked planes available on short notice. "Turn that up," he said, impatiently. Hanson, seated the closest to the computer monitor, lurched forward in his seat and tapped the volume control several times on the computer keyboard. Immediately, the voices of the agents in the room could be heard, introducing each other. Then, two men and a woman were led into the room by an agent with a badge and were seated at the front of the room.

"There's the guy we've been seeing in our surveillance of this Ben Ritter. Hopefully, he knows where this guy has disappeared to since he has been following close on his tail," Stamos reasoned. "The other two are friends of his son.

Hanson, as soon as these three leave, I want tails on all of them."

"Done," was all Hanson needed to say. He would put the Merlin drones on it in addition, and with a few strokes of his encrypted texting app to Sam, the command was quickly arranged.

The agent in charge of the questioning emphasized the usual legal disclaimers and other mambo jumbo that the investigator translated into plain English to Tommy and Isabella. The audio from the interview possessed the characteristic echo of every interrogation that Stamos had ever witnessed. He was still having difficulty understanding every word, especially over the jet engines, so he strolled to the front again and turned the volume up to maximum. He didn't want to miss a single word as he sensed the ultimate importance of this interview. He so wished this plane had been the faster, more modern G7, so he could have conducted this interview himself.

The agent in charge then dove swiftly and deeply into the question at hand, "So, we are here to glean any information from you that you know about this Ben Ritter. Can each of you tell me how long you have known him, and any information on his present whereabouts?"

The investigator piped right up at that point, and said, "First of all, I have never met him. As you probably know I am part of an organization of investigators, and also part of an organization that helps immigrants and the homeless fight baseless deportation and other legal proceedings that they otherwise would not be able to fight. We have lawyers, investigators, and social workers involved. We first heard Mr. Ritter and his cronies were starting some trouble with our immigrant population. They were recruiting radical right-wing locals to foment violence toward our friends. I've been following them, and they appear to be a loosely organized group. As to where he is now, the last time I saw him was three days ago. He was staying with a friend in a rented home, and now they are both gone. We haven't seen any activity from the whole organization for two days. I think they have something big planned though, and soon."

"Yes, we just started to become familiar with him right about the time he disappeared," the rather careless agent divulged. "Can you name any associates you have found him to be involved with and any information on criminal activity?"

"Well, there are dozens in this organization and the friend is also from Idaho. I can give you all their names, the ones we know anyway."

"And how about you, I think you are the intermediary between the son and this investigating organization?" the agent asked.

Tommy cleared his throat, "Yes, other than the information you already know, I only know that he has visited his son a few times, and his son is worried that he is up to no good. He has been silently in the background at some anti-immigrant and anti-native rallies. He is a slimy character in Idaho, racist, and violent through proxies only, probably couldn't harm a fly on his own."

"Any other information you can give us?"

The investigator, sensing his friend's lack of further input, spoke again, "Only one thing, and it is a photograph. On the day he disappeared, Mr. Ritter took painstaking measures to elude any followers, but we were able to tail him anyway. And he met with these two men, whom I have a picture of here." He reached into a binder and brought forth several hundred photos, which he flipped through to the last page where a few photos revealed grainy long-distance shots of two men meeting with Ben Ritter. "Together they left toward the airport, and I haven't seen any of them since our surveillance that day, and this time they did elude us. Mr. Ritter left his vehicle at that location, and they left in a souped-up pickup truck. We think it had Idaho plates. This guy was tattooed from head to toe with a beard and sunglasses, yet was well-dressed in popular attire. Could be a leader of some sort. This other guy looks Middle Eastern, also well-dressed, also with a long beard and shades."

"You're right about that. We'll check into it. Can we scan these photographs?" asked the agent, who handed them

392

off to another agent, who promptly stood up to leave the room before receiving an answer.

"Of course. As long as I get them back," said the private investigator, pointing to the photographs as they left the room. He grimaced at the thought of losing his weeks' worth of work. Upon assurances that he would indeed regain possession of the photos, he then turned to Tommy and Isabella and commented, "Good luck with your concert tonight. I won't be able to attend but will be thinking of you."

The agent sat back in his chair, looking like he was trying to think of any further questions. "You guys have a concert tonight? You are musicians in Charlie's band, right?"

"Yes, it is a get-out-the-vote concert for the election this year," Tommy proudly stated.

The agent, with a wave of his hand and an off-hand comment about the election, dismissed the information, and with some formalities of exchange of personal and contact information quickly dispensed with, the three informants were led away from the room to retrieve the photos. Left inside were three agents, who began to comment on the uselessness of the interview.

One of the agents stood up to leave, commenting, "Maybe they will turn up again soon. We'll just have to keep our eyes open."

Remembering the false flag and subterfuge of the past Russian operations, Stamos interrupted the three agents with a request. "Can you send us those photos that you have immediately? Hanson here will send you the link."

"Yes, sir. We can have them to you in minutes. They are uploading to our secure servers now and we will transfer copies to your servers also. It shouldn't take us more than a few more minutes."

"I want those photos circulated to our Merlin colleagues also," Stamos directed to Hanson. "Those two are important, I can feel it. What about that concert tonight? In addition to fanning out around Vegas to protect these individuals who we know are targets, let's look into this location. Find out where it is and who is attending. If I were Russia, and

I wanted to stage a terrorist false flag attack, that is where I would do it. Are there any other events today elsewhere? In Georgia, Arizona, Michigan, Pennsylvania?"

Sam answered him from afar, "I will have a full digital team investigate this angle, this avenue, post haste."

"We are landing in ten minutes, and we will hit the ground running," was Hanson's answer. "Merlin has a small set-up in Vegas, as the field teams and drones are command-ed from Arizona. We begin there and we can participate in the protective operations that they have ongoing for the future victims.

Stamos ritually packed his tactical bag with his usual and necessary ammunition, and it seemed he hadn't even blinked his eyes twice when the plane touched down. He had better hurry if he planned to achieve his trademark running jump off the moving jet, which he did not intend to give up now. He needed to stick the landing here in Vegas to mark the city as his own. As the plane pulled straight into the government hangar, it was barely inside when he opened the door, lowering the stairs, motioning and reassuring Hanson and the ladies to jump too as they shielded their eyes from the jetwash that created a cyclone in the cavernous hangar.

Their waiting entourage was a little bigger than expect-ed. Four Suburbans, engines running and air-conditioned, provided a welcome refuge from the fiery oven of the hangar they had to endure for just a few seconds after leaping out of the moving plane. Hanson directed the team to the SCIF vehicle, and Stamos waved the ladies into the heavy armored truck, which, while not originally planned for six, fit the crew snugly.

As the last door slammed with a vacuum seal, Stamos announced, "Okay, you guys are coming with me. Let's head straight to the concert location. Get Sam and Huy on the phone, this is it! I can feel it in my bones. We need to be on the ground there. Lights on, code three!" he commanded the driver.

Claire and the rest of the crew buckled in, and she was in tune with her long-time friend. "Sean, let's analyze the targets. It won't be this guy, Ben, because he is known. We need to be looking for these other two that they were trying to hide."

"Yes, we need to identify and find these two. They are the key to the final play." Stamos now knew in his mind how this would play out. He just needed to prove it in time and they could save thousands of innocent civilians. What was out of his hands were any other locations that could be mass casualty targets. If this was not the target, they needed to have eyes and ears open all over Vegas and even the rest of the country looking for anything suspicious. He knew now that he would have to place his trust in the other teams in potentially twenty-nine other remote areas of the country.

"What do you have in mind?" Sam asked as he tried to read the mind of the agent with the most Russian experience.

Stamos reasoned, "My thought is, they would need to release this inside the stadium or amphitheater. There has to be an incendiary device to distribute the toxin. In the ventilation system, or at the exits might also give them high casualty rates."

"We will need to count on the hope they haven't already placed it in the building," Claire reminded him.

"You are right, I am hoping that is not the case too. Sam, did you receive the pictures of Ben and his two friends? Can you run your own diagnostics on those two? Our guys are working on it also, but two heads are better than one."

"You got it," was the succinct reply.

"We need to get to the stadium ASAP, fanning out through the crowd looking for something suspicious. And we can use the drones, too. And with facial recognition, we can concentrate on these two bearded individuals. Let's get to work on finding them. I just hope we can find them before they can act."

Natalia spoke up, "Remember the investigator said they were heading toward the airport. What if that is the clue and Vegas is not even the target? What if they flew somewhere else? Shouldn't we have Sam and Huy search the Las Vegas airport cameras for clues?

Stamos agreed, "Sam and Huy, can you look into this angle also? See what you can find there. This was two or three days ago. They could have flown anywhere. My hunch is they stayed."

Stamos closed his eyes, again filing through the deep recesses of his mind for a snippet of a memory that made sense, that would crack this case. Countless perpetrators and victims of Russian murders flashed before him, each providing a confusing backdrop to what could easily be a stinging defeat. But this time he would not let it be.

—•≫ ≪•—

CHAPTER 38: PRE-CONCERT NERVES

—•≫ ≪•—

The pacing back and forth in the dressing room ceased for the night for Charlie, Jasmine, Isabella, and Tommy, as they entered the rehearsal room behind the stage to the raucous cheers of their fellow bandmates. The fateful night they had impatiently anticipated for months was now descending upon Sin City with dazzling lights already aglow, sending bright beams of light to the heavens further lighting up the flashy town. Despite the scorching heat, the promenades outside the Ellipse were crowded with the youth and vigor of Las Vegas and surrounding areas. It was readily apparent the arena would fill to its nearly 20,000 capacity. The entertainment district was teeming with jubilant, dancing teenagers, college kids, and idealistic peace lovers of all ages.

The scene was so encouraging to Charlie and Jasmine that they exchanged approving winks and hugged each other tightly as they excitedly watched the large screens on the wall of the rehearsal room showing the people gathering outside. While their ticket agents relayed otherwise, they half-expected to see only aging hippies limping into the arena. In the past few years, the media had perhaps unfairly depicted the youth of Nevada and the country as a whole as disinterested and aloof, wrapped up in their own selfish social media lives.

Isabella came closer, wrapping her arm around Jasmine, and whispered words of encouragement into the always receptive ear of her best friend, "You are going to bring down the house tonight with your stunning voice!"

Jasmine brought her hands to her chest in a prayer-like gesture, and the word, "Thanks," escaped her lips as she gave a hearty, reciprocal squeeze to the diminutive backup vocalist she had known and loved since her arrival to this desert town from Trinidad years ago. The two had been an integral part of one of the most famous island country bands in the world as backup vocalists, and only recently Jasmine had broken out of the mold as backup and created her first solo album to the rousing acclaim of the critics.

Tommy, noting the time by tapping his wrist, reminded his partners, "It's time!" He raised the honey-infused peppermint tea to his lips for one last soothing swig before their vocal exercises commenced.

Jasmine and Charlie, who practiced a nearly identical pre-concert routine to their friends, set down their preferred homemade concoction of Turmeric tea and breathed in simultaneously, followed by a forceful exhalation of their turmeric-scented breath.

After several minutes of escalating intonations, the four voices reached a fever pitch, sounding remarkably like an elegant Italian operetta. Their fellow instrumentalists, who until then had been milling about mindlessly tuning their instruments, gathered around the center of the large backstage rehearsal room. A few of the percussionists picked up a simple beat with deep bass bongos, accentuating the already celebratory vibe. A long pause ensued, as the black, sound-insulated walls enveloped them in relative quiet, with only faint sounds of the crescendo of chanting fans outside.

Breaking the silence, Jasmine sang in the most heavenly voice, "All together now, spirits lifted up to the sky! Let's blow the roof off this place!!" She paused for only two quarter-notes with a quick breath and continued with a crescendo denoting her voice's readiness, "No one will silence our song!"

The four fell into an embrace as the rest of their friends coalesced around them, a cohesive ensemble that would soon bestow their best version of musical happiness upon the city of Las Vegas. Tommy could not keep his eyes off the video screens showing the throngs of smiling youth showing their support for the cause of democracy and voting. Jasmine always liked watching the screen that showed a live stage view of all the seats that would soon be occupied by a lively crowd. The gates would soon be open, and she would then glean every ounce of energy from watching the people waiting for the show, just feet from where she would be belting out her soul. What a spectacle of positive energy this was, of hope eternal, of the future of mankind, each one dancing to the beat of their own drummer, but altogether as one.

Unbeknownst to the artists and fans below, two drones, flying high above the venue, hovered with actively scanning cameras, operated by the skilled pilots of Merlin Logistics. Doing their best impersonations of youthful, exuberant concert-goers, Stamos, Hanson, Natalia, Claire, Samantha, Sage, and Mía had joined the parade of revelers on the promenade. Claire's usual festive and colorful attire matched the atmosphere the most, followed closely behind by the summer coed garb of the rest of the girls. As one would expect, Stamos struggled to fit in with the crowd, but his tactical bag always had changes of clothes for all kinds of weather, so he managed to find a pair of Bermuda shorts and a black short-sleeve tight-fitting workout shirt that worked decently enough for the occasion. Hanson just couldn't, or wouldn't, and trailed behind like a bumbling father, hence blending in quite nicely with the older crowd.

Sam and Huy were now joint commanders in this mission, each in their respective headquarters. Sam, sitting on the edge of his chair in the desert headquarters, commanded the first drone to switch to facial recognition mode. In so doing, the video feed on the monitor to his left added a partition with text that, as the camera zoomed in on the crowd, flickered for a few seconds before it began to supply real-time identity information. The gates to the venue would open in scarcely thirty minutes, so they had precious little time to ferret out any nefarious activity.

One by one, the drone pilot focused in on the passing faces, which were identified on the screen almost simultaneously, with an address and a few pertinent facts, such as marriage, children, and occupation or employer. Most of the revelers were local college students and artists, distinguished by a lack of occupation or employers that were restaurants, bars, or casinos. Some were local political leaders, and Sam was astounded there weren't more tourists and casino patrons from across the country in the mix.

Impatiently and rising out of a pressing, anxious need to do more, he narrated a summary of those the drones identified so the FBI agents, the two Merlin field teams, and Stamos and his team on the ground could hear the search results. There was not another place in the world Stamos would rather be than right here, in this moment, to have the chance to save even one soul. His focus was arrow-tight today, on each and every iris, nose, lip, body posture, expression, anything that would trigger his innate sixth sense of wrongness. He had built a career first in law and then espionage on his perception of those around him and it had saved his and others' lives countless times over the years.

Meanwhile, the second drone added chemical sniffing mode to its arsenal. Huy liked to joke that it could sense a fart from 2000 feet, and in truth it actually could. The change in the chemical composition of the air would need to be significant, necessitating a rather large release of intestinal gas. Unfortunately, in this instance by the time the drone detected a nerve agent in the air, it would prove too late. The nerve agent Novichok and other similar compounds were volatile and known to have secondary victims, including the attacker. If the substance were to be released into the air with a device, one would expect the attacker to wear a gas mask, which would have to be carried in a backpack alongside the nerve agent.

About one out of every ten participants' faces did not

trigger recognition by the sophisticated software, flashing a red "NON-RECOGNIZED" in the space on the right-hand side of the screen, frustrating Sam to no end, to which he commented, "It could be sunglasses, new facial hair, weight loss. Whatever it might be, we need to scrutinize these folks."

Stamos, feigning like he was speaking to Claire, who was skipping joyfully along the sidewalk right next to him, finally broke radio silence, "Remember we are looking for someone who doesn't belong here, someone who doesn't fit in. Go with your gut feelings. I don't think they are going to do targeted attacks here, their goal will be to inflict mass casualties with a massive gas release. Look for someone with a backpack. You know they don't allow backpacks in the concert."

Claire feigned an infatuated gaze into his eyes, simultaneously searching the crowd with eyes disguised by her white cat-eye sunglasses, while she gave him an acknowledging wink, "Look for someone who is not skipping or dancing like me, someone who is acting uncomfortably, like my robot friend here."

In Stamos' defense, he could not bring himself to join significantly in the celebration, instead focusing on every minute detail within his field of vision, only occasionally emulating his drum circle days on the beach with his old friend with a few bobs of his head to the music. He had been trained by the best in the business to blend in and had become an expert in disguises in Eastern Europe to imitate the locals, but this situation fell outside his repertoire. He spoke several languages but clearly did not speak the modern slang of today's youth.

Every face and posture scanned so far appeared to harmonize with the concert vibe, and the drone facial recognition confirmed it, disappointingly. Not a soul present was from Utah, Idaho, or anywhere else suspicious that they could hang their hat on as a suspect. Precious time ticked by with each facial recognition failure, and to Sam, even the drone software seemed to reflect the anxiety of the moment, the information flashing on the screen appeared more pronounced, bolder even as he leaped from his chair and began pacing the floor again.

As Sam switched pacing from right to left for the umpteenth time, the blue digital clock above his video screens clicked to a frightening 06:29. His voice pitched and cracking, Sam announced, "Gates are opening in less than a minute! Do you want me to try to delay it?"

Stamos, without losing a step, thought about it for a second, "No, that may raise suspicion, and this crowd may start heading to the gates anyway. Let's get back to the gates!" he exclaimed, placing his arm around Claire and performing a one-eighty behind a group of six exuberant girls arm-in-arm dancing to the bass beat of a Bluetooth speaker.

Heretofore making their way away from the gate against the grain to view as many faces as possible, he knew they had better quickly return to the main entrance to scrutinize everyone a second time prior to entry. Luckily only two entrances separated the crowd from the interior of the amphitheater, making it easier to search the crowd. Fanning out toward the gates, time was now critical.

Ahead, close to the South gate, Stamos spied two men they had not yet seen who manifested seriousness and nefarious purpose, setting off alarm bells in the depths of his brain. "Up ahead!" he exclaimed, trying not to yell or alarm anybody. "Those two at the South gate. Does anyone else see them?"

Sam switched his focus from the facial recognition drone to the drone with a wider view of the crowd, which zoomed in on cue to those accumulating near the gate. Two clean-shaven bald individuals had made their way laterally, positioning themselves right in front of the gates, escaping detection. One clearly Caucasian, one olive-skinned, and these two were as out of place as two priests in a brothel. They both sported tattoos and as the zoom brought the pair into a closer view, initially the camera was slightly out of focus. When the pixels cleared, and the 8k camera proved its worth, a clear Don't Tread on Me snake suddenly appeared as the taller white man turned his head to the right.

402

Sam's voice cracked a little as he squawked a little too loud into everyone's ear, "That's them! The two from the pictures. Clear as day, they just shaved their beards and their hair. They are bald and have sunglasses on. One has a fanny pack of some sort, no backpack. Let me see if I can get facial recognition on them!"

Sean Stamos broke into a slight run, as he was at least a hundred yards from the gate. If the gates opened now, they would have at least thirty seconds on him, more like a minute if he was forced to navigate the crowd, Stamos thought. In a dreadful sight, the gates opened like floodgates just then, and the pair disappeared through it, along with a throng of fans.

"Not to interrupt your chase in the desert, but our three individuals in Georgia just showed up at a concert too," Huy, speaking from Atlanta, did in fact interrupt, but Stamos knew the importance of that juicy morsel and did not mind the interruption of his pursuit.

"What kind of concert is it?" he queried, managing to multi-task while he bumped into a few people, now fighting aggressively through the surging crowd without apology.

Huy, his voice cracking a little, answered, "It's a peace festival in the outskirts of Atlanta."

Trying not to voice words that would alarm those around him, Stamos could only say, "We need to take these two down now before they get into the arena!"

"Don't worry! We are on it! We have both drones and the field teams actively pursuing them. The FBI SWAT team and hazmat teams are en route. I also have Point on the line, and he is further activating the Sentinel System, and we are targeting all concerts in each of our thirty realms, so to speak." The Sentinel System was a quick strike team to combat chemical or bioterrorism with strategically placed antidotes available in stockpiles for mass casualties.

On the screens displaying the Atlanta targets in front of him, Huy now had the tactical advantage of having watched the unfolding scene in Vegas, therefore he alerted the field teams to watch for a similar modus operandi.

Point joined the conversation from Quantico, "The FBI

teams are 4 minutes out. You have our permission for take-down now if you can manage it! I have AD on the line here in Quantico. We have several other concerts where we are activating similar responses. One in Michigan is quite concerning. It is also a get-out-the-vote concert. That seems to be their MO here."

Huy added from Merlin Atlanta, "I'll get the Merlin drones and teams on it right away coming from Detroit. We have no idea who we are looking for at any of these locations. Interesting that in both of our present situations, they are using lone leaders for this mission. I am going to break away from your operation to guide the Atlanta mission and will also hand off Detroit to Chip and Torey. Good luck ladies and gentlemen!"

Before Huy turned off his comms, Stamos could hear him barking out commands to Chip and Torey in Detroit for their mission. Chip and Torey. They had their all-stars in Detroit, Stamos thought to himself ever-so-briefly before a sudden twist of his torso was required to avoid a collision with a concert-goer. He swiftly regained his balance and re-turned to full stride toward the gates.

On the fly, the seven on the ground in Vegas were joined by Merlin team members and FBI agents in full tactical gear. Between the two iron gates, they spotted a service entrance where they could gain access less conspicuously. With a flash of their badges and expressions of urgency, security was alerted. Once inside the arena, the walkways were packed with people and a hundred different routes their targets could have taken. It was only a matter of time before they would find these perpetrators, as the two bald men would stick out like a sore thumb, so to speak. Still, Stamos knew quick thinking would rule the day and he made an executive decision, partially to protect his inexperienced apprentices.

"We're going to have to split up in pairs. Remember they could have disguises or hats," Stamos reminded every-one as he grabbed Claire by the arm to lead her toward the stage. He pointed to the tactical members, "Each of you, take a lady with you! They have better eyes than all of us!"
404

Claire looked back at the departing group and with a wink, said, "Be careful, power ladies!"

Sam was flying blind inside the arena, with only a few tactical members and their body cameras to rely on to direct the operation.

Backstage, the eagerly waiting bandmembers finally spotted the crowd filing into their seats on the large monitor, as they moved closer to view the excitement on the faces of their fans. Charlie, who previously paid no attention to the monitors, moved closer to them next to Tommy and Jasmine. He wrapped his arm around Jasmine in a show of support for her biggest solo effort yet.

"I like to see the expressions on the faces of the ones in the front row. They are going to be right there with us, carrying us through, setting us on a higher plane for the show!" he added

"Me too!" added Jasmine, just in time to see the first several fans stake out the front row. "There they are! My god, I have never had such jitters even in front of football stadiums!"

"Look at those two! Tell me they aren't staying in the front row! They look like mob hit men!" Tommy said. Almost interrupting his joke, he stuttered, and grabbed Isabella's arm, "Wait a minute! Look at those tattoos! Look at that snake! Those are the two from the pictures, shaved and wearing hats!"

Isabella ran up to the monitor to get a better look. "We need to alert someone. Call security!"

Tommy began to run for the side stage door, "There's no time for that! We need to act now!"

Isabella ran after him, yelling "No, Tommy!" Charlie and Jasmine, confused looks and all, followed after. She was only a few steps behind him, and no sooner had she opened the door, than Tommy stopped in his tracks ahead of her. She ran right into the back of him, as did Charlie and Jasmine, like a rush-hour traffic pileup. Standing in front of Tommy were what looked like two fans, but one was holding a badge in his hand.

"Tommy, I'm with the FBI," Stamos announced officially as he showed Tommy his badge

"What a coincidence! Those two men are here! In the front row!" Tommy yelled, then realized he should be quieter on the side stage since the music in the arena was not very loud yet. He lowered his voice, moving closer to Stamos, "They are right over there in the front row!" he pointed past the black curtain.

"Okay, we will handle it," Stamos said calmly as he spoke into his comm. "Everyone, they are in the front row. We need to handle this quickly, but we can't let them know we are alerted, otherwise, they could release the toxin."

"They have toxin?" Tommy said, incredulous.

"We are going to pretend to be fans in the first and second rows. No tactical gear. We are just going to take them out from behind. Tommy and Isabella, can you join us? Charlie and Jasmine, you remain behind. We can't risk them identifying you and becoming spooked"

"Yes, of course!" Charlie said shockingly, "But how do you know my name?"

"It's your father, Charlie! They know your father!" Jasmine exclaimed.

"Somehow, I already knew that! Well, be careful!" he blurted out, as he grabbed Tommy by the upper arm.

The two newly deputized musicians joined Stamos and Claire, who were already headed out the side door to the end of the concourse of the arena. Nonchalantly, they blended in with fans and made their way to the stairs headed down to the front row. Stamos took note of how many fans were already in the arena, which appeared half-full already. "Damn that was fast, this place is almost full! I see them! In the hats! There's room right behind them. Tommy and I are going to be in the second row. Claire and Isabella, go to the front row and grab their hands as we take them from behind so they can't release anything. Go for that fanny pack, too!"

Claire, whose heart was racing now as it had never raced before, improvised her lines as they neared the front row, "I'm so excited! We're in the front row!" as she grabbed Isabella's hand. Just then one of the bald men began to exit the row, leaving the more diminutive individual with the fanny pack behind.

"Do you see that, Sam?" Stamos said, pointing his finger toward the graphics on the curtain in front of them, hoping that Sam would catch his cue. He carefully noted any possibility that the exiting man could possess any nerve agent on his person. His pockets appeared to have a few items, but nothing bulky.

"I see it, we will apprehend him as he leaves the arena. We have obtained some facial recognition on these two. The one who remains is Iranian Republican Guard. There is your false flag!" Sam knew Stamos would be right on the money with that prediction.

Stamos' jaw fell open as he hoped Claire would not become nervous with that news. This would mean their adversary would be trained to kill. He suddenly became even more concerned for the safety of his oldest friend in the world. He looked deep into her green eyes as she glanced back at him, searching for the bravery he knew she possessed, receiving only nervous, darting eyes in return. She and Isabella crossed in front of the remaining target, who was more preoccupied with looking around at the exits. Stamos surmised their quarry was casing out his exit plan. Stamos was certain the future plans for this man would not be to leave the arena as he would be getting the most lethal dose without a gas mask. The fanny pack was on his left side, six inches from Claire, who turned toward the stage but kept her eyes on Stamos in her peripheral vision. She jumped up and down passionately with Isabella's hand in hers, which also served to calm the adrenaline coursing in her veins.

Stamos waited until the other man left the arena, then held up three fingers behind the head of the man in front of them, and slowly dropped one and then two of the fingers. On cue, one second later, he reached around and placed a perfect choke hold, which initially appeared would hold, but Stamos knew better and prepared for the coming onslaught. Tommy also saw it coming and was able to place an arm behind the back of the man in an arm bar. With sheer size and strength, he neutralized any possible attempt by their enemy to fight back, but the man's damn hands were still very close to his fanny pack.

Claire and Isabella, frozen for hardly a second, sprang into action, grabbing the man's fingers, trying to prevent them from reaching the zipper, but they were too late as he now had ahold of a small device. "He's got something in his hand!" Claire yelled. "Grab it!"

Isabella, with all the might of her ancestors behind her, dove in front of Claire, grasping the device, and shocking even herself, ripped it from the attacker's hand. In the process, unfortunately, the device bounced from her right hand to her left hand and then flipped into the air above her head. For a brief moment, it appeared it would fall right back into the attacker's hand. Tommy, spying the glass and metal vial at face level of his tall frame, reached out with his free arm and snatched the device out of thin air, falling headfirst over the seat as he did so.

"I've got it!" he yelled, staring up at Stamos from the ground, just as he noticed their attacker was beginning to slump over into his chair. "Well, looks like your choke-hold finally worked." Faces above him appeared to be cheering, silhouetted by the blinding red and white stage lights. Tommy felt a relief fall over his soul at their good fortune. He sensed the approval of the spirits above as he closed his eyes to connect with them.

Stamos looked down at the device held in Tommy's bleeding hand. The plunger was intact, but the glass vial had an obvious crack down the side. All too aware of the impending emergency, he yelled into his comm, "We need 9-1-1 STAT, bring in the hazmat and SWAT teams now. We need to clear the arena now!"

"I'm on it!" Stamos heard Hanson exclaim in the comm from the top row of the arena. "We have our perp number two in custody up here. We are taking him to the containment area. Meet outside the arena to your left," he commanded.

Stamos grabbed Tommy's hand, cradling it in between his own hands. "We need to exit the arena now. Off to the left, toward that door! Now, everyone!" He pointed to Claire and Isabella to clear the crowd.

Tommy cracked open his heavy eyelids to the incredulous eyes of Isabella and his new-found friends. Hundreds of onlookers were already scrambling for higher ground in the arena. Two tactical FBI team members took over taking the Iranian attacker into custody, which consisted of dragging the unconscious man up the steps at stage left.

"We're going to need the antidote and a fast route to University Hospital. We'll be outside in ten seconds, but we don't have much more time than that," Stamos eyed the clearest path out of the arena and shook Tommy out of his trance. Was it a trance? Could he already be succumbing to the nerve agent? Tommy's eyes opened with a start, and he scrambled clumsily to his feet, staring down in disbelief at his crimson-stained hands.

"Alright, we have EMS right outside your door, ready to assist. Hazmat will be there in thirty seconds. They and the command SWAT vehicles are making their way down the promenade." Hanson now broke into the fastest sprint he could manage down the steep steps toward the red exit sign. Luckily the top of the arena had partially emptied, and an unhindered pathway lay ahead, at least at the start.

In the ensuing chaos on the floor of the arena, Claire and Isabella began waving their arms frantically, sprinting out of the arena ahead of Tommy and Stamos, commanding everyone to clear a better path for their now stumbling men. They held open the heavy, black exit doors as wide as possible, watching in horror as their partners' condition deteriorated by the second. Once outside the arena, linked by bloody hands and followed closely behind by their female partners, they made it to a camouflage-green Humvee and an awaiting ambulance before collapsing on the ground. Three Army medics adorned with white hazmat suits caught them mid-fall at the rear of the vehicles, guiding them softly to the ground.

At the same time, Hanson finally departed the building, now joined by Natalia, Samantha, Sage, and Mía, but they were slowed by a throng of panicking people blocking their way to the medics. Outside on the promenade, confusion reigned as skipping and dancing had entirely given way to running and panic. Hanson led the way like a fullback through the line, their arms locked in single file, desperately trying to make their way to assist the two heroes. Over the heads of the crowd, they could barely spy the ambulance in the distance, frustrating Hanson, who began to push harder through the oncoming crowd.

One of the white-clad medics methodically placed an orange padded metal box on the ground beside Tommy's hand and shepherded the device into its interior, swiftly closing the inner air-tight lid. He then disposed of his outer set of gloves inside the box and closed another pair of clamps on the outer enclosure. His partner carefully lifted the box, placed it in a small compartment marked with a bright red biohazard sign at the rear of the Humvee, and locked it with a key attached to the belt of his suit.

Stamos, before losing consciousness from lack of oxygen and carbon dioxide building up in his brain, stuttered the words, "Novichok, need... Antidote... oxime..." He struggled to grasp the wrist of the medic before he could no longer keep his eyes open and his hand went limp, falling like dead weight to the ground. The medics immediately secured both their airways and intubated them. His counterpart connected the clear plastic bag to the airway and began squeezing breaths into the now-paralyzed heroes. There was not much time to waste before seizures and brain damage could ensue. The medic looked around at his backpack full of syringes and vials in two separate compartments, carefully preparing two intramuscular injections of atropine and pralidoxime and administering them into the thighs of both men. In no time, they were transferred onto simple wooden stretchers, and the pair was loaded into the Humvee for the short ride to University Hospital.

As the dust obscured their view of the Humvee and ambulance speeding away, Hanson and the ladies, just arriving at the frantic scene, could only watch in disbelief. Still gasping for breath, they tried to comfort Claire and Isabella, who were locked in a grieving embrace and whose tears flowed steadily, dripping off their cheeks onto the grass next to the promenade. His mind searched for some encouraging words to say, finally landing on, "They have the antidote here thanks to the US Army and CDC Hazmat Response Teams. I'll give you a ride to the hospital. Very important ladies, if at any time you feel any unusual symptoms, let me know immediately. We have a lot of work yet to do to save more lives. We will work on that on our way."

Natalia also sought to reassure her fellow journalist friend, "You know, I've witnessed nerve toxin in my country years ago. With antidotes provided this fast, the outcome is more favorable than ever." She simply neglected to mention the zero survivors she had witnessed in her native country. For obvious reasons, the antidote was unavailable in hospitals in Russia and was reserved for the army.

Claire managed a tiny smile aimed her way, slowly wiped the tears from her eyes, and showed her appreciation, "Thanks. I needed that," before becoming speechless again. Her tears slowed and she noticed their taste was not as bitter as when Stamos lay unconscious before her. The return of that visual to her mind brought the bitterness back and a relapse into several seconds of sobbing. Through her fingers, she glanced up at the group surrounding her for a moment to see the shock and tears accumulating in their eyes. She gathered that she needed to quickly pull it together for the team's sake.

Still leaning heavily on Isabella's shoulder, Claire gazed up at the few wispy clouds scattered about the blue sky, wondering with a dreadful pit in her stomach if she would ever see the smile on her best friend's face, for he was her only connection to her fading childhood. That wonder quickly turned to hope as Isabella sensed her desperation and informed Claire that her ancestors were now in charge of the fate of their two partners. Claire believed in her heart there existed a powerful force of destiny determined by one's relationship with a higher consciousness, and it might as well be one's ancestors as her new friend believed.

Claire had already known that fate had a way of dealing the highest cards to the love of her life. She could only hope that the next few cards dealt to him and the rest of the group would be aces and she was determined to provide the karma from all of their ancestors for the best outcome possible.

—•✥ ✥•—

CHAPTER 39: TWO OUT OF THREE

—•✥ ✥•—

Despite the temporary loss of one of their commanders, potential victims across the nation remained in dire danger, allowing no time to lament. Shocking as the video feeds were of one of the strongest men any of them had ever known being reduced to his knees and unconscious within minutes of the attack, Sam and Huy fought to contain their emotions in favor of protecting who knows how many other stadiums full of unsuspecting souls. Uncovering other false flag operations became priority number one, narrowly supplanting the protection of individual victims listed in the documents that were distributed by the Russians.

Within an hour, Hanson was already on a plane to Arizona, accompanied by Natalia, Samantha, Sage, and Mia. Once onboard, he immediately contacted the AD in D.C. on a conference call with Huy, Sam, Torey, and Point, the latter of whom had assumed the role of director of the mission from the FBI side. Point was beside himself, hence his coat and tie were nowhere to be seen and his pressed white shirt disheveled and half-unbuttoned in the past twenty minutes of tense worry over the fate of his de facto best friend in the world.

Point began with an emotional bent, "Hanson, I am so relieved that you and Stamos activated the Hazmat response team so quickly. If we had not done so in the hours before this mission, Stamos would not be alive right now. For that, I thank you from the bottom of my heart."

Hanson recognized the truth to that statement and acknowledged the grave unknowns of the next twenty-four hours. "I also want to thank the AD, because without his support, this mission would not have succeeded as it has thus far. Speaking of which, we have two other mission-critical events happening right now. Huy, can you tell us where you are on this?"

Huy, who had his microphone muted on the video call, was silent for a few seconds while he unmuted his line. Juggling several evolving missions at once, he had precious little time to relay the results. "Well, gentlemen, here in sunny Atlanta we have two field teams and one FBI SWAT team en route, ready to take out our targets. Hazmat team is also en route, five minutes out. We will contain the perps within five minutes' time, fellows. I guarantee it!"

"Okay, proceed, sir. Godspeed! You are excused, sir. We shall follow with bated breath!" Point exclaimed in his best English accent, mimicking Huy's debonair James Bond-esque mission recap. "Torey and Chip, what do you have for us?"

Torey Severin and Chip Merlin, whose team had heretofore been silently building a dossier on their enemies in Michigan, Ohio, and Pennsylvania in a late flurry of activity, planned to use that list along with facial recognition to identify their quarry.

Torey explained, "We are working on it, I am on the ground here in Detroit, searching for the needle in the haystack. We have some ideas, and we have three field teams scouring this get-out-the-vote concert for the expected false-flag operation, anything out of place. This is the only event going on this week in Detroit, so as you can imagine, it is packed with kids."

Chip added his usual English metaphors to the conversation while trying to concentrate on the drone footage of faces in front of him, "We are quite blind at the moment, with so many cards face down. Unfortunately, that is the hand we have been dealt, so we need to play it the best we can."

Point managed a short laugh before putting forth some words of encouragement from on high that he had probably seen in an old World War 2 movie, "Well, it does no good to look at your opponent's cards anyway so lay your own down."

Meanwhile, in the Atlanta situation, all the cards were on the table as they closed in on their newly identified targets, who had almost lost the pursuing agents several times due to the thickness of the crowd. The horrendous physical shape of one of the fugitives ultimately was working against them, in any chase to a finish line.

Apart from the different shape of the arena and the grand oak trees lining the wide sidewalks leading to the multiple stage areas, drone footage from high above the sun-soaked scene could have been mistaken for that of the Vegas Ellipse just moments ago. Concert-goers were decked out in the most unusual digital music regalia imaginable as they skipped and danced to the music being pumped to them from speakers all around. The flashiest, skimpiest outfits were all the rage for the women while the men all seemed identically dressed in black or white jeans and shirts, with hats or bandanas the only flashy accessories.

Huy now had the three individuals in his sights in the distance with two teams in hot pursuit near the outdoor amphitheater on the outskirts of Atlanta. "Okay, all. You know the MO here, likely the two white men will leave the area right before the other one releases the nerve gas. If we don't apprehend them before that, all is lost. Agreed? So, first chance you get, take them out. Don't let them get inside the gates!"

The body cameras on the screen in front of him seemed to pick it up a notch or two in speed, as no more than a minute later several of the cameras displayed in real-time, three out-of-place men being followed more closely from behind.

While they did have the requisite bland male outfits, they were missing the colorful headgear like the rest of the crowd. Bald heads and clean-shaven faces with large sports sunglasses might disguise their identity from official facial recognition software but there was no mistaking these targets.

Two team members moved ahead of the targets and two team members flanked the group on each side. Huy directed the three with the most hand-to-hand combat experience to make a move from behind on his mark.

"Pay attention to that fanny-pack!" he relayed as he watched the life-and-death operation go down from afar. In seconds, the scene played out with a flurry of struggle that was difficult to decipher from Huy's point of view. The body cameras alternated quickly between showing the sky, the attacker's body, and the ground. Ten seconds later, all three monitors showed their targets laying prostrate on the ground outside the amphitheater, handcuffed and legcuffed, and the fanny-pack safely out of harm's way. "FBI hazmat is on their way. Don't let that fanny-pack out of your sight!"

Far less chaotic than Las Vegas, most of the Atlanta concert-goers had no idea there was anything out of the ordinary happening. Even the ones nearby thought it was a usual concert drug bust, with contraband narcotics being confiscated from the fanny-pack. They carried on their merry way into the concert grounds, as the FBI agents commandeered the pack with the nerve agent and whisked it away to the waiting hazmat team in the parking lot. All body cams and drone footage displayed the same scene, a dozen agents in a circle around the targets lying prostrate on the grass. The drone camera panned out with the thinning crowd streaming away and into the arena.

Point wiped several beads of sweat from his brow, as he shouted his highest approval, which consisted of a guttural sound, again uncharacteristic, "You're damn right we got your ass!" followed by a few pumps of his fists in the air. Fist bumps were passed around from the several computer scientists who also happened to be in the room performing dossier research. He sought to bring the temperature in the

416

room down a notch, back to reality, back to the task at hand. "Okay, two down, hopefully only one more to go! Michigan, give me some more good news!"

"Chip, check in, please," said Huy, also seeking to shift gears to bring Detroit into the focus,

"Torey and his teams are in place, we have two drones in the air, and the venue has not opened their gates as yet. We are scanning the crowd for anyone who does not blend in. We are hoping for the same MO."

"Right my friend," Huy replied as he rearranged the drone and bodycam feeds from Detroit to his primary larger screens in front of him. "Time is running short. Gates are opening soon! Let's go for the trifecta here!"

Point, anxiously viewing the same scene, received a whisper from Sebastian and a paper output from ARTI and hence interrupted the conversation, "We just intercepted some chatter about a .... He is an infamous character in Michigan and could be involved. I am sending his mugshot from a few years ago. Remember, picture this hairy guy shaved, with hat and sunglasses, and that could be our man."

The drone feed continued to process facial recognition data for all to see on everyone filing through the general promenade outside the gates. With multiple stages, the process would only become more difficult after the fans were allowed in. For now, people were spread out over a smaller area outside the festival grounds.

Torey, whose bodycam displayed him squeezing through a tightly spaced crowd, was traversing the areas closest to the gates. The jostling and hectic nature of the feed made it seem like he was more anxious than he actually was. He began to pick up the pace a little with each passing minute. Like any concertgoer jockeying for position in line outside a stadium, he encountered occasional resistance from some of the intoxicated larger male fans, as they eyed him with contempt and some choice words. His equally imposing size made it a little easier to navigate even the most hostile situation

He broke silence briefly but softly to announce he was turning around at one of the gates to make his way laterally to another gate. "Still no sign of our peeps. Focusing on hats." His exceptional height enabled him to peer over everyone as he was changing direction, all the better to see the faces of everyone looking toward the entrances. Unfortunately, due to the unusually sunny weather earlier today, almost the entire crowd brandished a hat on their head.

It was unclear who first blurted out the words, Point, Huy, or Chip as Torey winced upon the simultaneous loud vocalizations in his comm. "I see them! They're in!" was the collective vocalization. The din created some confusion and disorientation at first, as he was not privy to the drone feeds that his counterparts enjoyed. Just knowing he and his team were closing in on their prey generated the most surreal adrenaline surge he had not felt since his days in the military, and from the look on his face, his angst was probably obvious to most of those near him at this moment.

From the drone's bird's eye view, the two awkward, extremely white and obese individuals were struggling to keep up with the crowd and their third Middle Eastern partner who was leading the way with a now-visible fanny pack partially hidden by an oversized t-shirt.

"They are first in line at the gate, and people are being let in," gasped Huy as he glanced at his watch which belied the advertised opening time by several minutes. As painful as it was to watch, he calculated that Torey's team was a full five minutes behind even at an all-out sprint, which was impossible given the crushing forward momentum of those in the queue. By the time Torey made it through the ticket line, half the people would have been allowed into the overly spacious venue.

"Drones one and two, zero in on those three. Don't let them out of your sight! Come on Torey, Field Team One, get in there!" Chip commanded.

"Why don't we have hazmat on the scene? How far out are they? We need them there ASAP. If we don't get to them before they release the gas, there are going to be mass casualties!" exclaimed Point, unbuttoning one more button on his now wrinkled white shirt.

418

Not a single soul was prepared for the visual that appeared next on all screens from Detroit to Atlanta, for it would become engrained in their memories for years to come. The two obese individuals peeled off from their companion as soon as they entered the main stage area. There were probably a thousand fans in the immediate vicinity, the drone capturing the gathering sweaty, yet smiling faces all around the bald man with a ballcap and a fanny pack, who was eerily staring straight ahead toward the stage with a stoic expression on his face, his hands in his pockets awkwardly.

Point, sensing the impossible odds, swung his whole body around, turning away from the screen, looking up toward an assistant in Quantico, "I've seen enough, people! We need to move to containment. Hanson, as soon as Torey and his team gain entry, order the gate closed! Call in hazmat emergency response! National Guard is already on standby, bring them in!" he ordered as he watched Torey flash a badge at the shocked gate attendant, forcing his way through the metal detector.

Chip could be heard on the comm directing one of the drone pilots, "Drone One, Zoom out, please. Mark the target. Drone Two, mark the other two targets leaving the area."

In an instant, in each command center in Detroit, Atlanta, and Quantico, drone feeds zoomed out to a wide angle for a few seconds, displaying the magnitude of the crowd that had accumulated all too quickly. A red circle on the screen kept a placeholder of their target, who now was a speck among the few thousand attendees gathering. At the bottom of the screen, five blue circles appeared, slowly moving toward the small red dot above. They were moving in more quickly now, with a better pathway, but a hundred yards remained.

One of those blue circles, Torey spoke first, "I've got a line on him, first one to the target, take him out! No holds barred, crush him! Team Two, follow and apprehend the two others."

With the long central aisle opening up a little toward the front, Torey now broke into a full sprint, his long legs opening up in long strides. There couldn't be fifty yards between us now, he thought. Just half a football field as the drone camera narrowed its field of view to just one red and one blue circle getting closer and closer to each other.

On the zoomed-in feed of their target, their worst fears were about to be realized. Looking around suspiciously, the bald man with the ball cap slowly reached into the nylon pack and pulled out a now-all-too-familiar gray plastic contraption with a clear vial attached at the bottom. The drone zoomed in further and the object in his hands appeared to have a trigger mechanism that became more obvious as the index finger moved over it.

Huy's heart dropped at that instant, as he struggled for a half second to utter half the name of his top commander, "Tore...Tore... Torey, he has the nerve gas in his hands! Get there now!"

The blue dots were moving oh-so-close to the red dot, mere seconds out.

As the man pressed the trigger, all were expecting a visible release, a white jet of smoke, yet not a trace of visible gas emerged.

"Don't be fooled, he is releasing it now. It is invisible and odorless!" Huy relayed.

Point was not fooled a bit, as he was already on the line with the hazmat team of medics just arriving outside the venue. Four Humvees screeched to a halt, prompting several medics with green army fatigues and large green field packs on their backs to scramble toward the gates. The gates by now were congested with upset, sweat-dripping patrons chanting, "Let us in!"

FBI SWAT team members cleared a corridor for the expert nurses flown in from Fort Stewart, Georgia' who began to seal their tan-colored helmets and breathing apparatus onto their body suits on the fly. The sight of the space suits ended the chants and created pandemonium, however, luckily a large empty space existed away from their path for the crowd to disperse.

The grass field venue in front of the stage resembled a battlefield as hundreds of individuals were already stumbling, gasping for breath, with the already collapsed target convulsing in the arms of the decorated war hero, Torey Severin.

"We have the two perps in custody now. The target is unconscious. Everyone clear the area for the hazmat medics now," Huy commanded, his heart sinking into his abdomen further with each passing second.

This was the US Army show now. The number of survivors would be directly related to the number of injections that could be doled out to the victims in the next thirty minutes. There would be a dose-related effect of the toxin, radiating outward from Torey's location, away from the stage. Four more Humvees and nearly fifty ambulances arrived immediately and within minutes the first injections occurred. Army National Guard personnel by the hundreds filed in like ants to a picnic, all donned in white hazmat gear as well. There was no time for protocol, hundreds of endotracheal tubes were brandished and inserted into the throats of hundreds of concert-goers, providing a direct airway for oxygen to enter their air-starved bodies.

Limiting the survival statistics that day would be the sheer manpower required to operate the soft, clear plastic manual breathing pumps called Ambu-bags. Each victim who had been injected with antidote and intubated needed to be carried out of the zone of contamination by hazmat Army personnel before the rank-and-file emergency medical techs could attend to the victims and transfer them to the hospital. This required three personnel per patient to carry them while manually squeezing the air from the balloon-like ambu-bags at a rate of twelve breaths per minute.

Watching the spectacle from the drone's-eye-view indeed did look like an ant colony attending to a natural catastrophe. Huy now asked the difficult question, "Point, Hanson... Will it be enough?"

"Only time will tell, my friend. Only time will tell," Hanson answered from afar, himself sprawled out at his chair at the conference table of the landing CIA jet, partially in shock from the dire circumstances halfway across the country. As he peered out the window at the passing cacti along the runway, he really could not be too sure. This was uncharted territory. Two out of three was not a good statistic, percentage-wise. Letter-wise a D at best.

Bringing the doom-and-gloom show back to the future tense, Point looked up at the ceiling and breathed out an intense amount of stress before addressing the obvious next steps, "Alright teams, that must not happen again. We need all hands on deck for the next phase. Be watchful for more nerve gas operations, but let's activate the rest of our take-down measures. For each victim we save in the next 24 hours, I will personally reward the team with a bonus so big your head will spin!"

Regardless of the bonus, the next 24 hours would spin all of their heads until they were dizzy anyway.

CHAPTER 40: ARIZONA TAKEDOWN

Undeniably, unfinished business remained in the desert outskirts of Phoenix, and the success of the mission and survival of so many now cascaded down to his shoulders. Unsettled, with a growing fear of further failure, a myriad of scenarios circled Hanson's mind as he struggled to gather in the enormity of the situation. After the ever-so-brief detour to lay eyes on the condition of his charge, Stamos, the one he was tasked with protecting at all costs, Hanson had assembled the team, corralled all necessary resources, and hastily returned to Arizona. Still, the unease he felt leaving the man who was his responsibility could not be measured. As he landed in Phoenix with FBI and Merlin teams in tow, his mind could not erase the indelible image of his leader prostrate requiring a machine to breathe. He and the others prayed for his speedy recovery but knew they had more than just one life through which to measure their success.

As the airplane approached the hangar at the small base of operations airport in Northern Phoenix, Hanson and Natalia arranged bags and bags of tactical gear stacked neatly next to the secured airplane door. The barren landscape had changed since they had left a few days ago, with a sudden, brisk wind carrying dust and sand through the air, making visibility an issue. He could barely make out the hangars in the distance, let alone any surrounding features. The effect was briefly disorienting, for the scene could have easily been mistaken for Iraq or Afghanistan.

Taking a page from Stamos' playbook, Hanson forced open the door while the plane was still barely in motion, deployed the small stairway, and leapt to the ground running, albeit slightly less gracefully. Following his lead, Natalia and the rest of the heroines each grabbed one of the oversized duffles, mimicking their spy boss's technique. Despite the sandstorm, they easily navigated the taxiway toward the waiting Suburbans inside the open doors of the hangar. With serious smiles all around, without a doubt, this mode of arrival highlighted the urgency and gravity of their tasks at hand. Hanson finally fully understood the psychological boost his boss's airplane acrobatics gave to the team, setting the tone for the next phase of this operation.

Meanwhile, only a short distance away, the tone in Las Vegas remained a somber one indeed. The grip that death had on Stamos was lessening with each passing hour, though it still eerily seemed to relish the evil and unending touch it had on his soul. The result was a dizzying ebb and flow of any tiny signs of his recovery. Claire, pacing the hall outside his and Tommy's rooms, had become frustrated at her feelings of powerlessness as a witness to what looked like sleeping victims caught in the grasp of nightmares.

Passing in and out of conscious thought, Stamos could just make out the faint, burnt-edge image of the beast before him. The pale outline seemed all too familiar, yet at the same time unrecognizable. Perhaps his adversary appeared both friend and foe, masquerading as the friend of peace, stability, and law and order while stoking the embers of fear, war, and lawlessness. How could he, a mere cog in the wheel, possibly defeat such a foe? And how would he know he had won, having no measure of score or even a time clock to be certain when the end of the game had come? He knew in his heart the clock would never strike zero, and the struggle would continue on as it always had, since the beginning of mankind. The inevitable, unending conflict simply could not deter his will to conquer all those on the dark side of history.

On the outside, the room was quiet now, less effort was being spent on fighting off death, and the battle was turning to one of time and recovery. The doctors grimly informed them that only time would tell whether the antidotes would work. For Claire, the last few hours had passed so agonizingly slowly that she worried that it could take weeks to see any improvement. While Stamos had opened his eyes there seemed to be no purposeful brain activity, other than occasional rapid eye movements behind closed eyes. Perhaps he could be dreaming, she told herself. No inkling of neurologic recovery could be discerned from the otherwise lifeless body on the life support machines.

Suddenly, a tiny yet momentous change occurred, as first one, then multiple finger movements were followed by a flurry of eye movements that seemed to be tracking and focusing on objects in the room. Her heart fluttered as she leaped to her feet outside the window, yet the glimmer of hope would be fleeting. She sensed in his eyes an extreme will to survive just then, but just as quickly he drifted off into sleep, his eyes closing and restless eye movements resuming. Her jaw tensing in a concerted determination, Claire attempted to lend all of her strength to his in a transfer of energy and willpower. There was no doubt in her mind, the love of her life would win this battle, and she would never let another day go by without expressing that feeling to him. Too long had she kept her love bottled up inside.

Undeterred by the recent outcome in Michigan and the condition of their leader, scarcely a matter of two hours later, the reassembled crew in Phoenix under Hanson's local command gathered their forces for the fight. The drones had returned to the air after refueling and arming, as evidenced by the aerial desert feeds in front of him, this time with red target crosshairs in the middle of the screen. Standing resolutely behind his command chair, Hanson's eyes carefully studied Natalia, who had insisted on joining the extraction team, as she assembled her tactical gear in preparation for whatever resistance she might encounter.

She gave him a serious glance and a thumbs-up, loading and holstering her G26 as she and the Merlin team exited the command center, adorned with backpacks, duffles, and rigid cases that would make any SWAT team envious. Hanson reluctantly returned the thumbs-up sign from his chair, as he, for a brief second, considered vetoing the reporter-turned-professor's involvement in the operation. He didn't want to reveal the worry on his face, but poker was not his strong suit. This mission had experienced too many failures to risk civilians in this endeavor. Alas, the decision was not his, for she practically owned the company they had partnered with.

As soon as she was out of sight, Hanson blocked the exit of two members sporting the official white FBI letters emblazoned on their backs. "Protect this one. I put this on you. She is not to be in the line of fire. You got that?" he demanded, receiving a nod and an aye-aye in response. That short return did not assuage his concern in the least, his eyes briefly studying each of the other ladies now added to his digital team. "Don't you dare tell her I said that," he added, hands on his hips. He promptly turned toward his monitors and prepared to address his teams,

"Extraction team is en route. Field teams, remain in place. We have one extraction, four arrests, and four protective orders, and that is just in the next hour. Let's get busy! Drone teams, be ready for combat assist if necessary. Digital teams, continue your investigations," were Hanson's initial commands. Various teams proceeded to check in and report any anomalies. "Huy and Sam, are you ready?"

"Yes, we are ready. I have every realm covered. Simultaneous takedowns across all realms." was Huy's response.

Sam, from his command seat, agreed in the affirmative, "It's go-time!"

Point, from Quantico, inspired the teams across the nation, "Takedown is now. We have more than enough information to take into custody every known target. Let's bring

426

them in. And let's save this young captive we have in front of us. Huy, any sign of a trap?"

"No, none. Looks cut-and-dry. We have the field teams in place in Arizona for takedown alongside the FBI. Elsewhere we have most of our targets in our sight. Hanson, Natalia. Report when ready," Huy commanded.

Hanson, glancing at Sam across the room from him, erased the concern from his face and began the operation in earnest, "Extraction team will commence in fifteen minutes. Huy, arm drones and fire on my mark."

Natalia studied the drone feed displayed on the tablet in front of her as the Suburbans sped down the relatively quiet desert highway. While she was not the commander of this extraction team, her clout could be felt by Huy's deference to her. "We are ready, our GPS reads only five minutes to the staging area. We can begin soon after that. Right?" she queried the de facto team leader, eliciting a positive response.

"The sandstorm has quieted for now, but there is another expected wind disturbance arriving soon from across the state, and light is fading fast. Let's get this underway, the sooner the better," Hanson interjected.

Huy agreed, "Drones, assume attack positions, decrease altitude to 500 feet."

The two drone feeds quickly morphed into infrared, with barely visible outlines of around fifty individuals manning the two buildings near the captives, who had not moved an inch since their first sighting of them. First withdrawing to a more distant position, they then descended as ordered, which brought the targets into closer view. A third and fourth drone feed each outlined a different operation; a detail arose that apparently caught Huy's attention. He gave some orders to those teams for an imminent arrest before sequentially authorizing the commencement of more than dozens of nighttime raids across the country.

The moving parts of the massive operation would have been dizzying to even the most seasoned CIA operative and Point certainly was not one. His blood pressure probably was not measurable, he surmised. His own command screens were not as many as Huy's, but he believed he had a decent command of these moving parts. "Huy, proceed as planned. Ultimate care for preservation of life, please. I want this phase to be more successful than phase three. No failures accepted."

"Agreed," Huy retorted.

Throughout Georgia, South Carolina, Florida, Wisconsin, Michigan, Pennsylvania, Nevada, Utah, and certainly Arizona, the machinations of law enforcement gathered steam. It seemed not one of their targets was aware of any imminent danger, as they were caught and apprehended without incident, each and every one, without exception. Point and Huy followed each operation over the next few minutes, before concentrating on the Arizona feeds, which suddenly became closer and closer as the drones encircled their targets.

Hanson gave the go-ahead with a resounding, "Commence operation, on my mark." He paused, and almost yelled, "NOW!"

Four Suburbans entered the view within seconds from the highway into the compound, the first crashing through a gate as two individuals dove out of the way of the onslaught. The two Suburbans of the extraction team entered about ten seconds later. Natalia had a front-row view of the action as twenty heavily armed agents fanned out in offensive positions in the front and rear of each building. They encountered little resistance initially from the ill-prepared individuals who were not heavily armed. Several men emerged with handguns drawn and immediately were dispensed with.

The extraction teams remained in their vehicles at first, as incendiary and smoke devices were deployed at the front entrance.

"Extraction teams, enter now. Drones, clear a path, if necessary," Hanson ordered confidently.

It turned out that was a prescient order, as four men appeared at the door, with automatic rifles just as Natalia and her team exited their vehicles toward the same door. Small flashes could be seen from the sides of the drone feeds, showing rapid gunfire, which had an immediate, probably fatal effect on the four targets, who were propelled against the side of the building, guns flailing.

Natalia, never one for following orders, flanked four of her tactical team members on the right through the white smoke, to the doorway of the building on the left. Unlike the rest, who brandished their semi-automatic rifles, she sported her 9 mm in front of her, preferring a more accurate approach. Out of the corner of her eye, she caught a hazy glimpse of gunfire and the outline of one of their targets. She verified the fire was indeed unfriendly and not one of their own, took quick aim at the lower right shoulder, and fired two steady shots.

The grotesque, violent reaction somewhat surprised her, having not shot anyone in real life with live bullets before. Her only previous training was with rubber bullets or paintballs which paled in comparison, yet she dared not deviate from the plan with even one more second of emotional thought. Satisfied that her adversary was incapacitated, she crouched in a defensive position at the right of the door.

Hanson, at the edge of his seat now, directed the show. "Good work! Only two armed targets remain inside the building. They are to the left of the door. Drone One, take them out."

The heat signature of the two bodies inside the building appeared to be waiting in ambush for any intruders, however, in seconds they fell to the floor motionless. The corrugated steel buildings proved no match for the armor-piercing ammunition. With the path cleared of any opposition, the extraction team entered the building, with each man yelling, "Clear!" in their quadrant of the building.

Natalia sprinted in a beeline to the diminutive woman tied to the chair in the corner, sliding across the smooth concrete on her knees the last few feet. "Are you okay? We are here to help. I'll cut this off." Her knife made quick work of the zip ties that were cutting at the bloodied wrists of the groggy, yet relieved social worker, who immediately collapsed from the chair across Natalia's outstretched legs. Natalia held her in her lap, checking her pulse. "Open your eyes, please. Can you talk?"

Two brown eyes cracked open just then and a faint, "I'm okay," emanated from the chapped, wrinkled lips as Natalia wiped the sweaty grime from her face. What an ordeal this brave woman had to endure the last several days. Thank God they made it in time, Natalia thought as she surveyed the smoke-filled room. The smell of gunfire and incendiaries had barely replaced the stench of body odor of the trash that had recently filled this room.

Point and Huy, thousands of miles away, had mirror-identical body postures as they each had access to the dozens of body camera feeds across the country including the Arizona drone feeds. Each operation already had its marching orders, independently commanded by a field agent, so no direction was necessary from the command center. With muted, concerned expressions, they each stood, with one arm crossed to the other armpit and the other elbow propped on that arm, holding up the chin, in a quasi-thinking-man's pose, as they looked from side to side at their underlings, who were equally stunned by the efficiency of the takedown operations unfolding across the country.

Each monitor displayed in turn the near-simultaneous operations. A wooded farmstead in Georgia, a historic antebellum mansion in South Carolina, a small warehouse in Florida, and a country auto detailing business in Michigan, among dozens of other locations, all housed their quarry. In each case, the result was the same, relatively little resistance was displayed.

Breaking the silence, Point sensed an opportune time for direction from above, "Come on people, no stone unturned, no victim left behind!"

Huy, breaking his pose to wipe the sweat from his brow, moved anxiously up and down his urban Atlanta command center, painstakingly inspecting each and every monitor for any signs of mistakes or bad outcomes, nodding as he went. Only then, would he respond, "All operations proceeding as planned. I don't see any hiccups yet!" On monitor after monitor, FBI agents in heavy tactical armor, all with Merlin field teams embedded, could be seen, mostly apprehending suspects, but some simply protecting the listed potential victims.

"Stellar!" Point exclaimed. "While we have one huge notable failure, this day will go down as the biggest success of the FBI in protecting its citizens from a foreign attack ever. Nice work, gentlemen! However, keep it up! Don't take the foot off the pedal. Let's wait for the dust to settle before we count our cards!"

As those cards were played in the next few days, the dust did settle, the view became clearer, and there were more failures. But of the thousands of planned victims, less than a hundred would die including those in the nerve gas attack. The tedious work of sifting through the cases to separate those who may have been framed from those who were true criminals would fall into the lap of each US attorney's office. Point had no problem with allowing the evidence to fall where it may in those cases. Kudos to the Russians for finding some pedophiles in the midst of his fellow innocent citizens and putting them behind bars.

Prosecuting the perpetrators of kidnappings and murders would prove a national moment of pride in the justice system. Swift, severe punishment could now be meted out and spectacles would be made of the most egregious offenders. Certainly, there were still those among the media who would support their enemy, casting doubt upon the evidence that was indeed cut and dry. Steven Point would come to loathe the spotlight of Congressional oversight and news interviews as he traveled back and forth from D.C. to Las Vegas to attend to his partner's recovery.

—◦∢⟩ ⟨∢◦—

CHAPTER 41: BUNDLE OF NERVES

—◦∢⟩ ⟨∢◦—

With all of their synapses overloaded with acetylcholine caused by the nerve agent, the two heroes continued to require full support with sedatives and muscle relaxants, but these measures were slowly being weaned off. Even though their acetylcholinesterase enzymes were being reactivated by the antidote and acetylcholine-blocking activity provided by other medications, Stamos and Tommy's recovery was not at all certain as Claire and Isabella accompanied their men into the makeshift private ICU the hazmat team required. For two days, they could only watch from outside the windows, viewing the life-sustaining machines and green and red squiggly lines on the monitors, indicating at least proof of life. A special Walter Reed Army Hospital team was flown in with expertise in the disposal of potentially contaminated urine and feces.

Yet slowly but surely, by the second day, Sean Stamos' open, shifting eyes turned to focused eyes on Claire and the doctors providing his care. For the second day in a row, she could hardly blink her eyes, she was so intently monitoring for any further sign of response or improvement. He had closed his eyes that afternoon for an hour, so she utilized the rare moment to catch a bathroom break. Upon returning, she was shocked to see his eyes were open and there were tears streaming down his face, certainly not what she was expecting. She strained to see his eyes, and as he turned his head toward the glass, his moving lips startled her even more. The lip reading was not difficult to discern the most basic lip and mouth movements. They were the unspoken three words she knew were on both of their lips their entire lives. The tears of joy began to flow down Claire's cheeks, and her smile could not be contained.

Heretofore, the team of four Army nurses remained inside the rooms in eight-hour shifts, sweating inside self-contained breathing apparatus. Meanwhile, the containment system was slowly being relaxed, allowing the medical personnel to enter the room with plain plastic gowns, gloves, and masks. Soon, Claire would be able to sit with her best friend as he sat in a chair and received therapy to strengthen his muscles. The dimly lit room was now illuminated brightly during the day with LED lights to stimulate the senses and promote wakefulness. Within hours, both Tommy and Stamos were off all breathing machines and were shifted to a semi-reclined position in their beds. For another few days, they would require feeding through nasogastric tubes, providing liquid nutrition directly to their stomachs. Remarkably, that afternoon, Stamos requested to stand at the side of the bed, resulting in abject failure but the determination displayed on his face was encouraging.

That evening, finally Claire felt comfortable enough to sleep inside the hospital room, knowing the eventful day had worn Stamos to exhaustion. She awoke before the first light of day could enter the large window as the nurses began the day's evaluations and treatments. Eyes already open, Stamos could only be described as tenacious, as he grimaced through his self-directed new exercise regimen of arm and leg raises.

As their eyes met, Stamos surprised his friend again. "I am going to walk today," he said with a strong intonation and diction that was probably better than his normal voice.

"Yes, I believe you will! You know I want to tell you how

much you mean to me and have always meant to me." Claire struggled to express herself through her tears. Freckles glistened in the now bright room as the nurses flipped the switch for the day's activities.

"How is Tommy?" he asked Claire and the nurses, adding, "Are there any others affected?"

"He is also recovering and there is literally no one else involved in Nevada. Isabella and I had no symptoms whatsoever. Incredibly lucky!" She chose not to divulge the Detroit casualties that had occurred. Maybe tomorrow, she thought, though she was sure she or someone else would be forced to reveal that truth by the end of the day, especially if he was allowed to receive briefings.

In Detroit, a similar, yet different, devastating scene played out in Torey Severin's room. By the seventh day, little neurologic recovery had occurred. As could be expected, he and the Iranian decoy had received the highest dose of the nerve agent. No matter how much antidote or supportive treatments they could administer, the swelling in the brain proved too much, despite invasive treatments to relieve this pressure. Doctors there struggled to contain seizures and even inserted a drain deep inside the brain to release the pressure. An entire 400-bed hospital was filled with victims, each in their own private contamination suite. The same division of the Army that had provided rescue services manned this entire hospital, having been taken over by decree.

While Stamos was flexing every muscle and joint that he could think of, Claire was pacing the room, glancing at the progress every few seconds. For the fourth time, by request, she recounted to him what had occurred to him over the past few days, describing the scene and who was apprehended. She could tell he was about to beg for a briefing from his superiors and she would not be able to stop him. Behind Claire, a commotion began that disrupted the day's routines. Army nurses and doctors began to scatter and stand at attention.

First to enter from the long hallway, several men in black suits and earpieces flooded the room, collecting names from badges, and typing them into a communication tablet. Both Claire and Stamos took exceptional notice, knowing what would follow would not be a standard visitation. Three familiar men in suits entered next, one of whom, his partner Steven Point, could not be distinguished from the Secret Service agents who had just entered before them. A huge smile graced Stamos' face as he could not believe his eyes. He did not display his usual demeanor, even in the presence of the director and the assistant director of the FBI at his side.

The three men suddenly parted to the side like centers boxing out a lane on the basketball court. Behind them, two men appeared, serious demeanor and conversation displayed on their faces. One blast from the past and one he had met only once, introduced to Stamos at the White House by the former, his old friend and mentor. They conferred with one of the doctors as the Secret Service chief ushered them toward the patient with an approving nod and an outstretched arm toward Stamos.

"Well, now, this is your second encounter with this stuff. Looks like you received a bigger dose this time. You look great, probably better off than the last time in a dark alley. I hear this time you saved the day, old sport!" Bret Chelsvig's barrel chest heaved in a guttural laugh while inappropriately slapping Stamos across the shoulder blades.

"You old salt! Get over here and hug me you big bag of wind!" Stamos could not contain his appreciation for his mentor's guidance that certainly once again saved his life.

Stamos sat up straight in his bed, his hospital gown flowing down to the ground has he swung his legs weakly over the bed to the floor. Immediately two nurses, who were used to the antics of their patient, sprang into action to prevent catastrophe. He hardly required assistance as he stood to embrace his old friend. Point appeared quickly to help him stand with a shoulder to lean on. The numerous anticholinergic medications made it difficult for him to produce tears, but a precious few escaped his eyes, rolling down his cheeks as he painstakingly greeted every nurse in the room.

As Stamos sat down on the edge of the sterile white hospital bed, the leader of the free world addressed the room, "Ladies and gentlemen, you all are a shining example of the good of this country and your life's work will not go unrecognized." The Secret Service ushered him out of harm's way, with the uncertainty of exposure in the room. He turned around as he exited, shouting, "Chelsvig, somehow, I knew you had a big part in the successful containment of this threat! And Stamos, I am summoning you to the Oval Office next week so we can trade stories."

"Where can we grab some wings and a pint of Guinness around here? How can I recover without that?" Stamos asked, causing a burst of laughter from all in the room. His arm and leg muscles were fasciculating, causing a spasm, and he collapsed backward onto the bed. "Maybe too soon!"

The President exited the room, surrounded by his protective detail, leaving the lifelong friends to chat among themselves.

"Where is my good friend, Tommy?" asked Stamos, to which Claire responded with gestures toward the door across the hall. With that, Stamos attempted to walk again, unsteadily at first, with minimal support. He managed to clear the threshold of his room, where he could see into the next room. Stamos waved his hand weakly, releasing it from Claire's grip, which caused some listing to the right side, before grasping Claire's shoulder. Tommy remained bedbound, but awake, turning his head toward the door, and smiles and nods were exchanged. Isabella maintained her vigil at the side of his bed.

Pivoting to return to the room, he addressed his old friend, Point, with a pat on the back. "Thanks, old chap. I knew we were going to bring the house down on this one! I hear we had some losses in Michigan but far better than it could have been if it wasn't for you."

"It's all preparation, Hanson, Huy, the directors..." Point paused, raising his arm, so as not to forget the political figures in the room. "We did lose a good one from Merlin, it looks like Torey is not going to make it."

Stamos bowed his head and looked upward to Point,

"Yes, a damn good one at that."

"So where do we go from here?" Stamos asked.

"Let's regroup next week, I will continue the unfinished business of mopping up anyone we have not cast a net on yet." Point flashed a wry smile and quickly exited the room with two FBI agents decked in tactical gear in tow.

Stamos nearly collapsed again onto the hospital bed before Claire caught him. "And you," he started, wrapping one long arm around her shoulders. "You are never going to escape my view. I love you, love of my life!"

They embraced again, closing their eyes, the biggest smiles evident through the tears, ending only with kisses they had waited too long to initiate.

❧

CHAPTER 42: SAIL AWAY

❧

The question coursing through every corner of her sun-soaked brain at this moment was as foreign as any question she had ever asked herself. She would never have imagined in her wildest dreams he was who he was and that he felt exactly the same about her as she did him. Could she eschew her simple, independent life, the one she had come to know and love, for a man who had carried on such a clandestine existence? Her carefree ways, which made her feel vibrant and alive, were about to become shockingly, incredibly complicated. Could she even fathom what lifestyle modifications would be required to handle his unique kind of stress? Furtively, she glanced at the intense pain she sensed in the depths of Stamos' brown eyes, silhouetted by dark, hollowed eye sockets, and prominent cheekbones, remnants of the prolonged neurological recovery he had just endured. Though the worry center of her brain needed not the visual reminder, those outward signs of bodily injury and near-death experience could be a predictor of the physical dangers that they both would be risking. Could they?

In a self-love exercise, Claire purposefully blurred her

vision to focus inward, to better concentrate on her inner feelings. Beyond his vague outline, as his foreground image blurred into the landscape, hues of blue and green took over, his now indistinct features blending into the sea and rock behind him. She breathed in deeply, ignoring her sense of smell, to avoid the aroma of the sweet rum, chocolate, and nutmeg frozen Bushwhacker concoctions presently being served. She was instantly relieved she rarely drank alcohol so she could open this direct line of communication with her mind, soul, and spirit. She relished in the self-realization that she could never blame any of her thoughts on the release of inhibition due to the effects of ethanol. She held fast to the sweet oxygen within her lungs, along with all of the positive energy she could gather from their lives together, weighing it like a scale. Closing her eyes, she exhaled slowly yet forcibly, measuring any negative energy as it left her body.

The negatives seemed to be immensely dwarfed by the positives of the trust, equality, and oneness that she felt with Stamos. Eyes now wide open, she redoubled her focus on his eyes, surrounded by the small wrinkles and more penetrating scars that etched each corner of his skin, uncovering his true self. She studied every facial defect, wondering about their cause, as she imagined the experiences that had opened chasms, eventually coalescing into those wrinkles and scars. In the end, it was his striated, brown irises that revealed all though, as his eyes locked with hers in a sweet ocular embrace. It was in that moment, and she recounted that it was true for all moments staring into his eyes that came before, she knew the answer she sought. She trusted no one with her heart like she trusted this kindred soul. As she looked to the right over his crimson shoulder, her focus was interrupted, unable to ignore a similar staring contest between Chip and Natalia. Perhaps their sappy love was likewise reduced to melted chocolate in the blazing sun.

A second harrowing brush with death paired with victory over her evil homeland had come to pass for these two late-blooming lovebirds and now, for the second time in only a few years, they desperately attempted to escape the public eye in the Caribbean. Two short years ago, they ensconced themselves in this same location on the Wizard I with Sam and their security contingent, but at this moment it felt more than right to bring a few close confidants along for the ride. To all involved, the connection among these old and new-found friends was not a passing fancy, but a feat to be celebrated. The oh-so-different personalities of the actionable Stamos, reserved Point, determined Natalia, aloof Chip, shy Sebastian, and the other heroes were now decidedly blended into a family, and it was not just their trauma bond that held them together. They were all drawn together to serve a higher purpose, combining their kindred spirits as one force, using any means possible to fight for human decency. The inflection point of the financial fraud of two years ago had turned their lives upside down and this newest tragic outcome would not be that different.

Natalia turned her gaze toward the blue heavens, only minimally obscured by the few nebulous clouds dancing through the sky, reflecting yet again on her destiny and the journey that had brought her to another momentous decision. While so many of the external events of her life would appear, on their surface, to be exerting undue influence, she was fully aware every bit of her destiny was within her control, and she intended to continue in her righteous fight.

If uncertainty could be a certainty, Natalia knew deep down in her soul she could not return to academic life at Georgetown, at least for the time being. She had scarcely embarked on her once-in-a-lifetime scholarly vision quest before taking off on this crime-solving adventure, and she wished upon all possible wishes that she could continue teaching young, impressionable journalists like Samantha. However, her pragmatic side perceived that might not be possible in the age of social media outrage and cancellation culture, as she caught a glimpse of Samantha, Sage, and Mía giggling to themselves without a care. Even though most of the world deemed her to be on the right side of history, the propaganda machine of her native country had already begun spinning the story as one of fake news, blaming the whole affair on these meddling, lying journalists. In the past few weeks, the memes had landed on this side of the Atlantic, taking her completely by surprise.

The resultant firestorm of negative posts, threads, and conspiracy theories propagated by bots based around the world would have flummoxed most young women, however, Natalia's steel backbone had her confronting the lies via the social media machine for what seemed to her like weeks on end. The ensuing crescendo of lies became so deafening that the situation ultimately required a crisis management firm known for its heavy reliance on social media influencers and journalists to combat the falsehoods. It was a wise choice, the increasing din of negativity could have destroyed their lives personally, professionally, and perhaps even literally. They had each other, though, and they had their intact belief in a just world, which they knew they shared with the majority of the world.

Another silver lining in their lives was the Wizard II, as the pair could finally enjoy their recently acquired dream yacht. The shining light in their lives was a 350-foot schooner with three sailing masts and probably enough room for the entire Merlin investigative team. She had just been delivered to the islands and was built of solid aluminum and steel construction. Moored about 100 feet off the beach of Merlin Cay in the British Virgin Islands, they could throw a conch shell and hit the private island of that other famous British billionaire. As the bright island sunshine shone down on her masts and teak deck, gentle waves lapped the hull, and a cool breeze provided a respite from the heat of the sun. The large stern compartment lay open at the water line, with two center console boats and several jet skis floating alongside her. Situated on the top deck at the stern, her palatial bubbling jacuzzi was as big as some swimming pools on land.

Nearby, Stamos quietly focused his attention, one by one, on all of his most trusted confidants in the world, he resolved to thank them individually and profusely. From the steadfast Natalia, to the kindred spirits Chip and Sam, and finally, to Claire, the soft spot in his heart for all time. He

442

vaguely became aware of a harsh red hue blinding his vision, suddenly realizing the color of his skin was rapidly morphing from FBI alabaster to island crimson. Tomorrow would be hell to pay for his lack of sunscreen application. As was characteristic, he never seemed to think about his own health or well-being, instead concentrating, out of a sense of duty, on those around him or the world at large. His impending sun poisoning notwithstanding, he felt at peace with his choices to date; however, from now on, there were only two souls he would place at the head of the list.

One could count a dozen reasons he could lament the state of humanity at this juncture, but in truth, all was good with the world in his mind. The struggle and strife he constantly sought out and endlessly battled would clamor on without end, but as Dr. King once said, with effort, that arc of justice would eventually bend toward the right side of history. But it would only bend at the behest of good and honorable people willing to take a stand, grasping one end of that arc to bend it with their will, against the powerful opposing forces. While he would never end his personal quest for justice, it might soon take on a different appearance, for he thoroughly believed he was now counting his last days as a federal agent. As his eyes surveyed the Brits in the crowd, he envisioned that retirement to be quite similar to the present life of Chip and Natalia's chief, Sam, who had recently offered him a position in a partnership with Merlin Investigations.

Despite the inward persistent soul-searching within each of them, the entire group carried on laughing and having the time of their life, relaxing to the melodic beat of the steel drum band near the bar. The Caribbean backdrop was conducive to both soul-searching and a resetting of priorities. The chief lesson in life was the ever-present difficult choice between valuing those they loved and those worth loving over the comforts of everyday life. Family was family for God's sake and at any moment, those who were less powerful and deemed unimportant could be taken from this earth without warning or rationale. The world was decidedly rough and unfair that way; without principled and ethical people in powerful positions, unequivocally, the arc of justice could instead bend in an altogether untoward way.

"I, for one, intend to enjoy the bubbles while I still can. No sense in brooding about the failures of the past! We conquered our demons, won the largest battle of our lives, and vanquished our enemies, if only for the time being! Who's with me? It's HOT in the hot tub! Burned my foot!" Stamos exclaimed as he dipped his toes, taking an exaggerated step backward, quoting an old Eddie Murphy bit. As he did so, Claire, chuckling at the outrageous imitation, arose to join him in the jacuzzi.

There would be plenty of room for the twelve of them in the enormous jacuzzi, with sparkling wine from the Merlin vineyards in Switzerland flowing nonstop. Chip and Natalia, simultaneously in another jinxing moment, asked Stamos and Claire, "So what is next for the odd couple?" Natalia and Chip had nicknamed them that ever since they got back together. They seemed so different superficially, yet so philosophically identical.

Claire blushed a bit at first, glancing up at those brown eyes she had known for so long. "First, we are going to allow our skin to heal, while we spend a little time in these islands, immersing ourselves in their reggae roots."

Stamos nodded in affirmation, splashing water on his red shoulders while poking the skin to reveal his sunburn. "I have an announcement to make, everyone. I've been thinking about my future for the past few weeks, and I have decided not to make a decision yet. Therefore, henceforth I will be taking a sabbatical, however short or long that may be," Stamos smiled, first gazing at the green-eyed angel settling into the jacuzzi beside him, before looking off into the approaching sunset on the horizon. His lips now dangerously close to hers, he stole a little peck before revealing, "It's been since the last time you and I were together that I've been able to relax enough to absorb the vibe of this island music. Sitting here next to you, I feel alive once again. My soul can't help but dance to the rhythm of those steel drums when I'm with you."

Claire, eyelids holding back the flood, yet with the biggest smile that had ever graced her face, confessed, "I couldn't think of any place I'd rather be with you. I could get used to working from the islands. WNN could use a bit of an island mix in their culture pages. And I will finally have time to work on some poetry."

"Take your time, Stamos, and when you begin to miss the action, we have a leadership position for you at the Merlin Security division." Chip flashed his wry smile at Stamos while struggling to raise himself out of the plush white chaise chair. Natalia followed suit to gain access to the soothing temperature of the churning waters in the hot tub.

Point, taking some offense, yet happy for his friend, confided, "I understand, my friend. I couldn't think of a better outfit to lose you to. But first, I too need some bubbles to go along with this music." He swiftly dipped his toes first, then slipped slowly and completely under the water, holding his nose as he blew bubbles from the depths.

The half-expected revelation could not suppress the mood emanating from the water. In minutes, the entire group was performing their best imitation of pink, boiling shrimp, laughing at the mindlessness of it all. Maybe a shrimp's life was not so bad after all they had been through.

Claire, having warmed her soul in the water, sensed the time was right, stood up, her bright green, glittery one-piece dripping wet, and slid into her colorful cover-up that was lying on her chair. and approached the microphone that perched alone on the teak deck in front of the band. The steel drums continued their high-pitched melody as her iridescent green eyes searched the few clouds in the sky for inspiration, suddenly swelling with tears as she knew the subject of her first impromptu beat poem in weeks. Her curly auburn hair, uncharacteristically tied in a purple hair-tie, was as untamed as ever in the humid, salty air, for she had not given a thought to taming it here in the islands where she would not have a care in the world except the love she had re-discovered.

Claire's fair skin was covered in her trademark red, green, and yellow coverup over the green glitter swimsuit that

445

accentuated her captivating eyes. As if captured by her spell, all in attendance, female and male alike, followed every sinuous flowing move toward the band. She grasped the microphone stand, bringing it closer to her mouth while closing her eyes. The rasta-inspired silky fabric scarcely covered her subtle curves, the breeze lifting it gently away from her skin. Emanating from deep within her chest, a deep harmony burst forth, morphing into a soulful high-pitched intonation, her lips pursed together as if trying to contain the vocal energy.

"Mmmmmm Mmmmm Mmmmm..." she continued, returning the notes in a circular motion back down to a contralto, "Aaaaahii iAaaaahii Aaaa..." The steel drummer, sensing the implied blues vibe, set a slow background rhythm for her next vocalization, each and every sound matching Claire's voice, as her style blended between beat poet and a Beyonce-inspired forceful, guttural rant.

> Love's toils ne'er ending
> Evil e'er to rebound
> Beating hearts rendering
> Passion's future abound
>
> Beginnings win anew
> Endings overcome asunder
> Strength of precious few
> Gathering 'ere one another
>
> Kindred spirits reignite
> Passion from blunder
> Causing flint to light
> Faces stern like thunder
>
> Heaved upon the fire
> Evil, times will fall
> Yet steel still for hire
> Most cannot recall
>
> Love from horrid ordeals

Is tenuous victim bond
Love from common ideals
Is friendship to be fond

Being bound by hope
Risen from tragic dire
Victorious now to cope
Out from under mire

Future cannot but wait
Breezes align weaving souls
Binding scarred hearts in fate
Tides off ebb e'er flows

Emerald water cleanse
Rhythmic beats combine
Through far-reaching lens
A love transcends all ltime

Heat of passion melts to merge
Bodies swiftly consummate
A full moon's tides surge
Washes over to inundate

Left remaining love eternal
Hands in hands above pillow
Lips embrace glowing inferno
Like winds through burning willow

Whispering love's promise
To carry another higher
Not only loins filled with bliss
But hearts and minds forever afire"

Claire's eyes opened wide, gazing first at the approaching sunset with all of the passion of her soul. She then focused on what was just in front of the auburn sky to what sat before her, her love, now a mere puddle boiling in all he had heard.

To Stamos, she could have been floating ten feet off the teak deck, staring right through him, to the other side of the universe. He could melt in her eyes forever, knowing now that his soulmate had always been there waiting. Both flush with emotion, their faces, necks, and chests ever more crimson by the minute. He had never felt such emotions as he was just then and could not wait for the passion that awaiting future held.

This motley crew spent the afternoon enveloped in the music of the steel drum band that Claire had arranged from the local islanders on Virgin Gorda. She was in her element singing the night away and even asked Natalia if she could continue to bring aboard local talent during their indefinite sabbatical. She envisioned each morning she and Stamos would spend a few hours taking the tender ashore on Virgin Gorda, Tortola, or Jost Van Dyke exploring the local music scene and recruiting for their very own daily island soul infusion. In the weeks that followed they hoped to discover some real talent, none more so than the kids of Jost Van Dyke and a small music school there which was started by the legendary Foxy Callwood. They loved it so much that for a week, the Merlin Wizard II relocated offshore of White Bay so that they could be closer to these ingenious, artistic children.

So thus began the uneventful sabbatical that Sean Stamos and Claire Taub had been dreaming about for the past few weeks. What could happen in one of the world's most famous money laundering havens?

The End